The Earl
and the Artificer:
Book Three of the Ingenious
Mechanical Devices

꧁ꕥ ꕥ꧂

Kara Jorgensen
Fox Collie Publishing

Copyright © 2016 by Kara Jorgensen
Cover Design © 2016 Lou Harper

First Edition, 2016
ISBN 978-0-9905022-4-1
EBook ISBN 978-0-9905022-5-8

To my classmates and professors, who helped me take this from a thesis project to a book, and to Steph, who put up with my whining and helped more than she could know.

ACT ONE

"Every man is surrounded
by a neighborhood of
voluntary spies."
–Jane Austen

Chapter One
The Ninth Earl

Elbow-deep in steamer engine innards and covered in grease was not how Hadley Sorrell expected her honeymoon to begin. The wedding and journey to Dorset had been surprisingly smooth, but their luck never lasted. She should have expected the steamer to pop and belch smoke in the middle of the road. Glancing over her shoulder, she watched her husband stare off, his grey eyes locked on the rolling waves as they lapped against the piebald coast in the distance.

"Hold my leg, so my dress doesn't blow up," she called. "Eilian!"

"Sorry!" He snapped to attention and held her billowing gown, his prosthetic hand resting behind her knee, as she looked into the hood. "Are you certain you don't need help? I feel bad just watching."

"It's fine. I don't think there is room in here for you, anyway."

Leaning into the front of the cab, she brought her face close to the boiler as the heat of the kettle stung her cheeks. The metal coils of the heating element had melted into a blackened cake that smelled of burnt hair. Using the sides of the hood for leverage, she pivoted back until her satin boots met the road's white gravel. Staring down at her cream dress, already streaked with soot and grease, she sighed and wiped her hands across it before smoothing a lock of henna hair behind her ear.

"I can't fix it. It's burned out."

"We could take the bicycles into town. I don't think it's that far."

"Let's just wait for Patrick to come back. You know he won't be long."

As Hadley lingered in the road, reconnecting the pipes and organs from the disemboweled car, Eilian listened to the pastoral silence. Under the waves and the rustling trees, there was a faint noise he couldn't identify and it was growing louder. Gravel hissed on the other side of the bend. By the time the steamer broke from the tree-line, it was barreling down the narrow lane. Eilian waved his arms to catch the driver's attention, but he never slowed. Wrapping his arm around Hadley's waist, he darted and turned, falling back onto the grass in time to watch the car hurtle past in a blur of steel and wood.

"Good Lord, he nearly ran you down!"

Hadley sat in her husband's lap, arms and legs wrapped around him. As she tried to uncurl her legs from his lap, the muscles of her thighs locked and shook. Resting her head against his collar, she inhaled the sweet, earthy scent of sandalwood that lingered on his skin and let him hold her a little longer. *If he had been slower*— She shook away the thought.

"It's no different from London. They would sooner run you over than look at you. Help me up, and I'll finish before someone else comes."

"No, let me do it. I'm already part metal. What's one more limb?" he replied, kissing the top of her head and carefully disentangling himself from her skirts.

Watching Eilian from the grass, Hadley smiled to herself. The mechanized fingers of his right hand flexed at a thought, reattaching the engine's cords and tubes with ease. It had been a year since they met, when she came knocking on his door with a tape measure and an idea for an electric prosthesis. They had shared a tent in the dusty lunar gorges of Palestine while she was disguised as a man, but there would be no more charades or mutterings from his mother about scandal or imagined impropriety. Now, they could finally be together. A thrill laced through her breast at the thought of such liberty.

"Incoming!" she called as a steamer chugged down the lane, slowing to a stop a few yards away.

Eilian stepped out of the way, his eyes trailing to the black-haired woman in the driver's seat and beside her, his butler clamoring out the door. Patrick burst from the cab, sputtering apologies and half-formed phrases.

"Pat, slow down. I can't understand a word you're saying," Eilian said as he joined him at the steamer's hood.

Taking a deep breath, Patrick pushed his glasses up his nose and collected his thoughts. "Sorry, sir. She's willing to take you and Lady Dorset up to Brasshurst Hall. I'll stay behind and wait for the mechanic."

The woman with the full features of a Caravaggian saint climbed out of her cab, her voluminous skirts rustling with each step. Her dark eyes ran between the young man with the wayward hair to the woman in the stained dress at his side. "Sorry to intrude, but your valet said you were headed for Folkesbury? I am headed that way now if you would care to join me."

"That is very kind of you, Miss—?"

"Mrs. Rhodes," she replied, walking back toward her steamer while the butler dithered between the trunks and bicycles tethered to the back of the hissing steamer.

Eilian held the passenger door open for Hadley to slide in. "I hope we aren't inconveniencing you."

"Not at all, I was heading back home. Brasshurst Hall is on the way."

A pang of guilt rang in the pit of Eilian's stomach as he watched Patrick grow smaller behind them.

"I was surprised to hear you were headed for Brasshurst. No one has been up there in ages. I almost didn't believe Argus—my husband—when he told me the earl's servants were coming up from London to clean the house. Are you his guests?"

Hadley's lips twitched into a grin, and she shot her husband a knowing look. "He *is* the earl."

"Oh." Mrs. Rhodes's eyes left the road long enough to search the nobleman's face for any sign of offense while her own cheeks burned. "I beg your pardon, Lord and Lady Dorset. I— I was expecting someone... older."

"No harm done, Mrs. Rhodes. You were probably thinking of my father. I have only been the earl for a few months, and I— Is that the house?"

Over the tops of the closely clumped elms and oaks, the spire of a tower rose. As they cut through the brush, Eilian's eyes widened. Knowing his father, he had expected a conservative Georgian brick manor with a square roof and a smooth face, but the house was like none he had ever seen.

Brasshurst Hall was an asymmetrical monster. It had a Gothic portal and face on the front, a Palladian annex shooting off the side complete with columns and pediments. Straining his eyes, he could make out the latticed windows of a sultan's harem floating above another layer of cathedral spires and pointed arches. The weathered grey-brown cloister stone was half-covered with ivy and wisteria. Following the gravel drive across an old stone bridge, the orangery appeared. The greenhouse's glass and metal body bulged from the side of the manor like a verdurous boil. No wonder his father chose to move them to London.

When the steamer slid to a stop, Mrs. Rhodes swallowed hard, looking between her passengers. "I do hope you will call on us while you are in Folkesbury, Lady Dorset. My cousin is staying with us, and he has been eagerly awaiting your arrival. He lives in London, too, near Bloomsbury. You may have heard of him. Nadir Talbot, the novelist."

"Yes, I think my brother read his last book, the one about

Cleopatra. He enjoyed it very much." When the woman's eyes lit up, Hadley continued, "Thank you so much for giving us a lift, Mrs. Rhodes. I will most certainly pay you a visit once we are settled."

Watching the steamer roll away, Hadley sighed as the grin fell from her cheeks. She would have to pay calls in a few days, drifting from house to house pretending she was the Countess of Dorset and not Hadley Fenice of Fenice Brothers Prosthetics. It was hard enough to pretend she was an aristocrat for a few hours at their wedding. How was she supposed to keep it up the entire time they were in Dorset? At least her etiquette books were packed in her trunk and Folkesbury seemed like a small town. Maybe no one would notice that she wasn't a born aristocrat.

Eilian's metal hand pressed against her palm. "So, what do you make of it?"

"It's... different," Hadley replied, her gaze running over the bright blue brace and ledge door set into the deep rings of the Gothic facade.

"I'm beginning to wonder if insanity runs in my family." Eilian opened the door and turned to her with open arms. "Well, shall we?"

"You're going to pick me up? Are you sure you can carry me?"

"I have before."

Slipping his arms around her shoulders and behind her knees, he hoisted Hadley against his chest. She wrapped her arms around his neck and braced herself in case his prosthesis couldn't bear her weight. Whenever he picked her up or held her close, part of her still wanted to look around to ensure no one was watching, yet she didn't want him to stop.

"This is a silly tradition, Eilian. You don't have to do this."

"I want to; it's good luck." He kissed her cheek and pushed the door with his back. "The Romans believed carrying a bride over the threshold would protect her from evil spirits..."

Eilian froze in the doorway. The tunneled hall was dark, looming over them and pressing close to his head. While the floor had been swept and the old rug laid out, the ribbed arches were webbed with spider's silk. As the dust motes danced and surged around them, he tightened his grip on her. Turning toward the sun's rays, he reached to close the door but left it for fear of the shadows rushing in or what might lie beyond the threshold.

"I think we are a little late if we want to beat the evil spirits." Hadley's eyes roamed over the clots of long dead insects and debris spun into the grooves of the stone ceiling as he set her down. "I thought the maids were supposed to come and clean up."

"They were. Maybe I didn't send them early enough. There are only three of them, and I had no idea the house would be this large... or filthy."

Taking Eilian's hand, Hadley stepped into the great hall. The house groaned and yawned somewhere deep within. Hadley raised her eyes to the high Gothic windows and skylights she had seen on the drive up, but they were so choked with ivy they barely emitted enough light for her to make out the family coat of arms carved into the hearth on the other side of the room. A pile of furniture covered with once white sheets stood in the corner, blocking off the entrance to the dining room. The wood-paneled walls were caked in grime while the pointed arches in the upper arcade were cloaked in curtains of cobwebs as opaque as silk screens.

Rubbing her arms, Hadley stared into the mouth of the massive hearth. A granite lion's head snarled back at her, a spider skittering from his drawn lips to his meager mane. She pulled a handkerchief from her purse and stood on tiptoe to wipe the crest above his head. An otter and a fox stood on either side of a shield surrounded by acorns and leaves. In the fox's paw was a key while the otter clutched a scallop. Between them an oak sprouted, and a banner stretched across its roots. With her finger wrapped in the linen square, she scrubbed at the stone until the thin letters peaked through. It all had significance. If only she knew what.

"Eilian, what does it say?"

The earl squinted, tracing the letters with his fingertip as he pronounced the familiar phrase. *"Salus in Arduis.* A refuge in difficulties. Maybe in better days. Come on, let's see if we can find the library or the orangery."

Walking into the windowless hall, Eilian felt along the wall for the gas lamps' switch but found only the dusty edge of a picture frame. He reached behind it, but when something in the shadows brushed against his hand, he lurched back, bumping into his wife. Raising his eyes, he met the face of a man in a powdered wig as the lamps lit with a gurgling sigh. The third earl stared down at him from the wall, the grey irises beneath the cocked brows and the signet ring on his finger were all that tied them together, and he still hadn't been able to wear his father's ring yet. He swallowed hard. So these were his ancestors. These were the men he had to live up to.

Eilian took a step forward but stopped, moving back with his eyes locked on the painting.

"What are you doing?"

"His eyes follow you." He shuddered and tried it with the fourth earl's portrait further down the hall. "Do we really have to stay here? Can't we just go to Greece instead?"

Hadley rolled her eyes, avoiding the women hanging in a row on the opposite wall. Why look at them when she knew what she would see? They were a line of noblewomen, born and bred to be the wives of aristocrats, all perfected in oil and exuding a hauteur she couldn't hope to emulate. She dreaded the day when she and Eilian would sit for their portraits, when their faces would be placed beside his ancestors and everyone would see the glaring deficiencies in the ninth Earl and Countess of Dorset. Reaching the end of the hall, she tugged at the pocket door. With each inch it slid, the thrumming hum of an engine grew louder, but on the other side stood the library. Eilian drifted in behind her, his eyes wide as they followed the bookcases up the wall where they melded with the coffered ceiling.

All of the houses prior eccentricities and sins were forgiven at the sight of the library, which rivaled his back in Greenwich. He ran his hand over the edge of the cabinet before turning the key and pulling it open. Books by Pliny, Archimedes, Al Jazari, and the Banū Mūsā brothers stared back at him. Carefully pulling the last tome from the shelf, Eilian cradled it against his chest with his prosthetic arm and turned the fragile vellum pages with the tips of his fingers. His gaze darted over the tight lines of Arabic and intricate schematics as he settled in at the divan under the window. He wondered who else had cared about ancient engineers.

Hadley's cream gown floated at the edge of his vision until she knelt on the chair beside him and wiped at the window. She swatted at his shoulder, but his attention never wavered from the page.

"Eilian."

He had never been able to find a pristine copy in Arabic, even in Cairo and Constantinople. His friends at the Oriental Club would be envious if they knew of his find.

Hadley gripped his shoulder and squeezed. "Eilian, look!"

Glancing up, he met her wide blue eyes, the freckles across her nose stark against her sudden pallor. She motioned for him to peer through the hole in the dust. Between the trees and dense foliage of the greenhouse, a figure sat in a wingback chair beside the algal pool.

"Someone's in there."

Chapter Two
Derringers & Disappointment

Hadley swallowed hard. "Did you hire footmen?"

"No, the only male staff I have are Patrick and my gardener."

"That isn't the gardener, is it?"

He shook his head.

She put a finger to her lips and backed away from the window, her eyes locked on the head swaying above the chair's back. As Eilian crossed the room and grasped the rough fireplace poker, he frowned at the hearth. Despite the dust and cobwebs coating the rest of the room, the ash had recently been swept from the firebox. Inching toward the double doors at the far end of the library, Eilian listened to the chug of an engine on the other side. Hadley followed close behind, fishing through her clutch. He stared at the beaded purse. *When had she started carrying that instead of her carpet bag?* Her face brightened as she pulled out a snub-nosed gun the length of her palm.

"You brought your derringer?"

"It's been useful thus far." She checked the chambers before snapping it shut. "You didn't think I would let you go in there alone, did you?"

Holding Hadley's gaze, he counted off with his fingers. At three, he drew in a deep breath and inched open the door to the orangery. A puff of hot air hit them as they stepped into the artificial jungle. Massive palms and bushy camphor trees blocked the sun, casting the greenhouse in a balmy haze. The stench of fetid water was overwhelmed by the scent of plants. Everywhere was the smell of earth and the things that belonged to it, concentrated and bottled under the glass dome.

Eilian pushed back a Jurassic fern and slowly followed the cobbled path toward the pool. Sweat collected under the leather brace around his upper arm, but he ignored the urge to wipe it and swept his eyes through the brush. With firecracker flowers and orchids of every shade and strange conformation crowding the path, he expected to hear the caw or flutter of a parrot, but the air was quiet, rolling and bubbling with the river and fog. As they rounded the corner, the man in the armchair came into sight. The hammer of Hadley's derringer clicked in Eilian's ear. He tightened his grip on the poker and watched the man turn. His sharp grey eyes never left his assailants as he stood and stepped around the chair.

"Who are you and what are you doing here?" Eilian called, feeling Hadley tense beside him.

His dark suit was impeccably pressed and the fabric even from a distance was fine, costlier than anything Eilian owned. Something in the intruder's aquiline features was strangely familiar.

"Is that any way to greet your cousin, Lord Dorset?"

"Cousin?"

"Put down the gun, Lady Dorset, before you hurt yourself."

Hadley's jaw clenched, but she kept the muzzle pointed at the grey-haired man at the edge of the pool. Catching her eye, Eilian nodded, and she exhaled, dropping her arm only to keep the gun at her side. Eilian lowered the poker as the man approached with measured steps.

The man's lined, silver eyes fell on Hadley's simple coiffure before lingering on her breasts and waist a moment too long. The new dress, while of good quality, was already dirty and the corset too loose, and though her features were pleasing, she was far from beautiful. The garter gun hung looped in her stained fingers. Where Lord Dorset had found such a creature, he could hazard a guess, but why would he *marry it?*

"I'm surprised your father never spoke of me."

"We didn't speak very often."

"Apparently. Lord Dorset, the *last* Lord Dorset and I were cousins. We were raised in this house."

When the man's cutting gaze reached Eilian's mechanical hand, the younger man tucked it out of sight. "How did you get in here? Did the maids let you in?"

His eyes narrowed as he straightened and cocked his head with a scoff. "I have a key, and even if I didn't, I know this house better than my own body."

"You still haven't told us who you are," Hadley said, resisting the urge to train the gun on him. There was something in his manner, the way all of his movement seemed to be in his eyes, that set her on edge. She had seen men like that in London— men who kept you busy with their eyes when you should have been watching their hands.

"Randall Nash, and you are Hadley Fenice, the illustrious toy *heiress* who has risen to countess."

Hadley winced. The embellished wedding announcement in the society pages had not been her idea. Her future mother-in-law had taken it upon herself to soften the blow of an inter-class marriage with money. Heiress had a better ring than craftswoman, even if it was false. At least the article brought in as many orders as their Christmas advertisement.

"Are you insinuating something, Mr. Nash?" Eilian asked, but before the man could reply, the butler's harried voice rang through the walls. His voice grew fainter as he retreated through the gallery. "In the greenhouse, Pat!"

Eilian and Hadley turned as a crash resounded behind them, and when they looked back, Randall Nash was gone. Using the end of the poker, Eilian pushed back the bushes growing at the edge of the pool but could find no trace of him. He stared down at the empty armchair. From the humidity of the orangery, the fabric had rippled and dampened, raising the varnish on the arms and legs. Beside it sat an open bottle of champagne, a chipped glass, and a book on Caesar Augustus.

"I wonder how long he's been raiding the wine cellar. He's definitely been in the library, too." The butler's flushed face appeared in the doorway. "Pat, did you know he was here?"

"Who?"

"Randall Nash."

"He's the estate manager, sir." Patrick pulled off his fogged spectacles and cleaned them with his handkerchief. "I had to write to him, so he could let the maids inside when they got here."

Hadley shuddered at the thought of the maids trapped in the house with that man. "Does he live in the house?"

"No, ma'am. On the grounds in the dower house."

"Good. Don't let him wander in unescorted, and make sure any doors leading to the greenhouse are locked at night."

"Yes, ma'am. Should I have Mrs. Negi make lunch?"

Hadley nodded, and Patrick disappeared into the library. As she reached Eilian's side, her eyes swept over the soaring vaults and the paths around the pool leading deeper into the greenhouse. What secrets laid buried beneath weeds and dust?

Slipping her hand into her husband's metal palm, she felt his fingers curl around hers. "Shall we explore some more?"

⚬๏๏ ๏๏⚬

Eilian groaned as he collapsed onto the bed. Hadley had put him to work dusting and moving furniture until he was too sore to move.

His body ached all over, throbbing in his lower back and heels despite soaking in the tub for the better part of an hour. How had he not realized when he saw her attack the grime on the family crest or the library window that Hadley would take it upon herself to clean the entire house? Exploring had merely been a ruse to find a maid and a bucket of soapy water. He ran a hand through his wet hair and let out a stifled chuckle at the look on the poor chambermaid's face when the lady of house stole her bucket and brush before she could protest. At least part of the house was clean or would be when the maids put their final polish on it. Closing his eyes, he slid lower until the hearth at the end of the bed warmed his sore feet.

He raised his head at the squeal of a board and found Hadley standing in the doorway with a red silk caftan hanging over her nightgown. Climbing onto the antique bed, Hadley settled beside him. Her light eyes ran over his face before following the faint burn scars that trailed like vines down his neck, across his chest, and under the edge of his dressing gown. With her free hand, she traced his sternum in a slow line, but as she reached the satin of his dressing gown, Eilian brought her hand to his lips.

"You still have your prosthesis on."

"Don't worry, I took it off and cleaned it. I just didn't feel like carrying all the parts." Sitting up, he shrugged off his robe and unhooked the springs of his prosthesis one by one. "So what did you think of our *guest?*"

"He gave me the creeps."

"And he has a key. We'll probably find him sitting at the breakfast table tomorrow."

Hadley shook her head. "Maybe we should change the locks. Here, let me get that."

Eilian held out his arm as his wife removed the triceps coils on the back of his arm and tugged at the knot in the leather couter. Those grey eyes laced with malice combined with the evident disdain for what he was brought back too many bad memories. The image of his father dressed in his tailcoat with his bison head and black beard as he loomed over the dinner table floated to the surface. *I forbid it.*

"He reminds me of my father."

"I hope your father didn't stare like that."

"No, no, but his tone, his voice—" He sighed as the leather corset encircling his arm finally slid off. "I had hoped we wouldn't have to deal with patronizing family members for a while. My brother's toast at the wedding was bad enough."

"Oh yes, being called an upstart in front of our guests made my day."

"If I had known how much he had to drink, I would have stopped him. At least mother gave him a proper earful for that."

"Well, unlike Dylan, we will only have to deal with Cousin Randall for a few more weeks. Then, it will be back to London or Greece or wherever."

"Now, that sounds like a real holiday." He watched Hadley arrange the pieces of his arm on the nightstand. "You know, I wasn't expecting you to clean the house, Had. I sent the maids up for that."

"I know," Hadley began, slipping her finger under the stocking covering what was left of his right arm, "but what if someone stops by? We can't show them into a filthy sitting room. They will think we're inept."

"But we kind of are. At least with these things."

Hadley stopped, locking eyes with her husband who regarded her with a lopsided frown. "They don't need to know that. Eilian, I know you don't care what anyone thinks, but *I* want to make a good impression."

"I do care. I'm just not very good at any of this."

"Well, I'm paying calls tomorrow, and if you want to accompany me, all you have to do is be your charming self."

"Fine. Then can we do something more fun?"

A coy smile played on her lips as she ran her hands across her husband's bare shoulders. "Oh? What do you have in mind?"

"I was thinking we could go for a bicycle ride around the grounds or down to the beach." His grey eyes brightened. "They call it the

Jurassic Coast, so maybe we'll even find some fossils there."

"Anything else?"

Eilian thought for a moment. "There might be some Roman ruins nearby. I don't know what else is around here, and we can't go too far with the steamer in the shop. Why? What were you thinking?"

Her face lurched into a stiff grin. "Nothing in particular."

Hopping off the Gothic bed, Eilian pulled back the covers. With his forearm unprotected and barely more than a titanium rod with a hand at the end, he kept it tucked against his chest as he shimmied into bed, careful not to put too much weight on it. As Hadley slipped off her caftan and settled in beside him, he grinned. He had forgotten how much he missed waking up to find her beside him or listening to her gentle snoring in the dark. Those months when they slept beneath the cool desert stars only an arm's length away seemed so long ago.

Wrapping his arm around her, Eilian pulled her closer until he could feel the warmth of her skin radiating beneath her cotton shift. She tipped her head back and caught his lips, cupping the back of his head and running her hand along the hilly terrain of his right arm. The heat rose in her breast with the brush of his hand against her cheek and down her neck, but as soon as his lungs tightened, he pulled away. For a moment, she waited, hoping he would continue. Instead, he reached into the nightstand and withdrew a copy of *The Royal Egyptology Society Chronicle*.

"Mind if I read? I can turn the lamp down."

"It's fine. I'll read *Mrs. Beeton's*."

Hadley found her stack of etiquette and advice books arranged on her bedside table. Grabbing her mother's worn copy of *Mrs. Beeton's*, she sunk lower until she was lying with her back to her husband. Her eyes followed the rickety, uniform type, but after a few lines, her mind drifted as she stared at the heading of chapter one, *The Mistress*. Tonight was their third night together, and while the sheepishness of crawling into bed together had ended the first night, something felt off. On their wedding night, they had been so tired that they fell into bed, lulled into sleep by rich food and exhaustion, and while traveling to Folkesbury, they had stopped at an inn where the only rooms left had a single bed. She slept with her face buried in his neck and his hand on the small of her back to keep her from falling off the narrow cot. Now that they were in Folkesbury in a real bed, clean and relaxed, she expected things to progress, yet it seemed to be the same as it had been for months.

"Eilian, I—" The words dropped as she watched the journal with its sharp-eyed sphinxes flutter in time with the slow, steady cadence of his breath. She plucked the paper from his lax grip, but he didn't stir. "Never mind."

Chapter Three
Keeping Up Appearances

Hadley gritted her teeth and gripped the handlebars until her fingers turned white as her velocipede rattled down the cobbled hill. Her beaded clutch bounced in the bicycle's front basket, threatening to fly out for a third time. The people of Folkesbury flattened against the thatch and stone cottages to let the earl and countess rumble by. As they flew past shops with painted signs swinging in the salt-kissed breeze, she tried to take note of what the town had to offer, but the moment she nearly collided with another child or wizened gentleman, her mental map muddled.

At the bottom of the hill, they slid to a stop in front of a house that had once been slightly grander than its neighbors. It was larger and set further back from the road with a walled garden and unobstructed view of the coast, but the roof appeared frayed in patches and the paint around the doors and windows had begun to peel. Leaning their bicycles against the stacked stones, Hadley drew in a calming breath as she swept her hair behind her ears and smoothed the front of her riding jacket. When Eilian dismounted and reached for the bell, she pulled him to her level and flattened his hair down, but the moment he ducked away from her hand, the wayward spikes popped back up.

"You can't fight it, Had," he whispered as he rang the bell.

A grim-faced butler ushered them inside and disappeared with the cards Hadley pulled from her cramped bag. Her eyes swept over the wooden beams that cut through the plaster and disappeared into the next room. A fire crackled on the other side of the velvet curtain which had become threadbare at the edge where years of hands had pulled it aside. A board whined upstairs as Mrs. Rhodes's head appeared at the top of the landing. Close behind, a man followed as she bustled down the steps. He was older than Eilian by at least five years with thick glasses, a paunch, and frizzy black muttonchops that connected into a mustache.

"Lord and Lady Dorset, we weren't expecting you so soon," Mrs. Rhodes said when she reached the bottom. "Allow me to introduce my husband, Argus Rhodes."

Mr. Rhodes held out his right hand but quickly switched to his left when he noticed the earl's metal hand.

"It's a pleasure to make your acquaintance, Mr. Rhodes." His brows furrowed as he turned the name over in his mind. "Did you recently write a paper for the Royal Egyptology Society? I think it was on Rome's influence on the Ptolemaic dynasty?"

"Why, yes. You've read it?"

"Not yet, but I was reading the Chronicle last night and came across the review. It sounds fascinating."

"Would you like to take a look at it? I have the manuscript in my office."

"Argus, show him the printer's copy instead," his wife replied. "It's in your desk, bottom-right drawer."

When the men turned to leave, Hadley stepped to follow them, but Mrs. Rhodes laid a gentle hand on her arm. "Men are always talking shop, aren't they? Let's leave them to it."

Before Hadley could reply, the woman led her into the parlor and offered her a seat. Ringing the bell beside her chair, she waited for the butler to appear again and asked him to bring them a tea tray. Mrs. Rhodes's dark eyes lingered on the younger woman's houndstooth trousers and riding boots as Hadley fidgeted in her chair.

"You rode a bicycle over from Brasshurst?"

"Yes, our steamer won't be fixed for some time, and I was afraid everyone would think me rude if I didn't pay some calls soon."

As the butler returned to pour their tea, Mrs. Rhodes asked, "Do you have any causes, Lady Dorset?"

"Not really. I mean, not officially. I think I may get into women's education or creating opportunities for female artisans. Being one myself, I would love to create a union of sorts. Wouldn't it be lovely? Women supporting themselves and each other."

Hadley looked up from her tea to see her hostess laughing into her cup. When Mrs. Rhodes noticed the countess wasn't laughing, she cleared her throat and focused on her tea.

"Then again, there's always the poor," Hadley murmured, her cheeks flushing.

"There are so many noble causes. I thought maybe you were part of the Rational Dress Society."

"Why? Oh, the knickerbockers. I'm not officially part of anything, but once you catch your skirts in the spokes, you understand why trousers are preferable."

Mrs. Rhodes nodded thoughtfully. "But aren't you afraid of bicycle face?"

Hadley sighed as she listened to her husband and Mr. Rhodes chattering in the next room. She knew little about the Ptolemaic rulers and would have had nothing to contribute, but she would have liked to learn. Instead, she was stuck hoping her companion would strike up a conversation about herself so that she could focus on what the men were saying. Mrs. Rhodes was waiting, watching her with the same languorous stare laced with domestic authority that she had seen in her mother- and sister-in-law. If she couldn't get through an afternoon with Mrs. Rhodes, how would she ever manage real society ladies?

❧ ❦ ☙

Eilian followed Argus into his study. While it sat off the parlor, it opened into a glass conservatory just large enough to place his desk and a few potted spider plants. In the bookcases were rows of atlases and encyclopedias, and propped between pots filled with alien lilies and scruffy marsh plants were books on history and pharmacology. Tucked in the corner far from the sun's harsh light sat a curio cabinet. Potshards, fragments of papyrus, and stone amulets littered the upper shelves. Below, busts of Caesar and half-worn Romans stared back from flattened coins that collected dust beside a nearly intact amphora.

"Do you read *The Royal Egyptology Society Chronicle* often, Lord Dorset?" Mr. Rhodes asked as he knelt beside his desk and opened the bottom drawer.

"Only since I joined it a few years ago. I like to see what others have uncovered. Sometimes it inspires my own research."

He flipped through the papers within before trying the drawer above it. "Are you an Egyptologist or a backer?"

"Neither, I'm a mechano-archaeologist. I've conducted excavations in Egypt in the past, but I tend to work more in Greece and the Middle East." A soft chuckle escaped his lips. "The last thing I expected to find in Folkesbury was an Egyptologist."

Slamming the drawer shut, Argus tried the last one and withdrew a typed manuscript. He ran his eyes over his name as a swell of pride rose in his breast, but when he reached the rows of text below, all meaningless and shifting, he quickly handed it to the earl. "You can borrow it for as long as you would like. It would take too long to read it here."

Eilian thanked him and let his gaze trail to the photograph beside the desk where Mr. Rhodes sat atop a camel with his wife riding sidesaddle beside him. Upon closer inspection, he realized the camel was stuffed and the desert landscape was no more than a painted screen.

"I hope you don't mind me asking, but why settle here? Surely you would have an easier time making a living near a city or a university."

For a moment, Argus stared at him. Swallowing hard, he fiddled with his glasses before turning to the side table. "Would you care for a drink?"

"No, thank you," Eilian replied and watched the other man's hands shake as he poured himself a healthy portion of brandy.

Drawing in a deep breath, he threw back half the glass and wiped away what clung to his mustache. "I— I only recently began pursuing Egyptology as an amateur. I've always been interested, but I never thought I would get anywhere with it. I could go elsewhere, I suppose, but it would be hard to leave this house. The house, along with the inheritance from my aunt, has supported me and allowed me to do what I please. That and the misses keeping the books. I don't suppose I could manage that in a city."

The earl nodded and drifted back to the bookshelves. Titles flashed through his mind, ticking off his mental inventory, until he reached a book on hieroglyphics he didn't own. "May I?"

"Of course." As he sipped his drink, Mr. Rhodes watched Lord Dorset flip through the pages of hieroglyphs with their translations written neatly beneath them. With each mouthful, his chest flooded with heat and the knot within it loosened. "The thing is, Lord Dorset, I'm self-taught. Anything I know about Egypt I learned on my own. I never went to university. I don't think I would have even gotten in then, so why would they want to hire me?"

"That makes two of us."

Mr. Rhodes raised his heavy brows.

"Don't look so surprised. My father tried to send me to university, but I left after a month. I decided to travel and get some first-hand experience instead, much to his dismay. At that age, I couldn't sit still. My tutors taught me Greek and Latin as a child, but I taught myself hieroglyphics, Hindi, Urdu, and Arabic on boats or dirigibles when there was nothing else to do."

"Don't tell Nash that, though he probably already knows."

"Why?" Eilian asked, slipping the book back into the shelf.

"He's a snob. He's well-educated and lords it over everyone. I wanted to ask him a few questions about the Roman economy at the time of the Ptolemaic dynasty since he used to be a big name at Cambridge, but when he saw me, he gave me this disgusted look and slammed the door in my face."

Eilian gave him a sympathetic nod. "I'm surprised he's a scholar. I would have sooner taken him for a burglar. Lady Dorset and I found him in the greenhouse."

Argus raised his heavy brows as he threw back the rest of his brandy. "Sounds like him. I don't think he's been right since the scandal."

"Scandal?"

"Apparently, years ago he tried to convince everyone he had grown a silphium plant. Said he found it right here in town"

"Really? Imagine that. Silphium in Dorset. Do you think he was telling the truth?"

"Nash is a nutter. The plant's been gone since Nero."

⚜

Why had she told Mrs. Rhodes they had only been married a few days ago? After recounting and fabricating details about the flowers, the courses served, the guest list—of which her hostess certainly knew no one—and their living arrangements in Greenwich, the woman was giving her marriage advice. Nodding and smiling as she went on about wives being a reflection on their husbands, Hadley let her eyes trail to the window behind her head. The wind wove through the grass, blowing bits of seeds and pollen over the bluff. If she made a run for it, would anyone stop her?

"Always make certain your staff is keeping an accurate ledger. You never know if—"

The front door squealed open and a motley figure strutted past the doorway.

"Nadir? Nadir darling, is that you?"

"Did you know someone left their filthy velocipedes against your fence? Should I alert the sergeant? Get him off his lazy duff for once," the voice replied.

"Nadir, we have *guests*. Come introduce yourself to Lord and Lady Dorset."

"Busy, Leona," he called, the stairs creaked in time with his steps.

Mrs. Rhodes's face blanched before reddening. "He must not have heard me. Nadir, come down here and meet our guests *now*."

The footsteps stopped and retreated down to the parlor door. The young man who pushed back the curtain was not what Hadley was expecting. Knowing he was a man who wrote romantic adventures women clamored for, she had expected someone older, more distinguished, or at least someone less of a dandy like her brother. While Nadir Talbot shared Leona Rhodes' black brows and Mediterranean complexion, his hair hung in loose waves to his shoulders and a shadow of stubble already outlined his jaw. Even in the warm weather, he wore a teal velveteen jacket over a lilac vest with a Damask rose tucked into his lapel. Her brother would have certainly envied Mr. Talbot's perfectly tailored wardrobe.

Locking eyes with his cousin from behind his sun-spectacles, Nadir dropped his walking stick into the stand near the door with a clatter and stood with his hands on his hips. He folded his glasses, barely giving Hadley a second glance, before proffering his hand and bringing the countess's to his lips with a graceful bow.

"I'm sure it is a pleasure to make your acquaintance, Lady Dorset, and that you are a very charming person, but I have things to do. My dear cousin seems to think books magically write themselves when no one is looking. Now, if you will excuse me, I will be upstairs getting some work done."

With a flourish, he deflected his cousin's dirty look and disappeared into the hall. Hadley suppressed a grin as Mrs. Rhodes stared at the curtain in disbelief. If only she could have been so bold as to excuse herself to the other room.

"Mr. Talbot seems charming," Hadley said sweetly as she poured each of them another cup of tea while Mrs. Rhodes' attention was elsewhere.

"I must apologize for my cousin; he is so dreadfully focused on his career. Those publishers are always breathing down his neck for the next book." She shivered and rubbed her arms, watching the fire falter and wave. Ringing her bell, she swallowed hard. "Nadir must have let the chill in. Barnes will take care of it."

Staring at the study door, Hadley willed Eilian to come out. What excuse could she make to leave? If she were by herself, she could have feigned fatigue or left for another appointment, but she couldn't leave without him. Mrs. Rhodes was staring at her as if waiting for her to speak again. Suppressing the urge to groan, Hadley turned her gaze to the window and the fields beyond it. The bell's jarring peels grew louder as the other woman shifted and sighed huffed excuses for her butler. Hadley rubbed her temple and let her eyes roll back to the fireplace. Sitting beside it just out of arm's reach was a stack of firewood in a brass bucket.

Mrs. Rhodes rang the bell again.

"For God's sake!" Hadley cried as she threw a log in.

Leona sunk back in her chair, eyes wide as if the countess had struck her. Eilian and Argus peered around the parlor door, looking from the noblewoman to the fireplace. Hadley's hair was askew and she stood with her hand out as if they had interrupted some impassioned moment. Swallowing hard, she tucked her hair back and smoothed her jacket before meeting her husband's gaze.

"Oh, dear. I hope you will forgive us, Mrs. Rhodes, but we are late for an appointment, right, Eilian?"

He frowned and glanced at his watch. He didn't think they had any plans. When he looked up, his wife's eyes were wide as she twitched her head toward the door. "Ah, yes, the solicitor. Mr. Rhodes, it was a pleasure to make your acquaintance, and thank you for letting me borrow your paper. Hopefully we can speak again soon."

The Earl and the Artificer

Once he had repeated his good-byes to the lady of the house, they were ushered outside with promises of seeing the couple again soon. As they waved and led their bicycles up the path, Hadley leaned close and hissed into her husband's ear, "You better not leave me alone with that woman again."

Chapter Four
The Letter

Nadir took the stairs two at a time, bounding past oil landscapes of waves, overgrown ruins, and pirates' coves painted long ago. Shutting the door on the bell jangling below, he tossed his jacket onto the coverlet and rolled the tension from his shoulders. As much as he didn't feel like dealing with guests, he hoped the earl and countess would stay long enough that his cousin would forget he was upstairs. Then, maybe he could get some work done without her barging in.

The sun shone through the old bleary glass, casting its gaze across his manuscript. Pages lay scattered on the desk and stacked in a hat box on the floor beside it, but when he shuffled the blank pages into a neat pile, he sighed. They still vastly outnumbered the pages he had written. A trip to the country was supposed to rouse his characters from their slumber, not send them further into the recesses. He stared down at the page of script and scribble. Well, if they wouldn't come out, he would chase them out. Sinking into the hardback chair, he cracked his knuckles, loosened his tie, and reread what he had written a week before.

His pen flew across the page, crossing out whole sentences and rewording others, but as he reached the end of the chapter, his gaze trailed to the world beyond the window. As much as he enjoyed the fresh air and scenery, he missed the vitality of London: the din and haze of smoke in his parlor when his friends stayed late into the night, the thrum of parties, the women. The country was too damn quiet.

Pushing open the pane, he leaned out with his elbows on the sill and drew in a gulp of salt air. He raked his hand through his hair and pulled his lucky talisman from his pocket. Turning the misshapen bead of Roman glass between his fingers, he sighed. What would he do if he didn't write something soon? Rogers was already breathing down his neck. His valet kept forwarding the letters his publisher sent to his house in Bloomsbury asking for the next section, but he had nothing to send. Of course he had the sales of his other books to fall back on for a time. He swallowed hard. That would only last so long until he faded into obscurity and another writer rose to take his place.

The door below whined, breaking him from his morose thoughts. Craning his neck, he watched the Earl and Countess of Dorset emerge from the house with his cousin close on their heels. She patted the Countess's hand, and the woman's face contorted into something between a grimace and a smile. His cousin had that effect on people.

"You must call on us again soon!"

"Please don't," Nadir whispered as they waved and walked their bicycles up to the road. At least his cousin would have someone new to bother.

As soon as Leona was back in the house, Lady Dorset admonished her husband, he couldn't hear for what, but the man bowed his head and nodded. Nadir clicked his tongue and settled back at his desk. He watched the blank pages futilely flap against his paperweight. Maybe a pot of coffee would help get things going. At the top of the stairs, he listened for Leona moving below. She rustled through the parlor, clicking shut her sewing box before the springs of her chair whined.

With Argus in his study and Leona's attention turned to her latest project, Nadir crept down the steps.

Slipping into the dining room and down the servant's stairs into the kitchen, he smiled at his luck; the butler was occupied elsewhere. In the cool space beneath the house, he set to work filling the pot and loading the coffee grinder with beans, both of which he brought from home. He should have brought his valet. At least then someone could make him a *real* cup of coffee. Barnes still ignored him and made dishwater coffee. As he counted the rotations of the crank, a gentle rapping came from the side door. Pursing his lips and drawing in a deep breath, Nadir put the grinder aside with a thunk. He had expected to find the butler or grocer red-faced and waiting impatiently at the door with a crate of supplies, but instead he found a woman. She reminded him of a splotch of ink, all middling hues of black and white with narrow features that were more shadow than line.

"Yes?" he asked, leaning against the doorframe.

The woman's nearly white eyes flickered over his bright waistcoat as her mouth gaped mutely and her gloved hand surged forward with a half-crumpled letter. Her thin voice faltered as she said, "I— I need to speak to Mrs. Rhodes, sir."

"I'll take it to her."

"No!" she cried and shrank back, pulling the missive to her breast. "My master wants me to deliver it to her personally."

Nadir's eyes ran between the little woman and the letter in her hand. Peeking from under her shabby wool coat was the white lace collar of a maid's uniform. "Wait here. I'll get her."

He stepped out of the way to let her inside, but the maid stayed rooted on the cobbled path. Closing the door on her, Nadir walked upstairs. For a moment, he considered going back to his room without saying a word, but the woman had piqued his interest. Plenty of women or their servants sent calling cards to Leona or Argus, yet none came to the servant's door or refused to relinquish their message. If only he had snatched it from her and slammed the door in her face when he had the chance.

34

At the parlor curtain, he hesitated and cleared his throat. "Leona, someone's at the door for you."

"Who is it?"

"I don't know. She said she would rather wait downstairs."

Even without seeing her, he could sense his cousin tense on the other side of the wall. Nadir backed down the hall and watched as Leona stormed out of the parlor, her needle whipping on its fabric tether. When she reached the servants' hall, she pulled the door shut behind her, but Nadir caught it and waited until she reached the kitchen counter before creeping down the steps behind her. Staying just out of sight on the landing, he watched the smaller woman cower as Leona wrenched open the door.

"What do you want now, you little toad?"

The maid's eyes widened as she held out the letter. "Mr. Nash sent me to give this to you, mum."

Leona ripped it from her hand and unfolded the note. From the stairs, Nadir could only make out her back and the side of her face, but skimming the page, her gaze hardened. As she refolded it, he swore he saw her hand tremble. "What if my husband had seen this? Does he have no consideration or shame?"

"He said I had to give it to you and only you. I never would have given it to Mr. Rhodes."

"Oh? And how would that have looked?"

She straightened up, gaining back what little height she had. "What should I tell him, mum? He told me not to leave without a reply."

"Tell him the devil can have him."

His cousin reached to shut the door when the maid put her foot in the way, wincing when the wood collided with her instep. "Please, I need an answer—a real one. He'll be cross with me and just make me come back if you don't respond properly."

"Let him know that I will meet him in the usual place at the usual time. He will know what that means." For a moment, she seemed to deflate, but her voice sharpened as she asked, "Did you read it?"

"No, mum."

"Then, you have your answer. Now, get back to your master, Pilcrow, before I call the constable."

The maid's eyes flicked onto the shadow on the stairs, but Nadir ducked further out of sight before his cousin could see. He listened as the door shut and a chair squealed as it was pulled away from the table. Nadir chanced a look. Leona sat with her forehead resting against her fist, watching the grey little maid through the kitchen window as she disappeared into the village. When she sat back, he noticed that she held the letter against the bodice of her dress. He had never seen her upset, let alone angry, yet any emotion that had been there before already seemed to be seeping away. She reread the short missive, her face impassive.

With silent strides, Nadir returned to the top of the steps and bounded down them again. His cousin looked up at him with a start and tucked the letter under her needlepoint, which she promptly picked up and began to work on.

"Who was at the door?" he asked as he moved back to the stove.

"No one. A woman looking for work."

"I could have sworn I heard voices just now."

She shook her head and carefully added another stitch. "You must have heard me muttering about the mess you left."

With a shrug, Nadir returned to the coffee grinder.

Dropping the fabric and pinning it under her elbow, she turned to watch him. "You were quite rude to Lady Dorset. You know they live in London."

"So?"

"They *know* people. They could help you, and you decide to be flippant. You're not a fool, Nadir. You know how important first impressions are."

Clunking the grinder against the counter, he barred his arms across his chest and faced her. "What do you expect me to do now, Leona? Beg forgiveness? Lady Dorset didn't seem too put out. The earl probably didn't even notice that I snubbed him."

"You're just lucky Argus was entertaining him. Tomorrow, I want you to go up to Brasshurst and bring her a signed book. Apparently, her brother is a fan of yours... if she hasn't already written to tell him how rude you are."

"And what if I don't have a book to spare?"

"You told me you always carry one, in case you run into some spinster or eligible lady you want to impress. Bring Lady Dorset a book tomorrow, or I will write to your parents and tell them to cut you off again."

"I'll have you know, I haven't asked my parents for money in two years," he cried as Leona picked up her needlework and letter and headed up the stairs. "My books are wildly popular, but you would know that if you actually read them."

"Bring her a book, Nadir!" she called from the landing.

Shaking his head, his eyes traveled back to the broken beans in the grinder. He inhaled its warm, bitter aroma, his mind perking at the familiar scent. If he was to follow Leona to her secret meeting, he would need it to be strong.

ઉલ્લ ૭ૐ

Nadir sat in the darkened dining room, fighting his body as it grew lax and heavy before snapping alert at the slightest sound. Tucking his coat and scarf closer, he fortified himself against the cold and took a swig from his flask. The brandy coated his throat, warming his chest from the inside out and making his head swim. From his perch in the furthest corner of the dining room, he could watch the front door and the servants' stairway, but in the shadows, his cousin wouldn't see him. Stretching and straining, he could just barely make out the face of the mantle clock in the moonlight. Two forty-five. Maybe she had been bluffing after all. He moved to stand but froze as the top step creaked in the foyer. Leona's plump form, swathed and veiled in black, appeared in the doorway. Nadir leaned further into the shadows as she opened the front door and slipped out into the night. Watching her through the dining room window's undulant glass, he waited until she rounded the corner at the end of the road before following.

The streets of Folkesbury were empty. Nadir rubbed his ears, unaccustomed to the silence, as he crept behind her, darting from doorway to doorway. Even at that hour, London had never been this desolate. Fog rolled in from the beach, trapping the flickering glow of the streetlamps in luminous clouds. Leona's silhouette bobbed through the mist, her heels tapping down the cobbled path as she moved away from the stone and thatch houses and into the brush. Out of the town's dim glow, Nadir could barely make out her form among the scruffy trees and long grass. His boot-soles slipped on the cool, salty spray of the fog as it lapped and whirled against the weatherworn stones. Perhaps brandy wasn't the best idea.

Fifty feet ahead near a copse of oaks, she stopped. Nadir knelt behind a tree as she looked over her shoulder and opened the shutter on her lantern. In the harsh light, he couldn't be certain if she really was his cousin and not some fae leading him into another realm. What could the letter have contained that would have brought her out in the middle of the night? Maybe he had fallen asleep in the dining room chair or maybe he was slumped over his desk and the maid's arrival had been a dream.

With the lantern lit, Leona picked up the pace, marching along the rickety fence at the cliff's edge. Wind whipped off the bay, catching Nadir's scarf and blowing through the wool and silk of his coat like it was not even there. As he took a step forward, his scarf tightened around his throat. When he slowly turned, he found his scarf had tangled in the branches behind him. Cursing under his breath, he tried to unwind the knit fabric from the tree while keeping his eyes on his cousin. The light grew fainter until finally he ripped the scarf from the tree with a sharp snap. Staggering back on the dewy stones, Nadir's foot slipped from under him and he collided with the road, crushing the bush behind him with a crack.

"Who's there?" Leona called, her brown eyes wide as she walked toward his hiding place.

Her lantern's beam swept across the road only feet away from him.

Nadir held his breath, fingering the bead in his pocket for luck. What would he say if she caught him? She would know that he had spied on her and that he followed her from the house. Then again, what cousin wouldn't be concerned if his closest relation left in the middle of the night?

"Nash, is that you?"

His ankle and tailbone throbbed, but he turned his head away to muffle his cry. A night bird warbled and was answered by its companion near the shore. In the stillness, waiting to be found, Nadir listened to the ebb and flow of the waves below and shut his eyes.

"I must be hearing things," she murmured. Her skirts swished and her footsteps retreated down the path.

Letting out a silent breath, Nadir stiffly climbed to his feet and padded behind her. As the hill rolled closer to the beach, the light around his cousin grew brighter but more diffuse. She moved as a ball of light like a will-o'-wisp, but when she stepped from the path, the light went out.

Nadir blinked in the sudden darkness. Groping forward, he reached for his cousin and met only the cold, chalky wall of the cliff-face. He rubbed his eyes, his heart pounding in his ears with panic. She had been there a moment ago.

"Leona?" he whispered before repeating himself a little louder. "Leona!"

With hesitant steps, he pushed through the brush, feeling for ahead of him for her skirts or a hidden door. There was nothing but the scratch of grass and the rustle of unseen creatures. She was gone.

He wasn't sure how long he stood there in the oppressive blackness waiting for her lantern to reappear, to prove that he wasn't dreaming, that she hadn't vanished. The damp soaked into his clothing, wracking his body with shivers as he stared into the void. He couldn't wait there all night.

Overhead, the moon blazed, illuminating the inky ripples of the sea and the fog coating the lane's shining cobbles. Limping up the hill to return home, Nadir stopped at the summit. On the cliff above him lit like a lighthouse was Brasshurst Hall. For the first time, one of its upper rooms twinkled with firelight. His eyes traveled from the glass dome of the manor to the space in the mist where his cousin had disappeared. Maybe he could spare a book after all.

Chapter Five
Ghosts of Brasshurst

Pulling a cog from the washbasin, Hadley polished its smooth, brassy surface until it shone. With her brows furrowed in concentration, she carefully brushed on a coating of her father's special oil before putting it aside with the others, which had been piled on a tea tray like a stack of gold coins. She sat back, looking at the pieces of the emptied grandfather clock, and wiped her hands on a clean cloth. At least now it should work again, once she replaced all the pieces. She drew in a deep breath and held her knees over her brother's hand-me-down trousers. The house was coming along nicely. Leaning back, she closed her eyes as the sun rained down from the skylights and warmed her cheeks. Now that the ivy was gone and the sheets of cobwebs removed, the rooms were airy and bright, as if they had never been shut up. While she set to work fixing the lifeless clock, she had sent Eilian to see what the other rooms still needed done and she hadn't seen him since.

Despite coming home from the Rhodes's house the day before with a smile on his face and Argus's paper in hand, he had been quiet all morning. She woke to find him sitting on the edge of the bed. His prosthesis had already been assembled and in his hand was the chunky ring that had once belonged to his father. The gold band caught the light as he turned it over to reveal the family crest etched in minute detail on the metal's surface. She reached out and ran her hand down the smooth flesh of his back. Just for a moment as he turned, she caught the heaviness in his eyes, when the grey of his irises held the gravity of all he didn't say. Before she could speak, he leaned over and kissed her forehead. Pulling back with a smile, he asked, "So what are we to do today?"

She thought that would be the end of it, but as they were eating breakfast, she caught him staring past her at the portrait of his great-grandfather and his children hanging above the fireplace. He brought a few forkfuls of sausage and eggs to his lips and then let the rest grow cold. *That* was not like him. Once he was given his orders to look for things to repair, he went off without a word. Sighing, she decided that if he was still in a funk when she finished with the clock, she would determine what the matter was.

Hadley gathered the last stack of clockwork parts and loaded them into the nearly naked hull. Reaching for the next batch, she paused, listening to the doorbell peal through the stillness. For a moment, she waited to see if Patrick would get it, but when it rang again, she wiped her hands on a fresh rag and answered the door. Standing on the other side was Nadir Talbot gazing at her from under long, dark lashes. In his fern suit and yellow cravat, he looked as if he could have sprouted up in the orangery.

"Mr. Talbot, what a pleasant surprise," she said with a smile but in a tone flat enough for him to understand her true meaning. "Please come in."

"I hope I didn't come at an inopportune time."

As he followed her into the great hall, she could have sworn he leaned on his walking stick more than he had the day before. His cardamom eyes traveled over the stone walls and ancient tapestries before falling on the disassembled clock. With the end of his stick, he reached to nudge the nearest pile.

"Don't touch that."

Nadir looked up at his hostess, his eyes drifting to her grey trousers. They weren't jodhpurs or bloomers but men's trousers. "My apologies, I did not realize you were trying your hand at horology, Lady Dorset."

"*Trying my hand?* Is that what you think I am doing?"

"Surely a lady of your esteem does not dabble with a broken clock when she could easily bring in a clockmaker to repair it."

The redhead scoffed and shook her head, a wayward tendril escaping her bun. "Mr. Talbot, you write books about women who are queens, pharaohs, courtesans, women who hold power, yet you don't think I can fix something as simple as a clock. Do you truly believe that your women are only intelligent because a man created them?"

"The women I write about are fictitious." He swallowed hard, watching the countess regard him with raised brows and crossed arms. "I have never written or met one who was capable of doing so."

"Well, now you have met a real one. Make no mistake, Mr. Talbot, I am the Countess of Dorset, but first and foremost, I am the owner of Fenice Brothers Prosthetics and Hadley's Hobbies and Novelties. A clock is nothing compared to what I create on a regular basis. Just because women choose not to, doesn't mean they can't. Now, what business do you have here, Mr. Talbot? While I'm sure you are a very charming person, I have work to do."

Nadir winced at the sting of his own words being used against him. "I do hope you will forgive me for making assumptions about your character, Lady Dorset. I came to bring a peace offering for my rudeness yesterday, but I probably should have given it to you before I misspoke." He reached into his jacket and pulled out a book decorated with filigree flowers and stars. "Leona told me your brother was a fan of my work, and I thought he might like an autographed copy. I have yet to inscribe it as I did not know his name. But if you don't want it, I can leave."

Hadley's temper ebbed as she exhaled. "That is very kind of you, Mr. Talbot. My brother's name is Adam."

Sitting on the edge of the sofa, he balanced the book on his knees and withdrew a fountain pen from his breast pocket. He signed his name with a flourish and watched her from the corner of his eye. Despite her deservedly cutting him, he found he liked Lady Dorset. It was refreshing to meet resistance rather than a demure tight lipped smile. She reminded him of his impertinent heroines. With her vibrant red hair and contrasting blue eyes, she was a striking figure. She wasn't beautiful, not in the classical sense as his women always were, but the air of power was evident in her upright bearing and charged stare. The women he met in London would titter about how they saw themselves in Cleopatra or Boudicca, and he never understood how when he could never picture them giving impassioned speeches or leading anyone to victory. In Lady Dorset, he sensed a different sort of woman.

"I was rather surprised to hear your brother was a fan. Most of my readers are women. I can't remember ever seeing a man at a reading, apart from my friends and the ladies' husbands, of course."

"Adam... Well, he's a romantic sort. As I told your cousin, he loved *Lotus on the Nile*. He will be delighted to receive this."

Nadir pushed down on his walking stick to get to his feet, feeling the aching strain of his sore hip and ankle, and left the book open on the end table to dry. "I do have an ulterior motive for paying you a visit, Lady Dorset. I was hoping to see the inside of Brasshurst Hall."

"Is it to be the setting of your next novel?"

"No, no, I grew up in Folkesbury. Leona and I spent many a summer collecting shells and fossils along the shore, and every time we returned home, we had to pass this house." His eyes roamed over the carved wooden columns and the intricate lattice of the upper arcades. "It has been shut up for as long as I can remember, and we always longed to know what it was like inside. Leona thought it must be a grand palace, but I, being prone to morbid thoughts, assumed it was haunted."

"It's definitely grand, but you should have seen it when we arrived."

As she spoke, Nadir's gaze drifted to the dining room. Something moved in the shadows. He narrowed his eyes, watching the light break and shift as a low whine whistled from an unseen source. Was that breathing he heard? He stumbled back, grabbing the end table and dropping his stick as a ghastly face appeared in the doorway. His face and hair were white and his breath came as labored as if he had been drowned. Lady Dorset continued on, but he couldn't hear with the colorless figure in black coming closer.

"Lady Dorset, I beg your pardon," the man panted, suddenly solid and very human. "I heard the doorbell but got lost. I am deeply sorry for any inconvenience I may have caused."

"It is quite all right, Patrick. When you catch your breath, would you please bring us some— Mr. Talbot, do you take tea or coffee?" she asked, pretending her guest wasn't white as wax.

"Coffee," he replied in barely more than a whisper, but his voice was drowned out by his heart beating in his ears.

Once the butler was out of sight, the countess's face brightened as she broke into peals of laughter. So much for Nadir Talbot's hauteur. "Morbid thoughts, indeed. You thought he was a ghost!"

"The light in this place plays tricks on you. Surely Brasshurst must have a few ghosts."

She sat in the armchair across from the hearth and motioned for him to take a seat. "I don't think so. At first I did, when the place was still covered in spider webs and dust, but now it seems so alive that I can't imagine anything hiding in the shadows. Was it really shut up when you were a child?"

"Oh, yes, it was utterly deserted not fifteen years ago and had been for some time. The orangery had grown wild with the gardens outside to match." Nadir raked his fingers through his unfashionably long hair, whisking it from his forehead to behind his ear. "I was taking a walk last night and was surprised to find the house alight. For my entire life it has been shuttered. We would try to peer inside, but except for the greenhouse, all the windows were sealed off and even the glass dome was filthy. I hope you don't mind me prying, Lady Dorset, but was there a reason your husband avoided Brasshurst?"

"Actually, we didn't know it existed. He was raised in London at their townhome, and his father never spoke of Brasshurst Hall. Why his father decided not to live here, I have no idea. Mr. Nash, the previous earl's cousin, has been overseeing the property. I'm ashamed to say that it fell into such disrepair."

His ears perked at the name. "Are you well-acquainted with Mr. Nash?"

"No, we have only met him once. Do you know him?"

"Only by name. I have been meaning to call on him, but he doesn't seem to live in the village."

"He doesn't. He lives in the dower house down the road."

Nadir looked up as the spectral butler scurried down the hall with a tray. He poured them each a cup of thick Turkish coffee before disappearing into the shadows of the dining room. Taking a sip, heat flooded Nadir's chest and throat. For the first time since stepping into the hall, calm washed over him. He breathed in the smooth, nutty bitterness and sighed. This was what he missed from home. When he looked up from his drink, the countess was smiling at him.

"Have you fully recovered from your fright, Mr. Talbot?"

"Yes, thank you." His gaze traveled to the clock, but seeing its missing face, he pulled out his pocket watch and pretended to look at it. "I guess I should let you get back to your clock, Lady Dorset. I have taken up quite enough of your time."

"Wait," she called as he eased to his feet. "Would you like a quick tour before you go?"

"Would Lord Dorset mind?"

"Not at all. Maybe we will even find him along the way."

⋆⋆⋆

The house was bigger than he ever imagined. From the outside all those years ago, Brasshurst Hall seemed monumental, but he was a child then. With the hawthorn and yew trees growing unchecked and the vines obscuring the Gothic stone, it was impossible to tell how far it extended into the greenery. Comparing the size of the rooms to his flat in the city or Leona's cottage, he tried to guess how many would fit inside Brasshurst. *Many* was the only answer he could form, yet what surprised him most was not the size but the amount of light. Most of the castles and manors he had visited were cold, drafty places where every room was lit with a fire to chase away the damp. Instead, Brasshurst radiated warmth and smelled faintly of the forest. Its layout resembled a cathedral, with a spine growing from the Gothic portal flanked by transepts on either side to allow a set of tall windows on at least one wall in every room.

His hostess seemed as in awe of the place as he was. Upon entering each room, many of which she still did not know the name of, she pointed out what she admired most. In one of the drawing rooms it was the pianoforte, which Lady Dorset thought had been beautifully carved and gilded even if she could not play it. In another, it was a series of landscapes set in Folkesbury with maelstroms, rolling waves behind green coasts, and overgrown ruins. Nadir found that they hadn't been done with any particular skill or by a great artist, but the countess was taken by the idea that perhaps one of her husband's relations had painted them. Throughout the manor, the moldings and tapestried walls had been decorated with stylized jungles filled with parrots and long-armed monkeys. While the furniture was not opulent, it had a claw-footed strength that balanced the flighty birds woven into the tapestries.

There was no question that Brasshurst was a unique house, but what held Nadir's attention was the view. On the east side, he could see the grey waves and glimpses of the forest surrounding the property while nearly every room on the west side of the house faced out into the wilderness of the greenhouse. The tall Georgian French doors of the drawing room overlooked the garden where the creeping tendrils of ivy had broken through the top of the glass and edged along the crown molding. Lady Dorset stared out at the greenery beyond as Nadir settled into one of the old tapestried chairs to silence his sprained ankle.

"What do you think of Brasshurst, Mr. Talbot? Is it as you imagined?"

"It's better. Bigger, too."

Her dark red brows furrowed as she watched him stretch and flex his leg. "Are you all right?"

"Yes, I'm fine. Just a little clumsiness on my part." His eyes rose to the glass door. "Is it as beautiful as it looks?"

"Come and see for yourself."

With a yawning crack, the doors opened, engulfing the drawing room in the cloying aroma of flowers. Easing onto his feet with his walking stick, he followed her into the mist. His eyes ran along the ribs and spine of the glass dome until they disappeared beneath the massive leaves of palms and yews and flowers of every color and size. Nadir walked down the stone path, careful to not aggravate his throbbing ankle by slipping on the mossy tiles.

On either side of him shattered columns rose from the dirt. The smallest were consumed by the garden while the taller pieces served as a support for flowering vines seeking sunlight. Under the dome's center sat a clearing decorated with mosaic tiles depicting squids, shellfish, and serpents. Somewhere nearby water gurgled, but from the middle of the floor, he couldn't see where. Lady Dorset stood waiting as he studied the plants lining the edge. Most were exotic flowers, others were common weeds, and some were simply ugly. Raising his eyes to the ceiling once more, he noticed that several windows in the manor's upper stories were trapped beneath the glass bubble.

"You should throw a party here."

"Here? Why would I do that?" she asked, returning to his side.

"You said no one has seen the house, and if you had a party, you could invite all of Folkesbury to see what you have done with the place. With it being shut up for so long, everyone must be dying to know what it looks like inside. Why not satisfy their curiosity?"

She nodded, frowning as she ran her eyes over the wayward plants. Her heart pounded in her throat. The thought was terrifying. Everyone in her home, judging her, her food, her house, her husband. There would be countless things to arrange, lists to be made, people to invite. Eilian would of course have to agree to it, and the servants would have to be trained. She didn't think they had ever served during a party, except Patrick, and they were understaffed to begin with. They could barely have anyone over, let alone host a party while the house was still being put back together. On top of everything else, she wasn't certain she could do pull it off. What if she failed?

Hadley smoothed a lock of hair behind her ear and swallowed hard. "I don't know. We are not planning on being here long, and it would be a massive undertaking."

"You're an intelligent woman; I'm certain you could figure it out. Picture this: the entire house is open to allow couples to stroll in and out of the garden to the parlors and drawing rooms. In the orangery, a band plays against that wall," he motioned toward an ancient potting bench leaning against the house, "while your guests dance among the creatures and conks. Is there a pond?"

"Yes, on the other side of the trees."

"You could have your gardener bring in lily pads or lotus plants or you could even float small candles on saucers. It would look like something from Monet."

His brown eyes brightened with visions of women in Worth gowns and men in tails twirling, absinthe flowing from a glass fountain held aloft by a silver faerie. What he could do with a house like this.

"My parents throw parties in their vineyard all the time, and Folkesbury is a lot smaller than Alexandria; you could invite the entire town and still have room. As the lord and lady, you would win them over and secure your reputations here, for what that's worth."

A knot coiled in Hadley's chest. *Or ruin them.*

Chapter Six
Duty

Pain bloomed in Eilian's arm, radiating down the stump until it burned in his metal palm as if the muscle refused to relax. Gritting his teeth, he clenched his eyes and drew in a constrained breath. It had been months since his body reminded him of the flesh and bones that had been seared beyond salvation. The last time he could remember the phantom pain occurring was when he finished settling his father's estate and he realized he was now the earl. Even in death, his father still managed to cause him grief. He had expected the pain to return on the day of their wedding, but any worries he had dissolved when he saw Hadley enter the church. She showed up without looking as if she wanted to run and that was all that mattered.

Staring at his prosthetic hand, Eilian watched the titanium fingers uncurl to their full length before slowly retracting. With each exertion of his will on his prosthetic hand, the invisible muscles loosened. He groaned as he creaked back in the old desk chair and stared at the portrait hanging on the far wall. It differed from the painting hanging in the portrait hall. There his great-grandfather appeared stoic and ever the proper grey-haired nobleman. In this portrait, he was only a few years older than Eilian. Laurence Sorrell posed against a rocky outcropping spattered with moss and vines. His legs and back were tense and his jaw clenched as if he had been cornered against the cliff face. The artist had painted the sky brighter than Eilian thought possible in England, and resting in his hand was a sheathed saber. With his scarlet and gold officer's uniform, he looked as if he stepped off the battlefield, removed his bicorn hat, and sat for the portrait. His hair stuck up in wayward brown curls and clung to his cheeks as if they were coated in sweat. The hand resting in his lap was adorned with the same ring that now rested in Eilian's palm. Swallowing hard, Eilian turned the signet ring over in his hand and watched as the stylized family crest glinted in the sunlight. For months it had hung from his neck on a silver chain out of sight, only taken out to seal official documents.

He couldn't put it on. He didn't deserve the ring or all that came with it.

"How can I represent my family? A one-armed prodigal. How did you do it?" he asked the ill at ease young man hanging from the plaster. "I'm sure you were ready. I'm sure you were able to handle it. You probably didn't think twice about it."

After all, Laurence Sorrell probably wasn't the family pariah like Eilian. Being born first wasn't Eilian's choice, and if he had it within his power, Dylan would have been the earl while he would have simply been Mr. Sorrell. As the Earl of Dorset, his life would forever be tethered to the land by duty and blood. He was trapped on an island with the flood rising, snuffing out what was left of Eilian Sorrell. There was nothing he wanted more than to pretend to be *Mr. Sorrell* again. Mr. Sorrell could do as he pleased and be whoever he wanted. The Honorable Second Son Sorrell's life was an afterthought, a spare in case the heir couldn't wed and bed someone before he died. He sucked in his breath as a bolt of pain shot up his arm. Primogeniture was a farce and so was he.

Eilian looked around the tiny office. It was barely more than a closet hidden behind a panel in the parlor with space enough for a desk, a narrow shelf of ledgers, and an old brass telescope folded in the corner. He had pulled a ledger down to see what the others before him had done, but the numbers and acronyms never made sense. His eyes jumped between lines, blurring and muddling the figures no matter how hard he tried to concentrate. Rubbing his eyes with his knuckles, he groaned. How could he be the earl when he couldn't even figure out the household accounts or do what Hadley had asked? All she wanted was for him to check for cracked plaster or broken clocks, yet he found himself hiding in a closet and interrogating a painting. Ever since they arrived at Brasshurst, Hadley had bustled from task to task. She was constantly cleaning, mending, or socializing, while he was left unable to act. He felt utterly useless.

❦

Patrick Sinclair stood in the doorway of the private study watching his master. Even with his back to him, he could see by the sag of his shoulders and the dip of his head that something was amiss. He had hoped that a trip to the country would lift Lord Sorrell's spirits. Since arriving back in England after his father's death, he had vacillated between elation and sorrow, just as he had after the amputation. Losing his arm had made him aware of his mortality, but the loss of his father cemented it. With mortality came fear, and with fear came misery. Eilian's contagious grin and youthful exuberance were nowhere to be found. He stared ahead, flicking the ring between his thumb and forefinger.

"Sir?" Patrick called softly from the doorway. "Sir, are you all right?"

Eilian shook his head and rubbed the muscle of his sore arm. "What am I doing here, Pat? I'm not ready for any of this."

"You knew it would happen someday."

"I know, but I thought I would be older," he stifled a bitter laugh, "or dead before that happened."

The butler furrowed his brow. "Don't say things like that, sir."

"But it's true. I never thought it would actually happen. Did you really think I would survive malaria or the crash?"

"I did."

"Of course you did." His grip tightened on his arm as he rode out a wave of pain. "Pat, I just don't know what I am supposed to do."

"Have you spoken to Lady Dorset about it?"

"Do you mean Hadley or my mother?"

He pushed his spectacles up his narrow nose and cleared his throat. "Your wife."

"I don't want to upset her. She's already worrying about being a lady. I can't have her worry about being an earl, too."

"Her ladyship was looking for you in the portrait hall. Shall I tell her you will be joining her shortly?"

"Yes, thank you, Pat," he whispered as he slipped the ring and its chain into his collar, out of sight.

"Sir, is there anything I can do to help you?"

His lips curled into a stiff smile. "Switch places with me. I always considered you to be my older brother."

"If I could, I would." Taking a step into the drawing room, Patrick stopped and turned to face his master again. "Please speak to her, sir. She can help you more than I ever could."

As soon as he was out of sight, the butler hurried down the hallway and into the passages behind the walls created decades ago for servants to go about unseen. He had told his master that Lady Dorset was in the portrait hall to buy a few minutes alone with her. If Eilian got to her first, he would brush everything off with a blithe grin. If Patrick could be fooled into thinking Eilian was fine when he had cholera, then she would most certainly be fooled. In Greenwich, it was infinitely easier to keep an eye on his master. The house and staff were small enough that he could be butler, valet, and driver; but Brasshurst's size alone made it impossible to stick close by. He had shadowed Eilian since they were boys and he was a footman in his parents' house. As a servant, Patrick had been trained to recognize what would be needed before anyone asked, and from a young age, it was apparent that Eilian Sorrell needed help the most.

Bustling behind the wall, he passed the thrumming engine that powered the orangery and the stairs leading to the catacombs beneath it. Every few feet, light broke through narrow slits cut into the walls, casting strange shadows in the dank hall. At the end of the tunnel, Patrick pushed open the paneling and arrived outside the dining room. He brushed the dust from his elbows and shoulders and waited out of sight until his heart slowed. Catching his breath, he rounded the corner to find Lady Dorset replacing the last of the gears in the grandfather clock.

"Did you find Eilian?" she asked, watching the blur of white hair from the corner of her eye.

"Yes, my lady, he'll be here in a moment." He straightened and craned his neck to see if Eilian was coming. "Lady Dorset, I was hoping to speak to you. I know it's out of turn, but it's very important."

She turned to find Pat's face grave. She was so accustomed to seeing him flustered with nerves that to have him stand before her with his light brows furrowed and his demeanor calm scared her. "Of course, go ahead."

His eyes darted down the hall again. "I'm worried about his lordship. He has been out of sorts lately."

"I noticed that this morning. Do you have any idea what's wrong?"

"It's the earldom, my lady. He's feeling the pressure of his new position, and his outlook is becoming very bleak. It's the worst it's been since the dirigible accident, and that troubles me."

Hadley sighed. For once Patrick wasn't overreacting. "I knew I should have asked him what the matter was when he skipped breakfast."

"He wouldn't have answered. His lordship doesn't want to upset you." He paused. For a second he thought he heard footsteps in the hall. "May I ask you for a favor?"

"Anything."

"Tomorrow, please get his lordship out of the house for a while. Apart from your outing to visit Mr. and Mrs. Rhodes, he's been inside since you arrived. He needs to get out for a little while. I know you are very busy, but please go for a walk or ride together. It should set things right."

"But if he wants to go outside, why doesn't he? He's a grown man; he doesn't need my permission."

"He doesn't know what to do, so he's following your lead. You stay inside, he stays inside."

"Well, why didn't he say anything to me? I would have done it if I knew."

"I don't think he knows what he needs." Patrick dropped his voice as Eilian drifted toward them with his head down. "Please don't tell him I told you."

"I won't," she mouthed as the butler disappeared into the dining room.

Eilian stood in his shirtsleeves and waistcoat with dust-ringed cuffs. When he saw her, he gave her a gentle grin, but the hint of cheer never made it to his eyes. "Pat said you were looking for me."

"I was wondering where you had gone. Dinner is ready."

Taking his hands, Hadley pulled him closer until he wrapped around her with his chin resting against her temple. For a moment she thought he wouldn't embrace her when suddenly his arms cinched around her waist and the warmth of his body sighed into hers. His cool lips pressed against her cheek and hair before his head came to rest between her neck and shoulder.

"I love you," she whispered into his collar, running her hands up and down the length of his back.

"I love you too. I'm sorry, Had."

"For what?" She asked as she pulled away and led him into the dining room, watching Patrick place two plates of chicken fricassee on the table.

"I got distracted. I only inspected three rooms," he replied as they settled into their seats.

He sighed and pushed a mushroom around the edge of his plate. Anger flared in Hadley's breast. She had asked him to do one thing— *one thing*—and he hadn't done it, but she drowned out the thought with what Patrick had said. It was obvious that something was wrong by his faraway eyes and slack frown. She knew what caused it and hated that she could do nothing to fix it. Even with a replacement arm, a wife, and a title, he wasn't happy. In his mind, he still wasn't an earl and never would be.

"Did you hear the doorbell ring a while ago?"

Eilian shook his head.

"Nadir Talbot, Mrs. Rhodes's cousin, came to bring me a signed copy of his latest book. He heard that Adam enjoyed his work and thought he would like it."

"That was very generous of him. I'm sorry to have missed him again."

Watching him finally stab a bit of tomato and chicken, she continued, "It turns out he grew up in Folkesbury. He said Brasshurst has been shut up for as long as he can remember, so I gave him a tour."

"What did he think? Was he as afraid of it as we were?"

She chuckled to herself. "I would say so. He thought Patrick was a ghost, but he seemed quite taken with it. He even suggested that we throw a party, so everyone could see the house restored to its former glory."

When she looked up, Eilian's eyes were wide and his face had turned a sickly grey. "A— a party?"

"I told him it was a foolish idea, but he was pretty persuasive. It would be a great way to meet all of your tenants and show everyone that you intend to restore Brasshurst."

"Do I?"

"As I said, it's a foolish idea. We are in no position to throw anything larger than dinner for Mr. Talbot and his cousins." She waited, watching the pain surface in his face. He took a bite of chicken and clenched his eyes shut. His breath hitched, and as he swallowed, she noticed how the whites of his eyes glistened at their edges. Now was not the time. "I was thinking that maybe tomorrow we could go down to the beach. We have been stuck inside for days, and I don't think I can stand another day of dust or clocks. What do you think?"

"I don't know. Aren't you busy? Maybe I should stay home. I still need to check for repairs."

"But I want to spend the day with you, away from all this."

Eilian locked eyes with her, relief loosening his features. "All right then, if you're sure. Are we taking the bicycles?"

"We will have to; the steamer is still in the shop. I bet we could fit a picnic basket in the front of my bicycle. How does that sound? A picnic on the beach."

The color drifted into his cheeks and eyes. He was far from himself, yet somewhere in his eyes, a glint of hope appeared. It wasn't strong or sure, but it was there.

Chapter Seven
Picnics & Prostheses

Drawing in a lungful of sea air, Eilian felt the knot in his chest loosen. The sun warmed his cheeks as he threw back his head and closed his eyes. Only a few feet away the water roared over the jetties, being caught by a thousand tiny arms until it sloshed over his bare feet in an icy surge. Eilian stood rooted on the shore, feeling the press of the slick pebbles under his numbed soles as another wave sprayed over the hem of his trousers. If he closed his eyes and banished all thought, he could feel the ocean's pull. It urged his feet and body forward toward the channel to be swallowed up by the earth. All it would take was a few more—

"Don't go in too deep! Remember your arm can't get wet!" Hadley called, spreading a blanket across the detrital sand.

As she unpacked the wicker basket of sandwiches, chutneys, and sweets, along with bottles of lemonade and wine, she watched her husband at the water's edge. He picked up a broken clam that lazily spun in with the tide and pitched it into the bay. It skimmed the surface before hitting the jetty and breaking in two. Patrick had been right; the change was undeniable. By the time they reached the path and got the velocipedes rolling downhill toward the coast, Eilian's face had regained its color and his eyes had brightened with glee. At the bottom of the bluff, they were forced to walk their bicycles through the coarse sand, rumbling over the seashells and bits of stone that had drifted the world over before coming to rest on the Dorset shore. Every so often Eilian would stop to examine a shell or to check if an upturned rock was a really a fossil in disguise.

"Patrick has really outdone himself. I don't know how he fit it all in here. Finger sandwiches, bread, curds. Is that curry?" she asked as she uncapped a jar and brought it to her nose. It was still warm.

Eilian kicked the sand from his feet and settled on the edge of the picnic blanket. "You should thank Mrs. Negi for that. She cooked it and probably assembled the basket."

"You know, I still have never met her."

"She keeps to herself, but if you're still thinking about throwing a party or dinner, you may want to speak to her. She... she doesn't like having things sprung on her." Grabbing a slice of bread, he loaded it with curds, chutney, and a dollop of curry. "Much like you, she has a temper, but if you were descended from Rajput warriors, I would expect you to have one, too."

"Rajput warriors?"

He nodded, licking the sauce from his lips. "Her ancestors were palace guards. At the time, I was traveling through Northern India and I stopped to have dinner with a British family my parents knew. They were the local officials, trying—successfully, might I add—to usurp the princes' power. One night we dined with the local prince. Thing is, the entire time I had been with the family, all we had was British food apart from dessert, and when I was invited to dinner with the prince, I thought I would finally get to taste real North Indian cuisine." As he spoke, he assembled another sandwich dripping with mango chutney. "Apparently, she was tired of English food, too. As we were leaving, I heard her arguing with the head servant about never getting the chance to cook the food she was hired to make, and he told her to leave. I asked her if she would like to travel with me as my personal cook."

"And she just went with you?"

"Oh, no, of course not. Who in their right mind follows a twenty year old anywhere? Anyway, after I convinced her that I could pay her and that I really wanted to hire her as a cook, she agreed. Her husband had died some years earlier, along with her only child, and she needed the work." He chuckled to himself. "Most of my servants are cast-offs. I don't understand why any of them were let go in the first place."

Hadley smiled to herself and wondered what stories were attached to his maids. From what ill fate had the three girls been plucked? Raising her gaze from her cold chicken sandwich, she spotted a familiar dark head. At the far end of the cove, Nadir Talbot ambled along the path, his cane ticking in time with his step. His scarlet coat and plum vest glowed in the sunlight as if he were dressed for a party, but what betrayed his formal attire were his sun-spectacles. In his free arm, he lugged a portable writing desk, a valise, and a camp chair slung over his shoulder, which required straightening every dozen steps. As he crossed the sand, he stopped, letting the wind whip his black curls and open collar like the debauched hero of some Gothic novel. When he turned toward them, Hadley raised her arm and beckoned for him to come over.

"Mr. Talbot, going for a stroll?"

"Searching for inspiration, Lady Dorset," he called as he walked over. "My heroine will be coming ashore from a foreign land in a few pages and I thought the smell of the ocean might evoke something." He barely spotted her bright red hair above the two bicycles leaning against a massive boulder, but as he drew closer, he realized she wasn't alone. The man beside her sat half in the sand in only his shirt, waistcoat, and trousers, which had been rolled to his knees. His shoes and stockings sat beside him while his jacket had been slung over the seat of his bicycle. He supposed he was the Earl of Dorset, but from his sandy feet and state of under dress, he couldn't be sure.

Hadley smiled to herself. It seemed strange to have the two men in such close proximity. Nadir Talbot gleamed like a ruby while her husband in his linen shirtsleeves and light brown trousers, looked like a laborer. "Eilian, this is Nadir Talbot, the writer. Mr. Talbot, this is my husband, the Earl of Dorset."

Eilian quickly wiped his hands and mouth and climbed to his feet. "My wife speaks very highly of you, Mr. Talbot."

"And you. I hope you didn't mind that Lady Dorset gave me a tour of Brasshurst. It's quite a *unique* specimen." Reaching for the earl's hand, his eyes landed on his prosthesis. Despite being identical in size and shape to its twin, his right hand was nearly black and perfectly smooth. The segmented titanium fingers were curled into a loose fist, and where it met the wrist, two rings sprung from either side where long, tightly curled springs were attached by bent hooks. The fingers unfurled as their hands touched. From being in the sun, the earl's metal palm radiated a dull heat. "That is a beautiful prosthesis, Lord Dorset. If you do not mind me asking, where did you come across it? I have never seen one open like that."

"My wife created it." His lips curled into a stiff grin as he rubbed his hand over it self-consciously, but when he looked in the Mr. Talbot's eyes, he found only curiosity. "That's how we met. She designed and built it for me."

The writer laughed. "So this is what you create on a regular basis, Lady Dorset. Now I understand what you meant about the clock." He tilted his head, searching for a bulge or string beneath the nobleman's shirt. "How does this contraption work? Is there a spring or lever?"

"No, it's electric. There's a battery in the holster."

"But how does it open?"

There was something about Nadir Talbot that put Eilian at ease. It could have been that he acted like Adam Fenice and looked like the Egyptian men he worked with in his excavations. Perhaps it was that Hadley trusted and liked him. His questions about his arm seemed to arise from natural curiosity rather than repugnance or ignorance, and Eilian thought genuine interest should always be rewarded.

"Would you like to see it?"

When Mr. Talbot nodded, Hadley watched in shock as Eilian unbuttoned his sleeve and rolled it over his forearm and up to his shoulder. He almost never showed others his prosthesis, yet he allowed the writer to step closer and examine it.

Nadir's keen eyes traveled over the springs that began at his wrist and looped through half a dozen more sets of metal rings before connecting to a leather bracer on his upper arm. Sticking out from the side of the couter was a pouch large enough for a battery. All that was left of his forearm was a metal rod surrounded by spring muscle bundles, and while he couldn't see what was beneath the leather brace or cotton sleeve under it, he was certain his upper arm was still intact. The design was simple and strong. Metal, leather, and flesh melded to rebuild what had been lost. Nadir watched as the fingers bloomed open before curling shut once more.

"How did you do that?"

"A doctor inserted gold needles into my nerves. If I think about my hand opening, it does. Well, it's more like I feel it opening."

"Fascinating. So you had surgery?"

"Yes, they had to attach the porcelain joint with," he cleared his throat, "donated tissue."

"I'm impressed, Lady Dorset, thoroughly impressed. I may need to include one of these in a story someday. My readers would love it, especially if they knew it really exists."

"That's very kind of you." Hadley's cheeks pinkened. "Would you care to join us? We have plenty to spare."

He looked from the earl to his wife and then at the spread of edibles that lay across the blanket. There had to be a dozen tins, jars, and linen parcels of food, and each looked better than anything Leona could muster up. "I wouldn't want to intrude."

"Please, join us, Mr. Talbot," Lord Dorset said, motioning toward an empty space adjacent to his wife. A soft smile spread across his features as he rolled down his sleeve. "Then you can tell us all about your book."

"All right, but only for a little while. Then, I must be off and actually write something."

Dropping his valise and camp chair next to their bicycles, he settled in beside Eilian and Hadley. Between neat bites of finger sandwiches, he told them of his latest idea. After seeing the vast orangery of Brasshurst, he had decided to alter his current manuscript from another Greco-Roman drama to a Babylonian tale of a young peasant woman sent to the king's harem only to be thrust into a world of hanging gardens and exotic riches. Of course it would be a romantic tale full of intrigue and mystery as the girl rose to queen despite attacks from the other women of the harem and the king's scheming priests.

"My brother will love it. May I tell him of your idea?" Hadley asked as she unpacked the glasses and poured each of them some lemonade.

"Of course. Just don't give away the ending, though it will probably change by the time he reads it."

The back of Nadir's eye burned as he resisted the urge to wink. If he had been talking to the well-to-do widows or the young women barely out in society who usually frequented his and his friends' parlors, he would have done it as he had hundreds of times before. Even if Lord Dorset hadn't been there, he wouldn't have dared to do it. In her blue and yellow dress with her hair artfully bundled under a straw hat, it was hard to imagine Lady Dorset standing before the grandfather clock in men's trousers and an oil rag in her hand. After seeing her like that, so at ease in both roles, it seemed impossible to approach her the same way as he would other society ladies. At least her husband didn't appear to be the jealous type.

Hadley leaned back, soaking in the ocean's gentle murmur and the sun's warm gaze as the men rooted through the tin of desserts. She had hoped Eilian and Nadir Talbot would get along. For the second time in her life, she and Adam were separated, but this time, it was for good. There would be no returning to Baker Street except as a guest. It was odd to wake up and not have someone to critique her outfit or help her pin her hair before she went out. Mr. Talbot's dandified dress and air of cultivated eloquence would be as close as she would get to Adam in Dorset, and it only made her long to see her twin more. Opening her eyes, she watched the waves lap against the coast as it curved away from Folkesbury.

She squinted. Someone was walking on the far end of the beach. As the figure slowly processed across the sand, she realized there were actually three people. The woman in front wore a forest green gown, the side of her face obscured by high mutton sleeves. Holding a fringed parasol over her mistress was a slight maid. With her colorless dress and jet hair, she could have been the woman's shadow, narrowed in the afternoon sun. Linked arm-in-arm with her was a well-built gentleman. From afar, he seemed handsome, even if he appeared old enough to be Hadley's father. He stood very straight beside her but lacked the polished gait of the aristocracy.

"Mr. Talbot, do you know who that woman is?" she asked as the party grew closer.

He craned his neck. His eyes roamed over her light blonde hair, which had been elaborately coiled and pulled back severely from her forehead. Her face was set in a scowl, giving her stately features a hard edge. Even though she didn't appear to be over fifty, she had the bearing of a much older woman. Her maid's eyes widened when she noticed Nadir watching them. Without question, he recognized her. She had delivered the letter to Leona, the one they both tried so hard to hide. His cousin had said her name, but for the life of him, he couldn't recall it.

"I don't know, but they appear to be headed this way."

The woman and her companions crossed the sand and stopped near the outcropping where the Sorrells had parked their bicycles. As her eyes ran over the velocipedes, she sneered, looking down her upturned nose at the picnickers. The Sorrells were not what she had imagined, even if her husband had warned her of their immaturity and lack of decorum. They were dining in the dirt without gloves or servants. Their lips and corners were tinted orange from their meal, and they were eating with bare fingers. Worst of all, the earl had shed his jacket and shoes in favor of sitting the sand in only his shirt sleeves.

"Lord and Lady Dorset, I presume?" she stated, coming no closer.

Hadley watched sweat bead down the maid's cheek as her arms shook from holding the heavy parasol steady, but her lady took no notice. "Yes, and you are?"

"Rubella Nash. I believe you have met my husband."

"Yes, we have."

Mrs. Nash's hard gaze never wavered from Hadley's face. It was impossible to tell if she was studying her or boring through her skull, but it unnerved her just the same, even if she refused to show it. Hadley glanced at the man at her side. His mustache had been artfully set and waxed into a fine curl. The man was far younger than Mr. Nash and much more attractive, but he was much too old to be Mrs. Nash's son.

"It is a pleasure to make your acquaintance, Mrs. Nash. We were not aware that Mr. Nash was married. If we had known, we would have called on you sooner. And you, sir, though I don't believe we have made your acquaintance."

"Sergeant Purcell, head of the Folkesbury constabulary," he replied, his speech clipped with authority. Purcell gave her husband's hand a firm shake before bowing to Hadley. Neither visitor even paid Nadir a glance. "Hopefully we will not meet again, your ladyship, unless in a social setting."

Mrs. Nash's eyes narrowed on the young couple. "We did not see you at church this morning."

"That's because we were not there," Hadley replied, forcing a soft smile.

"Did you not know where it was?"

"We *chose* not to go."

"Do Londoners not attend mass?"

Eilian and Mr. Talbot exchanged glances as Hadley took a deep breath and stiffly replied, "Not all, Mrs. Nash. We do not. We are secular."

She pursed her lips. Finally, Mrs. Nash said, "Then, you will not be joining the Society of Visiting Ladies? We meet every Wednesday at Billings' for tea. We're a decidedly *Christian* organization. If you choose to no longer be a heathen, then you may join us."

"Rubella, why not let her join?" the sergeant asked genially while giving Hadley and Eilian a sharp look. "You know how young people are nowadays."

"They need to know expectations here are different from the city." Without removing her gaze from the redhead's face, she snapped her fingers and the maid lurched forward. "I hope we will see you next week. Come, Pilcrow."

Nadir and the Sorrells watched as the Mrs. Nash and Sergeant Purcell sauntered out of sight with Pilcrow at their backs.

Eilian blinked, unsure if what he had seen had really happened. "Did we just get reprimanded for not going to church? My parents didn't even care if I attended mass."

"She called you a heathen!" Nadir cried. "*Decidedly Christian.* Like you would even want to—"

"Are either of you really surprised? Folkesbury is a small town, and we are all outsiders. I'm sure they have been keeping an eye on us for that very reason. Small town gossip."

"Too bad we aren't in Bath or Paris. They only talk about where you are, not where you aren't. Unless it is a party. Then, they wonder why you were not invited and what you did to deserve it."

Eilian frowned, nudging a pastry away. "Hadley's right, we are all curiosities. Still, it was unwarranted. I don't know how anyone can like the Nashes."

For a few minutes they sat in silence, finishing the last of their desserts and the remaining lemonade. Nadir's eyes flickered to his neglected writing desk where it rested beside the Sorrell's bicycles. A dusting of fine sand coated its top. An afternoon of good conversation and food would have been much preferred to a solitary half-day of writing, but the Babylonian king's mistress was dancing through his mind and he had to catch her before she left.

"I beg your pardon, Lord and Lady Dorset, but I really should be going soon. Unfortunately, I owe my publisher the first half of my book in a week or so, and I have barely begun my rewrites. Thank you for allowing me to dine with you. There is nothing I cherish more than good food and conversation."

Hadley inwardly sighed but smiled. "I'm so glad you could join us."

"I do hope we will see you again soon." As the writer gathered his valise and desk, Eilian asked, "Mr. Talbot, do you know if there is anything interesting to see in Folkesbury? Hadley told me you lived here as a child."

He thought for a long moment. "Not really. The ocean is the biggest draw in the summer months, but there are Roman ruins scattered throughout the woods. When we were children, Leona and I would search for the faerie caves that were supposed to be hidden amongst the trees, but all we found were old foundations and walls. But who knows? Perhaps you will be the first."

Chapter Eight
Woman Troubles

Nadir gently clicked the front door shut behind him and dropped his writing desk on the hall table. The day had gone better than he expected. At first he feared his picnic with Lord and Lady Dorset would eat into his writing time or dampen his mood, but it only inspired him. In the hours after they parted, he sat on the beach with his writing desk resting against a rock and slipped into the perfumed, dangerous world of Ancient Babylon—or at least what he thought Ancient Babylon to be. Maybe a steady stream of good company and good food were all he needed to finish this book.

Hanging his top hat on the rack, he listened in the stillness for his cousin or her husband. A loud stuttered snore ripped through the darkness of the parlor. Nadir drew back the curtain and found Argus asleep across the sofa with his hairy hands neatly folded over his paunch. A half-empty teacup cooled on the side-table behind his head, and his wire-rimmed glasses hung half-off his face, fogged from his hot breath. He considered waking Argus up to save his spectacles from being broken under his heavy cheek when he heard a clatter in his office. Slowly creaking open the door, Nadir peered in.

Every gas lamp and candle in the room had been lit, despite it being only a quarter past seven. While the desk remained tidy and untouched, the bookcase beside it had been nearly emptied and its contents scattered across the floor. Only the books at the edges were left standing, leaving a ragged gap that ran the length of the shelf.

"Blast it! Where did I put it?"

Nadir stuck his head around the edge of the door and watched his cousin. Running a hand across her brow, she released a tremulous breath and stared at the pile before her. She picked up each book in turn, checking the spine and cover before tossing it behind her onto a slanted stack. When she finished inspecting that sample, she leaned into the next shelf and felt behind the books. Her back straightened as she withdrew a small text. Its light grey cover appeared to be blank, but when she opened it to the front page, her eyes brightened.

"*Every Woman's Book*," she read aloud, frowning thoughtfully at the weathered page, "not quite what I was looking for. I could have sworn I put Carlile by Hanchett."

Tucking the thin volume under her skirt, she stuck her arm into the gap between the pages and the shelf. When she didn't find what she was looking for, she repeated it on the final one. Leona sat back and stared at the bookcases. Lying across the floor, she reached under the shelf. Between Argus's labored breaths, he could hear something running across the wooden boards. A black book slid out at the end of Leona's fingers like a planchette. From his hiding place, Nadir couldn't make out the golden letters across the cover, but it had to be the right book. She let the pages run between her fingers until she found what she was looking for. Silent words raced across her lips, but as her eyes widened, the board under Nadir's boot groaned.

"Doing a bit of redecorating?" he asked with a cheeky grin.

Her eyes shot to the door as she slammed the volume closed. "I— Oh, I hate it when you do that! What are you doing here?"

Before she could slip the book out of sight, he had crossed the space between them and plucked it from her hand. Leona shot up after him, her hands snapping for her book, but he raised it above his head and spun toward the door as he had so many times when they were children. This time, it wasn't a diary in his hands but a medical textbook. He cocked his brow and stared down at his older cousin. Her dark brows knit in anger and her breast heaved, yet beneath her blustering and scowling, her eyes were strained with fear.

"*Sexual Health?*" he asked, holding it out for her to take.

Her round cheeks grew hot as she snatched it from his hand and placed it on the mantle. "Yes, it's a textbook. I'm— I'm having woman troubles, thank you very much, and I would appreciate it if you did not pry while you're here."

"Oh." His face fell. "I hope it's nothing serious."

"No. At least, I don't think so."

"Have you seen a doctor?"

Leona cocked her brow. "If I went to Dr. Sturgis, the whole town would know."

"You could come back to London with me. I'm sure someone on Harley Street could sort it out."

"Really, it's nothing. Help me put these back if you care so much."

Picking up a handful of books, he stared at the spines. Half were her father's old apothecary manuals while the rest were books on Egypt. "Shouldn't these be in some sort of order?"

"Just put them back. Argus won't notice the difference."

"Have you told him?"

"Told him what?"

"About your 'woman trouble'?"

Leona froze with her hand on the shelf. Her voice came out pinched and strained as she replied, "No, no. You know Argus. He would worry so, and it's nothing. Please don't burden him unnecessarily, Nadir."

It wasn't a hissed threat or a tight whisper, as he expected. Her voice faltered, but her impassive face betrayed nothing. Nodding, he

70

restocked the shelves. For her sake, he hoped it really was nothing. As much as he said he hated staying with her, Leona was the closest thing to a sister he ever had and he had been looking forward to their time together after nearly five years of only sparse letters.

She cleared her throat. "How was your day? Did you get any work done?"

"Yes, quite a bit. I met Lord and Lady Dorset by the beach. They invited me to share in their picnic. We ended up talking for quite some time."

"That was very nice of them." Her face and eyes softened before tightening into a tired frown. "I don't think Lady Dorset likes me very much. Women usually like me, but she seemed miserable when they called on us."

With her eyes cast down and her face darkened with thought, she looked like her younger, more innocent self, the girl he remembered collecting shells with during his childhood. He wrapped his arm around her shoulders and gave them a squeeze. "She is an odd sort. Then again, you know you can be off-putting when you try too hard, but she will come around. I can even put in a good word for you if you want."

"Thanks," she replied as she replaced the final handful of texts.

"I don't think she dislikes anyone. Well, except for Mrs. Nash."

Nadir watched from the corner of his eye as Leona stiffened.

"Oh? Why does she dislike Mrs. Nash?"

"Because while we were eating, she chastised her for not attending church."

⊶⊙⊱ ⊰⊙⊷

The grass crunched under Eilian and Hadley's boots as they led their bicycles up the hill toward Brasshurst Hall. While they hadn't discovered the faerie caves Nadir mentioned, they had found the remnants of a Roman wall on the cliff above the beach. In places the mortar had chipped away only to be held fast by countless mossy fingers. To Hadley, the wall seemed barely more than bits of stone stacked one atop another like a poor man's fence, yet it brought her husband great joy. He measured its height and width against his hand and leg before following it up and down the hill where it disappeared into the earth and brush only to reappear several yards away. By the time they completely lost the wall to the countryside, both Sorrells were ankle deep in mud.

"What do you think it was?" she asked as Eilian lugged their velocipedes down the back steps into the servants' quarters.

"I'm not sure. It could have been part of a fortification or town. It would make sense since we found them on the hill, but I will need to go back and look again. Maybe I should do an excavation here."

"Does that mean Brasshurst was built where there used to be an ancient town?"

Before Eilian could reply, Patrick opened the basement door. Charlotte, the lanky maid who had been with him the longest, appeared behind the butler's shoulder but quickly curtsied upon seeing the earl and countess. Both servants' eyes widened as they trailed to the dirt that had wicked up the Sorrells' clothing. Hadley plucked the half-empty picnic basket from her bicycle and handed it to the waiting maid before working on her boot laces.

"Charlotte, in a little while, would you come to collect my dress for cleaning if you aren't occupied?" Hadley asked as her gloved fingers slipped over the sticky mud.

The light-haired maid left the basket on the dining table and gathered Hadley's soiled gloves and shoes. "Yes, milady. Will you need help redressing?"

"No, thank you. I will see to it myself."

"When you go up, fetch his lordship's trousers as well," Patrick added as he motioned for Eilian to hand over his caked boots. "I have already laid out clean clothing for both of you."

In their stocking feet, they padded through the servants' hall and up the darkened iron staircase that led to the upper floors. Cutting through the high, latticed windows of the harem-style wing, Hadley paused to watch the sun set over the trees. Beyond the panes and panels of dark wood, the sea engulfed Folkesbury in a cloak of fog. Hadley laced her fingers with her husband's as they rounded the bend near their bedroom. From the corner of her eye, she watched his lips curl into a smile as she squeezed his palm.

"Did you have a good time today?" she asked as he held the door open for her.

"Very much so. Thank you for arranging it." He released a constrained sigh, pulling off his jacket and setting it aside on a hanger. "It was nice to spend the entire day with you. It seems like I barely see you even though we're always here together."

She frowned. She hadn't intended to ignore him, but the house had been a bigger project than she had imagined. Shutting the door, Hadley stared down at the four inch line of mud running along the hem of her gown. Before she could ask, Eilian wrapped his prosthetic arm around her waist and undid the buttons running down his wife's neck one-handed. He kissed the top of her head and left her to disrobe. She stepped out of her dress and slipped off her camisole and dirt-peppered stockings. Standing in only her chemise and corset, she watched Eilian toss his muddied trousers onto the valet stand and his father's signet ring on the nightstand. Sunlight spilled through the curtains, pouring over his firm shoulders and down the lean musculature of his torso and arms until it stopped at the edge of his cotton drawers. The deep scars that marred what she could see of his right arm fanned across his ribs in webbed vines before dissolving at his waistline. When they were first in the Negev together, she remembered them being redder, but over the past few months, they had paled to his natural skin tone. It seemed so odd to her now that they never once touched all those nights they were alone in the tent.

"Close your eyes," she said, standing before him as he sat on the edge of the bed to remove his wet socks.

He stared at her for a moment, unsure of what she intended, but when she didn't budge, he obeyed and shut his eyes. Her hand grazed his thigh before coming to rest on his shoulder as she shifted her weight across his knees. With his eyes still closed, he wrapped his arms around the small of her back.

Hadley took in her husband's face. When he was looking at her, it was hard to not be drawn to his quick grey eyes. With them shut, she could finally see the rest of him. She ran her fingers through his thick brown hair, which was still damp at the roots with sea spray and sweat, and planted a reverent kiss between his brows. Her hands traveled along the aperture of his neck as she kissed each eyelid. When her soft lips grazed his jaw, his grip tightened, inching her closer until their bodies brushed. Her flushed breasts burned through her chemise where they pressed into the muscles of his chest. The breath caught in his throat as her mouth kneaded the sensitive flesh of his neck. He shifted beneath her, his hand trailing up her back in time with her mouth. Reaching his chin, she gazed at him for a moment before finally bringing her lips to his. Eilian was hers.

Eilian pressed back, heat flooding his chest and abdomen as her hands wandered across his shoulders and into his hair. The moment he parted his lips to draw in a breath Hadley's tongue swept along his lower lip. She shifted onto her knees, kneeling over him as he mimicked what she had done. Against her will, a soft groan escaped her lips at the sensation of his tongue grazing hers. Her arm slid behind his neck and drew him closer until her hips rested against his stomach. They breathed in time as their hands ran over the curves of the other's body and their lips slipped and locked. Sliding his hands up her sides as he planted a line of kisses down her clavicle, his prosthesis caught on the strings of her corset. He tried to tug it free, but the lace held fast. When he broke away from her flesh to untangle it, her dark blue eyes fixed on him, waiting.

Eilian swallowed hard. He knew she expected him to remove her corset, but he couldn't. Another man would have jumped at the chance, yet it filled him with dread. His stomach churned as a cold sweat broke over his forehead and back. He didn't know what he was supposed to do next. Hadley instinctively knew, everyone seemed to know, and it came as naturally to them as walking. Averting his gaze from her silk chemise, he desperately sought to untangle his spring from the laces. If he didn't do something, she would. With one final roll of his prosthetic hand, it came free. Relief slowed his racing pulse as he sank back. Had she seen the panic in his eyes?

Resting his lips on her freckled shoulder, he swallowed against the gnarl in his gut. His wife was still waiting, but apart from the race of fear, his mind was blank. When he leaned back to meet her light-eyed gaze, the tension left her face only to slacken with disappointment. His hand shook as he traced her cheek and kissed her once more, but this time she barely pressed back.

His heart pounded. He hadn't meant to hurt her. He loved her. He loved her dearly and wanted nothing more than to spend his life with her, yet he couldn't bear to do it. Opening his mouth to speak, Eilian realized there was nothing he could say. How could he tell her that thinking about it made him so anxious that he felt sick to his stomach? How could he possibly talk about desire when he had never experienced it?

The back of his eyes burned as he carefully lifted her off his lap and slipped out from under her. "I can't. I'm sorry, Hadley, but I can't."

Her eyes darted over his fallen features, silently pleading for him to stay. His face grayed as he rubbed his upper arm and ducked into the dressing room without meeting her gaze. The door softly clicked shut behind him.

Sitting on the edge of the bed, Hadley drew in a tremulous breath. She cleared her throat and straightened her back before smoothing and re-pinning her mussed hair. As she picked her soiled dress off the floor, she stared down at her form. What had she done wrong? She replayed her part in their embrace, but she couldn't understand what would have made him leave. Slipping on a clean gown, she stared at the dressing room door. She could confront him, demand to know what that was all about, but what good would it do? The damage had already been done.

Hadley calmly stepped in the hall and walked toward the grand staircase. Surely there was something in the house that needed fixing.

Chapter Nine
An Unwelcome Guest

Hadley Sorrell's heels clicked across the polished floorboards. Her eyes swept into each open door, searching for a maid or even Patrick, but thus far, her staff had eluded her. In her hand she clutched two letters; one for each of the important women in her life. To her mother-in-law, she wrote about the possibility of throwing a party at Brasshurst. The dowager countess would know the feasibility of such a plan, and perhaps she would even offer to help her draft the menu or tell her where she could procure a few more servants. The other was addressed to Eliza Hawthorne. Ever since her mother died, her cousin had become her surrogate mother and honorary sister, and she was the only woman with whom she could speak freely. Days like these made her wish Eliza and James had come with them to Folkesbury. As a married woman and a physician, surely she could spread some light on what had occurred a few days earlier. Maybe it was a normal reaction, but she wouldn't know until she replied.

The Earl and the Artificer

For three days she had debated whether she should say anything. The night of the incident she stayed downstairs taking apart and cleaning the algae-encrusted mechanisms of the orangery's pond until she was too tired to reassemble the engine. She left the pieces strewn across the mosaic floor and returned upstairs to soak away the slime and what remained of her misery. When she slunk into their bedroom in her nightgown, she was surprised to find the room dark and Eilian beneath the bed's canopy with his face to the wall. He didn't stir as she sank into the mattress beside him, but she knew he was awake. His eyes fixed on the bed curtain while he cradled his stripped prosthesis in his other arm. She hadn't seen him since he locked himself in the dressing room, and watching his bare back rise and fall, she wondered if he had eaten dinner or if he had gone to bed after she left. Sliding under the covers beside him, she stared at the bed's gathered ceiling. Words hung in the air ready to be plucked but neither spoke. The hours wore on and the disquieted silence soon faltered into a stiff slumber.

In the morning when she awoke, he was sitting on the edge of the bed assembling his prosthesis. At the sound of the bed creaking with her waking movements, he turned to face her. He bent down to kiss her forehead like he did every morning, but as he drew closer, he hesitated, giving her ample time to pull away if she chose. When she didn't, he reverently kissed her on the brow. Leaning back to meet her gaze, Eilian's eyes were soft with guilt.

"I'm sorry," he whispered.

Hadley cupped his cheek, her thumb scratching across his stubble. "I know."

For the past three days, he had disappeared into the recesses of the house only to reemerge upon being summoned for meals. When they were together, their conversations were sparse and the kisses chaste. Releasing a long breath, she wondered how long it would go on like this.

Hadley stuck her head into the parlor. The pale blue upholstered chairs stood empty and the hearth cool. She could have sworn she saw a shadow move within, but no one was there. As her eyes roamed over the darkened corner of the room, she took a step forward only to collide with something solid. Jolting back, she stumbled into the coffered wall, dropping her letters, but a gloved hand caught her arm and kept her on her feet.

"I beg your pardon, your ladyship. I didn't mean to startle you," Patrick began as he released her and picked the missives off the floor.

"It's fine, Patrick. Actually, I was looking for you. Would you or—" She stopped when she noticed that his lips were drawn straight and behind his spectacles his gaze was tense with worry. "What's going on?"

"There is a *situation* in the greenhouse."

"What sort of situation?"

"Mr. Nash is back. Shall I find his lordship?"

This again. "No, I will take care of it."

Squaring her shoulders, Hadley marched down the hall. Even if she still had trouble finding their bedroom at night when fatigue made all of the hallways meld into one, the orangery was the one room she had no trouble locating. Hadley paused, listening to the pool's engine thrum. Now that she had cleaned and oiled its internal workings, its rhythm was less cacophonous, but it was still loud enough for her to hear on the other side of the house. As she rounded the corner of the light-cut hall and crossed the empty drawing room, voices rose on the other side of the French doors.

"Touch one more plant, and I will break your bloody arm."

"I didn't come all the way from London to be threatened by the likes a you, ole timer. Her ladyship tol' me to weed an' prune, an' that's what I'm gonna do."

"*Her ladyship*," Nash spat, "is not in charge."

Hadley ground her teeth. Mr. Nash was lucky she left her derringer in her bedside table.

Throwing open the door to the orangery, she stormed inside. As she followed the path past the oceanic mosaic and into the murk of the pool's chamber, the men's voices grew louder. Standing at the edge of the pool were Randall. Nash and Mr. Bernard. The heavy-browed gardener stood with one hand on his stout hips and gesticulated threateningly with a pair of shears in the other. Randall Nash had his back to the countess, yelling into the gardener's face despite his added girth. His curled grey hair and fine suit were unmistakable from behind. As she broke through the foliage, Mr. Bernard's beady eyes brightened.

"Here comes her ladyship now," he replied with a smug smile. "She'll set ya straight."

Nash's eyes narrowed as he turned to meet the Countess of Dorset's glare. With the penetrating gaze of a great horned owl, he sliced through her form, cutting across her knees where her jodhpurs ended in wool stockings and piercing her breasts where they pressed against her shirtwaist. Resisting the urge to straighten her clothing or hair, Hadley came to the edge of the pool with her head high and her back rigid. How dare he invade her home and bully her staff.

As she had seen Eilian do, she turned to the gardener as if Nash was not even there. "What seems to be the problem, Bernard?"

"He won't let me do m' weedin'. Says you ain't in charge."

"This is ridiculous. Mr. Nash, what problem can you possibly have with our gardener pulling weeds?"

The older man's gaunt face convulsed, contracting into a pinched grimace. "I don't have to explain myself to the likes of you. You have no right to destroy this house."

"I'm not destroying anything!" she cried. "All I want is to weed the garden to ensure that it looks nice for our guests."

"Leave it alone."

"It has been left to go to seed for decades. Am I supposed to leave it that way?"

"You are supposed to mind your own business, Lady Dorset."

"Don't talk to her ladyship that way," the gardener snapped, looming over Nash, who seemed to take no notice.

Hadley raised her hand. "It's fine, Bernard. Mr. Nash, if you have a problem with me, I would prefer it if you came and spoke to me like a civilized person. If there is a certain plant you are worried about, say something."

"Why should I speak to an upstart like you? This isn't your house. You have been here for less than a month and think you own the place."

Rage climbed up Hadley's ribs, squeezing her lungs and pumping her body with heat. "No matter what you may think, Mr. Nash, this is *our* house now. Harland Sorrell is dead. Eilian is the earl now, and I am his wife. *We* own Brasshurst Hall and everything within it whether you like it or not. Nothing you do or say will change that."

"We shall see about that. You think you're entitled to—"

The gardener took a deep breath, about to start again when Hadley laid her hand on his arm. She smothered her anger with a civil smile that would have scared Eilian or her brother and said coolly, "Thank you, Mr. Nash, for letting me know what you think of me, but I have no need of your opinions as I have plenty of my own. I speak for myself and my husband when I say that you are no longer welcome at Brasshurst and we no longer require your services as the estate manager. Now, please leave before I have Bernard throw you out."

Nash's sharp brows knit as he scowled, shaking his head and tutting in disgust. "You are making a grave mistake, Lady Dorset. I don't think you understand the consequences of your actions. Your husband will be very disappointed in you."

"I know full-well what I'm doing, and no self-important busybody is going to insult me and tell me how to run my household. Get out, or I will call the constabulary and have you arrested for trespassing."

His hands twitched into fists at his sides. Before she could get out the final word, Randall Nash turned on heel and stormed off into the greenery. Without waiting for Hadley's command, the gardener charged after him, disappearing into the dense brush. Hadley ran a trembling hand down the front of her shirt. When she heard Nash was in the house, she had expected conflict, if their first meeting was an indication of his temperament, but his words and gaze had cut her deeper than she anticipated. *An upstart.* Is that what people really thought of her? That she was Eilian's mistress or servant turned wife? Even if she had been, she wouldn't have deserved that sort of harassment. In London, where people knew who they were, where they lived, and could guess how much they each earned, did they think she was nothing more than a scheming woman climbing the social ladder by marriage? No matter what they thought about how she got there, the truth was she loved Eilian, and despite what happened the other day, she knew he loved her too.

Stifling her thoughts, Hadley turned to where Bernard had been working. A mound of dead stalks and milkweeds sat at the edge of the pool. Her eyes ran over the discarded bits of grass before returning to the bed of alien flowers and ferns. It was obvious that the gardener had only clipped what couldn't be salvaged, so why had Nash reacted so strongly? It wasn't unheard of for old men who were set in their ways to overreact to even the smallest changes, but to threaten to break a man's arm over weeding a garden was past overreacting. There had to be a reason. She narrowed her eyes as she scanned a row of tightly curled ferns but lingered on a thickly stalked plant that rose from the dirt behind it like a three-tiered fountain filled with daisy heads.

"I lost him, your ladyship," the gardener wheezed as he loped back to her side.

"Thank you for trying. Do you know how he got out or is he lurking somewhere?"

"I don't think he's hiding. How he got out, I haven't a clue. Like a bloody magician, that one."

"Bernard, while you're tidying up, if you find a plant that you are unsure of, leave it be, but if you come across a box or strange object, bring it to my or his lordship's attention."

He nodded, his eyes trailing to where the redhead stared. "Should I be lookin' for anythin' special?"

"I don't know yet. Mr. Nash is guarding something, and I would like to know what."

Leaving the gardener to his work, Hadley cut through the greenery and into the cool, bright rooms of the main house. As she crossed each threshold, she glanced inside to make certain they were empty. Mr. Bernard's reassurances that Randall Nash had escaped gave her little comfort. She couldn't bear the thought of the man peering at her from some darkened corner, watching her in the one place she could let her guard down. Upon reaching the parlor, Hadley pulled the pocket doors shut and sunk into the sofa. She closed her eyes and lay back with her arm thrown over her face as if she had swooned. Nash trespassing, Eilian acting strange, and the self-imposed agony of an impending dinner party were too much for her all at once. If only swooning meant she could admit defeat and hand her problems off to someone else.

"No more," she whispered as she rubbed her eyes.

"No more what?"

Hadley shot up. She spun to the right and left before finally looking over the back of the chair only to find her husband staring at her with concerned eyes. Over his shoulder he hefted a brass telescope on a wooden tripod. His grey eyes flickered over her face. Leaning the telescope against the fireplace, he sat across from her and felt her forehead with the back of his hand.

"Your face is flushed. Are you ill?"

"No."

"Something's wrong."

"No, it's just that nothing is going right. How did you even get in here?"

"Back in the corner, behind the paneling, is a little office. I have been working in there all day, going through some of my great-grandfather's things. Look, I found a telescope." He smiled, but when she sat back and stared at the ceiling, he prodded softly, "What happened?"

"Patrick came to fetch me because Mr. Nash came back."

"Why didn't he find me? I would have taken care of it."

"I told him *I* would handle it, and I did. He's gone now, disappeared like he did last time. Bernard looked but couldn't find him."

"He was in the garden again?"

"Yes, he was all put-out because I told Bernard to weed—" Hadley stopped when she noticed her husband's brows furrowed thoughtfully.

"What is it?"

"I'm not sure. It may be nothing, but when we visited Mr. Talbot's cousin, Argus mentioned that Nash told everyone he grew silphium."

"Is that some sort of poppy?"

"No, it was a medicinal plant from Ancient Rome. The last one was given to Nero, but the species was supposed to have been harvested to extinction. Can you show me where he was in the greenhouse?"

She exhaled and sank lower into the cushion. There was nothing in the world that would make her get off the sofa. "Ask Bernard. He was there when Nash came in."

Leaving his wife on the couch, Eilian trailed down the hallway, dashing past the portrait gallery of past earls. In the library, he unbolted the door to the orangery and pushed into the suffocatingly thick air. Sweat instantly prickled his scalp and clung to his shirt as he followed the path to the edge of the pool. With the engine back in working order, the pool no longer reeked of fetid water and had gone from nearly black to a healthy algal green. The heavyset gardener knelt beside a carpet of flowers, ripping out weeds with roots as thick as turnips and tossing them onto the growing mound beside him. When he realized Eilian was watching him, Bernard mopped his brow and climbed to his feet.

"Your lordship. I tried to catch the villain, sir. I really did, but he's a slipp'ry one."

"I know you did. Where did you see Mr. Nash?"

"Well, he was right there, sir," he replied, pointing to the far side of the pool. "Then, he came over here when I didn't stop workin'."

Nodding, Eilian paced along the water's edge. His grey eyes darted over the palms and brush before migrating to the smaller plants. If the ancients gave silphium plants as gifts, they would have to be small enough to transport. From what he could remember from the etchings of it he had seen on coins found in Cyrene, it grew on a thick stalk and had heart-shaped seeds. Nothing here looked right. While he couldn't name any of the English wildflowers or exotic plants from the Far East, he knew they weren't silphium. The garden hadn't been laid out in any sort of order, and while it was obvious that the trees and larger specimens had been planted first, the smaller flowers appeared to have been placed where there was room enough for them. Eilian walked to where Bernard said he had first seen Nash appear. What had the man seen that he couldn't?

He watched as the gardener threw aside a vine that had nearly choked out a Chinese lantern plant before moving onto the next one. "Look at this beaut. You don't see weeds this big every day."

Raising his eyes to the gardener's calloused hands, the words died in Eilian's throat. A plant half as tall as a corn stalk and as thick as a man's arm rose from the middle of the bed. Veering off from the main stem were undulating leaves and diffuse clusters of yellow flowers. Bernard reached into his pocket and pulled out his gardening sheers.

"Wait! Don't cut it!" Eilian cried as he ran back to the other side, his foot slipping on the slick tiles. He caught his balance, staggering into the pile of clippings and scattering them across the water's surface. "That's not a weed."

Eilian's hand shook as he gingerly bent the head of the plant closer. One of its flowers had gone to seed, transforming from a blossom to fleshy green pods. Carefully working one of the segmented seeds free, he turned it over in his metal palm. The orangery's engine died away beneath the pounding beat of his heart in his ears. While the seed was more elongated than it appeared on the ancient coins, it was clear that it was shaped like a heart.

Chapter Ten
Silphium Hearts

A plant long thought extinct had been growing in his family's ancestral home for God knows how long. Eilian could barely believe it, but there it was sprouting at the edge of the pool. Like most of his discoveries at dig sites, he couldn't be certain if he was right, but he felt the inkling of truth in his bones. He was onto something. Pulling down books from Hippocrates, Pliny, and Theophrastus, Eilian pored over the ancient texts. His notebook rapidly filled with half-conceived ideas, possible leads in other works, and what he knew to be true about the plant. The massive desk in the library was soon stacked to the brim with crumbling books and ink-covered parchment. When he ran out of room, Eilian transferred them to the floor near the hearth where he could surround himself with everything he could possibly need. By the time Patrick came in with his afternoon tea, half of the locked cabinets stood open and he had to step over a pile of books three deep to reach his master.

Not often did the ancients agree on anything, but Eilian was certain that silphium had been used as a medicinal plant. According to Hippocrates, it had been used to treat all sorts of ills: wounds, fevers, warts, sore throats, coughs. Pliny's account supported that the plant had gone extinct at the time of Nero when it was given to him as a curiosity, but the natural historian added that one of its additional uses was to promote menstruation. Eilian stared at the text for a long moment, unsure of what to make of that. He would have to ask Hadley about it later.

Despite all of the information he garnered from the Romans and later from secondhand medieval sources, he still couldn't be sure what the silphium looked like. If only his ancestral home had been in London, then he could have called upon a dozen numismatists who would certainly have a coin from Ancient Cyrene or Rome depicting the plant. If he sent a letter now, even if it went by express dirigible, it would take at least a week for a reply and more than likely they would only send a sketch or written description and not the actual coin.

Sitting amongst his books and notes, Eilian frowned. He had to tell someone; he had to run the idea past someone else to prove to himself that he wasn't crazy. Hadley had listened with interest when they discussed his preliminary findings at breakfast, but now, she was busy compiling menus and reading the women's magazines she picked up in Folkesbury's bookshop and he didn't want to disturb her. Ultimately, her knowledge of ancient history was limited and she wasn't much help past acting as a sounding board. He wanted someone to share in his excitement. Cracking his neck as he climbed over the stacks of books, he paused when his eyes met the pile of papers on his desk. Why hadn't he thought of him before?

Eilian tossed on his jacket and dashed down the hall. Propped against the wainscoting near the servants' door, he found his velocipede waiting. At the top of the steps, he lingered on the threshold, watching the rain patter down in a steady tattoo. He could go back upstairs and wait for the storm to pass or he could change into his Norfolk suit to keep from ruining another pair of trousers. Without a second thought, he kicked away from the portico and peddled down the muddy lane toward Folkesbury.

⋄⊙⋄ ⊙⋄⋄

Leona Rhodes held the needle poised above her embroidery. From beneath his thick spectacles, Argus was watching her. She wanted to ask him what he was staring at, but doing so would only imply that there was something *to* look at and that was the last thing she wanted. Maybe he wasn't looking at her, maybe it was only paranoia, and he was simply staring into space. Then, he smiled. For a second, she hesitated, the nausea thickening her throat. With a swallow, she smiled demurely and turned her attention back to her embroidery hoop. If she went to look for Nadir, would Argus think it strange?

Her head shot up as the doorbell jangled in the hall. Barnes trudged past the parlor, ruffling the heavy curtain as the front door opened. She held her breath, her heart thundering in her chest at the thought of the dark little maid at the door with another letter. Thus far she had made sure to keep out of sight, but what if Nash decided he was tired of discretion? A man's excited voice rose from the hall, and she sagged into the armchair with relief as Argus turned his attention to the foyer.

The butler pulled the curtain back just far enough for his broad face to poke through. "Lord Dorset is here to see you, sir."

Nodding, the couple rose to their feet as the earl was ushered in. His dark suit had been soaked through with rain while his trouser legs were spattered with mud. Eilian ran a hand through his hair, returning it to its usual configuration of sickled spikes. Despite his rain-soaked face and clothes, his smile and eyes were bright.

"Lord Dorset, what a pleasant surprise. What brings you to our home in such dreadful weather?" Leona asked, relieved to have the attention off her for a time. "Did you bring Lady Dorset with you?"

"No, not this time. I came to speak with Mr. Rhodes on a discovery of some importance. That is, if you aren't too busy."

Argus shook his head and led him into his office. Eilian's eyes ran over the shelves before coming to rest on the cabinet of Roman coins and pottery fragments. The pudgy man once again offered him a drink, which he declined, but as Argus poured himself a glass, Eilian knelt before the case. His grey eyes gleamed as they came to rest on a tiny, lopsided coin. The edge of the image had been rubbed smooth as if by a nervous hand or the course of water, but in the center, the engraving was unmistakable. An alien plant complete with a stout stalk and a cluster of round flowers at its top grew from the metal. It wasn't identical.

"Mr. Rhodes, may I see that coin there? The one with the plant."

"Of course, help yourself."

Opening the cabinet, Eilian gingerly plucked the coin from the shelf and placed it in his prosthetic palm seed side up. With his free hand, he dug into his pocket for the heart-shaped pod. His hand shook as he laid them side by side. The shape, the texture, the ring of raised flesh around the edge was all the same. It was as if the artist had drawn it based on another's description and not from the real thing.

"What do you make of it, Mr. Rhodes?" Eilian asked, holding out his prosthetic hand to allow the other man to study the coin and pod.

"It's a bean?"

"It's a seed. A *silphium* seed."

His palpebrous face darkened as he put his glass on the mantle and adjusted his spectacles. "It can't be. It died out with Nero, probably burned with Rome."

"Pliny was wrong. How was he to know someone brought one to Britain?" Eilian dropped his voice. "I found it growing in Brasshurst's orangery. Nash was telling the truth."

"But— but how did it get there? How do you know it's the real thing? I mean, neither of us are botanists."

"I don't, but look at it, Rhodes. You can't deny that the seeds are the same, and the plant—if you squint your eyes—looks just like this."

Argus shook his head, retrieving his drink from the mantle and holding it close. "I don't know..."

"Many historians have made greater discoveries than this with less proof. We can't pretend as if it was never found."

He swallowed hard. The earl's eyes gleamed and his prosthetic hand flexed and gestured in time with his left as smoothly as if it were still flesh and bone. He was impassioned by his discovery, and Argus Rhodes, who had never had colleagues, didn't know how to respond to that.

"Are— are you going to write a paper on it? After more research, of course."

Eilian cocked his head, watching the Egyptologist from the corner of his eye as he returned the coin to its rightful place in the cabinet. He wasn't nearly as excited as he expected him to be. Did he not understand the implications of discovering a plant that had been so important to Rome's economy that they mourned its demise?

"Ancient botany really isn't my field of study, but aren't you intrigued by the idea of finding out why this plant was so important to the Romans? Haven't you ever wondered why they harvested it to the point of supposed extinction?"

"I suppose." Refilling his glass, Argus settled into his desk chair. "Have you spoken to Nash yet?"

"No. Part of the reason I came to see you is because I wanted to ask your opinion on how I should approach Mr. Nash. You have dealt with him more than I have, and I don't want to publish a paper or bring the plant to the world's attention without his permission, even if it is on my property. I wouldn't feel right about it."

"He's never going to let you. You may as well take that seed and grow your own. He's been claiming that plant existed for years, but he's never shown it to a single soul."

⚬ℚ ℚ⚬

Leona smiled to herself as she pressed her ear to the plaster between the study and the parlor. Now she finally had something she could wield against Nash. Going to the constabulary would have only ended in exposing her own sins, especially when the sergeant was such a dear friend of Mrs. Nash, but the plant was more than she could have hoped for. A few more kernels of information were all she needed to gain a little leverage.

When the earl left and her husband settled down after dinner, she would slip into his study and take what she needed. She made a mental note of every name Lord Dorset mentioned while her husband sat mutely on the other side of the wall. Even if Argus, with his limited imagination, couldn't appreciate the fortuitousness of Lord Dorset's discovery, she did.

⁓ᘛ ᘚ⁓

Pilcrow stood outside the Gothic face of Brasshurst Hall, staring up at the ivy-scarred stone. While the vines had been removed upon the ninth earl and countess's arrival, the ghosts of the plants remained as veins across the great house's face never to heal but as a testament to years of neglect. It wasn't the size of the house that made her pause; she was accustomed to feeling small even in the dower house, which was scarcely an eighth of the size of the manor. It was that their eyes were watching her from the portal. She had never been a woman to give into fancies or superstition, but after following Mrs. Nash to mass and hearing the sermons of fire and brimstone year in and year out, how could she not feel the hollow-eyed saints casting their gaze upon her from the ring of the portal? In her breast pocket out of sight was a note to the lady and master of the house, which she was to deliver directly to one of them and not to a servant as usual. Her hand shook as she reached for the bell pull, hoping it would be the lady of the house who answered. She could weather a slap, but she always feared the pitiless knuckles of an angry man. Maybe if she let herself disappear into the doorway, the stone saints wouldn't see what the Nashes were making her do.

She licked her cracked lips as briny rain dripped off the roofline, down the brim of her hat, and onto her nose. When no one seemed to be coming, she tucked her coat closer and trotted away from the bright blue door. Mrs. Nash wouldn't be venturing out of the house in this weather, so maybe she could stop at the tavern for a hot meal and a bit of time to herself. As she reached the gravel path, a voice called out behind her.

The maid turned but froze upon seeing the figure in the doorway. She had never seen hair so red. It was as dark as blood, but it brought out the light dusting of freckles over the woman's nose and ruddy cheeks. Her eyes were a bright blue, and while they could have been striking to the point of being unnerving, they were softened by her rounded features and expressive brows. The dark blue skirt and jacket she wore over her plain shirtwaist were simple but well made, unlike her lady's fussy dresses.

"Wait! Do come back. I'm so sorry I didn't get to you sooner, but I didn't hear the bell. Who are you looking for?"

"Lord and Lady Dorset, mum," she called.

"I am she." As the umbral maid drew closer, Hadley's eyes widened. "Please come inside; you are soaked to the bone."

Before Pilcrow could protest, the countess was ushering her inside with one hand and closing the door with the other. Lady Dorset shook her head as she appraised the maid's thin form, which appeared even more drawn and frail when wet. Her wool coat hung from her bony shoulders while her threadbare hat sagged where water had run from the brim. The hollows of her cheeks cast hungry shadows across her ashen skin. With a little prodding, the countess convinced her to remove her coat and follow her into the great hall.

"Please, take a seat by the fire. How long were you waiting?" Hadley asked after speaking to Charlotte who appeared at the tug of the bell-rope. Drawing close to the hearth, she laid the water-logged coat across the grate. "I hope it wasn't long. I heard the bell, but with my husband and butler out, I didn't realize no one let you in."

"I was only there a moment, mum."

Pilcrow's eyes ran over the massive hearth before skimming over the columns of the upper arcade and skylights. She glanced down the darkened hall to see if anyone would call out to stop her as she sat stiffly on the edge of the embroidered chair. It had been years since she sat anywhere upstairs. If Mrs. Nash knew she was sitting in the earl's house like an honored guest, she would be furious.

"You're shaking." When Charlotte reappeared with a tray of tea and placed it on the side table, Lady Dorset quickly poured a cup for Pilcrow and handed it to her with a gentle grin. "I can't believe your master sent you out in this weather. Wait here."

Disappearing down the hall, the countess returned with a wool blanket. With a snap of the fabric, she carefully wrapped it around the maid's shaking shoulders. As she crouched beside the chair to ensure it was tucked close, the maid shrank back into her seat. If it had been made of a darker fabric, the woman would have disappeared, but there was nowhere to hide against the red Damask. At Hadley's touch, Pilcrow flinched, averting her gaze to her lap, and drew the shawl closer.

"Thank you, but you needn't trouble yourself for me, your ladyship. I'll be fine."

"Have you eaten? Our servants will be having something soon, and I'm sure they could spare you a plate."

"No, thank you, your ladyship," she replied, her words betraying the ache in the pit of her stomach that she had grown accustomed to, "I already ate."

"Your name is Pilcrow, isn't it? You're Mrs. Nash's maid, I think."

"Yes, mum, her lady's maid."

"So what brings you to Brasshurst in the rain? I do hope it isn't the church business."

For a moment, she tried to avoid the countess's probing gaze by taking a long sip of tea. The warmth flooded her chest and chased away the damp cough tickling her lungs. In the inner pocket of her coat was the letter Mr. Nash had given her. All morning he had picked through his stacks of London papers, combing the society pages and announcements for anything he could discover about the Sorrells. When he had reached an article reporting a strange meeting at the

British Museum where Lord Sorrell's fiancée had simultaneously confessed to cross-dressing to travel to the Middle East and discredited Sir Joshua Peregrine, an archaeologist of feeble renown, Mr. Nash's brows arched and his thin lips curled into a wry smirk. What exactly was in the letter she couldn't be sure, but it was never anything good. Half of the village hated her. As she passed, they would mutter an oath under their breath or shoot her black looks that seemed to accumulate on her person until she appeared more specter than woman. They would never dare to treat her masters that way even if she wished they would, so punishing her would have to do.

Pilcrow's grey eyes flitted between the grate where her coat hung limply and the countess's bright face. She had dried her coat, offered her food and tea, given her a blanket, and even remembered her name, which was far more than the Nashes had done for her in the twenty-three years of service with them. It would be easy enough to slip the letter from her pocket and toss it in the fire before she left. No one would be the wiser. If Mr. Nash asked, he could confirm that she had been to the manor and talked only to Lady Dorset.

The words hung in her throat, but with another sip of tea, her chest loosened, allowing them to work free, even if they were soft and stilted. "Since you're new here, mum, Mrs. Nash would like to offer my services to you in case you require anything."

Chapter Eleven
Ancient Paths

The wind blew through the trees, carrying with it the sea's salt and the musk of wet earth. Donning his best suit and hat, Eilian followed the gravel path across the lawn and into the ornamental garden. Along the way, he passed the moss-consumed walls and foundations of buildings long forgotten. He considered straying from the path, but if he wanted Nash to take him seriously, he would have to stay out of the dirt, at least on the way there. The white rocks crunched beneath his shoes as he mounted the hill. Halfway to the top, Eilian stopped.

Standing between Brasshurst and the dower house was a miniature cathedral complete with Gothic facade and minarets that mirrored the ones affixed to the front of the hall. Much like its parent, ivy had grown around it until the figures ringing the portal were crumbling beneath their roots and shoots. Even without leaving the road, he knew it had to be the family crypt. *Sorrell* was barely legible above the door, eroded to a dull outline after centuries of rain and sea spray. He swallowed hard, stretching and flexing his prosthetic hand before the pains could start. Would his body one day rest there? All of the men and women who hung on the walls of the gallery rested there, still in neat rows. His father had been buried in London while he was away. It was a small comfort to know that the door hadn't been opened since his father inherited the earldom and that the bones of his ancestors had remained undisturbed for nearly thirty years.

The world died away as Eilian lingered outside the mausoleum. His eyes trailed over the lopsided headstones that lay on the periphery, half-buried by brush where servants and distant relatives rested at the earls' and countess's sides. He had always imagined he would die somewhere far from them, maybe in India from the plague or from a dig accident in Greece. When the dirigible crashed in the countryside and he saw the bowels of the airship alight between its mighty ribs, he couldn't fathom that it would end here. To be trapped in English soil forever was the worst fate he could imagine, and in those moments when he was certain his life would end, did he really hope the flames would consume him until he could be scattered to the wind?

Heat lanced through his missing muscles, ripping him from his morbid thoughts. Eilian rubbed his arm as he cut through the twisted yews and ancient oaks to reach the glen before the dower house. When they arrived at Brasshurst, this was the house he had expected. Instead of being a conglomeration of mismatched styles, the dower house resembled the cottages in town with a thatch roof and stone face, but the windows had been rendered with Gothic lines and leaded glass. An ornamental garden surrounded the house, painting the lawn in delicate pastel pinks and purples. A figure floated past the glass in the upper windows, disappearing and reappearing as they crossed the upper arcade. Drawing in a controlled breath, Eilian stepped onto the porch and checked his reflection in the mirrored surface of the doorknocker. He pushed his hair down as best he could and knocked.

Minutes passed, but no one came even after he knocked again. Eilian walked back to the tree line, confirmed that the figure was still moving within, and tried the door. The knob turned easily, creaking open to reveal a familiar but scaled down version of the great hall, complete with a grand stone fireplace and columned arcades on the upper floor. Light streamed in from the wall of windows behind him, catching the strands of gold in the tapestried chairs. Taking a step into the room, Eilian craned his neck down the hall where a door stood open. The sun danced across the coffers and plaster, yet he could not tell if anyone was within. He listened for the nearly unperceivable tread of a servant as he crossed the great hall, but no one came.

"Anyone here?" he called, following the edge of the rug to the empty hallway. "I tried the knocker, but no one came. Hello?"

Passing a row of locked doors where light streamed in dusty beams from empty keyholes, Eilian waited at the threshold. In the back parlor, Randall Nash sat amongst dozens of stacks of newspapers. Much like their owner, each had been carefully pressed and creased before being set aside. They sat in grey piles nearly half a man high at the sides of his chair and around the perimeter of the room. On the table near the window, thick albums sat two rows deep with the edges of oversized slips of newsprint jutting from the tops of pages.

The older man's face was blocked by a two month old copy of *The Daily Telegraph*. Eilian kept his grey eyes locked on Randall Nash as he crossed the boards on silent feet and sunk into the armchair directly across from him. When Nash lowered the paper to turn the page, he jolted back, crushing the paper in his grasp.

"Who let you in here? I told Pilcrow I was *not* to be disturbed," Nash snapped as he tossed the ruined newspaper aside.

"I knocked, but no one came."

He glared at the young man sitting across from him. "Did you think maybe there was a reason for that?"

"Well, Mr. Nash, now you know how it feels to have your privacy violated by an uninvited guest," Eilian replied, surprised by his own boldness.

"What do you want? Did that wife of yours send you to confront me?"

"She doesn't know I'm here."

"That isn't a good way to start a marriage, *Lord* Dorset," he muttered under his breath as he searched the earl's face.

He was far too confident to be there because of his letter. When people came to settle the matter, they were furious or cocky, thinking they could intimidate him, but they were never this secure. She must not have told him. Nash smiled to himself. He could use that.

"I came because I believe you."

His face contracted into a sneer. "Believe what? I don't need you to believe anything."

"The silphium plant. I, too, believe it isn't extinct."

"Who told you that?"

Eilian watched Nash's face tighten with strain. "Mr. Rhodes told me there was some scandal or something in the past, but I think you're right. After you left the other day, I found it in the orangery beside the pool."

"Oh, that's why you have come," Nash began, nodding as he climbed to his feet and loomed over Eilian. "You want to lord it over me. You want to destroy my plant unless I do what you want, eh? Well, you have another think coming because—"

"Good lord, no. I want to do nothing of the sort. I'm— I'm an archaeologist, not an extortionist," Eilian sputtered, gazing up at the seething man with pleading eyes. "I wanted to ask for your permission to study it, maybe even send a seed to a botanist in London, but that's all. Why would I destroy it?"

"Do you take me for a fool, Lord Dorset?"

"No! I took you for a rational human being. I thought that if you listened and understood that I only wanted to continue what you started and bring it to the attention of the proper scientists and historians, you would—"

"Get out of my house this instant!"

"Mr. Nash, please listen to me a moment longer." Eilian spoke as he walked backwards around furniture and down the hall as the older man urged him toward the door. "I'm not trying to steal your discovery; you would receive most of the credit. I simply want your permission to move forward. I didn't want to go behind your back, which is why I came here in the first place. We are both scholars; we could even work together if you want."

Eilian's back collided with the front door. Even though Randall Nash was three and half decades older and several inches shorter, the earl shrank back, groping for the knob behind him with his prosthetic hand. He had never been as afraid of his father as he was of this man. His father's outbursts were predictable—anti-imperialism, sympathizing with anyone who wasn't British—but Nash was a different animal. His reactions were over the top and reeked of potential violence no matter the size of the offense. A slender shadow appeared from one of the locked doors in the hall, but when she saw her master's teeth bared and his hand raised in rage, Pilcrow ducked back into the other room.

"There is nothing that would make me want to work with the likes of you. Just because you put on a clean suit and comb your hair, doesn't make you worthy of your family name and it does *not* make you worthy of my respect!"

The backs of the earl's eyes burned as he ground his jaw. Randall Nash was done intimidating him. "You're right. It doesn't make me worthy of a title, but I never asked for that; it was given to me by chance. But you can keep your respect. I don't want it." Eilian doffed his hat and straightened to his full height. "Good day, Mr. Nash. You won't have to worry about hearing from me again."

Turning his back on Nash, Eilian slipped out and slammed the door behind him. His breath hitched as a bolt of pain ran down his arm. He drew in a lungful of cool air and let it wash through him to staunch the burning. Before him stood the garden of candy floss flowers and the misshapen yews whose bodies hid the spires of the family crypt. Leaning against the corner of the house out of sight, Eilian's eyes traveled to the gravel path. From where he stood, he could see the white line that led down to the hulking manor with the edge of the orangery's glass dome appearing above the roof. Stepping toward the yews, Eilian vanished into the mist and murk. He would take the long way back.

⁕ ⁕ ⁕

Nadir glanced up from his portable writing desk and out at the sea as it lapped against the beach, whisking shells across the sand in a lazy waltz. Something still nagged at the back of his mind. He had yet to figure out how his cousin managed to disappear the night he followed her to her mysterious meeting. It was like something out of one of his blasted stories or a nightmare. From the pain in his ankle and backside the next day, he knew he hadn't been dreaming, so he had to have missed something. Placing the papers inside his desk and locking the catch, he slipped it under his chair. The beach had been deserted all day, and it was unlikely that anyone would tamper with the chapter he worked on.

Climbing up the path toward Folkesbury, Nadir followed it until he stood just below the ridge, out of sight of the village. He studied the path before him. She had come this way past the rough undergrowth and low trees, of that he was sure, but somehow he thought it would be easier to work out the twists and turns of her path in daylight. Soon, he found nothing looked the same. Slipping on his dark sun-spectacles to simulate the midnight darkness, he pushed through the brush and followed the drunken fence posts up the bluff. That night, it had seemed to take hours to reach their destination as he waited and watched, but within moments, he found the tree branch where his scarf caught. Minute fibers of indigo wool still hung from its forked fingers.

He slipped off his glasses and pursed his lips as he envisioned Leona standing no more than twenty-five feet away from him with the lamp in her hand and her cheeks painted in deep shadows. Stepping into her place, he stared into the clusters of gnarled and salt-stunted trees but saw nothing. There was no door or path for him to follow. But how could that be? He had seen her step off the path and vanish. Moving into the grass, Nadir's eyes caught a shadow on the cliff face. It had been impossible to see from the path as trees and the lip of the cliff stood in the way, but cut into the stone was an arch. His head scraped the ceiling's smooth surface as he entered the tunnel, running his hand along the rounded diamond-shaped stones that had been laid centuries ago. Sunlight streamed into the shaft and reflected off the scant coating of water that hid the floor. Keeping one hand on the wall, he walked into the gloom.

Dusty cobwebs tangled in the waves of his hair as he kept his head down, following the tunnel until he could no longer rely on the sun to light his way. Water splashed with each step, yet it never seemed to grow any higher than the soles of his shoes as he ventured further into the rock. The diamond tiles soon faded into blackness, and with each breath, the air grew thicker with humidity and must. Nadir's lungs tightened against his well-tailored suit as the air pushed in on his ears to the point of pain. His pulse pounded in his temples as he proceeded forward, guided by the tips of his shoes, which he could no longer see. Even his hand on the wall was no longer visible, but he trusted the cold bricks beneath his palm and the gentle splosh of water beneath his feet. In the dark, he couldn't be sure if he had passed forks in the void or if the tunnel traveled straight under the town, but during his trek, he felt the ceiling rise away from his skull as if the room had widened before narrowing again a few yards later. He cursed himself for not bringing a torch. It had been foolish of him to assume Leona only brought it to find her way down the bluff. She had lived in Folkesbury her whole life and could have followed the cobbled paths through the woods or the trails around the earl's land with her eyes shut.

A voice carried over the stillness, so faint he couldn't discern if its originator was male or female, but it didn't matter. He froze, pressing his back against the wall as he waited for the blaze of a lantern to appear. A thousand thoughts of who could be hiding in the tunnel flitted through his mind until his legs locked with fear and he drew a fist back in case he had to fight. With his other hand, he rolled his lucky bead between his fingers. Waiting in the thick air, his heart pounded in the ears and drowned out the voice. When no one appeared, Nadir took a lurching step forward.

The Earl and the Artificer

As his hand slid over the smooth surface of a curve, his heart leapt at the sight of a shaft of light streaming from the ceiling. The clean air above chased away the stench of still water and eased the fear that entrapped his breast. Standing beneath the warm light, Nadir looked up to find a brass grate no bigger than a brick embedded in the stone three feet above his head. His teal suit was coated in a layer of dirt. He reached to brush the dirt away when he realized with disgust that his hands were equally filthy. Nadir ducked into the shadows as voices rose again and boots clacked above his head. This time, they were undeniable.

"He is insane. There is no other way to put it."

Listening to the echoed words ricocheting down the vent, he cocked his head. He recognized that voice.

"Well, what happened? Did he give you permission?" a woman replied from the other side of the room.

"Of course not. You would have thought I asked him for his first-born the way he carried on. He acted like I was an extortionist or something, went on about me using the plant against him, that I would destroy it if he didn't do what I wanted. I can't say I understand it."

"That's a big leap."

"That's what I thought! Then, he threw me out."

Boards whined above his head as mud-encrusted soles stopped on the grate. Bits of grass and dirt drifted down like dust motes, peppering Nadir's suit. The man sighed, pacing over the shaft with his head down before coming to a stop a few feet away. Nadir let out a slow breath and stepped away from the wall again. It took all his self-control to keep from wiping the flecks of dried muck sprinkled across his nose.

"So what are you going to do now?"

"I don't know. I can't let it go. If that plant is the real thing, it could be one of the most important discoveries of our century. What if it's the key doctors need to cure consumption or malaria? Of course, Nash would never see it that way."

"Why not just pretend you never spoke to him? It's a plant after all, anyone could have found it, and no one can stake a claim on something that has been there since the Roman Invasion."

"I don't know, Had. It feels dishonest to claim it as my own."

Nadir's eyes widened. He was under Brasshurst Hall, right below Lord and Lady Dorset's feet, and they had no idea he was listening in on their conversation. He had to get out and go back to the beach, but he didn't dare move for fear they would notice the gurgle of water or the blur of black and teal under the grate. Why had Leona come to the tunnel if it led to Brasshurst?

"If he is as unstable as you say, he has no right to be the deciding factor in your decision. The silphium is growing on your property, which means it's yours. Eilian, you are an archaeologist, and if you know there is a trail to follow, I think you should. Damn what Mr. Nash says," she laughed warmly. "Why let him stop you?"

Eilian's feet crossed the room to his wife in two long strides. The room fell silent. The familiar soft click of lips parting meant they were kissing, and like a voyeur, he was eavesdropping on their intimate moment. Nadir covered his reddening face and leaned out of sight, too afraid to move and disturb the water on the floor. He could picture the earl drawing back with a gentle smile as he rubbed Lady Dorset's arms to maintain contact a little longer. It seemed like something he would do.

"You're right, Had. Anyway, I have a seed of my own. I could grow a silphium plant myself if worst came to worst, and he would have no right to that plant, now would he?"

"So does that mean I shouldn't invite him to the party?" she asked, her voice lifting with a grin.

"No, definitely not. He would probably try to turn our guests out of doors along with us if he had the opportunity."

"I don't think Mr. Nash cares whether he gets an invitation or not. If he catches wind of the party, he will be there. You can count on that. Now if only we could figure out how he keeps getting in."

"I have searched that room top to bottom, and for the life of me, I can't figure it out," he replied, his voice trailing away.

Two sets of feet crossed over the roof of the tunnel and out of earshot. When Nadir could no longer hear the lilt of their voices or the soft groan of ancient boards, he sighed and let his head rest against the wall. He ran his hand across his face, but drew it back in disgust when he coated his lips and nose in the tunnel's grime. The path ran from the beach to Brasshurst, but where did it go? Nadir narrowed his eyes, trying to peer past the beam of light to see what lay beyond in the gloom. Where was Leona headed that night? She could have met someone in the tunnel along the way, but if they were just meeting, then why didn't they go somewhere more convenient and less... dirty?

Nadir sharply exhaled and stepped out of the comforting shaft of gaslight. Following the tunnel around another serpentine curve before straightening again, his heart leapt as the shadows engulfed him. The darkness was absolute. His senses betrayed him, keeping him from orienting himself. The echoing drips of water that could have been ahead of him, behind him, or in his head for all he knew. A rhythmic clatter shook the bedrock around him, and suddenly he was seized with the urge to turn back. He feared the tunnel would grow narrower and narrower until it trapped him or the marrow between the tiles would falter after a thousand years and come crashing in upon him. His lungs burned as they rapidly expanded and contracted, straining against his ribs. He tugged at his silk tie to relieve the tightness in his throat. Was the air growing thinner and colder the further he inched? He could turn around, but if he did, would he be able to tell if he was facing the way he came? For all he knew, the shaft could run through all of England or it could end only a few hundred yards ahead, just beyond the next curve.

There would be no turning back. Stretching his arms out to touch both sides of the wall, Nadir closed his eyes. This darkness was his own, and in it, he steadied his pounding pulse by reminding himself that the shaft had stood for hundreds of years and there was nothing to worry about. Thus far, he hadn't found any rubble or heard the creak of imminent destruction. He promised himself that if he didn't find a way out by the time he counted to a hundred, he would follow the wall back to the coast.

"One... Two," he called, his voice echoing away endlessly in the void. He swallowed hard and kicked through the water. At fifty, he still saw nothing, yet it felt as if the outlines of the tiles were growing more distinct and that the ceiling had lifted away from his scalp more than once. Suddenly he blinked, realizing he could see his hand at his side smeared with grime. Nadir picked up the pace. His eyes burned as light streamed in from the tunnel's crumbling end. Outside trees obscured the entrance, but when Nadir emerged, furiously shaking the cobwebs from his hair with dirt-stained hands, he found that he was surrounded by tall swaying grasses and ornamental yews. The tunnel fell away into half-stacked walls with piles of diamond-shaped bricks strewn around them before disintegrating into the grass.

Panic lanced between his ribs as he stopped mopping at the teal fabric of his suit and looked around him. Where was he? At the thought of going back through the tunnel, his fear of cave-ins and creatures surfaced once more. If he had to, he would, but if he could find someone he could pay to drive him back to Folkesbury, he would choose that instead. Anything to not go back in. Following a trail of dirt no more than a deer path, he froze at the top of the hill. He recognized this place.

As children, he and Leona had stalked this house. They had wiped the film from the lower windows with their sleeves and gathered bouquets of flowers from the overgrown garden to play wedding. It had been abandoned then with wisteria climbing the chimney pots and along the heads of the yew trees, but now, it breathed with life locked beyond the Gothic panes. An old man with the face of a horned owl moved within, fretting irritably between the windows in the back parlor without ever seeing the young man standing in his yard. Around the corner of the house, Nadir spotted a familiar gravel path.

Walking back toward the beach past Brasshurst, his brows furrowed. What did Leona have to do with the dower house that she wouldn't want her husband or cousin to know about? Whatever Nash wanted with her, it wasn't right.

Nadir would have to have a word with him.

ACT TWO

"Women are naturally
secretive, and they like to do
their own secreting."
–Sir Arthur Conan Doyle

Chapter Twelve
The Countess & the Cad

Hadley smiled as she glanced up from her breakfast to find her husband's eyes bright again. He sat with a book propped in his prosthetic hand, his eyes locked on the page while his left hand brought forkfuls of meat and egg to his mouth. Occasionally he would set down his fork to jot down a line in his notebook, but he never wavered from his project. Perhaps she should have been annoyed that he was ignoring her in favor of his work, but she wasn't a morning person and had very little to say at that hour. It was comforting to see him return to his old self.

"Anything wrong?" Eilian asked, finally pulling away from his book on ancient plants when he felt her eyes upon him.

"No. I was just thinking how lucky I am to have you."

His cheeks and neck burned. He wanted to ask her if she was sure about that. There were too many aspects of life in which he was acutely aware of his short-comings. Instead he smiled. "*I* am the lucky one."

"Is your research going well?" she yawned with a smile, pouring herself another cup of coffee.

"Not sure. I can never be certain whether medieval philosophers are telling the truth or speaking in riddles. Thus far, I still believe our silphium is the real thing. I have no evidence to the contrary. I only wish I knew for sure."

"What's so important about this plant? From the looks of it, it isn't ornamental."

"It seems to have been medicinal. At the peak of its use, Rome was prospering, yet their population didn't grow despite that there weren't any plagues or wars. This plant is the reason."

Hadley's sleep-addled mind perked at the thought. "Imagine how useful that would be today."

Before he could reply, a mop of white hair appeared through the panel in the wall. Patrick carried in a silver tray laden with envelopes. He placed a stack in front of Eilian before giving the remainder to Hadley. Her eyes skimmed the handwriting on the front of each letter. A few were cards congratulating her on her marriage from those who couldn't attend their nuptials, but at the bottom, she found two she immediately recognized. One bore Eliza Hawthorne's neat script while the other, which was written in ornate arabesques on prim stationary, could only be from Eilian's mother. Fearing what Eliza's might have said, she dropped it into her lap to read later and tore open the other letter.

"Is that from my mother?"

Hadley's eyes widened. She hadn't even gotten it out of the envelope yet. "Yes, how could you tell?"

"I tend to recognize what I dread most. At least she only writes to invite me to parties or to tell me about family business. Which is it this time?"

"A party, but I brought it on myself. I asked her if I could borrow some of her staff."

Watching her scan the lines of looped script, Eilian ground his teeth at the sight of a matching letter in his own stack. "And?"

Despite the panic curling like smoke in the back of her mind, Hadley smiled. "She's willing."

⚬⚬

Hadley drifted down the cobbled street. Her eyes flitted over shop windows and the weathered signs swaying above them though her mind was far away. What had she done? She had asked her mother-in-law for extra servants, and the dowager countess had agreed. Somehow she had hoped the woman would refuse, and she would have to call off the party. She still could.

In front of a cockeyed building shoved between a draper and a butcher shop, Hadley stopped. Despite its tilted windows and mossy roof, the building radiated warmth and the cloying scent of Earl Grey and scones. On the sign beside the door, a tea pot with a banner advertised Billings Tea Room and Bakery. Hadley fingered her clutch, hearing the familiar clink of coins within. There were plenty of errands to run, but she had time for a cup and a cake.

The bell jingled as she slipped inside. Passing the empty tables, Hadley eyed the counter laden with sweets, petit fours, and scones beneath glass domes.

"May I help you, ma'am?" the young shopkeeper asked as she carried out a batch of steaming crumpets.

"I would like one of those, please, and a scone, and half a dozen petit fours."

"I assume you would like those in a box," she replied with a cheeky grin and a tilt of her head.

"Yes, they are for my husband. He would love this place. Leave the scone, please. I will have that here."

As the girl turned away, the bell rang and a sweep of cold air rustled Hadley's skirt.

"You have seen her?"

"Oh, yes, at the beach. Ghastly creatures, no decorum at all. She's certainly dragging the family down with her poor-breeding, though the husband isn't much better. She hasn't even paid me a call."

"How impertinent."

"Is the countess at least pretty?"

"She's young. Now, where is that girl? She knows we come in the same time every week, yet she never has a tray ready."

Hadley resisted the urge to turn around. She knew who it had to be. It was Wednesday after all; when the Society of Visiting Ladies met at Billings. Tears burned the back of her eyes.

"Miss," Hadley called, suppressing the tremor in her voice, "please put the scone in the box. I— I forgot that I have an errand I have to run."

The shop girl nodded. She said the cost of the order, but Hadley barely heard her.

"Apparently she's thinking of throwing a party while they're here," Rubella continued. "I hope we receive an invitation."

"Oh?"

"If she's going to make a spectacle of herself, I want to see it."

Dropping a handful of coins into the girl's palm, Hadley drew in a tremulous breath and snatched her box from the counter. She hesitated, pretending to rearrange her clutch. To leave, she would have to face Mrs. Nash and her friends. Hadley cleared her throat and straightened her back. She wouldn't let them get the better of her.

Her boots clicked across the floor, but when she reached their table, she stopped. Raising her gaze, Hadley locked eyes with Mrs. Nash. The older woman paused mid-sentence but didn't betray any regret she may have felt. The other women of the Society of Visiting Ladies looked from Hadley to Mrs. Nash, waiting to see who would strike first.

"I do hope you come to the party," Hadley said with a smile. "A woman of your esteem would be greatly missed, Mrs. Nash."

Before the woman could respond, Hadley turned on heel and marched out the door toward the cottage with the walled garden. With adrenaline shaking her hands, Hadley rang the doorbell. The stone-faced Barnes let her in, but before he could fetch her, Mrs. Rhodes appeared at the parlor curtain in a fine pink dress and a matching flowered bonnet. Her face blanched as she realized that the countess had come to call.

"Lady Dorset, to what do we owe the honor?" she said, her tight voice betraying her welcoming smile. She reached for her hat before letting her hand sink back to her side. "I was just on my way out to have lunch with Mrs. and Miss Campbell, but you are welcome to join us. I'm sure they would be pleased to make your acquaintance."

"I don't want to keep you, Mrs. Rhodes," Hadley began slowly, her eyes trailing up the stairs to where she imagined Mr. Talbot to be hiding. "I actually came to ask you for a favor. I know we don't know each other very well and it's a lot to ask, but I wanted to know if, one day, you would be willing to help me compile a list of everyone in town. In a few weeks, I hope to throw a party, and I don't want to miss anyone. As I said, it's a lot to ask, and if you are too busy, I would understand."

Leona watched the redhead fidget with the white bakery box dangling from her hand.

"You can borrow my address book; it should have everyone. Barnes, please fetch it for her. Is there anything else you require?"

"Is Mr. Talbot in? I was hoping I could speak to him."

"Let me fetch him." *Nadir? What could she want with him?* she thought as she mounted the steps and knocked on his door. "Nadir! Nadir, darling, someone wants to speak with you."

"I told you I am not to be disturbed! Tell whoever it is to go away," he yelled through the wall.

"It's Lady Dorset."

His chair scraped across the floor followed by a series of bumps and thumps. After a moment, the door whined open and her cousin appeared looking much more put together than he did when she last saw him that morning. When he had been furiously writing and berating her for bothering him, he had only been in his shirtsleeves, but for Lady Dorset, he had donned one of his bright suits and matching cravats. He buttoned his cuffs and was about to saunter past his cousin when she sunk her nails into his arm.

"Ow! What is your problem?" he hissed as she dragged him away from the stairs out of earshot.

"Is there anything going on between you and the countess?"

"What? No, of course not."

Her full cheeks flushed with anger as she grabbed the tender flesh on the underside of his arm and pinched through his suit. Nadir tried to wrench his arm away, but Leona held it fast.

"Stop that! Do you think I'm that much of a rake?"

"I have heard plenty of rumors, Nadir. You had better not be involved with Lady Dorset."

"Can a man and woman never be friends?"

"No."

He rolled his eyes, letting out an exasperated groan. He grasped his cousin by the shoulders and met her dark gaze. When their byzantine eyes met, she pinched her lips until they nearly disappeared and glared at him. As he cocked a black brow and grinned, Leona's resolve faltered. Her lips curled against her will, but she quickly stifled her smile with a half-hearted scowl.

"Please tell me there is nothing between you."

"Nothing but friendship," he replied softly. "She seems to want a companion, and I like her. She's... eccentric. You know how I enjoy the company of interesting people."

His cousin wrapped her fingers around his upper arm, ready to pinch him again. "You promise that is all?"

"Yes! Really, Leona, how can you think I'm such a cad? I would never get involved with another man's wife. Their daughters, on the other hand, are a different story."

"You're horrid." Leona slapped his arm before looping her own through it. "Hurry up, or I will be late to the Campbell's house."

"You're the one holding us up."

At the bottom of the stairs, Lady Dorset waited with the leather address book clutched to her chest. A grin brightened her countenance as her eyes roamed between Leona and Nadir. While the shapes of their faces and lips differed, it was clear from their expressive almond eyes and matching noses, which began narrow and gradually widened into an arrow at the tip, that there was a family resemblance. Nadir had the rich golden brown skin of the men Eilian worked with in Palestine and the striking angular features that caught women's eyes no matter the man's skin color. His cousin could have easily been an Italian or Greek, maybe even a dark Englishwoman. By her countenance, Hadley assumed that, unlike Nadir, at least one of Leona's parents was of English descent.

As they reached the lower steps and Leona released her cousin's arm, her booted foot caught the carpet-runner. Nadir watched her fall, but before he could catch her, she hit the steps. Instinctively throwing her arm across her stomach, she slid down the last three stairs and came to rest on the wood floor in a heap of silk and crinoline. The countess darted over as Nadir ran down the last few steps. Leona quickly pulled herself to her feet using the banister and steadied her panicked breath.

"Leona, are you hurt?" Nadir asked, reaching for her arm but was quickly shaken off.

"I'm all right! I'm perfectly all right!" she cried as she fought against her shaking limbs to slip on her gloves and walk to the door. Nadir and Lady Dorset watched her with wide eyes, poised to administer any aid she could need, but she brushed off their concern with a shake of her head. "I promise I'm fine. Now, I really must be off, or I will be late."

Before either Londoner could stop her, Leona bustled out, leaving them alone.

"Is she all right?"

Nadir shrugged. "Who knows with her? She's probably embarrassed to have fallen in front of you. Let's go in the parlor—"

He pulled back the curtain blocking the parlor only to find his cousin's barrel-chested husband snoring softly on the sofa. Tugging the drape shut, he turned back to the Countess of Dorset and lightly guided her down the hall.

"On second thought, it's a lovely day. It would be a shame not to sit outside."

Leading her by the arm, he walked her out the back door and into the little walled garden. It was barely more than a patch of cobbles with enough room for an iron table and two chairs. In each corner stood a terracotta pot of half-dead petunias. Nadir sneered at the shriveled brown flowers sitting amongst sprigs of weeds. If Argus was going to loaf around all day, the least he could do was keep the house presentable. He made a note to pay a visit to the florist after the countess left.

As Hadley thumbed through the address book, skimming the names and addresses with mild interest, Nadir gracefully seated himself on the hip-high wall. For a moment, he considered mentioning the dusty tunnel running beneath her house, but he thought better of it.

"My cousin was under the impression that you came to see me and not her."

Hadley closed the book and folded her arms over it. "I hope I didn't offend her. To be honest, you *were* the one I came to see."

His sharp brow arched.

"My mother-in-law has agreed to let me borrow a handful of servants from her when I throw my party in a few weeks."

"That's wonderful. Now, I can finally wear my new tailcoat." He paused, noting how the redheaded woman fiddled with her clutch and gloves. "Somehow I doubt you walked all the way down here to tell me that."

"No," she began slowly, "I wanted to ask for your assistance with throwing the party."

"I doubt a woman like yourself needs *my* help."

The countess's face fell as she smoothed a lock behind her ear. "A woman like myself has never been to a real party... apart from my wedding."

"Oh." Sinking into the chair opposite her, Nadir cocked his head, regarding Lady Dorset with a frown. "What about Lord Dorset? I'm sure he could help you."

"He's not the sort who enjoys large parties. While he would never stop me, he isn't much help. Eilian can't even remember the names of different canapés or wines he's had." She released a nervous laugh. "My title may be countess, but I'm brass with just enough polish to pretend I'm gold. I had hoped that someone with your experience would be willing to help me sort some of this out. I'm sure you have hobnobbed with plenty of people."

"That I have. If you would like my expertise, Lady Dorset, then I would be happy to give it, especially since throwing a soirée was my idea."

"It will be far from a soirée. Mr. Talbot—"

"Please call me Nadir."

"Nadir, when you stopped by, you mentioned that your parents throw parties in their vineyard in Alexandria. What are they like?"

A smile crept across his face as the garden faded into the Egyptian night. Insects chirped all around, hidden in the rows of vines, but as the musicians picked up their bows and flutes, they were downed beneath strings of notes and the clatter of conversation, the tink of wine glasses.

"The servants would hang colored jars with candles on the fence posts surrounding the vineyard, where they would shine like a thousand oversized jewels. Between the fields, there would be a series of chandelier-lit tents where the guests would sample my parents' favorite new vintage and dance to an orchestra that would play European and Egyptian melodies. Waiters would filter through the crowd with canapés and grapes. Of course, all of this would be done at night when the air was cool and crisp and smelled faintly of fruit and wood."

"It sounds magical."

He nodded, his gaze finally returning to the shabby garden with a lurch, as if he had not expected it to be there. "It was."

"Are both of your parents from Egypt?"

"Yes, well, my father likes to tell people that he is half-English and half-Egyptian, like that means something to them. Even if he was, he would only be the bastard son of some faceless Englishman named Talbot. Leona, on the other hand, really is half-English, and for the most part, she passes."

"Passes?"

"They assume she is merely a swarthy Englishwoman, and I'm glad for it." When the noblewoman still looked puzzled, he continued, "Anyone can see I'm not English. My father made certain we had a British surname and only let me speak English, but it doesn't change the fact that I'm obviously not from here even if I was born in Dorset. You would be surprised how quickly you can be expelled from some of the best schools in the country when you misbehave and are not British. No amount of eloquence or money or friends can change the fact that you are not one of them."

Hadley sighed. She had expected Nadir to become upset or impassioned by the sudden turn in the conversation, but he simply sat across the table from her, rolling a glass bead between his fingers as if they were discussing the most mundane of subjects. Is that how it felt to deal with inequity for so long? To have the hatred dull to the expected sting of a switch? Maybe that was what Eilian meant when he railed against the empire's mistreatment of its colonies.

"To a lesser extent, I know how you feel. But what about your friends? I'm sure they don't feel that way about you."

"I don't know what they truly think, and I don't think I want to. My aesthete friends call me exotic." He shook his head, pursing his lips in thought. "Animals or clothing are exotic. I tend to lose my appeal when they realize I'm much more like them than they first realized. It's funny. They would pay a king's ransom for a mummy or a chair with my ancestor's face on it, but I'm worth much less than any of their friends, if it ever came down to it."

"I can't imagine that to be true. There's no reason to discount you. You're successful and charming. Look at the books you have written. People love them."

"Perhaps, but I wouldn't want to see what would happen if I was put in a situation where I needed them." He spread his hands across the tabletop and leaned closer. "Enough of that, I have monopolized your time on my woes long enough. Let's discuss the party. When is it?"

"I was hoping to have it maybe a week and a half or so from now."

"We can work with that. You will need to get the invitations out as soon as possible and contact musicians and the florist. I assume you aren't picking flowers from the orangery."

"No, definitely not. Can I get all of that in Folkesbury, apart from the musicians?"

Nadir crinkled his nose in disgust. "The nearest florist is in Poole, which is where I would suggest you get everything. It isn't London, but it will do."

"I can't ride my velocipede to Poole, can I?"

"Not unless it has an engine. Luckily for you, your ladyship, I brought my steamer."

∗ ∗ ∗

Quietly pulling the door shut behind him, Nadir listened in the stillness for any sign of Leona or Argus in the dining room or parlor. He grabbed hold of the banister and staggered up the stairs, trying to avoid the squeaky boards. At the top, he froze as the clock struck ten, filling the small house with its rhythmic clamor. Lurching the last few feet to his bedroom door, he slipped in and hoped that the whining hinge was drowned beneath the clock's gonging. He couldn't bear to speak to Leona. After their conversation that afternoon, she would surely think that he had spent the entire day and part of the evening with Lady Dorset even though they had parted company hours earlier.

His head swam as he pulled off his coat and threw it across the bed. He had gone for a walk along the shore after their outing to clear his head. In Poole, they had picked out flowers and stationary and visited the market. While Lady Dorset seemed to finally relax once he steered her toward what he and his friends would have chosen, most of which she dismissed for her own choice, he couldn't stop thinking of the vineyard in Alexandria.

What he hadn't told her was that the party he remembered was nearly twenty years ago. He had escaped from his governess's ghost stories and run down the candle-lit lane to find his parents. He hadn't thought of Egypt in years. After spending most of his life in England, the thought of being in the abysmal heat was more than he could bear, yet nostalgia made him long to return. No amount of wave-watching or walking could chase away the idea. What was the point in traveling there? It had never been his home. His parents lived in England, his publisher was here, his house was here, his life was *here*. After downing half a bottle of wine and something brown that tasted like lamp oil at the pub, he concluded that the only Egyptian paradise that would ever welcome him existed in one of his books.

Pulling off his shoes, he turned them over to let the sand trickle out into a tiny dune beside his bed. As he unbuttoned his waistcoat, the door creaked open, but he ignored the voluptuous figure behind him with her hand on her hip.

"Where have you been? I thought you would have been back for dinner."

"The countess and I went to Poole to order supplies for her party. She wanted me to thank you again for letting her borrow your address book," he replied without meeting Leona's narrowed gaze. "Oh, that reminds me, I have new plants for the garden in the back of the steamer. You really shouldn't let them go to seed like that."

"You reek of liquor."

"So? I went to the pub. I'm allowed to go where I bloody well please, Leona." Nadir turned to find her scowling at him, her lips nearly invisible. "What do you want?"

She clinked a china cup onto his desk, sprinkling droplets onto the pages of his manuscript. "I came to bring you this. I should have dumped it on your head. Good night, Nadir."

Without another word, she slammed the door behind her. Nadir rolled his eyes and sank into the stiff seat of his desk chair. He carefully soaked up the drips of tea with his blotter before turning his attention to the words beneath them. Nadir skimmed the scene he had written the night before and readied his pen to continue. If he was to write a chase, he would need to at least be somewhat sober. Downing the tea in two gulps, he penned his heroine's clandestine escape from the king's harem by feigning death, but as she was about to be nearly caught, he yawned and rubbed his eyes. Nadir's breath came in languorous puffs. His mind wandered and the ink seeped from his pen where it lingered on the parchment. He leaned back, stretching his neck and arms to fend off the fatigue. Maybe he had misjudged the potency of the wine. Closing his eyes, his body loosened and the pen dropped from his hand.

ഷ്ലോ ඉର

Something shuffled in the darkness, thumping up the steps and across the loose boards. Nadir's body jolted upright in the chair at the sound of a door slamming nearby. He blinked, the pain of the noise echoing through his skull. Looking over his shoulder, he found that his door was closed and no one else was there. He rubbed his eyes and checked his desk clock. Three hours had passed.

Cracking his stiff back and neck, he collapsed onto his bed and lay facedown in his pillow, too tired to turn off the lamp. As he waited for sleep to overtake him again, a sharp inhalation broke the still air followed by the wet tremor of a sob. Thoughts of his books, Lady Dorset, and Leona's fall tumbled together as he was pulled under.

But why was the harem girl crying?

Chapter Thirteen
The Lieutenant Colonel

Party preparation was in full swing. Everywhere Eilian turned, he found maids scrubbing or polishing, noisily clanging their brushes against metal buckets. Scooping up his notebook, he crossed the bare halls. The carpet runners had been stripped away to be beaten out back while the statues and paintings had been smothered with white cloths. In a way, the house appeared to be regressing, returning to the entropic state they found it in, save for the spiders, yet there was nothing left for him to do. Hadley stood like a general on a domestic battlefield—directing staff maneuvers and ordering supplies—and he expected no less from her. After all, she had run a business practically on her own for years and built her line of toys into something sought by rich and poor alike, so a party should have been an easy feat. Still, he hoped there would have been a place for him. He didn't mind menial tasks, and during the first few days of preparation, he cleaned the library from top to bottom, washing the shelves' glass panes before oiling and polishing the books within. He had even smoothed things over with Mrs. Negi who was in a black mood after discovering she would be cooking for several hundred alongside the spare kitchen help from his mother's home in Grosvenor Square.

Now on the sixth day, he was no longer needed. Keeping his head down, he made his way to the parlor and was relieved to find the room empty. The sofa and chairs were cloaked with sheets, but standing in the corner just far enough away from the wall to catch the light filtering through the mullioned windows was what appeared to be a pot of dirt. After being insulted and derided by Nash, Eilian returned home determined to collect his own silphium seeds. His professional integrity wouldn't allow him to send the flowers or seeds from the original plant to London, but he didn't feel the slightest pang of guilt as he harvested a handful of seeds, several of which he dried out on the windowsill while the rest went into the empty pot. Picking up the watering can, he checked if any green had broken the surface. If he could grow his own silphium plant, then maybe it was possible that the species could be revived again and he could send it out for analysis. Part of him wondered what the consequences of his discovery would be, but if the Romans used it for hundreds of years, then surely it could only benefit society.

His eyes trailed to the wall beside the fireplace. With its intricate scrollwork, massive mirror of Venetian glass, and busy wallpaper, the faint outline of the study door was barely visible. Pushing on the edge of the plaster, a faint click sounded behind it and the door swung open. Every surface was coated in a layer of dust, except for the tabletop which Eilian had cleaned when he discovered the room and the blank space against the wall where the brass telescope had once been. It was a relief to know that the maids hadn't yet discovered the hidden cubby. Eilian slipped inside, leaving the door open far enough to let in air and light while still being able to be quickly shut if someone entered the main parlor.

Opening his notebook, he separated his notes from the stack of letters he had yet to open. Most were nothing more than updates about his late-father's shipping company or bills from the various merchants Hadley procured for the party. A smile spread across his lips but rapidly faded to a grimace as he withdrew a letter from the mechanic and saw the figure it would cost to fix the steamer. It would be ready to be picked up in town at his earliest convenience. Hope bloomed in Eilian's chest. Maybe they could return to London soon. He deflated with a sigh. No matter how much he wished to return to the city, they would remain in Dorset until after the party and probably a week or two more. He never imagined London to be a place he would want to return, but being trapped in Folkesbury made him realize how much he missed his home and even the familiar garden paths of Grosvenor Square and Greenwich. There was smog and noise and frippery, but there was more variety in London than any city he had ever visited. Now that he and Hadley were married, he would be tied to England due to her businesses and his duties, yet he found he was looking forward to staying in Greenwich for part of the year. During the offseason, they would travel to the Near East or around Europe, and when she had to build her inventory, he would stay to help her or work on his mechano-archaeology research. For once there would be balance in his life.

Eilian put aside the bills to be taken care of later. At the bottom of the pile was a letter from his mother. He considered sticking it in the back of his notebook, but what if she was writing to tell them she could no longer spare her staff? Reading the letter, his eyes slowed as he reached the body of the missive. A tremor passed through his hand. He let the letter fall and rubbed his brow.

The announcement has not yet been made public, but Dylan stopped by the yesterday to tell me some wonderful news: Constance is with child! The baby will be born sometime in December if all goes well, and in the meantime, your brother and his wife have settled in a lovely flat near Grosvenor Square, close enough that I can visit my grandchild whenever I please. Nothing could be better, except perhaps a second grandchild in the near future.

Eilian groaned and closed his eyes. He knew what his mother

meant. His chest tightened at the thought. Dylan already had a life of his own and punctually met their mother's expectations. He was happy for his brother, truly he was—Dylan and Constance would surely shower their child with love—but what he craved was freedom, not children. Even though he happened to be the elder brother, Eilian felt as if he was not much more than a child himself. Starting a family seemed so far off that he and Hadley hadn't even discussed it. When speaking of future plans like traveling or expanding her business, children were never mentioned.

A ripple of fear gurgled through his gut. If he truly loved his wife, how could he willing put her in mortal danger? Maybe Patrick was rubbing off on him, but he was afraid. *If all goes well.* So much could go wrong, and he couldn't bear the thought of no longer waking up beside her or hearing her brisk step through the halls just to fill an obligation.

Rubbing the back of his neck with his prosthetic hand, something cold slithered across his neck and down his chest. Eilian rose and tugged his shirt from his trousers only to have his long silver chain snake out. The signet ring bounced off the chain and across the floorboards before skidding under the desk. Frowning, he stuffed his shirt back in and dropped to his knees. The ring glittered in the far corner. He reached for it while keeping his head against the desk's front, but his fingers barely brushed its cool surface. Getting down on all fours, he crawled under the dusty desk.

"Now, I've got you," he whispered, his fingers finally closing around the ring, but as he raised his gaze, he bumped his head in surprise. Lining the back wall were three dozen journals. No two were the same in size, color, and level of wear, but on each spine a white numeral had been carefully painted. His elbow ached as he leaned on his prosthesis to pull out the first two volumes. Shimmying out from under the table, he dusted his knees and placed the books on the desk along with the chain and ring. Eilian threaded the chain through it again, but as he reached the clasp, he realized the links around it had been torn open. There was no way around it. With a sigh, he slid the ring above his wedding band, flexing his fingers until it rested comfortably below the joint.

Pulling the study door a little closer, he inspected the stack of books. The first journal was barely more than a hand-length long, small enough to easily tuck into a breast pocket. He turned it over in his hand, noting the spatters of dried dirt on the edges of the pages and the degraded condition of the stitches that bound the spine. The ink on the inside cover was smeared and stained with water, but through it Eilian could make out:

If found, please forward to Brasshurst Hall, Folkesbury, Dorset, England. Property of Lieutenant Colonel Laurence Sorrell—

The battalion number that followed had been washed away long ago. Eilian's eyes trailed to the portrait of the young man seated against a boulder. So this was Laurence Sorrell. Carefully cracking the pages apart, he found that most of the journal cataloged the daily happenings of the Napoleonic War: the condition of the men; their surroundings, which were often drawn in detail along the edges of pages only to intrude upon the words; the things he missed most on the battlefield.

January 2nd, 1809

Starving. Can't wait to have real food. Cottage pie, perhaps...or pheasant.

He chuckled to himself at the short entry, which was surrounded by drawings of bread and what looked like a cauldron over a fire. Things hadn't changed much. Glancing over more complaints and half-decipherable battle maneuvers, he stopped when the pages suddenly appeared free of drawings and mud. Laurence's handwriting no longer seemed scribbled in haste. Ink pooled at the ends of his words as if he sat deliberating whether to commit them to paper. He could picture the curly-haired soldier wrapped in a blanket penning the entry by candlelight. The night would have been punctuated by boom of cannons and rifles in the distance, and the air would have tasted of sulphorous smoke.

March 14th, 1809

Gabriella has written to tell me that my father is dead and I am expected to return home at once. Why? Why should I abandon my men to return to a man who will be long dead and buried by the time I reach English shores? The letter itself was sent nearly a month ago. For a month I had no knowledge that I was now the earl, but I should make haste. I will leave when I am good and ready. My purpose is here. No one in Dorset needs me as much as my men do now.

Eilian frowned. He could sympathize with his great-grandfather. When he received the letter from his mother in Beersheba, it felt as if his life had been ripped out from under him. In one moment, he found himself fatherless and shouldering a burden he had tried to escape from for a decade. Neither he nor his great-grandfather had the experience of most men. There was no sickbed to wait at or decades to watch their fathers wizen with age all during which they could gather experience. Eilian's gaze trailed to his prosthetic hand. Then again, he ran as far away as possible from his father the moment he could.

Thumbing a few pages forward, the drawings of soldiers and greenery once again disappeared.

March 21st, 1809

I never thought my family would stoop so low. I have been accosted. For months I have complained of the noblemen who have decided to try their hand at playing soldier. They are the ones who think having a title allows them to watch the war from their social clubs. They hide at the general's camp, if you can call it that when it has beds and a roof, and have servants fetch them wine while their men roast whatever creature they can find and march in sole-less shoes. Now, I have been forced into their ranks by my own flesh and blood.

This morning I received a letter summoning me to the general's camp. I expected to be given new orders or even boots to bring back, but instead, I was met with toasts and carousing. They were congratulating me on my sudden rise in station. How can they celebrate a rise in stature if it comes at the expense of another man's life? Wellington at least seemed to understand that. He brought me into his office to speak privately, and I was horrified to find Thomas waiting there with a painter. They made me sit for a portrait to commemorate becoming the seventh earl right then and there.

It was the most uncomfortable experience of my life. I would rather trudge through a hundred muck-strewn roads than be scrutinized for hours against my will. The painting will never see the light of day.

My brother seemed thrilled to find me well and whole, yet I can't help but be churlish. Being on the continent, I had hoped to escape all of them: mother, father, Gabriella, Thomas. My deep love for them doesn't negate the fact that I am most myself when there is distance between us, and while I yearn to see my nieces and nephews again, I wish my return was only a visit.

Now, I shall be drawn back against my will as if Fate's wheel turned only to reel me back across the channel to Dorset. Maybe I will be lucky, *and the French will sink us. If only Thomas wasn't joining me. What my life will become on the other side of the sea, only the Fates know.*

"What *did* you become?" Eilian whispered as he peered under the desk at the other thirty-three volumes neatly numbered and arranged out of sight. From his portrait in the hall gallery, he knew Laurence lived well into his golden years and appeared to have become the quintessential gentleman he imagined when he thought of earls or dukes, but how did he get there? Prying the stained pages apart, Eilian read on. There was only one way to find out what became of the Seventh Earl of Dorset.

Chapter Fourteen
Love & Desire

Hadley scrutinized her reflection in the vanity mirror. Her eyes slid over every pore and freckle, her heart quickening as the list of flaws mounted. Swallowing hard, she met her own weary gaze. At least she liked her eyes and nose. She pushed on her cheeks and ran her hand along the edge of her jaw. They would say her cheeks were too full, her jaw too masculine. Licking her finger, she smoothed her auburn brows. It felt strange to suddenly try to care so much about her appearance. She had never felt the need to bother with it. No one looked at her, and she didn't really want them to.

She had resigned herself to becoming a spinster with the business as her only companion, and spinsters didn't need elaborate coiffures or fancy gowns. Living with Adam hadn't helped either. How could she possibly measure up against a man whose clothes fit better than hers and whose hair was done with more care than anyone she knew? Occasionally, she did try. After her older brother, George, died and she was forced to attend meetings with potential buyers, she added new trimmings to her old gowns and had Eliza style her hair to ensure that the only flaws they could find were in her product.

She ran her hands over her arms, which were far too strong from lifting molds and heavy automata. Her calluses caught as her palms brushed. Over her cotton nightgown, she traced the shape of her full breasts and trailed over her sides until she came to rest on her hips. After more than a decade of wearing a corset, she should have been narrower, but the restriction was infuriating and she could never bring herself to pull it too tight. Maybe she would take up the Rational Dress Movement after all. It had to be better to be mocked in the society pages than to be so limited.

Resting her head in her hands, she sighed. The party was only four days away, and she still hadn't decided whether she would strive to be what people like Mrs. Nash would respect or the woman she truly was. A woman who loved to indulge in a dress that matched her eyes but much preferred to work with her hands and wear trousers. She wouldn't wear them then, but if one woman had already scoffed at her ideals, others certainly would.

Her gaze returned to the woman in the mirror. With a shake of her head, waves of dark red swirled and settled against her skin, highlighting the lines of cheekbones and the cupid's bow of her lips. Biting them until they pinkened, she smiled and smoothed the edges of her hair. If nothing else, she was striking, and if Adam could work with that, so could she.

Slipping Eliza's reply from the vanity's drawer, she retreated to her bed. She sank into its plush folds as she reread the missive for the tenth time. Nearly every night she had meant to bring it up with her husband, but it didn't seem like the right time. How did one discuss these things, especially when they had never even gotten that far? Hadley straightened as a thump echoed from behind the dressing room door. When the door squealed open, she threw the letter into the bedside table and fluffed her hair. She watched as Eilian crept inside in his pajamas but upon seeing her awake and waiting for him, a lopsided smile spread across his features. Crossing the room, he dropped a stack of mismatched books from under his arm onto the dresser and leaned across the bed to kiss her.

He plopped down beside her, wrapping his prosthetic hand around hers. "I'm surprised to see you still up. You looked exhausted at dinner."

"I was, but now, I am wide awake," she replied. She had fallen asleep on the chaise in one of the drawing rooms while looking over the final menu. When she awoke, she found Mrs. Negi glowering over her, the menu crumpled on the floor, and the chair's white sheet wrapped around her. "What have you been up to?"

"Patrick and I walked to town to retrieve the steamer. Apparently the boiler damaged several other parts, but it's fixed now." His grey gaze traveled over Hadley's face. Despite her bright smile and quick movements, her eyes betrayed the fatigue lingering behind them. "Is there anything you want me to do tomorrow, Had? I feel as if you are shouldering so much with this party, and you needn't do that. I can help— I *want* to help."

She rubbed her face and fluffed her hair at the roots. "I know, I know. Tomorrow, I promise I will think of something. I'm not accustomed to delegating."

"And I am not accustomed to being useless." Rubbing her shoulder, he reverently kissed her forehead. "Let me help."

As she nodded and watched him walked to the weathered books sitting on the dresser, her eyes locked onto the gold ring sitting above his wedding band. "Are you wearing your father's ring?"

"Only by necessity. My chain broke, and I didn't want to lose it."

"Maybe it's a sign."

"I doubt it."

Her cousin's letter called to her from the drawer. She had to say something. When he returned with book in hand, the words worked free from her mouth against her will, "Eilian, before you start, there is something I need to speak to you about."

He cocked an umber brow and settled beside her. "Is everything all right?"

"Yes. Well, no, not exactly. I want to discuss what happened the night your arm got caught on my corset."

"Oh, that," he replied, raking a nervous hand through his hair. "What about it?"

"I just want to know what happened. Was it something I did?"

"No, of course not."

Without meeting his gaze, she reached into the nightstand and pulled out the letter with shaking hands. "I hope you don't mind, but I wrote to Eliza."

Eilian's face fell. "Had, did you really? Do you know how embarrassing that is? To have everyone know our intimate business. I'm sure she told James, too."

"I didn't know who else to turn to!" she cried. "You wouldn't talk about it, and she's been married for years. I thought she might have some advice."

"What did she say?"

"That it isn't rare for a man to be hesitant, especially one who is very respectful." She swallowed hard and smoothed her hair behind her ears. "Eliza also said that you may not want children yet, so you might be worried about that. I mean, I don't want them yet either, but apparently there are ways around that. I will let you read it yourself."

Sweat broke across Eilian's back as he took the letter from his wife's hand. The more he read, the harder it was to fight the thickening in his throat. Swallowing against the nausea, he rubbed the back of his neck where the skin burned against his will. He glanced up at Hadley to find her watching him, as if waiting for him to rejoice at this epiphany, but all it did was make him feel ill. To Hadley, it must have sounded so simple on paper, but to him, it was as indecipherable as one of his great-grandfather's battle maneuvers. Eilian wiped the sheen of sweat from his forehead and drew in a measured breath to stifle the bolt of pain lancing down his arm.

"What do you think? None of it sounds too bad."

"I... I don't know. You're all right with all of this?"

131

"Of course, aren't you?" Hadley searched his face, noting his downcast eyes and quickened breath. "You're not?"

His eyes trailed back to the paper before he shook his head. "No, I don't think I can do this."

"Can't do what, exactly?"

"Any of it. Honestly, Had, I'm not comfortable with any of this."

"But— but why?"

"Because thinking about it makes me feel ill."

The words had escaped before he could think to stop them. Hadley stared at him, blue eyes wide in confusion and hurt. Looking down at his mismatched hands, Eilian tried to squelch the burning behind his eyes. There was nothing he could do to change how he felt. It wasn't her fault that she wanted to make love and he didn't. He was the odd one, the one lacking.

Her lips twitched as she asked, "Do *I* make you ill?"

"No, please, Had, don't ever think that. It isn't you, it's— it's the act itself. None of this has anything to do with you."

"It has everything to do with me. You won't even touch me."

"Of course I touch you. I kiss you, hug you, help you dress."

Hadley's voice cracked as tears moistened the corners of her eyes. "But you don't touch me *in that way*. Do you not feel that way about me? Do you not want me?"

Eilian froze, his stomach knotting and churning. How could she think he didn't want her? He had invited her to join him in the Negev because he couldn't imagine going months without seeing her. He had proposed to her and married her. She was the only person he ever knew that he wanted to spend his life with, so how could she think that?

"I do want you," he replied, holding her hand between his. "When have I ever rejected you?"

"Eilian, you're rejecting me right now!"

"But..." He opened his mouth, unsure what to say, as she pulled her hand away. Bile rose in his throat. How could he make her see that he rejected the act, not her? "When you say 'feel that way,' what exactly do you mean?"

"That you desire me. You don't even seem to want to touch me."

"If you wanted me to, why didn't you tell me to?"

"Because you're my husband and you should want to!" She dropped her voice. "What about men? Do you feel *that way* about them? I won't be angry. It would at least make sense that you seemed attracted to me in Palestine."

Sitting in stunned silence, he watched his wife's lips tremble with his hesitation. "No, should I?"

She wiped at her nose with the back of her hand and sniffed against the staunched tears. As Eilian inched closer, she turned her face from him. Her lips contorted into a grimace, and when she could no longer suppress them, hot tears trickled from her eyes. Eilian wrapped his arms around her as she rocked with silent sobs.

"I didn't mean to hurt you, Had. I only wanted to be honest with you. It isn't you, though. I have never felt that way about anyone."

"That's of little comfort," she replied, pushing the cold metal of his prosthesis away.

"I don't know what you want me to say, but this is how I feel. It wasn't until recently that I found out that not everyone feels as I do."

She drew in a tremulous breath and straightened, her voice coming in grating bursts as she said, "Eilian, you aren't stupid. How could you have not known that?"

"How was I supposed to know when I have never felt it?"

"Maybe you would feel differently if you actually tried."

Her hand shot out, reaching for the buttons of his pajamas. Before she could work it loose, he swatted her away and hopped off the bed.

"Stop! Just stop!" Eilian released a constrained breath. His fear and nausea hardened into anger as he stared into her defiant eyes. "I would love to try if I didn't feel as if I were about to vomit. Despite what you may think, I'm not exaggerating, Hadley. Do you not care at all about how *I* feel?"

"I don't understand what's happening between us."

"Then, that makes two of us. Look, I need some space. I need to get away from all of this," he replied as he refastened his buttons.

Gathering his pillow and dressing gown, he refused to meet her gaze. "I will sleep in one of the guest rooms tonight. Good night, Hadley."

"Are you suggesting that we will never—?"

He paused with his hand on the door, swallowing down his rage. "No, I would never do that to you, but I need time to figure this out. All I ask is that you allow me to go at my own pace. If you can't accept that, I will be moving my things into the guest room."

Shutting the door behind him, he leaned against it and closed his eyes. He lingered for a moment to see if Hadley would pursue him, but to his relief, she stayed in bed. There was nothing in the world he wanted to discuss less than another personal failing. But could he really call it that when he could never remember a time when he felt differently? Opening the nearest bedroom door, he stripped the dusty cover from the bed and collapsed onto the mattress. He ran a hand through his hair and stared up at the gathered silk canopy hanging precariously above his head. Maybe it would come crashing down in the middle of the night and end his misery.

Attraction. Desire. The words were bandied about but their meaning never made clear. He should have known then that something was wrong. His attraction to Hadley was stronger than it had been to any other woman. He loved her tenacity, her curiosity, the way she self-consciously smoothed her hair and clothes when she was nervous. It made him want to spend his life entirely in her company. But what did others feel when they looked at her? He thought she was beautiful and clever, but it was impossible to fathom that phantom feeling of desire. Apparently she felt it when she saw him. His stomach knotted at the thought.

His inability to experience desire wounded her. It wasn't something he could control. Like a colorblind man, he had no idea of what he couldn't see until it was reflected in another's perception and he realized the magnitude with which they felt what he could never know. Hadley would assume that he did not desire her in the way she did not desire his brother. While she could never understand the complete absence of a feeling that was natural to her, he wouldn't be able to construct that feeling from others' testimonies.

On his wedding day, his brother had ribbed him about the wedding night, and while he smiled and chuckled along, he knew he hadn't fully understood what he meant. There was some anticipation of the event that he did not feel. Eilian closed his eyes, his body sighing into the old mattress. It was naive and foolish to have assumed that anyone felt as he did. They never did before, so why would they now?

Chapter Fifteen
Opportunity Makes a Thief

Hadley lay in bed with a copy of *The Strand* resting against her thighs. Her eyelids drooped despite her best attempts to follow Mr. Holmes's latest case. It seemed fitting to read a story about a runaway bride. Even with the lamp burning in the corner of her vision and Hatty Doran's mysterious disappearance, her head lolled forward, snapping up momentarily as she regained her place on the page. The house had fallen silent long ago, but she didn't want to sleep. If she slept, it would be morning and she would have to speak to Eilian or pretend the night before never happened. Neither option sounded preferable. As she reached to turn the page with a sluggish hand, a loud clank echoed through the house. Sitting up, her eyes drifted over the furniture and door. Had she imagined it in that moment between sleeping and waking? No, she was certain she heard something fall.

"Eilian? Eilian, is that you?" she called, thinking he had stumbled over something in the guest room, but no one responded and no footsteps padded on the other side of the door.

Opening the drawer without taking her eyes off the door, she withdrew her derringer and slowly slid out of bed and into her slippers. She crossed the boards on soundless feet, cracking the door enough to peer into the darkened hall. Light streamed from the bedroom but was drowned beneath the deep shadows at the other end. The only noise came from the faint hiss of the gas lamps behind her and the steady thrum of the engine in the orangery. In the stillness, it clanged and rattled as she inched toward the doors at the darkened end with her gun pointed ahead of her.

A scant glimmer of light shined off the polished floors and wood-lined walls as she crossed the empty hall to the row of guest rooms. Her eyes swept over the doors flanking either side for any sign that someone might be hiding in one, but when she opened the first door, she found her husband sprawled across the bedspread sound asleep. Two springs had unhooked from his prosthesis during the night while the rest remained assembled and tucked around a pillow. Her gaze softened as she reached his face, which was already peppered with stubble and lay lax against the sheets. Reaching out, she shook his shoulder.

"Eilian," Hadley called, patting his side and cheek, "wake up!"

"Is it morning already?" he mumbled into the blanket, but when his vision cleared and his eyes came to rest on the glinting derringer, he snapped into consciousness. Scrambling to his knees, his heart pounded as he fumbled with his prosthesis. He looked toward the window to gain his bearings, but all he could make out was the pre-twilight blackness.

He drew in a constrained breath as his grey gaze traveled from Hadley's knit brows and tight lips to her gun. "What's going on?"

"I heard something. I thought maybe it was you, but obviously not."

He shook his head, rubbing the sleep from his eyes. "Want me to go look? Maybe one of the servants dropped wood or a bucket."

"At this time of morning?"

"Right." Eilian pulled his dressing gown over his pajamas. "Let's look. It's probably nothing."

"Maybe thieves broke in or Nash."

"If it's the latter, feel free to shoot, but please refrain from killing my staff," he yawned, plucking the iron shovel from the edge of the hearth.

Eilian followed his wife down the hall, but as they flung open each door, ready to attack any intruders, they found the wing of bedrooms empty. The only footsteps or breaths they heard were their own. The hard fear in Hadley's eyes ebbed when the last door closed. She could have sworn she heard something, but when searching the upstairs revealed nothing, she couldn't help but wonder if she had been dreaming after all. But if she was mistaken and someone remained in the house...

"Shall we go downstairs?" Eilian asked, his voice reverberating in the gloom of the upper arcades.

"Ssh, keep your voice down! They might still be here," she whispered, glaring at him over her shoulder.

With a renewed resolve, she raised her firing arm and crept ahead. Eilian stayed at her side as they peeked into the statue and vase-filled niches along the arcades of the great hall. Moonlit fog filtered in from the skylight, illuminating the spectral furniture in the room below. As the shadow-drenched staircase came into view, Eilian put his hand on Hadley's arm. She stopped, her mouth poised to reprimand, when he put his finger to his lips. Her light eyes widened as quick steps crossed the boards, growing louder until a figure emerged from the hall below. Eilian and Hadley leaned back from the pillared arches while the man crossed the room. His taper flickered in his hand, casting queer shades dancing on the family crest and lion's mouth of the hearth. When the stranger disappeared into the dining room, Hadley met Eilian's gaze.

"You distract him," she whispered, cocking the gun's hammer. "I will go downstairs."

He caught her arm and pulled her back to his side. "No. There could be more of them. We will do it from up here. I would rather have him run out the door than go after you."

Releasing a tense breath, Hadley nodded and trained her gun on the dining room door. Shadows roiled and drifted in the blackness below the arcade. Her heart drummed in her throat as she waited with her finger on the trigger. Drawing in a deep breath, Hadley released it slowly. She had to calm down or she would shoot him the moment he appeared. As she readjusted her hand, candlelight drifted back into the great hall. Eilian locked eyes with her, and with a nod, her gaze sharpened as she stared down the barrel at the man below.

"Identify yourself!" Eilian yelled.

The man below jumped, looking around before raising his gaze to the upper arcade. His white hair and silver-rimmed spectacles glistened in the scant light of the flickering candle as he spotted them leaning behind the wooden pillars. "It's me, sir! I thought I heard something."

Hadley exhaled and dropped her arm. She had never been so relieved to see Patrick. Quickly descending the staircase, they joined the butler in the great hall. Standing amongst the covered furniture in the dark, the house took on an otherworldly hue. The blackness beyond the hall leading to the gallery and library were absolute.

"Why didn't you turn on the lights? Hadley nearly shot you."

"I'm sorry, sir, but I didn't want to wake the whole house. Did you hear it, too?"

"I heard something, but I'm not sure what. Are all the servants accounted for?"

The butler nodded. "I woke Charlotte, and she said the other girls are in bed and haven't moved all night. I've been going room by room, checking the windows, your ladyship. I thought maybe a tree or branch broke through a window, but they're all closed and the doors are locked, too."

"That's good, at least. You didn't happen to see anyone while you—?"

Hadley froze as the unmistakable crack of shattering glass erupted behind her. They slowly turned, their gazes trailing to the pitch-black hall. There was no question; someone was in the house.

"Stay behind me," Eilian whispered as he held the shovel like a cricket bat and crept toward the gallery.

Fear inched up Hadley's form, sending a tremor down her arm as she held the gun ahead of her with both hands. She drew in a constrained breath. With the disorienting pulse of the pool's engine, it was nearly impossible to tell if the noises she heard were footsteps or merely an offbeat churn of the weathered cogs. As Eilian flipped on the gallery's lamps and illuminated the generations of nobles, her body relaxed under the familiar glow. The room was empty.

At the library's pocket door, they readied themselves for an ambush, but when it was thrown open and the light turned on, it appeared as if no one had entered it since Eilian cleaned it. That only left one possibility.

"You checked the back rooms, Pat?"

"Yes, sir. The parlors, the back drawing room, the morning room, the kitchen, the servants' quarters. I didn't go upstairs though."

"We did."

Eilian and Hadley exchanged strained looks. Neither wanted to go into the orangery. With the fog from the pool and the cover of the foliage, anyone could be hiding in there and they might never find them. Eilian swallowed hard. For once he hoped to find Nash lounging beside the pool with another bottle of champagne.

"Should I fetch the police?" the butler whispered, his eyes running between his master and mistress.

"Not yet. We need you to keep an eye out by the door. If you see anyone, yell."

At the library's double doors, Eilian waited, watching Hadley's chest rapidly rise and fall. "Had, you don't have to come in if you don't want to."

"I do. I just need a moment." Closing her eyes, she drew in a deep breath and focused on the piece of steel in her hand. It would protect her. She believed in her skills and knew what she was capable of. Hadley swept her hair behind her ears and cleared her throat. "Ready."

Eilian opened the door a crack and gazed into the darkness.

Inching along the wall with his hand, he searched for the switch that would turn on the auxiliary lanterns he had seen hanging on the metal armature that held up the massive dome. He ripped the stray vines from the switch and with a sharp click, the lamps exhaled to life. One by one the globe-sized bulbs alighted, radiating an eerie green light through the moss-coated glass. It wasn't much, but it was enough to make out the overgrown path that cut through the trees. In the alien glow, the fog churned, creating faces and shadows between the trunks, but as Eilian and Hadley stepped through the mist, the nightmares disappeared only to be replaced by darker shades once they left the safety of the library door.

Hadley's eyes darted across the brush, searching for any sign of movement. Every curl of mist caught her eye, but nothing appeared. The deeper they moved into the darkness, the louder her heart pounded. A little voice whispered that no one was there. Maybe a hedgehog or rat had broken into some forgotten cupboard and shattered a glass. As they rounded the corner where the mosaic floor lay, something caught Hadley's foot. Before she could catch herself, she stumbled forward and hit the ground hard, knees-first. She held her breath as her derringer skidded away, hoping that it wouldn't go off.

"Are you all right?" Eilian whispered, rushing to her side. "What happened?"

"I tripped."

Climbing to her feet, she brushed off her nightgown and glanced down at what caught her foot. She had expected to find a stray root or misplaced shovel but instead found an overturned iron candelabrum. It was one of a set she had brought down from the attic for the party. As Eilian righted it, she frowned thoughtfully. The candelabrum weighed over fifty pounds and had a wide decorative base. The vibration of the engine couldn't have knocked it over. Fear curled around her ribs at the implication.

"This must have been the noise Patrick and I heard. Where's my gun?"

"It's right here," he answered as he retrieved it from the edge of the path. "I really don't think anyone is here. We haven't heard anything or seen anyone. If they made this much noise before, I don't think they would be able to keep quiet for this long." He gently rubbed her arms, but she continued to clutch her gun and eye the gardens around them for the intruder. "Maybe they broke in, realized all of the doors were locked, and left."

"But I heard this first! I know I heard it. I was still awake. We need to keep looking, Eilian. I can't go back to bed without knowing for certain that no one is here."

"All right. Let's circle back. If we don't find anything, Pat will go and bring the police back. How does that sound?"

"Fine."

She crossed her arms and stared at the path ahead of them. Her thoughts churned in an infinite loop of fear that would only break and capturing the thief or the sun rising to chase away the unknown. Then, the shadows would recede and everything would be as it once was. Eilian wrapped his arm around her shoulder and drew her closer, reverently kissing the top of her head. Against her better judgment, she allowed him to draw her forward around the path toward the pool. She huddled against Eilian's side, shivering as a biting breeze cut through her cotton gown. Her eyes narrowed as Patrick came into view again.

Slipping away from Eilian, she broke from the trail and cut through the thin patch of trees between the girders and the pool. The wind tousled her hair as her eyes locked onto the shattered pane. In the spectral green glow, she could make out the sea breaking against the bluffs in the distance and the spray of shattered glass across the lawn. Hadley backed away from the window to allow the moonlight to shine onto the orangery's floor, but no glass was left beneath her feet.

It didn't make any sense.

When she emerged from the brush, she found Eilian standing beside the pool with Patrick's candle in his hand. His grey eyes were wide as he stared into the patch of earth where orchids and birds of paradise sprouted. Even when she reached his side, he didn't stir. She followed Eilian's gaze, but the spot was empty.

"What's wrong? Did they take anything?"

He raked a hand through his hair and swallowed hard. "The silphium is gone."

Chapter Sixteen
A Sleepless Night

Hadley and Eilian watched from the chaise in the library as three policemen paced through the greenhouse under Mr. Bernard's watchful eye. The sun shone into the glass globe, revealing every errant footprint and wilted flower. Patrick had been sent to fetch them in the early morning hours, but when the police refused to come until daybreak, he drove to the mechanic and returned to Brasshurst with a large sheet of metal. Careful not to disturb the broken glass, Hadley and Eilian had welded the metal over the frame where the pane of glass once stood to keep the delicate plants from dying in the spring chill. A few hours after dawn, the police finally arrived bright-eyed and smelling of breakfast while the Sorrells glared at them with weary scorn. After waiting hours for them to arrive without going back to sleep or having a bite to eat, they barely cared if the culprit was caught. All they wanted was to have their lives and house back.

"I know I said this already, but I am so sorry this happened,

Eilian," Hadley said as the sergeant gave one of the younger men orders and walked toward the library door.

"At least I saved some seeds. It isn't gone, not indefinitely yet. Hopefully the one I planted will grow." He sighed. "Imagine what we could have learned from it. If the other doesn't take, all of my research was for nothing. If only Nash hadn't been such a stubborn fool. Now, we will never know what it could have done."

The library door squealed open, letting in the overpowering scent of musky cologne before revealing the well-groomed Sergeant Purcell. His mustachios had been perfectly trimmed and waxed to fine, curled points. Despite being in his late-forties, his military baring and blue eyes gave him a semblance of youth. Hadley could see why Mrs. Nash would have preferred his company to that of her husband. The sergeant gave them a curt bow and wiped the sweat from his brow with the back of his hand.

"You're sure all they took was the— what did you call it?"

"Silphium, and yes, from what I can tell, that is all they took," Eilian snapped. He knew where this was going. The sergeant had already tried this line of questioning twice.

"And you say all of the doors were locked from the inside when you came in?"

"Yes, I told you before that my manservant checked. Did you find anything?"

Purcell licked his thumb and flipped back through his notepad. "I want you to think hard about this. Is it possible that one of your servants unlocked the doors, stole the plant, and locked up again?"

"Why do you insist that one of our servants is a thief?" Hadley scolded.

"It's the most probable outcome, your ladyship," he began, his voice honeyed. "You never really know—"

"Don't patronize me, sir. I will have none of it." She pressed her fingers to her forehead, her eyes narrowing to a fierce sliver. "I have been up half the night because someone broke into our home, and you and your men didn't have the decency to get out of bed and figure out what happened or at least give us some semblance of safety. Now, you come into my house and accuse my servants of mischief. I will have none of it."

"Lady Dorset, if all of the doors were locked, then how did the thief get into the greenhouse? Hmm? It had to be an inside job. You said yourself that the broken window was shattered from the inside."

Hadley's hands curled into fists at her sides, but at Eilian's reassuring touch, she let out a puff of hot air and gritted her teeth. "As I mentioned when you first got here, we think there is a trap door or false panel in the orangery, but we haven't found it yet. The thief could have gotten in and out through there without having to unlock a thing."

"A trap door, right. Then they just happened to break a window. If you have it all figured out, do you have a suspect in mind, Lady Dorset?"

Eilian wrapped his arm around his wife, shielding her from the sergeant as much as he was protecting him from her. Before she could answer, he replied, "Our servants have no reason to steal from us. None of them even know what silphium is, and besides it has no real value. There are only two people besides us who know—"

The words died in his throat as his eyes fixed on the window to the orangery. Up the path from the drawing room came Nash's gaunt form. His grey head swept over the pair of constables standing amongst the plants before coming to rest on the library window. Eilian was on his feet and out the door before Sergeant Purcell could figure out what was going on. Meeting Nash at the pool's edge, Eilian blocked him from reaching the patch of dirt where the policemen and gardener stood watching them.

"Out of my way," he spat as he attempted to step past the earl but was matched step for step.

"Why? Have you come to look at your handiwork, Mr. Nash? I know you didn't want me to study it, but to tear it from the ground, so no one could have it— Are you that daft?"

Nash's brows furrowed as his grey eyes narrowed and his legs rooted in place. "What are you talking about?"

"The silphium, Mr. Nash. It's gone. I'm assuming I have you to thank for that and my broken window. You are the only one who frequents our greenhouse uninvited."

Pushing Eilian's prosthetic arm away, Nash marched over to the edge of the garden. As Bernard moved to stop him, Eilian raised his hand for the gardener to let him be. At the sight of the empty patch in the dirt where a dozen disembodied hair roots still reached for the light, Nash's eyes lost their cold intensity and faded to silent consternation as his mouth hung open. For a moment, Eilian feared the man might swoon or have a fit and fall into the algal pool, but he caught himself, staggering back a step and clenching his eyes as if absorbing a blow. Eilian stood at his side as the older man's mouth worked in half-formed phrases.

"Mr. Nash, do you know who did this?"

"It's gone. She said she would," he said to no one, his voice trailing into a whisper. "I should have— I should—"

Eilian laid his hand on his arm, and Nash whipped it from him as if he had been stung.

"I didn't take your blasted plant. You probably pulled it out and hid it away when I told you, you couldn't have it. Ask your pretty little wife about the letters she received. She probably did it to spite me." He shifted his attention to the two young men milling between the trees with their heads down and yelled, "And if I see any of you trespassing on my property, you will pay dearly."

Shoving Eilian hard in the chest, he pushed past without looking back. Eilian's heart skipped off rhythm as he grasped for the nearest tree, narrowly avoiding slipping into the pool. He looked up to see Nash storming up the path to the drawing room, muttering to himself and shaking his head.

Before Nash disappeared out of sight, the sergeant appeared at the library door and hollered, "Go home to your wife, you bloody bastard! You've caused enough trouble already."

Nash turned, eyes blazing. His thin hands contorted into clawed fists as he advanced toward the officer. Catching his balance, Eilian darted between them.

"Both of you please leave," the earl said, his voice calm but strained.

His eyes flicked from the academic to the policeman. Neither moved or removed their gaze from the other. The officer stood with his chest puffed out and his hand resting on his club while Nash eyed him with contempt.

"Now. Please go. Sergeant Purcell, I will not be pressing charges. Whoever did it is long gone. Please take your men and leave the premises. Same to you, Mr. Nash. You already know where we stand."

Turning from Nash, the sergeant smiled smugly and glanced over his shoulder at Hadley, who stood watching the men from the doorway with her arms folded. "I look forward to your party, your ladyship. I do hope you don't cancel it," pausing to widen his grin, he added, "and I hope to see you there too, Nash. You *and* Rubella. You really shouldn't keep her all to yourself. It ain't fair to the rest of us."

Nash's face paled and his eyes bugged. For a moment, Eilian feared he would strike the stalwart officer. He braced himself to absorb the blow or have to force the men apart, but instead, Nash gave the sergeant one last dirty look and left the way he came.

"Osgood, Lyall, pack it in!" Purcell yelled to his constables.

Releasing a tense breath, Eilian looked back at the library door. Hadley was gone. His gaze ran over the palm and pomegranate trees blocking the mosaic floor at the end of the path, but she was nowhere to be found.

"Bernard, please see the men out," Eilian called, ducking out of the greenhouse.

Trailing down the hall, he glanced into each room, hoping to find her standing at a window or meticulously deconstructing a clock or gadget, but all he found was Charlotte's younger sister in the parlor looking up at him with a cleaning rag clutched in her chapped hands.

"Lidia, have you seen Hadley?" When her brown brows knit in confusion, he added, "Her ladyship."

The mute teen shook her head. Walking into the great hall, he glanced into the dining room, already knowing she wouldn't be there. As he his eyes rose to the arcade, it dawned on him. How could he have been so stupid? He trotted up the steps and followed the floral carpet runner through the halls to their bedroom. Light shone from beneath the door, punctuated by shadowed steps as his wife crossed the floor within.

"Hadley, may I come in?" he asked, gently rapping with his metal knuckles.

The door flew open beneath his hand. Hadley glared up at him in only her chemise and corset, her pale freckled shoulders peaking from beneath the silk. "You don't have to knock, you know. It's your room, too."

His face reddened as he slunk in and shut the door behind him. "I'm sorry, but I didn't know if you were changing or sleeping. I didn't want to intrude."

She kept her back to him as she dug through her dresser, pulling out nightgowns and fresh undergarments only to drop them in a heap on the floor. As she found the stockings she was searching for, her shoulders sagged with fatigue, her flare of anger losing its momentum.

"I didn't mean to be curt, Eilian. I'm just frustrated. After all the work I put into planning and cleaning, this happens! I just can't believe it. Should we just call it all off?"

"You mean the party, right?"

Stuffing everything back into the drawer, she turned to meet her husband's anxious gaze. "Of course I mean the party. What did you think I meant?" Her voice caught as she watched him rub his arm and stare down at his feet. "Oh, Eilian. I would never do that. How could you even think that?"

"Because I couldn't blame you if you wanted to. It's perfectly reasonable for a woman to leave a man who neglects her. Men do it all the time."

Hadley drifted to his side and wrapped her arms around his chest. Pulling her close, his arms closed around her waist until their sides were flush. He rested his head against her neck as she ran her fingers through his hair, teasing it into unruly peaks.

"I'm not going to leave you," she whispered. "I love you, Eilian. It's just hard to take it all in."

"If it's really important to you, I guess I could try to do it," he replied, his voice tight and controlled.

"You don't have to *yet*. I'm not going to force you to do something that obviously upsets you. Then neither of us would enjoy ourselves."

His lips curled into a mischievous grin. "Then, I don't have to go to the party?"

"Nice try, but you aren't that lucky." Sighing, she shifted her hold and settled onto Eilian's knee. "So you think I should still have it?"

He nodded. "I don't think you have to cancel it. It was a theft, not a murder. The question is do you *want* to call it off?"

Hadley drew in a tremulous breath and smoothed her hair behind her ears. "No. I mean, I don't know. I'm dreading it as much as I'm looking forward to it."

"Then, cancel it. You don't have to do anything you don't want to do, and after what happened today, you have the perfect excuse."

"But the whole reason I'm throwing this party is to prove I can do it. If I cancel, then I've failed and proven Mrs. Nash right."

Her tired eyes burned at the thought of having to tell everyone in Folkesbury of her failure. Mrs. Nash and her Society of Visiting Ladies would have something to chat about next Wednesday, and that was far worse than breaking the news to her mother-in-law. Lady Dorset would probably be relieved to have her staff back.

"I just wanted to prove to myself that I could throw a party like Constance or your mother, that I'm not just some uncultured tinker."

"Had, is that what you think you are?" Eilian raised Hadley's chin until her scalded blue eyes met his. They gleamed with suppressed frustration and fatigue but never wavered. "You are the brightest, most tenacious person I know. Who else would have the smarts to keep her family's business going while still running her own without help from anyone? Who else would go so far as to dress like a man?"

"I don't know if that would qualify as smart."

"Call it clever then." He rubbed her arms, but as she opened her lips to speak again, he caught them with his own, silencing her self-doubt with a kiss. "So what if you don't know how to throw a party? I don't know how, and I'm sure my mother didn't either until someone taught her. You will learn with time. Soon, you will be the talk of London society."

A laugh escaped her lips against her will. "Let's not get ahead of ourselves. We still need to get through this one. Can you unlace me? I need to change before I prepare for our borrowed servants' arrival. They should be here by nightfall."

"That should calm Patrick at least. Had, Nash mentioned that you received letters from him. What was he talking about?"

Hadley held up her hair, so he could see the back of her girdle. "I have no idea. The only letters I have received are responses for the party and the ones from your mother and Eliza."

Leaning back, he untied her stays and gently tugged until her corset's grip slackened. Her body exhaled as she loosened it further with three well-placed pulls and finally unhooked the front. As she let it drop on the edge of the bed, she swallowed a yawn and took a step toward the wardrobe, but Eilian's gentle hand caught her wrist and pulled her back to his side.

"You have been up all night, Had. Why don't you take a rest?"

She hungrily eyed the bed's plush folds and rumpled pillows. Snapping to her senses, she half-heartedly pulled her hand away and began searching the dresser for clean stockings. "I can't. Who will tend to the servants and get them trained?"

"Patrick and Charlotte will do both. I don't think either of us could do a better job, and I'm certain Mother's servants don't need much more direction than getting the lay of the land."

"I supposed you're right." Hadley looked over her shoulder to find her husband removing his waistcoat and shirt. "What are you doing?"

"I thought I would join you. I only had a few hours of sleep." Tossing his tie onto the nightstand, he sheepishly said, "The guest room was rather lonely. It didn't feel right to sleep without you by my side. I was hoping we could pretend that last night never happened. That is, if you will have me back."

A smile crept across her lips as she abandoned her fresh clothing on the dresser and climbed onto the bed. When Eilian had removed his trousers and stood only in his drawers, she began detaching the springs and outer corset of his prosthesis. He sunk into the bed beside her and inched closer, extending his naked prosthesis under her neck and around her shoulder as she settled in with her head on his chest. Closing her eyes, she listened to the steady tattoo of his heart beneath the layers of roped burns and bone. She ran her hand across the lean muscles of his abdomen until she found his other hand resting against his stomach. Their fingers intertwined, and with little shifts and sighs, their bodies folded into the comfort of their natural grooves. In the stillness, she listened to his breathing slow with contentment. Despite their comfort, she felt the words climbing up her throat. She had to say it. He had to know.

"Eilian," she began hesitantly, "I'm not talking about right now, so please don't take this as me pushing you, but in time, if you ever become curious or consider doing anything, just know I will always be there. I'm not going to leave you or make you feel guilty about it again. If I ever do, I don't mean to."

His mouth shifted into a half-smile. Catching her hand, he brought it to his lips before lowering it to his breast where he tightened his grip. "I appreciate that, Had, and I want you to know that I will try. It may take a little while, but I am trying."

"I know."

Eilian snuggled closer and held her against his side. Drawing in a deep breath, he inhaled her familiar fragrance of cinnamon with a hint of gear oil. When he was certain she had nodded off, he gently ran his fingers through the silken curls of her henna hair. For his whole life, he did everything in his power to escape rejection and failure before they could tear apart what little love he had for himself. He had run from his father, his university, his duties, but he wouldn't run from her. No, for Hadley, he would stay and fight.

Chapter Seventeen
Expectations

"Leona! Leona, let's go!" Nadir called through the lavatory door, banging it with the flat of his palm. "We're going to be late."

"Go on without me," she croaked.

Stepping back into his bedroom, Nadir primped in front of the mirror. With the edge of his finger, he smoothed the smudge of charcoal beneath his lashes.

"I'm not leaving without you. I already told Lady Dorset you were coming. Anyway, Argus is waiting out in the steamer. If you're worried about Lady Dorset or any of those rubes you call neighbors, I wouldn't be. I'm sure you can dance a waltz as well as anyone... even if it is with Argus."

The bathroom door creaked open, and his cousin stumbled out, wiping her lips with a handkerchief. She drew in a rattling breath and slowly straightened to her full height. Gripping the front her butterscotch gown, she clenched her jaw as she rode out another wave of nausea. At least during her dry heaves, she hadn't stained it.

"You look dreadful," he said, his reflection watching her as he brushed the lint from his red velvet tailcoat.

"And you look like Lord Byron. I didn't know it was a fancy dress party."

Nadir snickered as he applied another swipe of black beneath his eyes, dragging the line to a thick point at its corner. "Good, then I've gotten my point across. What's wrong with you?"

"I'm sick as a dog, can't you tell?" Leona replied, leaning against the doorframe for support.

He shrugged. "It's probably all of that disgusting licorice tea you have been drinking. It smells foul."

"I have been taking it to make this go away. Don't you think the turban is a bit much?"

"No, it completes the look, and besides, Byron wore a turban. They will be expecting it of me."

Satisfied with his cosmetic calligraphy, Nadir eyed his reflection. In his layers of colorful silk and rich velvet, he was the picture of decadence. His friends in Bloomsbury would have applauded his daring, his rejection of English traditionalism in favor of art and beauty, but even he knew he was simply playing on the English's love of the exotic. There was no subversion in it anymore apart from refusing to blend. Part of him enjoyed flaunting his well-carved cheekbones and the nutty hue of his skin, which glowed when put against the bright silk of his turban. There was no rush like strutting into a party and having all eyes fall upon him, to hear the chorus of whispers asking, "Who is he?"

He averted his gaze from the mirror and turned his attention to his shoes. In the end, it was all a gimmick, a game to make others remember his face and name without associating either with dusty natives or crumbling piles of stone. Nadir Talbot wasn't some Egyptian boy whose parents boosted him up into society by pretending his skin wasn't too brown or that his features were too fine in some places and too wide in others. No, Nadir Talbot was exotic, an Aesthete who not only created art but was a work of art. He was to be taken seriously, not held up as some lucky victim of happenstance.

Swallowing hard, he ripped his thoughts away and stared at his cousin. A sheen of sweat glistened on her forehead as she stood waiting for him in the doorway. Her mustard gown stretched across her bodice, pulling at the armpits and breasts.

"Is that what you're wearing?"

"Yes," she replied flatly. "You wanted me out. Now, I'm out, and you're primping. It's getting late. Are we going or not?"

Adjusting his turban and practicing his smoldering gaze one last time, Nadir followed her out the door. It was time for him to make his entrance.

⋞⋙ ⋘⋟

By the time they arrived at Brasshurst Hall, the gravel drive was lined with idling steamers waiting to reach the manor's Gothic portal. On the drizzly night, no one had chanced walking through the muddy fields to reach the great house or risked their necks to share the gravel paths with cabs in the grey haze. If he hadn't brought his steamer, they would have been slogging through the mist on foot.

The house rose from the mist, its stone exterior taking on an ethereal sheen from the wavering glow of the gas lamps within as it spilled from the tall arched windows and overflowed from the skylights and orangery dome. Even from the old stone bridge, Nadir could make out the orbs of faerie lamps hovering in the jungle of the greenhouse. As he stared, they flickered and danced, occasionally blinking when an unseen figure crossed before them.

"Did I tell you that Lady Dorset modeled the decorations after *my* description of those parties my parents used to throw in the vineyard?" he declared offhandedly, but when he received only a stifled groan in response, he turned to find his cousin shifting uncomfortably in the seat beside him. "Leona, are you—"

Before he could finish, she grabbed the flesh on the back of his

155

arm and pinched it hard enough that he cried out. As he opened his mouth to speak, she put her finger to her lips and glowered at him. She nodded toward Argus who inched the cab forward unaware of what was transpiring in the backseat. Drawing in a constrained breath, she exhaled slowly and closed her eyes.

Nadir tapped the back of her hand until she looked up at him. He mouthed, "Are you all right?"

Her dark brows knit together as she grimaced and silently replied, "Don't say anything, I'm fine."

"I do hope there are drinks there. The earl and countess aren't temperate are they?"

"Even if they were, what do you need alcohol for, Argus? You see these people every day," Nadir replied with a scoff.

"I don't see them all at once. There will be so many people. Just look at all the cabs. Everyone's here."

"Thank God you don't live in London then. You would drink yourself to death."

"Nadir, leave him alone," his cousin replied in a strained whisper.

Sitting in silence, the procession of steamers filed toward the house and disappeared around the corner as liveried servants moved the cars out of sight. At the entrance, the footman opened the door to allow Leona and Argus to step out. Nadir drew in a calming breath, pursed his lips, and concentrated his energy into cultivating his signature stare. A waiting servant took their coats as they crossed the tunneled hall. In the cloistered space, the din of voices and music seemed so far away, but the energy hummed only yards beyond his reach. Hundreds of people waited just beyond the threshold and all that held them back was a layer of ancient stone.

Stepping into the great hall, the ceiling rose away and with it came the bouncing melody of a merry waltz. The men and women of Folkesbury mingled in clumps around the roaring hearths or in front of the grand paintings hanging over the tropical tapestries, laughing and chattering as if they did not see each other every day. The guests came in their least mended suits and best gowns. Some he recognized from the shop windows in Poole when he and Lady Dorset ventured there together. Others wore their Sunday best, reworked with new trimmings and mended to appear fresh. Leaving his cousin behind, Nadir cut through the crowd. With each step, he drank in the sights and sounds of the party, feeding off the cadence and energy of those around him. Perfume mingled with the savory aroma of food in the dining room and the tart champagne and wine waiting on platters. In the midst of it all, he closed his eye. He had to commit everything to memory, so he could put it to good use later.

With a satisfied grin, he found that his plan had worked. Once one pair of eyes fell upon him, the others turned to catch a glimpse of his purple, red, and gold attire as he swept through the hall. He paused long enough in each room to be seen before casually strolling through the open door in the drawing room to the orangery. It was just as he had envisioned it on his first visit. The massive mosaic floor had been cleared of pots and dirt to make room for a string quartet. Around the perimeter stood massive iron candelabras, but instead of having tapers stuffed into the bases on each arm, a colored glass globe containing a squat candle hung from them on decorative hooks. Blue orbs hovered around the dance floor as couples whirled in measured steps while red lamps trailed down the path toward the pool. Following the line of scarlet light, Nadir's eyes wandered over the milling crowd, and at the edge, he spotted the countess standing alone as the earl slipped into the house. Snatching a flute of champagne from a passing footman, Nadir sauntered over.

Hadley's eyes lit up at the sight of his familiar brown eyes and sharp cheekbones amid a sea of draped fabric. "Mr. Talbot, is that you? Somehow I knew you would be dressed to the nines, but I hadn't pictured something quite so ornate. Is it traditional garb?"

"Not in the slightest," he purred, turning for her so she could get a better view of his printed silks and fine jacket. "It's my own creation."

When she had finished taking him in, his gaze ran over her gown. It was nearly the same cornflower blue of her eyes. Traveling up her skirt and around her bodice were tendrils of white piping that formed an intricate lattice, laid to accentuate the lines of her form. Her dark red hair and lightly freckled skin popped against her elegant dress and white gloves.

"Eilian surprised me with this the other day. He saved me from one headache at least."

"Very nice. Your husband has excellent taste." Leaning closer, he whispered into her ear, "Any problems?"

"No, shockingly. Mrs. Negi and my mother-in-law's cook have come to a truce, the musicians showed up, everyone seems to be enjoying themselves, and my husband hasn't slipped upstairs to hide yet. What do you think, Mr. Talbot? You are the expert, after all."

He turned to watch the couples, young and old locking eyes and hands, turning in time with the music. "I think you have won them over."

ॐ

Eilian drew in a lungful of damp, earthy air. The orangery hummed with life. Couples strolled arm in arm down the paved paths with glasses of champagne or wine in their hands as if the mossy dome was a botanical garden. Even in the light of the jarred candles, the orchids with their otherworldly conformations thrilled their guests. Several had even asked the earl what this or that plant was, yet the robbery and his prosthetic arm seemed to be forgotten or ignored. Whether it was due to disinterest or good-breeding, he couldn't tell.

He circled through the main rooms, offering how-do-you-dos and pleasure-to-meet-yous to their guests. With each group he spoke to, the anxiety loosened in his breast. He had expected the party to be a miserable experience like the ones his mother threw, yet he found himself smiling and drifting through the crowd as if he had done it a hundred times. No one was trying to manipulate him into finding a mate or goading him into an argument. Being one of the hosts, he had expected to be worrying about food or whether they had hung the right pictures, but Hadley had every gear in place and oiled to run smoothly.

Patrick and his mother's servants made sure there was plenty of food and liquor flowing from the kitchen and wine cellar, and for the men, they had set up a room where they could play cards. It was a party and nothing more.

Smiling and nodding, he passed through a room of young women speaking eagerly around the samovar. Once he confirmed that Leona and Argus Rhodes were not there, he looped back out and moved on to the next room. He had hoped to discuss his article about the Ptolemaic Dynasty with him. While the review in *The Royal Egyptology Society Chronicle* had been favorable, something felt off. He couldn't put his finger on what it was, but something about the writing had nagged at the back of his mind since he finished it.

Returning to the entrance of the orangery, a grin crept across his lips. Hadley stood at the edge of the dance floor talking happily with Constable Lyall and his pretty young wife. At her side, Nadir Talbot's gaze flitted over the crowd as if searching for someone, but when he didn't see his quarry, he frowned and threw back his drink before fluidly placing it onto an oncoming tray. As the couple moved on to join the others lining up for the next dance, Eilian slipped in and wrapped his arm around Hadley's waist. Thus far, no one had seemed to notice that one of his hands was made of metal.

"Mr. Talbot, I must thank you for helping Hadley with the party. I fear I was of no use," Eilian said, watching the couples on the dance floor switch partners until he was unsure who belonged with whom.

"It was my pleasure, but Lady Dorset should take all the credit. She has done a wonderful job; the ambiance has exceeded my expectations. This alone should give me inspiration for a month."

"How is the book going?"

Nadir caught another glass of champagne as a footman strutted past. "Swimmingly, for once. Our lady has escaped the harem and reappeared in the court masquerading as a princess from a foreign land. I only have a few chapters left. That should get my publisher off my back."

"Is that why we haven't seen you?" Hadley replied, watching the writer absently finger the end of his turban. "I figured you were either stopped up or writing nonstop."

"The latter luckily."

"Mr. Talbot, did you come alone or are your cousin and her husband with you? I wanted to speak to Argus about his article."

"They should be here. Leona wasn't feeling very well, so they may be sitting somewhere."

"Is she all right?"

"Yes, just a touch of stomach trouble." He craned his neck to see over the crowd, but as his eyes reached the path from the pool, they narrowed. "God, why did *they* have to come?"

Chapter Eighteen
Keeping Secrets

Hadley and Eilian turned, simultaneously spotting Nash with his grey-hair and aquiline features ambling across the cobbles, sneering at the colored lanterns and merry villagers. On his arm, Mrs. Nash stiffly followed in a dower brown gown, her thin lips lined and pinched. As they cut through the crowd and everyone's eyes fell upon them, the atmosphere contracted and cracked. The gaiety felt only a moment earlier evaporated as the others straightened and fell silent. Dancing couples dissolved mid-song, drifting back to their original partner before disappearing into another room with a sidelong glance and a harsh whisper. Eilian shot his wife a questioning look.

"Yes, I invited them," Hadley explained, sweeping an invisible hair from her forehead. "I did it to be polite, but I didn't think they would actually show up. Should we say anything?"

"No," Eilian replied with a sigh and watched Nash settle into position at the corner of the mosaic where he could survey the room.

He hoped the sergeant would stay far enough away him to not cause another uproar. "I know his type. If he's anything like my father, he's looking for a scene, and we won't provide him with one. I won't let Nash ruin your party."

A wan smile played on Nadir's lips. "Though it seems tossing him out would bring most of the town a lot of pleasure."

With a laugh, Hadley tore her eyes from Nash only to land upon Argus Rhodes's broad form as he slowly led his wife into the domed room. She clung to his arm, her back hunched and her eyes crinkled at the edges as she shuffled in. His bespectacled gaze roamed over the crowd before he lifted his glass to his lips and took a long swig. A footman approached them with a plate of hors d'oeuvres, and while Argus loaded his wide palm, his wife greened and waved the canapés away.

Leaving the men at the dance floor, Hadley strode to Leona's side. The dark-haired woman gave her grimace barely disguised as a tight smile. She tried to straighten, but when she nearly reached her full height, she recoiled with a hiss.

"Mrs. Rhodes, are you feeling all right? Should I fetch a doctor?" she asked low enough that only the two women could hear.

"No, thank you," Leona Rhodes replied through harsh breaths, her chest tight with pain. "I'm fine."

"I don't mean to overstep my bounds, but you don't look fine."

Before Leona could respond, Hadley slipped her arm around her shoulders and dislodged her from Argus's grasp. When he realized who was taking his wife, he relinquished his hold and trudged over to Nadir and Eilian for companionship. Leona held her breath as another wave of pain ripped through her abdomen. The only tell-tale sign of her plight was her nails digging into Hadley's arm as they crossed the tiled floor. An iron chair stood empty only a few yards away, but already she seemed to be worsening. The pain coursed through her body and into her fingertips where Hadley felt its aftershocks, and the flesh of her face was no longer a healthy olive but a sickly grey coated with a layer of sweat. Helping her into the chair, Hadley motioned for the nearest footman.

"Fetch me a wet rag from the kitchen. No stops in between," she ordered before kneeling beside Nadir's cousin, who had wrapped her arms across her stomach and leaned forward into the pain. Hadley pressed her hand to Leona's brow and then her cheek. "Mrs. Rhodes, you have a fever. You shouldn't have come if you were ill. If you're worried about leaving Nadir or Mr. Rhodes, I can have one of our men drive you home, but honestly, I do not think you should be by yourself." She lowered her voice and asked, "Is it cramps?"

Leona bit her lip and shook her head, still clutching her stomach. Sucking in a breath, she looked past Hadley with tears glistening at the edges of her eyes. Her gaze suddenly hardened, but when Hadley followed it, she found Nash staring at them. She looked between Mrs. Rhodes and the troublesome gentleman, their expressions unreadable in the flickering lamplight. Letting out a stifled groan, Leona broke away from his grey eyes. Hadley squeezed her hand and stood up. What had possessed her to come in that state?

"Stay here. I'm going to find your husband."

Anger bubbled in Hadley's chest. Was the man daft or did he simply not care? A minute with his wife and she could feel the tremor in her hand with each stroke of pain and the heat that radiated from her fevered body. She hoped to God Argus Rhodes was merely a fool who was easily placated by reassurances. Being an idiot was much more forgivable than being a callous spouse. The men stood where she had left them with Eilian questioning the Egyptologist about his paper. The large man's black eyes were glazed with drink as he stumbled over his words. He rubbed his ruddy cheeks and muttered half to himself about the Ptolemy's lineage. Eilian arched a brow and leaned closer, still unable to make sense of his explanation.

At their side, she swallowed her anger and said as politely as she could muster, "Your wife is ill, Mr. Rhodes. She needs to return home *at once*. She is in no shape to be at a party. I suggest you leave immediately."

He stared down at her, his mouth hanging agape as if he didn't understand, but before he could reply, Nadir's shoulder collided with his. He shoved past and into the crowd, his silk turban unwinding behind him.

"Dear God, Leona! Someone call for a doctor!" he bellowed.

Hadley turned in time to watch Leona Rhodes slump off the garden chair and land in a heap of mustard muslin. Reaching her side first, Nadir rolled her onto her back, but as he went to pat her cheek, he drew back, eyes wide. Smeared across his hand was a streak of blood. Looking down at the floor beside him, his eyes followed a thin line of droplets that trailed from the dance floor to the chair, pooling beneath where she had sat to form a saucer-sized puddle of liver-colored blood. Behind him, a murmur of hushed voices grew louder as news spread of her collapse. They were growing closer, their bodies breaking the orbs of glowing light from the lanterns and closing off the air.

"Leona, stay with me," he whispered to her listless form.

She groaned and gasped, the cords of her neck straining against the pain, but her eyes remained shut. He had never seen her so pale. Against her black hair and his tawny hands, her face appeared nearly white with the only color in the heated flush of her cheeks. Breaking from the crowd, Lady Dorset rushed to his side with a damp cloth. She dabbed the sweat from Leona's neck and cheeks before laying it across her forehead.

Hadley's eyes drifted to the blood before returning to Nadir's face, which had blanched to nearly the color of his cousin's. Glancing over her shoulder, she watched the crowd press in for a better look. "We should move her up to a guest room. Can you lift her?"

He nodded, climbing to his knees. Her head rolled against his shoulder as he struggled to raise her to a standing position so he could get a better grip. Where was the doctor? Someone should have been there by now. His head swam. The earl was yelling, telling everyone to make a path for them. As Nadir slipped his arms beneath her legs to lift her, the breath caught in his throat. A sticky crimson mandala seeped across the back of her skirt, trickled down her stockings, and through her petticoat. On the front of her dress, a faint splotch slowly materialized, growing wider before his eyes. Raising his gaze as he hefted her into his arms, Nadir met Nash's probing grey eyes. While everyone watched in confusion, Nash stared, his cold gaze softening. He lingered on the blood before pausing on her breasts and the line where the fabric of her bodice and skirt joined.

He knew. Whatever was going on, he knew.

∘⋄∘ ⋄∘⋄

Nadir turned his good luck charm over in his hand, feeling its familiar lopsided surface roll beneath his fingers. His turban and jacket lay in a heap on the coverlet where they had been shed in a flurry of frustration and fear. His body, heavy with fatigue, sagged into the wooden chair, but at the slightest noise in the hall, he awoke. He ground the heels of his hands into his eyes, not caring if he smeared the black powder of his eyeliner across his face. He should have convinced her to go to London.

He had brought Leona home in the back of his steamer with the town physician following close behind, and the doctor had yet to emerge from her room. Argus had been too upset and drunk to drive and rode with the doctor instead. Luckily, halfway home Leona had regained consciousness, though Nadir couldn't tell which was worse: not knowing if she would wake again or listening to her sobs and gasps of pain while he could only drive through the drizzle and fog. Not much had been said after that. The door had been slammed in his face while Argus haunted the downstairs rooms. He couldn't bear to listen to his mutterings and mantras of Leona's good health or virtue. If he had to share a room with him a moment longer than necessary, he would strike the useless oaf. How Leona stayed with him, he couldn't imagine.

At the squeal of the bedroom door, Nadir leapt from his desk. Dr. Sturgis stood in the hall in his shirt sleeves with a bloody rag in one hand and his dinner jacket in the other. He had a boyish face even though he was in his thirties, but his eyes were quick and his manner short. For a town physician, he at least seemed capable. His light eyes swept appraisingly over Nadir's half-open shirt and soot-streaked skin.

"How is she, doctor?" he asked, unsure if he wanted to hear the answer.

"Are you the cousin?" When Nadir nodded, he went on, "She wanted me to speak to you. The bleeding and cramps will persist for another few days, but she will be fine. At her age, failed pregnancies are fairly common. Will you relay the news to her husband? He seemed distraught."

A failed pregnancy? Why had she not told him she was with child? "I will deal with him. May I see her?"

"Go ahead, but I gave her a bit of morphine for the pain. I don't know how awake she will be. I will return tomorrow to check on her."

When the doctor's slow tread plunked down the steps, Nadir pushed open the door. Despite the late hour, the lights had been left ablaze, and his cousin lay in bed with the quilt pulled up to her shoulders and a fire crackling in the hearth. Thick curls ringed her lax face, which had finally regained some of its color. She reminded him of the porcelain doll she lugged around as a child, a smaller, more perfect version of herself. Settling on the edge of the bed, Nadir gently brushed the hair from her eyes, but as he touched her forehead, she stared up at him.

"You look like a pirate."

Nadir shook his head and wiped at the streaks of charcoal. "How are you feeling, Lee?"

"Lee." A drowsy smile crossed her lips as let out a weak chuckle. "You haven't called me Lee since we had a governess."

"You have always been my Lee." When she pulled her hand out to push her hair from her face, Nadir held it. "Why did you go to the party if you were that ill? If you told me, I would have gotten a doctor."

She shook her head. Her voice came tremulous and strained as she replied, "I thought I could handle it. We can't afford it, anyway. I don't know how we're going to pay Dr. Sturgis."

"Don't worry about that. I will take care of it." He swallowed hard and squeezed her hand. "The doctor told me what happened. Why didn't you say anything about the baby?"

"Dr. Sturgis didn't tell Argus, did he?" she asked, her eyes bright with panic.

"No, I don't think so since he asked me to do it, but shouldn't he know? Did you not know you were with child?"

"I knew, but you can't tell Argus."

"Why? It was his child, too. Even he will understand that a miscarriage isn't your fault."

Leona bit her lip and turned her face from his, her fingers gripping his hand. "He can't know, Nadir. He just can't! We have always kept each other's secrets. Please don't tell him."

"What am I supposed to say instead? You swooning and bleeding through your dress is hard to explain away."

"I don't know. Tell him it was a bad month."

"There will be talk. I'm sure Dr. Sturgis will tell someone. The whole village will now by the end of the week."

"You know him. He will believe anything you or I tell him."

"Lee, what are you not telling me?"

When she turned back to him, the whites of her eyes burned pink and glistened with tears. "I can't say, but look in my sewing box."

Nadir followed her gaze to a tapestried box tucked under the chair in the corner. He crossed the room, averting his gaze at the waste basket stuffed with bloody sheets and her soiled gown, and knelt before the sewing box. Flipping open the lid, he held his breath, unsure of what he would find inside. At first he only found embroidery hoops, thread, and her half-finished pillow case, but as he moved them aside, bits of green poked through. Carefully untangling it from the myriad of threads, he drew out a long bundle. The plant had been cut into pieces with the roots, stalk, and heads in separate pieces but tied together with twine. It had been beheaded; its flowers had been cut off and all that remained of the top was a neck. The roots were missing in patches, and the once long stalk had been chipped away at both ends. He stared at the dissected plant for a long moment. Where had it come from? His brown eyes widened at the realization.

"You didn't?" he cried, looking from the stalk to his cousin. "Please tell me you didn't do what I think you did."

"You aren't going to tell her, are you?"

His hands shook as he reburied it beneath her projects and shut the lid. "No, I wouldn't want Lady Dorset to know my cousin is a thief. I can't believe you would do this. What would possess you? Are you trying to get us all in trouble? You better have a very good reason, Leona."

"Don't be mad at me, Nadir. I had no other choice."

He returned to her side and found her still facing the wall, unable to meet his gaze. All he could picture was the look on Nash's face when she fell. The cold gravity of understanding in his gaze.

"Tell me this: what does Mr. Nash have to do with all of this? I know he is playing some part in it."

"Even if I wanted to, I can't tell you."

"You expect me to keep your secrets, but you won't tell me any of them. I don't understand what is going on with you or why you would do something so foolish."

She clenched her eyes shut against a numb wave rippling through the muscles of her abdomen. "And you never will."

Chapter Nineteen
Histories

Tying his manuscript in twine, Nadir frowned. It was far from perfect, but he longed to be rid of it and enjoy the last few weeks of his holiday without kings and harem girls hanging over his head. He had jotted a few corrections and notations in the margins of what he might consider fixing later, but Rogers would have to take it as is. After he returned to London, he would put the final polish on it. His publishers had made enough money off him to give him a little leeway for once. Dropping it into its casket, he slid on the lid and pushed it out of sight. Now that Leona was recovering from her *illness*, he would be heading home before the summer crowded descended upon Dorset in droves.

He stared out the window at the coast in the distance. He would miss the clean air and the stab of rocky sand beneath his feet. It wasn't quite the holiday he had expected, but even with the odd circumstances, he enjoyed seeing his cousin for the first time in several years and spending time with Lady Dorset. At least he might see her again in town. Leona he might not see again for another five years. He would have to figure out how to prevent that.

In the hall below, the doorbell twilled. The door down the hall creaked open and his cousin's head peaked out. Her skin was still pale and the shadow of dark circles ringed her eyes, but at least, she could walk again without stooping or rushing to the lavatory. Spotting Nadir coming out of his room, relief eased her tight features.

"Stay put, Leona. I got it."

From the afternoon after Lady Dorset's party, a parade of women had made the pilgrimage down the hill to the house to deliver pies and baskets of food as if they feared he and Argus would starve to death with Leona bedridden. At first, she appreciated the company, but after the fifth visitor in one day, she willingly took her medicine and fell asleep to escape their gossip-mongering under the guise of well-meaning questions. As he walked down the steps past the old paintings and photographs, the bell trilled again.

"I'm coming!"

At the bottom, he straightened and put on his best company smile. When the door opened and he saw the Randall Nash standing before him with his expensive suit and ebony walking stick, the smile fell from his face. The man's quick eyes twitched at Nadir's change in expression.

"What business do you have here?"

"Is Mrs. Rhodes home?" Nash asked coolly.

"She is indisposed. As you know, Mr. Nash, she has recently been unwell and is still recovering. Is there a message you would like me to relay to her?"

His rough voice hardened. "I would prefer to speak to the lady myself."

"And *I* would prefer it if you left our property."

Nash narrowed his gaze. "Excuse me?"

"I said get off our property. Whatever you have to say to my cousin, you will have to say to me."

"This isn't your business, *boy*," he spat, his hand shooting toward the door. "Out of my way."

Nadir flattened against the doorway as the older man tried to weasel past him, using his walking stick to whack at his ankles. Reaching behind him, Nadir slammed the door shut and rammed his shoulder into the older man. Nash stumbled back, tripping over the cracked cobbles of the path and landing in the grass. He stared up in fury and alarm as he raised his cane to fend the writer off.

As Nadir stepped closer, Nash held it back as if to swing. "Stay back, or I will crack your skull!"

The cane jutted toward Nadir's abdomen, but he caught the shaft and pulled Nash forward onto his knees. The old man looked up, his gaze wavering before hardening once more. Despite his fear and age, Nash clung to the cane with all his strength, causing Nadir to have to tighten his hold.

Leaning close, Nadir growled, "Stay away from my cousin, old man. I don't know exactly what is going on between you two, but if you come near her again, *you* will be the one with the cracked skull."

With a shove, he released the cane and stormed back to the door. Constable Lyall and his wife lingered at the edge of the pavement, watching to see what either man would do next. Before he could see Nash rise and dust himself off or hear the slur slip from his lips, Nadir marched inside and slammed the bolt on the lock. At the top of the steps, Leona watched her cousin kick the umbrella stand before storming into the parlor.

"Who was it, Nadir?"

"No one of consequence."

⁂

Eilian lingered in the portrait hall, his eyes locked on the painting of his great-grandfather. He seemed so different from the young man who leaned uncomfortably against a rock while forcibly having his portrait painted. Now his hair had grayed to match his eyes and lines had sprouted from the edges of his eyes and the corners of his mouth. In the four decades between the two paintings, the discomfort had

171

disappeared, but what he had originally taken for an air of snobbery, he now recognized for what it was: contempt. He smiled to himself. Even after forty years of playing the earl, old Laurence still hated the pomp of it all. In the whole house, Eilian had only found three portraits: the hidden one of him as a young man, the official hall portrait, and the one hanging above the dining room fireplace where he posed with his wife and three children. While preparing for the party, they had found dozens of miniatures and paintings of men in powdered wigs and women in fancy gowns, yet his great-grandfather was nowhere to be found, leaving his legacy in ink instead of oil.

At the bottom of the portrait, a slip of painted paper stated that the subject was the Seventh Earl of Dorset. Eilian stared at it for a long moment. He had read it over and over in the covers of the journals, but something nagged at his mind. Had there been a mistake? He was the ninth earl, his father was the eighth. What had happened to his grandfather? His mouth twisted into a lopsided frown as he wracked his brain for any stories his father told of his grandfather. The tales he had been told during dinners where his friends from his club had come to smoke and talk were always of their exploits as young men. Courtships gone awry, secret dalliances behind parents' backs, near robberies by backwater bandits, but the man who came to retrieve the Harland Sorrell Eilian never knew was always called the Colonel. The Colonel dragged him home by the ear. The Colonel taught him everything he knew and kept him on the straight and narrow. Somehow he had always assumed the Colonel was his father.

Leaving behind the line of earls and countesses, he ducked into the library. His eyes trailed along the shelves until they came to rest on a massive tome bound centuries ago in filigreed leather. Eilian unlocked the cabinet and carefully laid the old Bible on the desk. Despite its age, it was better preserved than half of the books on ancient philosophers. It appeared as if it hadn't been cracked more than a dozen times in two hundred years. With the tip of his finger, he slowly opened the front cover to reveal a family tree drawn in spider writing before becoming bolder, then turning to his great-grandfather's thin and cramped hand as the tree spread across the page. His eyes ran across the minute names of Sorrells he had never heard of with birth and death dates he could scarcely imagine before coming to rest on William Sorrell, the earl who never was.

It read, *William Sorrell. Born 1811. Died 1845.*, and nothing more.

Eilian tapped the page over the name thoughtfully. His father had only been ten years old when his father died. No wonder he heard little of the man; his father barely knew him. To the left of William's name was an older brother, Alexander Sorrell, who had been born a year earlier and died nine years before him, and a sister, Beatrice Sorrell, whose name connected to a Fitzwilliam Nash and trailed to Randall Nash. He shared his birth year with her death year.

Returning to William, he traced the dangling branch Harland Sorrell hung from before it entangled with Millicent Holland. Eilian frowned. No one had added his name or Dylan's to the family tree or his father's death year. His stomach churned as he reached across the desk for a pen and carefully transcribed *1891* in his unsteady wrong-handed script. It only seemed right to close that chapter.

Eilian shut the book, raking a hand through his hair and staring through the fogged window into the orangery. What had he hoped to find in the family bible? He had gotten halfway through his great-grandfather's journals, but as they dissolved into short-hand ledgers of expenses and remarks about men he could only imagine had been his friends or neighbors, his interest waned. There was little advice or thought as to how he rose from soldier to earl. It seemed he took it as his new charge and simply did what he had to. Eilian spun the signet ring sitting heavily on his finger. That was of little consolation.

Eilian checked the death date for Great-uncle Alexander one more time before walking back to his little nook in the drawing room. On the top of the desk, the decades of journals sat in a neat row. Sinking into the chair, he pulled out one of the middle volumes to check the date and found that it was only a year before his grandfather's death. He thumbed through the pages, slowing as he reached his father's birthday. Between doodles of plants and a half-fallen stone wall, the squished, puffy face of an infant stared back at him.

March 18th, 1835

My second grandchild was born today. William and Jenny have named him Harland after her father. While I would never want another child to be cursed with Laurence, I do wonder why no one thought to name a child after me. Maybe Alexander will when he finally settles down, though he doesn't seem interested in anything other than books, botany, and riding through the grounds. Anna would have me convince him that now is the time to find a wife and leave off his "childish nonsense," but I know first-hand that the wanderlust will abate eventually. Even if it doesn't, women and children are remarkably portable.

March 30th, 1835

Little Randall is besotted with Harland. The child is without siblings or parents, and Harland will probably be his only chance at having a brother. Spending most of his day with a governess and a choleric old man is no way for a child to be raised. Jenny likes him. Maybe she and William will take him in, though Alexander would happily keep him as his own.

Eilian sighed. Alexander would never go on to have a child. His place on the family tree was barren, wedged between Beatrice and William's families. What had killed the young nobleman? A twinge of pain flashed through Eilian's arm at the thought of Alexander being killed by wanderlust. Flipping to the end of the journal, he watched his great-grandfather's handwriting falter. For more than a week, he had transcribed the date and nothing more. Ink splotches had dripped onto the page, leaked by a lingering pen. Finally on August 8th, 1836, he wrote:

My Alexander is dead.

I have avoided this task. Committing it to paper makes it real, and I still am not certain I won't wake and find him up to his elbows in dirt in the garden. No parent should live long enough to see their children die, and I have seen two. First, my daughter. Now, my son. Anna has taken to her bed and has not left since the accident. I can't bear to lose her, too. All I can hope is that our grandchildren will give her reason enough to live. Little Randall will not leave her side. Whether he understands death yet, I do not know, but he understands sadness and has spent the day trying to revive her spirits with stories and puppet shows.

We held the funeral without her. Despite my reservations, I know it was for the best. I could barely stand to see another coffin loaded into the family crypt, and I do not know what it would have done to her in her fragile state. Harland cried through the entire service while the vicar glared at him and me. How could he expect me to tell Jenny to hand her babe over to the nurse on a day when all of us felt the sting of a young life lost? Any woman would hold tighter to their child. She looked to me with panic in her eyes as she tried to soothe him, so I took him and we walked around the gardens Alexander loved so much. I did not tell anyone, but I doubt I could have sat through the service. With Beatrice, I was able to say my good-byes and keep a parting gift in little Randall, but I have nothing left of Alexander. He was gone before I could reach him.

Unlike Jenny, William was senseless to the proceedings. Showed up stinking drunk again. If he hadn't arrived before me, I would have sent him home on the end of my boot. At least his mother was not there to see it.

Hopefully grief is clouding his judgment because if this continues, I will be cutting him off. I do not care that he is to inherit now. My last living child will not kill himself with drink. I must think of a way to do this without causing Jenny or Harland to suffer by my hand. It is not their fault that William can't resist the bottle. I weep for my family's future.

It suddenly made sense now, why his father rarely drank even when his guests were rowdy and filled with red-nosed mirth. He couldn't remember him ever becoming drunk at one of his mother's parties when he merely could have stumbled up to bed. The habit had inadvertently passed to Eilian. When he did attempt to drink, it was usually under duress or to suppress the little voice in his head from telling him no. Luckily, that voice rarely spoke out of turn.

He was about to set the book aside when he spotted a familiar form peeking through the last few pages of thin parchment. On the back cover, a cage of metal and glass extended from the side of Brasshurst Hall. It was smaller than the monstrosity that existed now, but it was clearly the orangery with its tiny sprouting plants and clusters of trees.

August 31st, 1836

I have decided what I will do to honor my boy. Alexander did not leave me with grandchildren, but he left behind many children in his garden. He tended his plants faithfully, cultivating and breeding them with care. I can't bear to see them die this winter, so the garden will be encapsulated. Upon surveying the grounds, we discovered that the garden really does abut the ruins of a Roman bath. Alexander had told me about the marble tiles and broken columns, but I had never bothered to look. The builder suggested connecting a new engine and water supply to the old piping running beneath the tiles. If it is done correctly, the orchids and other exotics will never need smoke pots or protection from the chill. I hope to add to his collection, so his legacy can live on.

I also decided to buy one of those steamer contraptions. Lord Newbury and Sir Lisle are resistant to the idea of mechanical coaches, citing that they are unreliable and will surely go out of fashion in a few years. While all that may be true, I can no longer trust horses after what happened to my boy.

A pang of guilt rang through Eilian's mind. The orangery—the monstrosity—had been a memorial to a young man who was nearly his age when he died. Looking over his shoulder, he stared at the French doors leading out into the murky greenery. His feet carried him out the doors and down the path to the pool. The engine's pulse thrummed and somewhere beyond bees hummed, drifting from flower to flower. Pulling off his shoes and stockings, he dipped his feet into the water of the pool and closed his eyes. All around him flowers sprang a new. What had begun as a Taj Mahal for a dead boy became a palace of perpetual life.

Chapter Twenty
Unnatural

Hadley rumbled down the cobbled pavement, her hair whipping from her bun as she rounded the corner and narrowly avoided careening into Argus Rhodes. He smiled softly, tipping his hat to her as he continued on toward the market with an empty basket. At the edge of the property, she wedged her heavy bicycle between the stone fence and oak tree before peering through the curtains from across the yard. If she turned her head the right way, she could just make out the edge of Leona Rhodes's sleeve as she sat on the sofa in the parlor. Tidying her hair and squaring her shoulders, Hadley feigned an amiable smile and rang the bell. When the door opened, she had expected to see Leona or Barnes but was pleasantly surprised to find Nadir Talbot staring back at her.

"Nadir, I thought you had gone back to London," she said.

A wide smile crossed his lips, revealing a row of straight teeth. "Not quite yet. In a week or so, I will be packing up, but I would like to take in the sea air without worrying about palace intrigue or missed deadlines." His eyes ran over her tweed riding jacket and breeches, watching the rain darkened her shoulders. "My apologies, please, do come in, Lady Dorset. Are you here to see Leona?"

"Yes, I'm hoping to speak to her if she's up to it." Dropping her voice and wiping the moisture from her brow, she asked, "Is she well? I don't want to intrude if she is trying to rest. I'm sure half of Folkesbury has come to visit."

"She's nearly herself now, and I'm sure she would like to see you. She's right through here."

Pulling back the curtain, Nadir stuck his head into the room to make sure Leona hadn't snuck off when she heard the doorbell. His cousin sat with her sewing basket tucked behind her skirts and an embroidery hoop in her hands. She had already heard the countess's voice and caught a glimpse of her trying to peer into the window. Even if she had slipped upstairs, the noblewoman would have known. If it had been anyone else, she would have had Nadir turn them away anyway, but Lady Dorset had been instrumental in getting her help, or so she had been told the next morning when she was finally coherent enough to understand her situation. It was only proper to see her. As her cousin ducked out, the henna-haired woman entered, the heels of her riding boots clicking on the floor. Her light eyes lingered on Leona's face, taking in the signs of strain near her eyes and the slight pallor of her cheeks. She seemed to be more tired and drawn than before the party, but her eyes were brighter despite the fatigue.

"Mrs. Rhodes, I am so pleased to see you look well. You gave us quite a fright at the party," Lady Dorset said, taking the seat across from her. From the corner of her eye, she watched Nadir disappear down the hall out of sight. "I hope you are feeling better now."

"Much, thank you." Ringing her bell, the butler appeared and she sent him off to fetch them a tray of tea. "Nadir told me I have you to thank for getting me a physician that night. I hope I didn't ruin your party."

"Not at all. You merely added a bit of excitement to the night," she replied with a measured smile. Despite their best efforts to maintain the atmosphere, most of the guests who had been in the greenhouse at the time of her collapse left soon after and were shortly followed by the rest of the townspeople. At least it hadn't been her poor party-planning skills that drove them away. "I was more surprised that your husband and cousin had allowed you to come out in that state. Anyone with eyes could see that you were in pain."

"You can't blame Argus for it. I hid it from him, and Nadir tried to convince me to stay home. I didn't listen. I didn't realize how bad off I was until we were halfway to the party. Then, it seemed too late to turn back. It wasn't my intention to pass-out in the middle of your party. I hope you can forgive my behavior. It was uncharacteristically reckless."

The countess's eyes hardened even as her mouth curled into a smile and she bowed her head in a graceful nod. As Barnes brought in the tea and placed it before them, her gaze never left the dark-haired woman's face. Leona swallowed hard and kept her head down as she tended to their tea. The woman hadn't come merely to check on her. Of that she was certain. Something in the way she looked at her said she knew more than she let on. She was waiting. For what, Leona couldn't be sure.

"So," she began, clearing her throat, "you road your bicycle all the way from Brasshurst in the rain? I thought your steamer was fixed."

"It is, but I chose to go by velocipede. It helps clear my mind and burn up some excess energy. On warm days I don't think I could stand to sit in a cab anymore unless I had to." Hadley watched as Mrs. Rhodes nodded with a tight smile and took a sip of her tea. There was so much she wanted to ask, but did she dare? Hadley Fenice would never be so imprudent, but Lady Dorset would expect answers. Taking a sip, she added stiffly, "You seem happier than you were last time we spoke, Mrs. Rhodes."

"Do I?"

"Very much so, if not more nervous. I'm sorry if it's callous of me to say, but it seems odd for a woman who just lost her baby." When the woman's byzantine eyes widened and her hand stopped halfway to her mouth, Hadley whispered, "I know it's a rumor, but I know what I saw that night. That was much more than... a certain time."

Leona swallowed hard and wiped her tongue over her teeth, the moisture suddenly evaporating from her mouth. Panic rose in her breast, speeding her heart and raising a cold sweat across her flesh as the other woman stared back at her with calculated impassivity.

Her voice cracked as she replied, "I don't know what you are talking about, Lady Dorset, but if you are going to berate me, then you should—"

"I know you took the silphium."

"How?" The word escaped her lips before she could stop herself.

Hadley refilled the cups and repeated what Mrs. Rhodes had done on her own tea. "We should probably discuss this somewhere away from prying ears. Shall we go into the study?"

Nodding, Leona hesitantly stood and led her into the next room. Her hands shook and her abdomen cramped with a spasm as she crossed the threshold. The noose was tightening around her neck, but instead of Nash at the other end, it was Lady Dorset. She should have known it was coming. Noblewomen waltzed but business women pounced. As the door shut behind them, she turned, ready to face the woman with one last stand of strength, and found the redhead leisurely taking in the bookshelves and display cabinet. She snapped to attention as Leona released a stifled groan and sank into the desk chair.

"How— how did you know?" she asked, releasing a slow breath as it passed.

"Mrs. Rhodes, I was not trying to upset—"

"It's too late for that. Just tell me how you found out. Did Nadir tell you?"

Hadley watched as the other woman's eyes burned bitterly with betrayal. Despite her tight lips and hard gaze, her breast rapidly rose and fell against her will. She stepped forward and gave Leona's hand a squeeze. Her gaze traveled between the noblewoman's face and hand as if trying to discern her intentions. Why would Lady Dorset expose her and then comfort her?

Hadley Sorrell kept her voice low and calm as she explained, "No one told me anything. I haven't even spoken to Nadir since the party."

"Then, how did you find out?"

Hadley rested against the edge of the coffee table. "It was fairly easy to put together once I read the rest of Eilian's notes on silphium. A plant that 'promotes menstruation' goes missing days before you have a miscarriage. He had no idea what that truly entailed, but I do, and I don't believe that is a coincidence."

"We can pay for the broken window... over time."

"I don't care about that. It has already been repaired."

Leona Rhodes sat very still, her body locking against her will. If Lady Dorset wasn't after damages, then she had to want something more. "Are you saying you are going to turn me in?"

"No, and I'm not going to tell your husband or Nadir either. I'm sure you had your reasons, but I would have rather you came to me and asked for a piece of silphium. You could have certainly thought up some pretext for getting it instead of breaking in like a common burglar. Do I really seem so unreasonable that you couldn't speak to me?"

"I didn't want anyone to find out what I was doing." Locking eyes with the countess, she straightened and hesitantly asked, "If you don't want us to pay for the window and you aren't pressing charges, then why are you here? If there is anything else you want, trust me when I tell you we have nothing left you can take."

"It isn't something monetary that I want. Remember when we first met and I said that my cause was helping women? That I wanted to form an artisan guild just for them? You must understand that I'm not a noblewoman, I'm working class, but I was lucky enough to have crossed paths with Eilian in my business dealings. Unlike most men, he lets me do as I please and continue to work on my projects and company without restriction. Not every woman is able to do that after they are married. What I want to know from you is what worked. How did you use the silphium to achieve the desired result?"

She swallowed hard, seeing the blood again in her mind's eye as her body went into labor. "It's immoral to do what I did."

"I disagree, but I don't care about your reasons and don't want to know them. I only want to know the mechanism that achieved the result. You must understand, we have so few options that work and don't cause grave harm. From what I read in Eilian's notes, the Romans used it faithfully and they were able to regulate their population. Imagine how that would work in London and other cities where the only option is to risk your life in some back alley or commit worse atrocities later. With something like silphium, there would be less poverty and fewer orphans within a decade. Women would be able to even support themselves if they were able to control how many children they had without neglecting other areas of their marriages. I want every woman to have access to a natural method that actually works, and this is obviously effective."

"What's the point? They will say it's unnatural, and put a stop to it. Besides, it's gone now. I used up the useful parts testing it and burned the rest."

Hadley winced at the thought of the ancient plant being eaten by flames. "Eilian is growing another one. Luckily, he collected some seeds before you stole it. How could anyone deny that we were meant to have it when it has been provided for us to find? The Romans used it, and they are in fashion right now with scholars." Hadley leaned closer and met Leona's tired gaze. "All it takes is the right women finding out and spreading it to others. We could be a force for change with the right information and resources."

Drawing in an unsteady breath, Leona replied, "I will tell you, but you must promise never to tell anyone what I did."

⚬⚬◉ ◎◎⚬

Nadir watched from the dining room as Barnes passed into the curtained parlor with a tray of tea before ducking out and disappearing up the stairs. A wry smile crossed his lips. The kitchen was unguarded.

Slipping down the steps, he hoped the butler wouldn't interrupt him or make a snide comment on how much money he was costing Argus by purloining bits of cheese or leftovers, but as he crossed the last few steps, he froze and met a set of grey eyes gazing up at him from below. The thin shadow of a woman stood behind the table with her chapped hands resting on an envelope as crisp and white as the starched collar of her uniform. When she realized Nadir was the same man she met before, the edge of raw fear left her eyes.

"And what are you doing here? Another message, I see."

Her light eyes darted over the steps and over her shoulder toward the door before coming to rest on his rich, velvet jacket. "Yes. I— I have a letter for Mrs. Rhodes, sir. Is she at home?"

"Did Barnes let you in?" he asked with feigned disinterest.

On the final step, he dropped his foot with a thunk, letting it echo in the gloomy kitchen. Rain pattered down from the open door, casting undulating shadows on the cobbled floor. They split and flickered, merging with the edge of the maid's slight form. Pilcrow stepped back, unconsciously moving toward the door at the question. She should have waited outside.

"No, sir, the door was unlocked. My master said the letter was important, and I didn't want the ink to run, sir. I would get in trouble for that."

"You would get in trouble for trespassing, too." With a sardonic sigh, he held out his hand. "Give it here. Mrs. Rhodes is busy with Lady Dorset, but I can take it up when she's done."

Her mouth worked against the words that caught in her throat as she tightened her grip on the missive. "I can wait."

Nadir pursed his lips. For her size and station, she was a stubborn one. He had expected a woman who followed orders all day to give in. Languidly gliding across the cobbles, Nadir edged closer. The maid matched him step for step in reverse, her eyes never leaving his face. As her back collided with the wall, her face blanched to china white, but the hesitant resolve hardened in her gaze. Her heart pulsed against her ribs at the proximity of his breath and the brush of his hair against her forehead as he towered over her.

"Why not give it to me? Your master will never have to know," he whispered, his voice sweet and warm.

"But I will know."

His hand flashed forward, reaching for the corner of the letter, but she had seen him coming. The monochromatic woman spun away from him, facing the wall and twisting against his grip. Instead, his fingers caught the edge of her thin coat. The seam tore at the sudden motion, revealing her dull uniform beneath it. Pilcrow and Nadir stopped mid-step. Their wide eyes met in horror as he released her and took a step back. Still holding the letter tightly in her grasp, she checked her coat. Her mouth contorted into a grimace as she looked from the hole to the almond-skinned gentleman.

"I will pay for that."

Pilcrow's face sputtered and twisted until finally she yelled in a voice just loud enough to have an edge, "It doesn't matter. I'll still be the one mending it!"

His black brows knit and his eyes brightened at the thought. "If you give me the letter, I will give you twenty pounds. Then, you can buy a new coat."

Twenty pounds. She turned the figure over in her mind. That would be a year's worth of wages if the Nashes actually paid her what they promised. A whole year's salary for simply handing over an envelope that might fall into his hands the moment Mrs. Rhodes laid it down. She could buy a new coat and still have money left or she could save it until she could collect enough to leave and start over, but if Mrs. Nash found it when she rummaged through her room, she would confiscate it and interrogate her about where she got it. The horrid woman would call her a thief and toss her out without pay or references. As the hope drained from her mind, her grip loosened on the thin paper.

Before she could break from her thoughts, a hand clamped down on the other side. Her fingers tightened at the last second as Nadir pulled her forward, trying to tug it from her iron grasp. Even if he ripped it, she would rather have that happen than have him get it in one piece. He yanked her onto her tiptoes as he raised the letter high above her head. Beads of sweat collected on her forehead and the breath caught in her chest as she held it in. If she released it, she would let go. A cry escaped her lips as her fingers slid off and she collided hard with the wooden stool behind her.

Nadir stared triumphantly down at the letter. The envelope bore no name or markings. The back had been sealed with cheap glue and nothing more. Ignoring the maid as she rose on trembling legs and touched the blood seeping from the back of her hand where it scraped the stool, he held the papers up to the light. The few rows of neat script inside were barely visible through the dense paper, and where they could be seen, they overlapped incomprehensibly. With a satisfied smile, he stuffed it into his breast pocket out of sight.

"Give it back! It's not yours," the maid demanded.

Bright red blood dripped down her hand as she pointed a finger at him. Color rose in her cheeks, bringing out the russet sheen in her hair that a second earlier had been black. The shadows had condensed to fill-out the specter until her body became whole.

Her grey eyes glowed with rage. "Give it back!"

"My apologies, but it's mine now," he replied with a wide smile as he cocked his head and backed toward the steps. "I'm sure you can see yourself out."

Her hand dropped as he turned and trotted up the steps without looking back. She stood stunned. What could she do? The color drained from her face, landing in a tiny puddle of red at her side. Should she have chased him up into the house and taken it back? It would have surprised him—and her—but it was too late now. She knocked her fist against her forehead.

"Stupid. Stupid," she repeated as she righted the stool with her other hand. How could she have been so stupid? She should have known the man would have gotten it from her one way or another, and now, Mr. or Mrs. Nash would find out. Then, she would pay dearly for her idiocy and her coat. They would surely make her pay for that, too.

The Earl and the Artificer

Nadir sprinted up the stairs, slamming and locking the basement door when he reached the top. The letter crinkled in his pocket as he passed the empty parlor. He paused at the threshold, but when he heard women's voices drifting from the study, he continued on. *Pretend that nothing is out of the ordinary*, he reminded himself as he walked up the creaky, crooked steps with a slow, measured gate. He couldn't let Barnes see him too pleased with himself unless he wanted Leona to know. The butler was worse than a bloody parrot.

"Mr. Talbot."

Nadir stopped at the firm, plummy voice that brought him back to his school days of being brought before the headmaster. He turned to find the butler coming out of his bedroom. *Spying probably.* "Yes, Barnes?"

"Do you still want your shoes polished, sir? I was unsure which pair you meant. You brought so many."

"All of them," he replied with a smile as he slithered past and shut the door behind him.

Retreating to his desk, he rearranged his stacks of books and papers to block an unwanted visitor from seeing what he was doing. He shut the curtains before carefully tearing the letter open. If it was something benign, at least he could reseal it and slip it in with the post. As he pulled it halfway out, he hesitated. This was Leona's business. The letter was meant for her, and he had stolen it without a pang of guilt. There was still time to replace it before Lady Dorset left, but he *had* to know. Something was going on with her, something he didn't like.

His cousin hadn't said anything about her change in circumstances, but it was obvious by the state of her person and house. All of her gowns were several years out of fashion, her staff had been reduced to one, and the steamer she had been so happy to buy after her wedding had been sold even though they obviously needed it. Seeing her sneak out and disappear into the tunnel near the cove proved something was amiss. Then there was the look on Nash's face when she collapsed and the business with stealing the plant. Someone had to put an end to it. Argus would continue to bumble along unaware while everything went on under his nose, so that only left him. Glancing toward the door, he unfolded the letter.

This has gotten out of hand. We need to speak and finally put a stop to this nonsense. Meet in the usual place tonight at three. Tell no one.

Anger flared in Nadir's breast as he jammed the letter back into his pocket. No names, no formality, no question of where to go. How many clandestine meetings had they had? Well, Nash would be in for a surprise this time. If he didn't take him seriously before, he would now.

Chapter Twenty-One
Into the Dark

Sitting in the gloom, Nadir drew on his black coat and soundlessly slipped his feet into his boots. The house had fallen silent long ago, and each sound he made, no matter how small a creak or sigh, seemed to reverberate through the plaster. At the door, he listened for his cousin but heard only her husband's choking, throaty snores. Nadir opened the door a crack and stepped into the hall, careful not to make the hinge whistle. In the darkness, he could scarcely make out the lantern in his hand, but as he edged toward the stairs, moonlight filtered in through the front windows and shone off the framed portraits hanging across the wallpaper. He stepped over the loose board and padded over to the front door. Taking his walking stick from the umbrella stand, he pulled the ends apart just far enough for the hidden blade to catch the light. He closed it and tucked it under his arm, hoping it wouldn't come to that. Nash seemed like a man who wouldn't necessarily listen to reason but wouldn't take him lightly after a show of steel and coin. The latch's spring clicked loudly as he pushed open the door and walked into the cool night air.

The moon peeked behind murky clouds as Nadir kept his head down and picked along the deserted paths, keeping an eye and ear out for anyone who might notice his presence. In the village, nearly every house had fallen silent with the only light left to illuminate them coming from the electric globed streetlamps lining the pavement. He kept close to the fences and stone facades. Rounding the corner near the edge of town, he watched as three men in rumpled work clothes and shabby hats stumbled out of the tavern, its electric lamps shining bright and its tinny player-piano still playing at the late hour. Nadir stopped, locking eyes with one who glanced his way with bleary eyes, but when one of his companions made a joke, he laughed and staggered after them. Even if the man remembered him, it would be hard to distinguish what was real from what came from the bottom of a whiskey bottle. He swallowed against the dry knot in his throat and continued down the path toward the shore.

Half-fallen fences and scraggly bushes reached out with budded claws to catch his coat and hair as they drifted in the salty breeze. He stopped a few steps from the tunnel's entrance and drew in a long breath, savoring the calming tug and pull of the ocean below. With the taste of distant lands on his tongue, he lit the lantern with shaking hands and stepped into the brush. Even with shutter nearly closed, the harsh light gleamed against the dew-soaked rock like a beacon, illuminating the slick lichens growing in the grooves. As he stepped forward, his hand disappeared into the cliff's face.

Opening his lamp, he raised it ahead of him. The damp air sunk into his clothing, sending a shiver through his body as his feet splashed through the sole-high water. Nadir's resolve wavered. The endless abyss disappeared into the earth thirty feet beyond the reach of his meager lamp. Panic lanced through him at the thought of losing his way in the catacombs. He had heard tales of tourists becoming lost in Paris's underground necropolis only to be found months or years later, barely more than the piles of bones around them. Closing his eyes, he tucked the heavy walking stick beneath his arm and ran his free hand along the wall. The cold stone soaked through his glove, but a wave of calm washed over him. If Leona could make it through, so could he.

The peaked roof hovered inches above his head, occasionally tugging at his hair. As he passed rats' nests and things so decomposed he could no longer discern their forms, his stomach flipped. He had seen worse in London, but there he could cross the street to avoid it; here, he was forced to confront the world's ugliness. He stared into the darkness beyond his lamp, catching a whiff of a strange smell wafting from the far end of the cistern. Above the murk of stagnant water and centuries of moss, a musky odor rose. He crinkled his nose at the acidic, bitter notes of alcohol and stale sweat competing with spiced cologne. Water rippled over his feet as the smell grew stronger.

Darting to the other side of the tunnel, he scrambled onward. Metal grated against the stone wall behind him, sending his heart into a frantic tattoo. The stench drifted closer, but as he broke into a run, his lantern went out. Nadir heedless flung forward, feeling shafts of fresh air cut through the dankness as he passed under the parlors and drawing rooms of Brasshurst Hall. Ahead, the floor shivered with light, the ripples from his footsteps casting undulating patterns on the wall. Pale green light illuminated the water drifting beneath a half-rotted metal ladder affixed to blocks of staggered stone that formed a makeshift staircase.

At the edge of the shaft, he slowed his pace. In the otherworldly light, he found both sides of the tunnel deserted. His gaze rose to the opening. Another branch of the catacomb had been sealed long ago with massive blocks of marble, but above them, an engine thrummed despite the late hour. He had seen that absinthe glow. Something heavy thudded down the tunnel from where he had just come, echoing through the empty cavern, and the rank smell of sweat burned his nostrils. Nadir placed his light and stick on the top step before pulling himself up with the rusted rails. As he pivoted into the entrance, the catacombs fell away to reveal the vast dome of the orangery rising above him.

The liquid moon reflected off the glass, amplifying what little light could diffuse within the manmade fog. Relighting his lamp and setting it beside him, Nadir closed his dark eyes and slowed his breathing. With his heart pounding in his ears, he could scarcely tell whether it was his pulse or the heart of Brasshurst. Whatever the thing in the catacombs was, it didn't seem to follow him up. Maybe his imagination had played tricks on him. He pressed his hand to his pocket, feeling the aqua bead beneath it. There was no question in his mind that this was where Leona and Nash met. The tunnel led straight to his house, but no man would bring his untoward dealings so close to home. If they wanted to meet, it would have to be in the once deserted confines of the manor or the tunnel itself. Why else would Leona be so bold as to sneak into the orangery in the dead of night unless she had been there before?

Drawing up to his full height, Nadir clutched his lantern in one hand and his walking stick in the other. It was no wonder the earl and countess hadn't found the hatch yet. It had been surrounded by tall brush and was blocked on one side by a bull-sized boulder. He inched out of the thick bushes and massive ferns, his eyes sweeping over the slumbering plants for any sign of Randall Nash. A smile crossed Nadir's lips at the thought of the look on the old man's face when he realized that Leona had been left at home and what he would face would be far worse than anything she could have done. Even if he couldn't see or hear him, Nash was in there somewhere, waiting.

Apart from the gurgle of the pond and the hum of its engine, the greenhouse was silent. Nadir's eyes flickered down the path as he walked past the windows separating the dome from the delicate plasterwork and rich woods of the manor. Keeping the light half-shuttered, he walked toward the pool. He hoped Lord and Lady Dorset would remain fast asleep. Even if he expected that Lady Dorset would be at least somewhat reasonable, explaining his presence in their home at that late hour uninvited was a task he would have preferred to avoid, especially if it meant the possibility of having to reveal Leona's theft.

As he reached the crest of the trail, a light flickered at the edge of the tiled pond. It caught the light, creating tortured, deformed shadows that writhed around its wick. He squinted at the shuddering flame. Something lay beside it, but it was too dark to see. Following the dirt and cobbled path, Nadir's body locked at the water's edge. What he had imagined was a bough of wisteria or a fern dripping into the pool was really a pale hand.

The saliva dried in his mouth as he opened his lantern and stepped closer. A body lay twisted against the tile. A crimson pool surrounded the body, seeping into the tiles and following along the grout until it poured into the water in minute streams, narrow as capillaries. Nadir's heart pulsed in his temples at the sight of a bloodied hole torn through the fabric of his coat where a bullet had escaped. Walking along the man's side, he stopped at the grey head. He averted his gaze before he could see his lifeless features. *Nash.* He didn't need to flip him over to recognize the fine fabric of his suit and the curled but closely clipped hair on the back of his head. Nash was the one who was supposed to be there, and there could be no other. Laying his walking stick beside him, Nadir reached out and placed his fingers against the man's neck. The tide of blood inched toward his shoes as the pieces flooded into place. In a moment, all thoughts fled his mind, except one.

He had to get out of there. He had to tell someone what transpired. The smell, the chase, the letter, the body. It would mean waking up the Sorrells, but it would be worth it not to venture into the catacombs again and confront whatever lurked in the darkness. He stared up at the high windows. Would they even hear him if he banged on the windows? Maybe they had left one of the doors unlocked, but if he got in, who would he turn to? Climbing to his feet, he turned toward the path he had just come down.

He had only taken one step on the trail when a shadow slid out of the garden behind him, rustling the low branches of a pomegranate tree. He sensed him before he saw it, but his body didn't respond quickly enough. The specter raised something high above its head and brought it down hard. Pain thundered through Nadir's neck and skull, reverberating through his form as he stumbled onto his knees. His lantern skidded across the tile and sputtered out. He staggered. His head swam and his vision tunneled, sending the world into blackness.

⚬⚮⚭ ⚭⚮⚬

Calloused hands snaked across Nadir's face and around his chest. He tried to pry the man's hand off, but it felt as if he were trapped underwater. The air had thickened around him and his arms moved twice as slowly as he commanded them. Before he could stop him, the man pulled him up by the chest and held him in place like a photographer with a cadaver. Despite being raised to his feet, Nadir's shoes uselessly slid out from under him on the bloody tiles. His head lolled back against his will, heavy with confusion and throbbing pain. He fought to open one eyelid, which rose halfway before drooping again until a metallic click resounded in the gloom.

At the sound and the burn of cold metal being placed against his palm, his body rallied and stiffened against his attacker. As his senses cleared, his nose burned with the mixture of astringent cologne and sweat that he had smelled in the tunnel. Nadir flailed and struggled to push his shoulders into his attacker and throw him back, but with his weakened legs, he barely moved. The man's arm tightened around his waist and hand, holding him in place even as he writhed. He arched his back and felt the shorter man teeter backwards. With adrenaline pulsing through his veins in the nearly pitch black orangery, he threw his weight back again. The man stumbled and fell into the dirt beside Nash's body. Cool soil clung to Nadir's cheek as he landed hard to his side, his knee banging against a rock. Scrambling to his feet, he pulled out of his assailant's grasp and tumbled forward.

He took two hesitant steps before his feet slid out from under him, and he landed on hands and knees at the edge of the blood trail. The breath caught in his throat as he knelt frozen in horror at the warmth soaking through his trousers and into the lines of his palms. In an instant, he gathered his wits and ran toward where he believed the house to be. Through the heavy fog and his blurred vision, he could barely see a foot ahead of him, but he could hear the man's booted feet pounding after him. His body tilted and faltered, recovering as quickly as it staggered. Light glinted off the library windows as he rounded the path, but before he could reach it, a shot erupted behind him.

The boom reverberated through the trees and along the dome, sending leaves and bits of bark scratching across his cheek. Nadir sprinted forward as another shot rang out. By the time the noise finished echoing in his ears, pain seared through his left temple and rang through his skull. He clutched the side of his head and stumbled forward. The strength seeped from his limbs, and he slumped to his knees. Pulling his hand away from the wound, he found his palm nearly as dark as his coat. He strained to keep his thoughts together. Bolts of pain trailed across his scalp and down his neck while bile rose in his throat at the growing pressure in his temples.

He should get up. He should run toward the house and find help. He should move, but his legs refused to budge except to collapse under him. Wetness brimmed from the cut before trickling down the side of his face in slow rivulets. His eyes flickered shut against his will, the lids growing irresistibly heavy. The world grew quiet as the footsteps and smell trailed into the darkness and all that was left was the dull, rhythmic pulse of the engine. Closing his eyes, Nadir sunk to the cool soil and fell into the void.

ACT THREE

"The truth is rarely pure and
never simple."
–Oscar Wilde

Chapter Twenty-Two
A Writer of Little Infamy

"What was that?" Hadley cried as she shot up in bed, the words issuing from her throat before she was even certain she was awake.

"I don't know."

Eilian sat up beside her in the darkened room, the only sound their rapid inhalations. His wide eyes traveled the length of the room for the source of the phantom noise but found nothing out of the ordinary. Had she imagined the sound? No, he had heard it too, but the memory was already fading from his mind. As he leaned closer and brushed against her, her pounding pulse rushing against his arm.

A boom echoed through the stillness. Hadley ducked against him as Eilian covered her with his arms. In an instant, it was over. Locking eyes, they slipped out of bed without another word and donned their dressing gowns. As Hadley reached into the bedside table for her derringer, her heart thudded against her breast. She had heard that sound before. The retort ricocheting through the desert plateaus as she emptied a round into Edmund Barrister's ursine chest. Canvas tents whipped in the wind while blood spurted from the wound, spreading across his khaki jacket. She shut her eyes against the image of his body giving out before falling at her feet. Swallowing the fear tightening her breast, she slipped the gun into her pocket.

At the door, Eilian ran a shaky hand through his sleep-mussed hair and across his tired eyes. "Ready?" When she nodded and smoothed her nightgown, he wrapped his arm around her and whispered, "You needn't worry, Had. I'm willing to bet it's Nash again."

She furrowed her brows and frowned, she wasn't so sure. Stepping into the hall, they flipped on the gas lamps with each empty room they checked. At the top of the stairs, Patrick stood waiting for them. His white hair was wild from sleep and his pajamas' buttons were misaligned under his rumpled dressing gown. He yawned behind his hand as he clutched a heavy silk parasol. Hadley suppressed a chuckle at their manservant's choice of weapon.

"Are the girls somewhere safe?"

"Mrs. Negi is standing guard of them downstairs."

"Good. Did you find any damage on your way up, Pat?"

"The servants' quarters are untouched, as are the drawing rooms, parlors, and day rooms. Every door and window is locked."

Eilian's spirits sank at the implication. "So that leaves half of the upstairs bedrooms, the dining room, and the orangery?"

"Yes, sir."

"Of course. Where else would he be?"

They flipped on the light in every room until the manor blazed. No longer did they have to fear what lurked in the darkness or skulk with cudgels raised. Eilian was certain he knew who caused the mischief. Even if he didn't know what had been done, Randall Nash had to be behind it. No one else caused them any problems or tried to maliciously upset their lives, and the sooner they left, the happier Nash would be. No matter how many passages he read in his great-grandfather's journals, he still could not reconcile the innocent, loving child with the abhorrent man who did nothing but antagonize them and everyone around him.

At the library door, Patrick released the lock and turned on the auxiliary lights. The green glow from the high lamps and the bright lights from the rooms surrounding the orangery cast stark shadows over the trees and dome. The room stood as still as a picture.

"Nash! Nash, I know you are in here. Come out now, and I won't call the constabulary!" Eilian yelled at the threshold.

His heart thundered in his ears. Despite the stillness, the room felt charged, as if a battle had stopped the moment he opened the door. When no reply came, he left the shelter of the library and stepped into the stifling humidity of the greenhouse. Even without the sun's gaze upon him, sweat broke down his back and arms, but as he called again, a chill fell over him. A groan came from the trail just out of sight. He turned back to find Hadley at his elbow with her derringer at the ready. He shifted uncomfortably as they crept forward, his naked prosthesis feeling strangely heavy without its external springs or couter. The irritation died away as his eyes locked on a figure lying at the edge of the path. Before he could react, Hadley ran ahead, dropping her hand and gun.

"Had, wait!"

Eilian trailed behind her. His stomach lurched as vomit rose in his throat at the blood smeared across the man's face. Rivers of blood trailed over his forehead, across his eyes, and between his full lips as they parted to release a heavy breath. If Nadir Talbot hadn't been the only man of Egyptian descent in town, it would have been impossible to tell it was him with his dark hair matted and his face painted in blood.

"Mr. Talbot! Good lord, Nadir," she cried as she dropped to his side and turned him onto his back. Placing a hand on his chest, she jostled him until he released another groan. "Nadir, wake up."

"Pat, fetch Dr. Sturgis!"

"Should I fetch the police as well?"

"Yes but after. Tell Sturgis a man is gravely wounded." When the butler disappeared out of sight, he turned his gaze to the shadows beyond the dim glow of the auxiliary lights. The person who attacked

Mr. Talbot could still be there, waiting for their chance to finish them off next. He slipped his arm under Nadir's shoulder, but when he maneuvered his prosthesis to carry him back to the library, his eyes fell upon the bare titanium rod.

Eilian dropped his voice and leaned close. "Had, we need to get him out of here. Grab his left side. I don't know if we still have company."

They slipped their arms under his and dragged him toward the library. Nadir's body thumped along the cobbles as he weakly struggled to shrug off their hands. They laid him down on the rug in front of the hearth, but as Eilian turned from shutting the door, he recoiled at the sight. The amount of blood and torn flesh was worse than he had imagined. Blood dribbled down his face from the wound on his scalp. It cut from behind his ear to an inch from his temple where his flesh had shredded and peeled back to reveal the musculature and bone below. Before he could suppress it, Eilian ran to the desk and vomited into the rubbish bin as quietly as he could muster as not to alert Hadley. His throat burned as he wiped his mouth and rested a steadying hand over his stomach. He had to pull himself together. When he turned back, his wife had Nadir propped up against the sofa and was carefully parting his hair to get a better look at the wound. He averted his gaze as another wave of nausea gurgled through his gut.

"It doesn't seem too deep. I wish Eliza and James were here; they would know what to do." She pushed past him to fetch the scissors from his desk, but as she passed the garbage pail, she stopped. Her light eyes darted from the metal can to her husband's ashen face. "Are you all right? I can do this myself if you can't stomach it."

"I can help. I just can't look at it too much."

"All right. Hold his shoulder then, so he doesn't fall over."

Eilian swallowed hard and averted his gaze as he laid his hand on Nadir's shoulder. With the scissors, Hadley quickly cut off the bottom six inches off her nightgown and bunched it up against the bleeding wound. Nadir's eyes opened a crack, but as she pressed her hand to the side of his head, he clenched them shut and drew in a hissed breath.

"Where am I?" he mumbled, his words slurred against his thick tongue.

"Brasshurst Hall. You don't remember coming here?"

His glazed eyes widened as he looked past her. "No... I don't know. You're hurting me, Lee."

"It's not Leona; it's Lady Dorset. I'm sorry I'm hurting you, but I have to." She ran her hand along the back of his head to feel for injuries when her fingers drifted over a hot lump. "You have an egg on your head. Did someone hit you?"

He stared ahead for a long moment before nodding.

"Do you remember who?"

Images drifted through his mind, dim and just out of reach. It had been dark, and there had been that disgusting smell.

"Was it Mr. Nash?"

The breath caught in his throat. Nadir tried to catch the threads of his mind and draw them together despite the throb of nausea and pain. He had to tell someone. He *had* to tell. Gathering his wits, he said, "He's dead."

Hadley and Eilian locked eyes, their gazes traveling to the fogged window. Turning back to Nadir, Hadley raised his chin until their eyes met. The haze had nearly cleared for the time being, leaving the proud writer to grit his teeth and breathe in shallow gasps against the sear of pain in his temple.

"If you don't," Nadir paused to swallow down the pain in his head, "believe me, go check. He's by the pool."

Hadley looked toward the window again before returning to the bleeding wound and the growing stain on the cloth. Could she risk leaving him alone?

"I will go. Give me your gun," Eilian replied as he released Nadir's arm, happy to escape the sight of his torn scalp.

Reaching into her dressing gown, Hadley handed over her derringer. Her heart thundered in her throat. She watched Eilian fumble to position the gun in his real hand and slip into the orangery without looking back. Even if he ran into the culprit, she knew he wouldn't be able to protect himself. She reached to sweep her hair behind her ears but stopped short when she remembered they were coated in Nadir's blood.

"I think he's gone," Nadir said when she turned to him, her face blanched with fear.

"Who?"

He raised his hand, which still felt as heavy as his head, and held the rag to his wound. "The murderer."

"Oh. Did you see his face?"

"No, he hit me from behind. Then, it was dark. He grabbed me, and I ran. I— I dropped my lantern at some point. Not sure when. I should have thrown it at him." A bitter chuckle escaped his lips, rattling his throbbing head. He squeezed his eyes shut as a wave of pain radiated through his scalp and burned the cartilage of his ear. "Did he shoot me in the head?"

Hadley met his half-glazed eyes and nodded. "You were lucky this time. It isn't too deep."

"Lucky," he repeated under his breath, his fingers trailing into his pocket to retrieve the smooth bead.

"Nadir, I hate to ask, but I need to know before the police get here. Did you kill him?"

His dark eyes shot to her face. "What? Of course not!"

"Then, what were you doing sneaking into the orangery?" she demanded, her voice cracking. "If you got into an altercation with him and things went badly, I don't know if I could blame you. I need to know the truth before everyone gets here and turns the house into chaos again."

His bloodstained mouth hung open at the implication. At the rush of emotion, his head swam and the library tilted before righting itself. He swallowed hard and squinted his eyes until they focused.

"Lady Dorset, you must believe me, I did nothing of the sort! I snuck in to confront him, and that is all. All I wanted to do was give him a piece of my mind, maybe— maybe threaten him a little, but not kill him. When I got here, he was already dead or at least I thought he was dead. There was lots of blood."

"What happened after you found him?"

That part was still fuzzy. In his mind's eye, he could see Nash beside the pool with his hand dangling into the water. He drew in a ragged breath and closed his eyes to picture the scene, but as soon as he relaxed his body, the countess shook his shoulder, rattling his brain against his skull.

"Wake up!"

"I am! God, you're as bad as Leona."

"Don't you know you are not supposed to let a person who got hit in the head sleep? Now, focus and tell me what happened."

He groaned. "I don't know. Someone hit me, that much I remember, but after that, I'm not sure. I could barely see straight; he hit me so hard."

"How did you get in?"

Nadir swallowed and tried to hold his head still as the subterranean passage floated before his vision. "There's a tunnel by the beach. It leads under your house, all the way to the dower house. There's a trap door or loose tile that opens into the orangery. It was open when I got there. It looks like a sewage tunnel or something."

Hadley suppressed her surprise by busying herself with the bandages. She would have to take a look at that passage later. Cutting another length of fabric from her skirt, she carefully peeled the blood-sodden bandage away from the wound and handed Nadir the new one. As he shifted and repositioned his head, she caught a glimpse of the couch behind him. The cream brocade had wicked up the blood, creating a scarlet halo where his head had once been.

"How bad do you think it is?" he asked, pointing toward the gash.

"Bad enough for stitches. The bleeding is slowing down."

"I guess I will have to part my hair the other way now. Then again, to the right audience, maybe I could show off my battle scars. A writer has to gain a little infamy after they have been shot in the head and lived to tell the tale... even if it is exaggerated."

Her light eyes narrowed as she wiped her hands on her gown. "Mr.

Talbot, A man has been killed only a few yards away and you're thinking about showing off to your lady friends. Do you not realize how serious this is? Eilian could be in there with the murderer."

"Of course I do. I'm just trying to take your mind off it. I know you're worried about him," he replied, wincing as a bolt arced across his scalp. "That man would have overpowered you in an instant. Lord Dorset at least looks like he could hold his own. I'm sure he will be fine."

The anger seeped out of her as she sat back on her heels. In his dark coat free of cut flowers or vibrant colors, Nadir Talbot had lost his dandy's mask. He sat before her with his head resting against the sofa and the wad of once-white cotton pressed to his head, no pretention or preening left to hide behind. She had never noticed how much intelligence flashed behind his gaze or how his palms were stained with faded blotches of ink. A line of script cut across his thumb on his empty hand where it had rested across his manuscript until the words set in. With the fan of blood surrounding his head, he reminded her even more of his cousin. He could have been one of the Renaissance's doe-eyed saints, suffering but maintaining his unearthly glow. How had the gravity of his well-sculpted features been hidden so well behind layers of vibrant silk and velvet? For a moment, his brown eyes glazed before snapping back to her face as she brushed a few strands of blood-crusted hair from his forehead.

"I appreciate it, Nadir. How are you feeling?"

"Like I'm going to have a horrid migraine tomorrow."

"I'm surprised you aren't more light-headed from the bleeding. Hopefully Patrick will return with the doctor soon."

"Oh, trust me, I'm light-headed. I'm just trying very hard not to think about it. If I dwell on it, I may vomit." He drew in a long breath and let it out slowly as he readjusted his blurring eyes again. "I wonder how long it will last."

Picking up the used rag, she wiped a stream of blood trailing down his neck that had escaped his notice. She frowned when his hand trembled as he readjusted the cloth and shook out his wrist.

"It will probably wear off in a few days. You know, you still haven't told me why you were in there. How did you know Nash would be there?"

Nadir kept his gaze on the looping vines of the carpet beside them, tracing them with his mind to buy him time until he could figure out what to say. He had Leona to protect. He had failed before, but he wouldn't now.

"I received a letter."

Chapter Twenty-Three
Too Late

Through the trees growing beneath the dome, the dusky pink and blue dawn emerged to chase away the shadows lurking in the far corners of the orangery. Eilian held the gun ahead of him as he followed the path past where they had found Mr. Talbot. He had seen Hadley do it several times, but it felt wrong. It wasn't that her derringer was too small or that it fit awkwardly in his hand, it left him feeling exposed. If someone leapt from the cover of the brush, he knew he wouldn't fire. He would throw his prosthetic arm in front of him to protect himself before swinging with his real arm. Unhooking his fingers and twisting the gun into his palm, he stopped in the middle of the fern-like trees and listened in the still greenhouse for the assailant. As he expected, the only sound came from the murmur of the water in the pool and the engine behind it. Whoever had broken in was probably long gone now.

Forging ahead, he stopped as his foot collided with the thin metal of a lantern. With a crack, it shot off the path and banged into an unseen tree. The noise reverberated off the dome, shattering the fragile stillness. Before he would have frozen, waiting for the sound to pass, but there was no one left. As the path crested the hill, he sighed as his eyes locked onto the body lying face down at the water's edge. In the growing dawn light, he could make out the man's grey hair and long, thin arm, which dangled across the old stones. On his little finger, a gold signet ring glinted. Blood had pooled beneath his narrow chest and dripped into the water beside him. Somehow, this blood didn't turn his stomach. He should have felt queasy knowing his father's cousin had bled out while he slept, yet any nausea he should have felt was overpowered by the weight of guilt.

He hadn't known Randall Nash well. While he had been a nuisance with a miserable disposition, he had been family—practically his father's brother—and he was gone now. There would be no chance to salvage any semblance of a civil relationship. No one would tell him stories of his father's childhood or know what Laurence Sorrell was truly like. That entire generation of his family was dead, and now every Sorrell in the family bible would have their lives defined by birth and death. He had hoped to find bits of himself in stories of Laurence or Harland. Randall could have helped things make sense and confirm what he read in Laurence's journals. He should have done more to mend their relationship.

Swallowing hard, Eilian turned on heel and headed back to the house. He and Dylan were all that tied his family to the Brasshurst and Folkesbury. If either of them were to die— He banished the thought from his mind. Now was not the time for morose ruminations. Dylan and Constance were to have a child, and even if he never did, at least the house and all its history wouldn't go to seed again; he would make sure of that. At the bend in the path, he paused and watched the sun pierce the misty bluffs. Through the murk, the shadow of a steamer passed down the road to town while three others with their headlamps alight charged across the old bridge toward the house. The light-less steamer fell in behind them, following the caravan.

Inhaling the perfume of water and earth, Eilian braced for the chaos about to descend upon them.

⚜

"Two bodies, right?" Sergeant Purcell asked when Eilian met him on the front lawn.

The normally sharp policeman's mustache hung limp at the edge of his lips while his wool uniform, which had been pressed with care, had been thrown over a rumpled, collarless shirt. Behind him, his men looked as if they had rolled out of bed. One still wore a nightshirt under his wrinkled uniform while the other was dressed but looked as if he might fall asleep if left alone.

"No, just one."

The sergeant's light eyes sharpened. "Oh? I thought your man told my boys there were two."

"Randall Nash is dead. Luckily, Nadir Talbot is merely wounded. Dr. Sturgis is already inside tending to him."

"How fortunate for him. A double murder would have been a record for us."

When they reached the orangery through the drawing room, Purcell sent his men ahead. Standing before the nobleman, Purcell's eyes traveled toward where Nash lay as he opened his notepad. He gave the earl a onceover, probing him for any signs of guilt before lingering on the bloodstain on the cuff of his nightshirt where it had grazed Nadir's bloodied head.

"Lord Dorset, do you know anyone who would have wanted your cousin dead?"

"No, I didn't know him well."

"What about Mr. Talbot? Do you have any reason to believe he killed Nash?"

Eilian recoiled at the tang of sweat leaking from beneath the man's starched collar. Shaking his head, he stepped back, but the sergeant immediately filled the gap.

"I highly doubt it. I don't know why they were trespassing in the orangery, but I blame Nash for it. He broke in whenever he pleased, so I assume he set up the meeting." His wife was so fond of Nadir that he hoped what he said was true. "Nadir appears to be the victim of the same assailant who attacked Nash. I don't think it's possible that he could have shot himself."

⚬ᔆ℮ Ꙅᔆ⚬

By Purcell's smug, knowing smile, Eilian should have realized his interrogation wouldn't end at that. For hours, he, Hadley, and their entire staff were paraded in and out of the morning room, which the sergeant had designated as his makeshift office, all while still in their robes and pajamas. There he sat with his fingers tented in front of his now pomaded mustache, staring down whichever victim had been offered up for questioning. Little Lidia came out in tears followed by Charlotte who returned colorless, and during his turn, Bernard's rough accent reverberated through the walls. The only one who had escaped his investigation was Nadir Talbot, who had been sent back to his cousin's to rest at Dr. Sturgis's furious insistence. With each round of probing, Eilian watched Hadley's face grow redder while her lips whitened with rage.

"They're wasting time. This is ridiculous, acting like one of us did it when the real killer is probably halfway to London by now," she muttered, crossing her arms and storming over to the bay window where she perched on the cushion, away from the others.

Charlotte half-rose to follow her, but Eilian raised his hand to keep her at her younger sister's side. Crossing the room, he stood behind her and squeezed her shoulder as Patrick was summoned before the sergeant again. Rain pattered against the mullioned windows, casting streaks of grey across her freckled cheeks.

"At least he should be done soon. I can't imagine that this could go on much longer."

"Really? Because he asked me the same question four times. *Four*

211

times." Her shoulders sagged as she rubbed her eyes and leaned back against him. "We should have just buried him in the garden. I don't mean to speak ill of the dead, but I don't know if he is worth all this fuss."

A small smile played on Eilian's lips as he leaned closer and whispered, "Sorry, darling, but I can't blow everyone up to keep the police away."

"We're awful," she chuckled. "I know I'm being cruel, but it would have been easier that way. I can't imagine there are many murders here, and if he can't find who robbed us, I doubt he will figure out who killed Nash." She sighed, hugging Eilian's arms. "Poor Nadir. He doesn't know what he's in for tomorrow."

"If Purcell doesn't drag him out of bed tonight, he will be lucky. I don't think Dr. Sturgis has any say in what he does. Then again, he may not be done with us today."

Eilian's head turned to the door as it creaked open and Patrick's white head peaked out followed by Purcell's hard features. His light eyes surveyed the tense, careworn faces of the servants sitting on the couches before landing on the earl and countess at the window. As he motioned to his men to leave their posts by the door, Eilian tightened his grip on Hadley's shoulder.

"That will be all for today. If you are to be questioned further, one of my men will come to summon you. It would be in your best interest to go willingly."

A communal groan echoed through the room, but the sergeant didn't appear to notice.

"You may return to your duties, except for you, Lord and Lady Dorset."

With a nod to the servants, they filed out while their master waited at the window for Purcell to approach. Eilian swallowed hard but stood tall as Hadley rose beside him. The sergeant's gaze never wavered from his wife's form. If he could have, he would have kept his arm protectively around her for fear of what the policeman might threaten. Purcell sauntered over, fishing in his pocket for a moment before pulling out a miniature gun. Hadley reached out to snatch it from his palm, but he pulled it back out of reach.

"Yours, I presume, Lady Dorset?" When she nodded, he continued coolly, "We found it near where you said you stumbled upon Nadir Talbot. How did it get there?"

Her lip curled. "Am I being interrogated again?"

"I'm the one asking the questions, your ladyship."

"I told you, I ran over to help him. It must have fallen out of my hand when we moved him inside. Why did you not ask me this when you were hounding me before?"

"Why are you in possession of a derringer?"

Eilian's arm tightened around her as she replied sharply, "Because I live in London. If you were a woman, would you walk around unarmed with all sorts of vile creatures lurking about? It's for protection."

"Is this really necessary?" Eilian asked, edging between the sergeant and his wife. Even if he was a policeman, he was lucky she didn't have her derringer.

"It is. Mr. Talbot and Mr. Nash were both shot. Was it possible that you saw Mr. Talbot running in the orangery and shot him by accident?"

"No! I told you, we were awoken by a sound and then heard another gunshot a few moments later."

"That's what you say."

"That's what we *all* say because that is what happened. For the tenth and last time, we woke up because there was a loud noise, and as we got out of bed, we heard it again. We went downstairs with Patrick and found Nadir Talbot unconscious and Mr. Nash dead. Whatever you are looking for, Sergeant Purcell, you are looking in the wrong place. Now, if you will excuse me, I have better things to do than repeat myself."

Dislodging her arm from Eilian's grasp, Hadley stormed out of the room, her muddied silk slippers slapping against the wooden boards. When he turned back Purcell's sharp gaze was still locked on the door.

Eilian shifted uncomfortably and supported his disarticulated prosthesis with his other arm.

"You should learn to control your wife," the officer growled as he turned his penetrating glare to the earl.

Eilian bristled. "She's right, you know. No one on my staff has a motive, and even if we disliked Mr. Nash, Hadley and I were in bed at the time." He held his hand out expectantly. "You have no right to hold her gun. Give it to me."

Purcell's eyes bored into him, challenging the earl to stand down, but when he showed no signs of relenting, he huffed and dropped the gun in the nobleman's hand. "Only because it hasn't been fired, but neither of you are to leave town, got it?"

"Well, we will be staying for the funeral, won't we? Or have you not told his widow yet? You really should. You seem much closer to her than we are."

Without giving Purcell the opportunity to reply, Eilian left. Passing Patrick at the door, ready to lead the men out, Eilian trudged up the steps and cut across the upper arcades to their bedroom. Anger and sadness welled in his chest, twisting and knotting until all that was left was a clot of misery. They would be stuck in Folkesbury for God knows how long now when all he wanted was to go back to London— to anywhere really. Any place where he would feel useful and no one knew of his earldom.

On top of everything, Nash was dead. Any second chances he thought he had to reconnect with his father were gone now. It had always seemed so easy to fix. His father had loved him and would have welcomed him with open arms if he had changed his ways, but that never happened. It would never happen. Now, there were no more chances, no what-ifs, only what was. Nash's death had solidified that. Closing the dressing room door, he rested his head on the cool wood. He squeezed his eyes shut until the burning ceased.

Once again, he had acted too late.

Chapter Twenty-Four
The House of Stone & Bones

On the day of the funeral, the turnout was even worse than Eilian imagined. Less than a dozen people showed up to fill the pews in the old stone church, including Mr. Nash. Most would have blamed it on the rain, which pounded against the stained glass windows and beat through the clothing of anyone lingering outdoors for more than a few moments, but Eilian knew that despite living nearly his entire life in Folkesbury, Randall Nash had made few friends. Maybe that was his lot in life, to lose everything he ever thought he could possess: his parents, his home, his reputation, and finally his grandfather and cousin. What affection he had with his wife, Eilian would never know. In the front pew beside Pilcrow, she sat dry-eyed reciting prayers and singing hymns in widow black, paying little heed to the man stretched in the coffin before her or the mourners sitting behind her.

Eilian tried to keep his head down as if in prayer but found it nearly impossible with the coffin sitting only a few yards away. Every time he looked at it, he pictured Nash with the bullet hole in his back lying beside the pool, his grey eyes staring ahead as the blood drained out of him. Eyes so like his father's and his own. Ripping his gaze from the casket, he studied the elaborately vaulted timber ceiling before trailing to the dingy plaster that coated the church's ancient stone. What he wouldn't give to tear it off and examine the building's underpinnings. From the shape of the arches and the style of the figures in the windows, he guessed it to be from the fourteenth century. Under the pew in front of them, he spotted a flat, engraved stone as long as a man. *Surely the dead in Folkesbury must outnumber the living*, he thought as the vicar's droning voice sharpened, breaking his reverie. Now he remembered why he had avoided church since leaving home.

"Heavenly Father, welcome Randall Fitzwilliam Nash into your kingdom and—"

A ragged breath echoed through the stone and timber church. When he looked up expecting to find that his widow finally broke down, he found Mrs. Nash and her lady's maid reading as if it was a normal service. He glanced at Hadley, itching to look over his shoulder to see who cared enough about Randall Nash to mourn him, but with each shift or squirm, he felt the vicar's cold gaze upon him and Hadley's elbow in his ribs. As he put his head down, staring at the metal hand before him, another stifled sob broke from the back of the church. Skirts swished in time with the quick patter of footsteps, but by the time Eilian dared to turn, he could only make out the back of a woman as she slipped between the massive doors. Nadir rose from the last pew and followed her out.

◦◦੨◦ ୨◦◦

At the dismissal of the clergyman, they funneled out of the rows of wooden pews and into the rain, their exit marked by the thwump of umbrellas opening. Most of the attendees drifted down the cobbled path toward town, ignoring the group of hired men raising the casket onto their shoulders. As Eilian and Hadley followed the coffin processing from the church to the family crypt, a familiar face fell in beside them. The handsome Egyptian flashed a roguish smile and tipped his hat, sending a dribble of water over the brim. Peeking from the edge of Nadir's top hat was a flash of purple silk and a strip of gauze. Hadley's eyes returned to Rubella Nash at the head of the procession beside the vicar. On her right, Pilcrow held an umbrella over her head, seemingly oblivious to the current of water running along the ribbon of her hat and down the length of her narrow back, while on her left, a man had linked arms with her. From behind, Hadley couldn't be sure who he was. For all she knew, the woman could have had family nearby, but as he turned his head to speak to her, the manicured curl of a mustache appeared at his lip. Hadley released a silent groan. She had hoped not to see the arrogant fool again for the duration of their stay. Nadir raised a dark brow at her grimace, ready to back away if it was meant for him, but upon seeing him, she grinned and twitched a finger for him to stay at her side.

"What was that about?"

"I hadn't expected to see the sergeant today. Anyway, how are you feeling, Nadir?" she whispered as he fell into step with them.

"My head has been ringing for days, but I'm much better, thank you. Any leads on Mr. Nash's killer?"

She shook her head. "Not really. They found shells from three bullets in the garden, all from revolvers, but I don't expect Purcell and his men to figure out who did it. If Mr. Nash treated others the way he treated us, I can't imagine he was without enemies."

"Well, they're not exactly Scotland Yard, are they? They're at least thorough interrogators. It felt like I was sitting through the bloody Inquisition. Did you know they have forbidden me from leaving until this whole thing is settled? My publisher is livid. Several of my friends have threatened to come down and raise Cain to get Purcell to back-off. Not that I think it would do any good or that they would actually do it, but no one is pleased."

"He said the same to us. We may be taking up permanent residency at Brasshurst at this rate." Leaning in closer, Hadley whispered, "Honestly, I expected a better turnout. Nash was murdered after all, so shouldn't everyone have come to pay their respects or at least to gawk?"

"I thought the same thing, but then again, Folkesbury isn't London. They sweep scandals under the rug here, not call the press and print it in the society pages."

"Still, I expected a journalist or two."

A wry smile crossed his lips. "Watch what you wish for, Lady Dorset. They will probably be banging down your door tomorrow."

She watched as Eilian wandered off with the umbrella, his fingers unconsciously rubbing the gold band of his signet ring while his prosthesis held the fabric canopy a foot away from her. Frowning, she stepped back under it, pulling Nadir along with her. When she was certain Eilian was too far in his mind to hear, she asked, "How is your cousin doing?"

"Good as new, thank you. It's strange; it's like she's a new woman or she was until today. She wanted to come to the internment, but she didn't think she had the strength to get through it or that Mrs. Nash would like her there."

"I thought I saw her in the back of the church. Why would Mrs. Nash mind her there?"

Nadir shrugged, his brown eyes trailing to the muddied path before rising to Eilian Sorrell. The earl watched trees pass, veiled in his own thoughts. Stepping closer, Nadir said softly in hopes that the Sorrells would be the only ones who could hear, "The thing is, she was recovering so well. She seemed lighter—happier—than she's been the entire time I've been here, but this whole murder thing has upset her. I don't know if it's me getting hit over the head, which I doubt is the cause, or that old Nash was killed, but she's spooked. She started crying at dinner a few days ago over it, and I'm sure you heard her today during the mass, but she won't tell me what the problem is. Do you think you could talk to her later? I thought maybe she would say something to you."

The Earl and the Artificer

❧ ❦ ❧

Brasshurst's spires and contorted facades appeared through the gaps in the ornamental garden as the Sorrells crunched across the gravel path from the mausoleum. From the drizzle and sea spray, a grey mist rose from the lawns, casting the house in an otherworldly haze and transforming the orangery into a fortuneteller's ball. Life danced within, splitting into cascades of green and swirls of red before dissolving into clouds of mist. Eilian blinked the drops of rain from his eyelashes as he pulled off his top hat and wiped his face with his sleeve. Drifting from Hadley's side, he crossed to the edge of the road where oaks and yews twisted together with strangling vines and bulbous fungi. He scoffed as a cockeyed smile crossed his lips. How odd it was to see so much life.

Standing before the mausoleum's horned minarets and faceless saints, he couldn't help but wonder how many of them rested within. How many forgotten Sorrells came before him only to crumble to dust? Did anyone care about them once those they loved were dead, too? At the internment, they had followed the casket into the tight space, passing sealed niches carved with names, some so old they were clotted with webs so deep the letters were nearly indiscernible. In his years of traveling through Italy, he had seen miles of catacombs where husked bodies hung mummified from the walls or skeletons lay bedecked in jewels, but he had never felt his stomach sink at the sight of so many bodies. All that separated him from his ancestors were thin panels of stone. With each shift or tap, he feared he would rouse them.

The men from the village raised Nash's coffin into the vault as the vicar recited a prayer Eilian could no longer remember. He licked his lips, tasting the musty, damp air with each breath, but while the others kept their heads bowed, his grey eyes scanned the familiar names surrounding him. He felt as if he knew them. He could see them going about their lives at Brasshurst. Laurence in his red uniform walking up the gravel drive where Anna waited for him. Alexander bent over with a trowel, his arms encrusted in earth, his concentration never wavering from his plants. His father had escaped—for a time—only to meet the same fate miles away. One day would he, too, be stacked among his ancestors in one of the empty shelves, trapped in a house of stone and bones?

Eilian hoped not. His entire life had been spent running from that death. No, set him aflame like the Vikings of old or on the edge of the Ganges where he could return to the earth he loved. Laurence had been free for a time until the earldom came to collect him. Even after reading two dozen volumes of journals, he still couldn't imagine how Laurence settled into this life. To go from the battlefield to the house in a silent wood, which was soon filled with the chatter of children and local gentry, seemed impossible to reconcile with the proud soldier. Was that what his life would become? If the signet ring hadn't bounced beneath the desk to where the journals had been stashed long ago, would he have ever known that others who came before were so much like him?

The clergyman's words fell on deaf ears until he dismissed them with a solemn *amen*. When they left, the townsmen would wall his cousin behind a faceless stone. Fingering the worn gold of his family's ring, Eilian drew in a long breath, the taste of history dry on his tongue. As they processed out, he whispered their names only loud enough for them to hear. Jenny, William, Anna, Laurence, Alexander. *He lives whose name is spoken.*

"Eilian?"

Hadley's hand gently squeezed his arm as he came to. Rain pattered against his scalp, dripping through his hair before trailing down his cheek.

"You all right?"

He shrugged. "I guess. I'm just thinking too much."

"About?"

"Whether I will ever be like them," he replied, slipping his prosthetic arm into hers, and walking toward the house. "I don't know if I want to or not. Some days I want to be the nobleman my parents envisioned, but most days it sounds abhorrent, if not impossible."

Her hand slid over the smooth service of his titanium fingers, the cold metal radiating through her thin leather glove. "Is this about your arm? Replacing a piece of you doesn't make you lesser; it simply means you have changed. For better or worse is up to you to decide."

Against his will, his lips curled into a smile but this time without a trace of irony. "If it was merely my arm, it would be simple. I'm as whole as I will ever be in that regard, but this began long before that."

The rain drummed against the trees as if in time with the gravel crunching beneath their feet. The landscape and sky seemed so grey against the green of the lawn, finally rousing from its invernal slumber. Pink buds blinked from the dull wood along the edge of the road. Looking out across his family's land, his eyes swept over the meadow grass and out to the sea beyond the bluffs. It was out of sight, but if he stilled his mind, he could hear the swish of the waves against the coast. Soon it would all be alive again, and he would be fleeing before he could ever see it. He turned his gaze back to his wife and found her watching him with her red brows knit in concern.

"My entire life I have been told that nobility comes from blood and that I would become the earl because that's what I was destined to do as the eldest son. I grew up knowing this would all be my responsibility someday, yet I can't remember a time I ever relished it. Everyone acted as if I would suddenly understand how to be this earl they always spoke of— that I would grow out of being me. One day you will stop traveling. One day you will settle down. One day you won't think of any of this foolish nonsense." His eyes burned as he tightened his lips and flexed away the pain in his prosthesis. "How does one set aside everything they ever worked toward for something they never wanted?"

Hadley watched his face fall, his features all the more thoughtful and comely when softened with emotion. Stepping in front of him, she held his hands in hers. For a long moment, they simply stood there locked hand-in-hand, gaze-to-gaze, one pulse rising in harmony until the world beyond them fell silent. In this world, there was nothing but them. They were deaf to society's rules and expectations. As his hand trailed up her arm to pull her closer, she rested her palm against his cheek and slid it along his jaw. Her hand cupped the back of his head with her fingers working into his earthen hair while the other hand traveled around his side. Eilian closed his eyes and gave into the reassuring warmth of her lips as they met his. His hands slipped around her waist and back, reveling in the familiarity of her form and her body breathing him. When she began to ease from his grasp, he tightened his embrace and drew her into another kiss. He clenched his eyes against the moisture accumulating behind his lids and pressed harder, hoping it would cease before she could see.

His lips trembled as he relinquished his hold but kept his head down. A gloved hand skimmed across his cheek and wiped the wetness away without a word. Hadley rested her forehead against his, stroking the prickled flesh of his neck and jaw. He swallowed against the lump of emotion in his throat. If he looked up, she would see it too, and he couldn't bear to say anymore. Her arms tightened around him, holding him together when he no longer could.

"There is nothing wrong with you. There has never been anything wrong with you," she whispered against his ear, her breath warm against his cheek.

His voice cracked against his will as he replied, "I don't know how you can say that, Had."

"None of us will ever be what others want, but we have to please ourselves first, you know that. If it gives you any comfort, you are precisely what I want."

He let out a soft laugh and sniffed. Still holding her arms, he drew back to plant a reverent kiss on her forehead. "And you're everything I could have hoped for and more." The words hung on his lips. Even if she was right, he would never see it. He would never be one of them and no words could change that. After a lifetime of being told he was wrong, how could he believe her? "Come, let's go home before the rain gets worse."

The moment they reached the Brasshurst lawn, the heavens opened and rain poured over Folkesbury. As they held their hats to their heads and sprinted the rest of the way home, Eilian wondered what they would do now. Selfishly he hoped Hadley wouldn't try to make him go further tonight. After the funeral and the unwelcome sadness and fear of the future, all he wanted was to have dinner and settle into bed with his wife and a good book. While he admired Hadley's ambition and that she always had a plan or an item on her to-do list that needed her attention, tonight he hoped she would cuddle up with him in front of the fire instead. To feel the warmth of life was what he needed most.

Chapter Twenty-Five
The Lady in White

After shedding their soaked funeral attire and enjoying a feast of Turkish chicken and jasmine rice, the Sorrells retired to bed early. With a storm rattling the mullioned windows and the weight of mortality hanging in the air, Eilian removed his jacket and tie in silence. His eyes trailed to the dressing room door, knowing Hadley was just on the other side. What should he have felt when he saw her come out in only her nightgown and caftan with nothing more than a gossamer layer of cotton separating them? Another man's pulse—Nadir's probably— would have raced with anticipation while he stood there wondering if she would have been warmer in flannel. He had never understood why people railed against nude sculptures or ancient carvings crying that they were immoral. While he was studying them for technique, comparing them to what he knew of art history, and searching for symbolism, others were staring at them because— A grimace twisted his features at the possibility.

Cutting off his train of thought, Eilian quickly gathered his pajamas and robe. As he removed his shirt and trousers, he stared down at his chest where the skin had thickened in ropy scars or seared to form shiny patches of pink too glossy to be normal. He raised his prosthetic arm and felt his skin tug in protest. *If it hadn't happened, you never would have met her*, he reminded himself as the dressing room door squealed open and Hadley appeared in her bright red robe. Her light eyes slipped over his form, a smile gathering on her lips.

Standing behind him, she ran her hands over his firm shoulders before encircling his waist. She nuzzled his back. "Ready for bed? I don't know about you, but after today, all I want is a good night's sleep."

Eilian gave her a quick kiss as she walked back to their bed. Behind him, the coverlet sighed as she collapsed upon it and stretched into a yawn.

"I hate funerals. I've been to far too many in my life," she said, sinking into the blankets. "Are you coming?"

"In a minute. I'm just getting my book."

At the dresser, Eilian's eyes ran over the spines of his great-grandfather's journals, his gaze following the numbers undulating across their covers. He couldn't believe he was nearly at the end, counting down Laurence Sorrell's life in pages. Plucking the final book from the stack, he thumbed through on his way to the bed until he found where he had left off.

"Where are you at now?" she asked as he settled in beside her.

"His wife just died. Nash and my father aren't getting along. Big surprise."

"Ah, so soon you might find out why your father abandoned this place."

He nodded. "That's what I'm hoping."

As he slid lower and shifted until his body settled into the now familiar grooves of the old mattress, Hadley laid against his side with her head resting on his shoulder. Her calloused hands scratched across his stomach until she let out a drowsy breath and sighed into him. He smiled, wrapping his arm around her, even if it did make it harder to read.

She closed her eyes, and for a moment, he thought she had drifted to sleep, until she asked, "Did you ever find out how your grandfather died?"

"He drank himself to death when my father was ten. Jenny and my father permanently moved in with Laurence. Thank God I don't like brandy."

"Oh," she replied, her voice dropping with disappointment. From his flat reply, it was hard to tell whether he was ashamed or how she should respond. "It must be hard to read some of the entries. I don't know if I would want to know that much about my family. It must taint how you feel about them."

"I didn't think I would either, but reading this actually makes me feel better. It's the first time I have been able to connect with my family. Maybe it helps that I knew nothing to begin with, so it didn't change how I felt about anyone." Except his father, but in that case, he was hoping to find the man behind the tyrant. "I never held any illusions that my family was perfect. I was only interested because my father never said anything about them. He could have been raised by wolves for all I knew. Somehow, I thought we would have talked one day, but we never got around to it."

Hadley frowned. Even after six months, he was still grieving for the relationship he wished he had with his father. She paused, her finger lightly tapping his stomach as she decided if she should stray off topic and say what was on her mind, but she couldn't forget the way he squeezed his eyes and bowed against the pain.

"I was surprised to see how much the funeral affected you. I didn't think you had much affection for Mr. Nash."

"Nash was a miserable man *to us*," he said as he held up the book, "but to Laurence, he was his first grandchild. It's hard to reconcile the young boy tending to his grandmother to the man who berated us, but that's who he really was... before the world got to him. Then again, Nash was murdered, and while I can see how he could get on someone's bad side, he was family—the last one on my father's side. I would like to see whoever did it brought to justice, as unlikely as that is."

⚬⚬⚬ ⚬⚬⚬

Fire crackled in the grate at the foot of the bed. Hadley's body had gone lax against him hours ago, her arms limply outstretched across his stomach while her head weighed heavy on his shoulder. As he carefully turned the page, she let out a congested snore and squirmed against him before quieting once again. Eilian smiled and turned his attention back to the journal. This volume had been a bit of a disappointment compared to its predecessors. While it was still filled with sketchy caricatures of big-nosed people alongside drawings of plants and wildlife done with anatomical precision, the subjects of the entries had shifted from his family to the tourists coming to enjoy the summer shores. With his grandsons off attending Cambridge or spending weeks to months visiting other gentry in Bath or London, Laurence's attention had regrettably turned to the mundane.

Eilian sighed, skimming the gossip until he saw mention of a familiar name.

July 18th, 1856

Harland is apparently smitten with a young woman he met at the beach. One Millicent Holland, daughter of the Earl of Monmouth. She, her parents, and brother are in Dorset on holiday and staying in Poole. I had been wondering why my steamer and my stationary kept disappearing, but it appears that Harland has been using both to woo the young lady in question. I have to wonder what will happen when the Hollands go back to London. I fear my grandson will follow, and the house will finally be empty. Maybe I shall retire to the dower house. If

Harland marries, he and his bride should have the hall, but I'm getting ahead of myself, though I would like to see him settled as I am getting up there in years.

I'm not sure how I feel about the Hollands. The daughter passes well enough for pretty or at least fashionable and seems inoffensive. Her brother, the future Earl of Monmouth, is haughty and scornful, scoffing and scowling at Harland at every opportunity. It is probably his age as he is no more than seventeen. He reminds me of myself at that age.

Out of the lot, I think I like him best.

Eilian let out a snort. Well, at least he and Laurence felt the same about Uncle Malcolm. A smirk crossed his lips as he wondered if his great-grandfather had found young Malcolm handsome. He and his uncle were often mistaken for father and son. Maybe Laurence Sorrell would have liked him, too.

July 24th, 1856

The university's term can't start soon enough. Harland and Randall have been nearly coming to blows as of late. Since Randall left for Cambridge last year, he has been particularly snappish, especially toward Harland. In front of me they remain civil, but behind closed doors, I hear their voices raised in anger. I wish I knew what was going on, but—

Eilian eagerly turned the page only to find the back blank. He flipped it back and then forward again. Jolting upright, he thumbed through the journal for any loose pages that had been haphazardly stuffed in but found nothing. At his sudden movement, Hadley slumped off his shoulder, her blue eyes opening a crack as she watched him frantically shake the book before trying to pry apart the back cover.

With a grunt, she rolled over and tucked the pillow close to her head to block out the glow of the gas lamps and hearth.

"What's wrong?" she mumbled. "It isn't another break-in, is it?"

"Have you seen any more of these?"

She squinted through one eye at the book cover, barely legible in her hazy vision. "Hmm? No, why?"

"I think I'm missing one. Maybe I just misplaced it. Stay here, I will be right back."

Throwing off the covers, Eilian leapt out of bed and darted over to the dresser where his great-grandfather's journals sat in a row like careworn soldiers. In the mirror, he watched as Hadley reeled in the blanket and hugged it close against the chill of the waning fire. He turned back to ask her again if she had seen it, but by the time he did, her breathing had slowed to drowsy puffs and her arms once again laid limp ahead of her. With a small smile, he turned back to the diaries. As his eyes ran over the numbered spines, he counted off. All of them were there. Flipping to the last entry, he tried to recall the date he had seen scrawled in the family bible. No, his great-grandfather had lived for another four years after the last entry. There was no way the man stopped writing for no reason. He had to have misplaced one.

Without making a sound, Eilian shut the bedroom door behind him and quietly padded down the hall, slipping on his bathrobe as he followed the carpet-runner down the steps to the great hall. Standing on the rug before the hearth, he closed his eyes and felt the machine pulse beneath his bare feet. A wave of fatigue passed over him as the moonlight broke through the midnight fog and fell over him through the mullioned window. It had seemed like such a good idea to journey down to the hidden study to look for the missing journal, but with his hand on the spring that opened the paneling, he considered how easy it would be to turn back and settle into bed beside Hadley, to feel her body rise and fall with sighing snores. He didn't need the book. He wanted it, knowing that finding it would be the only thing to settle his mind.

He pushed down on the wall with a soft click and swallowed hard.

Maybe he wouldn't want to know what was in it. Maybe his father had done something terrible and Randall Nash could never forgive him. Maybe his great-grandfather had ultimately disowned him, and that's why he left Brasshurst Hall and never really discussed his childhood. No matter the result, Eilian had to know the truth.

The hidden door popped open beneath his palm. Switching on the lights, he ran his eyes over the shelves of ledgers one at a time, looking for anymore diaries, but among the rows of uniform black spines, it was obvious they weren't there. With a tired sigh, he dropped to his knees and crawled under the desk. A dull ache throbbed through his shoulder as he leaned forward on his prosthesis to get a better look. In the dim light, it was nearly impossible to make out anything beneath the heavy desk. He reached out with his real hand, feeling along the edges of the hidden shelf for the missing book, but when he withdrew his hand, he found it tangled with cobwebs and coated in dust. Ducking his head under the tabletop, he checked for hidden panels or false walls in the dark before backing out to check the drawers in case he overlooked the missing journal. He sifted through the piles of old letters and sketches, the thick paper stiff in his hand. It wasn't there. Eilian stood with his hands on his hips, surveying the room's few contents. Where else could it be hidden? His eyes brightened at the thought. *The library.*

He turned, ready to run down the hall to the other room, but he leapt back with a yelp. Standing in the doorway, blocking his entry to the parlor, was a figure shrouded in white. It stood so still he couldn't be sure if he was dreaming or if one of Brasshurst's ghosts had finally found him. His heart pounded as he backed into the edge of the desk, but when the creature tipped its gaze, he dissolved into laughter. Staring back at him from beneath the pale floral bedspread were his wife's blue eyes. Her red hair was plastered to the side of her face and gathered around her forehead in sweat-curled clumps.

"Had, you scared me half to death."

She gave him a dull, sleep-ringed glare. "I scared *you?* You scared me. I woke up and found the bed empty. After the break-in and murder, you decided it was a good idea to go strolling around the house. Do you realize how irresponsible that is?"

"I told you, but you were asleep. I'm missing one of the journals."

"So you decided to look for it at this hour?"

He opened his mouth but shut it without speaking. Controlling his impulsivity was not something he was particularly good at, especially when it involved something that interested him. "It sounded like a good idea at the time."

"You're ridiculous," she yawned. "Come on, let's go check the library."

"What?"

"You heard me. I know you will end up there anyway as soon as you think I'm asleep again, and I don't think I can sit upstairs waiting for you to come back. Let's go, I'm not staying up all night."

He smiled to himself as she gathered her blanket close and backed out. Shuffling past him, she disappeared down the hall and left him to shut up the old office. By the time he reached the library with its ever thrumming pulse, he found Hadley standing on a stepstool pulling books out of the glass cases one at a time to check their covers. In that moment, he loved her more than she could know.

Chapter Twenty-Six
Pretenses

From the corner of his eye, Nadir watched Leona with her embroidery hoop and needle in her lap. Her hand trembled, but she never stirred, as her mind was far away. She had sent Argus out in Nadir's steamer to the market, citing residual weakness that Nadir knew was long gone. Glancing down at his book again, he frowned. He missed the vibrant woman—the older cousin—he saw in those few days between her illness and Nash's murder. Now, she had been replaced by a Leona far more reserved and thoughtful than suited her age. Clearing his throat loudly, she finally looked up.

"Is there anything I can do for you? We could drive up to Poole, get you some new clothes or maybe some fabric for new drapes. I'm sure you could use them, and getting out of the house would do you some good."

She stared at him for a moment, her gaze drawn, and replied softly, "Thank you, Nadir darling, but I'm fine."

"You don't look it. You haven't been yourself in days, Lee. Now, I know something is wrong. Is it Argus? Did he say something unkind to you about your condition?"

"No."

"Is it Nash?" he asked as he sat beside her and pushed the embroidery hoop to the side.

Against her will, she winced, her eyes glistening before she could turn back to her work.

"It is, isn't it?" He reached out and gripped her arms, trying to catch her gaze. "Why won't you tell me? I thought you and I were becoming close, like before. We had been so dear to each other when we were children, like sister and brother, and now you've shut me out again." He shook his head, feeling the echoing ache from the bullet wound. "You didn't even tell me about Argus until you invited me to the wedding. Did I wrong you somehow?"

"My God, Nadir, that was five years ago!"

"It still stung! You were practically my sister—you still *are* my only sister—and you acted as if I didn't exist. You're the only family I have besides my parents."

"I've told you already, it was a very short engagement and not anything personal," she replied, her voice tight. "Anyway, you went to London to have your own life and I got married. What more do you think there is?"

"There has to be something. Why else would you marry so…so beneath you?"

A gasp escaped her lips before he could stop the thought, but he didn't regret saying it. She ripped her hands from his, and for a moment, he feared she would strike him. Instead, she glared at him and stabbed her needle into her project. Her eyes roamed over her cousin's face hoping to find the brightness of humor in his eyes but found cold confusion and hurt.

"How dare you say that about Argus! He is a lovely man and a devoted husband. He let you stay here with us, didn't he?"

"Argus would do whatever you told him. You will be lucky if he doesn't come back from the market with a handful of magic beans." Nadir braced himself for the slap he rightfully deserved as five years of holding his tongue tumbled out. "Honestly, I don't know what you saw in him. His family may have had money, but he certainly doesn't. Just look at this place. It's falling down around you!"

"Money may be a bit tight, but I certainly didn't marry beneath me. His family owns property and he has an inheritance." Her mind staggered, *had* an inheritance. Dropping her voice, she added, "If we're careful, it may last, but that isn't the worst problem for a marriage, is it?"

Nadir let out a bitter laugh. "It *may* last. Do you hear yourself, Leona? Our parents didn't come to England for us to live on mays and what-ifs. They wanted us to make something of ourselves, to do better than them. With your father's name and reputation, you could have married someone with a decent income and a brain in his head. It doesn't matter if Argus has a decent personality if he's a penniless dimwit. I know you do the books. I know he has no idea that you are running out of money and that one day he won't be able to live off his dead relatives. Does he even know how much he began with? Does he have no concept of money, too? I can't imagine either of you blew his inheritance on something foolish."

Leona's eyes narrowed as she shook her head. "He's a very sweet man. Maybe he is a little naive, but it's better than someone like you. You're always plotting, always suspicious of everyone else because you worry their motives are like your own."

"Plotting is how you get ahead, Leona." Nadir jumped up, looming over her with his hand on his hip. "You make plans. You don't sit on your duff and let the world take care of you, letting your wife write papers for you. What were you hoping to gain by that?"

"I only wrote it be—" Leona froze, her byzantine eyes wide. "Who told you I did that?"

"I'm not stupid. Anyone who knows you or Argus knows you wrote that paper for the Royal Egyptology Society. The man can barely read more than a few sentences of the newspaper at a time before he has to have a lie down." He put his hands up in defense at her accusatory finger. "It's through no fault of his own. I know he has problems, and I know for certain he could not and did not write that paper. What will you do if this scheme doesn't work and the money runs out?"

The words caught in Leona's throat, tension coiling around her tight-laced ribs until she could scarcely breathe. Nash had said that to her so many times, yet she still didn't know the answer. She threw her embroidery aside as she stood to face Nadir eye-to-eye. Her lips twisted and strained but no tears reached the surface.

Finally she yelled, "I don't bloody know. What do you expect me to say, Nadir? You're right, marrying Argus probably wasn't the wisest choice and I probably could have 'done better,' but I have to live with *my* choices now and deal with *my* problems. I'm doing the best I can to keep us afloat. Do you not see that?"

"Why didn't you go to your parents for help? They would do anything for you."

"How would that have looked?" She couldn't mention that her mother wanted nothing to do with her anymore. Her cousin couldn't know that.

Nadir's face softened as his lips parted to retort but fell into a sigh. "Why didn't you come to me, then? I would have given you money or loaned it to you without a word if you needed it. I can do it now. Just tell me— tell me how much it will take to spruce up the place or get you closer to buying another steamer."

"Nadir," Leona said, her resolve faltering at the sight of her cousin transforming from a pompous dandy back to the soft-curled boy she knew, "we are nowhere near being able to afford another steamer, even an old one, and we will probably only be able to afford Barnes for four more months. I can't ask you to help us get out of this hole; it will only drag you in with us. I have brought this on myself, and I must be the one to fix it."

"But why? Why are you punishing yourself?"

Her gaze swept over the floor as she walked to the front window, checking the road for any sign of the steamer. If she let him speak any longer, she would confess, and she couldn't lose anyone else.

Against her will, her voice rose in a tight cry, "I have done plenty you don't know about. I'm not the angel you take me for."

Picking up her skirts, she hurried out of the room, throwing the curtain back in her cousin's face.

He swatted the dusty drape away. "Then what is it?"

From the base of the steps, he watched her dart up the creaky treads and disappear. His feet stayed rooted in place while his hand wrapped around the newel post. Frustration and anger climbed up his limbs, squeezing until his teeth ground. All he wanted was to help her. It was all he had ever wanted. He released a trembling breath.

He yelled up, "You have been acting strange since Nash died. You can't tell me that there isn't some connection between the two of you. I know that he sent his maid to deliver notes to you. What was it? Did he help you with the paper?"

"Yes, are you satisfied now?"

"No, I'm not. People don't have clandestine meetings to work on a history paper!" He stopped with his foot on the step. "You think I did it, don't you?"

Leona appeared at the edge of her bedroom door, her head hung.

"You do! Leona, how could you think I killed him?"

"I don't think anything, but you were fighting with him, you went to confront him for me," she said, her voice trailing to barely more than a whisper. "I just hope it isn't true."

"Did you happen to forget that I was hit in the head and shot? When did I do it? When I was running for my life?" He took a step to follow her when a booming knock rang through the foyer. With a stiff huff, he turned and opened the door. "Argus, you oaf, how did you not bring a—"

His words dissolved as the officers surged through the door, ripping the knob from his hand and slamming him into the wall. The watercolor hanging over the hall table teetered and fell from its hook, shattering as they rammed him into the plaster. Pain rang through his skull as the world tipped and spun around him. Before he could catch his breath, they yanked his hands behind him and knocked him to the floor. Glass crunched and scratched through his waistcoat as the men pressed their knees into his back and forced his face into the carpet.

He squirmed, arching his back and throwing his weight only to have the constables twist his arms until tears seared his eyes and he feared his shoulder would dislocate. With a tink, his lucky bead dropped from his pocket, rolling toward the open door. Before it could reach the threshold, the sergeant's polished boot came down on it, crushing the ancient glass to dust.

"What are you doing?" he cried through clenched teeth. "Unhand me at once! I have done nothing wrong."

At the sounds of men and her cousin's frantic voice, Leona flew down the stairs. When she reached the bottom, Nadir turned his face away to keep her from seeing the fear and shame etched into his features. Cold metal encircled his hands as the men shackled him from behind and hauled him to his knees.

"What is the meaning of this?"

Sergeant Purcell continued, "Nadir Talbot, you are hereby under arrest for the murder of Randall Nash."

"What?" he and his cousin cried in unison.

"But he was shot, too! You saw it. He couldn't have done that to himself."

"That's for the court to decide, Mrs. Rhodes," he replied coolly. "He has an audience with the Justice of the Peace in a few days when he gets back from Weymouth. Until then, he will remain in our custody; to keep him from *fleeing* to foreign lands. You understand the risk."

The breath caught in Nadir's throat at the thought. Even after hours of questioning, he had never expected this. He had seen the murderer and was nearly killed, too, when the man shot at him, missing his brain by the width of his little finger. How could the man deny the wound near his temple that was still held together with thread or the peelings of invisible bells that only rang in his mind? Panic hammered through his heart.

"How?" Leona said, her voice high with fear. "On what evidence?"

"That's none of your concern."

One of the constables shoved him hard from behind, causing him to stumble forward and wrench his wrists against their manacles. Drawing in a tight breath, he caught his balance and carefully rose to his feet and finally to his full height. Nadir Talbot wouldn't leave the house cowering and stumbling like a common criminal. When Purcell reached for his arm, Nadir glared at him and tried to rip it from his iron grasp, but the man was too quick. The sergeant spitefully dragged him closer until his back collided with his gun holster. As he inhaled a mouthful of tangy, stale air, Nadir's body locked.

The possibilities of his incarceration became horribly clear. The noose dangled before him, the papers printed with headlines about the once-popular Egyptian novelist-turned-murderer being executed at Millbank. All of London would have his name on their lips but for all the wrong reasons. He had expected a scandal involving a nobleman's wife or daughter, but he had never expected this. With a forceful nudge from the constable's nightstick, Nadir took a halting step toward the door, avoiding Leona's tear-reddened eyes and ashen features for fear of reflecting his own.

"Nadir, what should I do?"

His eyes traveled between the stern-faced sergeant and his youngest underling, who looked from the sergeant and fellow constable to their captive as if unsure what to do. Sergeant Purcell glared at him, nodding toward the door, but Lyall kept his eyes on the cousins, refusing to move.

He swallowed hard against the knot in his throat. What could she do? No matter what he did Purcell would ensure he was found guilty. Nadir's voice caught as he uttered, "I don't know, but I didn't do it. You have to believe me, Lee."

"I know. I will figure something out, I promise."

As the policemen ushered him out the front door, he shut his eyes against the row of faces standing at the stone fence. Their eyes bored into him, stripping away what little resistance he had left. Upon seeing the grey police steamer, they had come to gawk, to see who would be hauled from the house. He wondered how many had hoped to see Leona handcuffed and head bowed.

What did they see when they looked at him being led from the house with a weapon pressed to his back and blood dripping from a cut on his cheek? In the eyes of those who didn't know him, he was nothing more than a criminal. A ruffian with shaggy hair and dark skin, a foreigner. Nothing he did mattered now. No facade, real or imagined, would convince them otherwise.

⚜ ⚜

Nadir tumbled forward, his hands and knees colliding hard with the rough slate of the jailhouse floor. Before he could stand, the iron door slammed behind him, reverberating through the dim, low room. Scrambling to his feet, Nadir grabbed the bars and pulled with all his strength, but the door barely rattled in its frame.

"Let me out! You have the wrong man!" he yelled, watching the three policemen disappear down the hall. "Purcell, I know what you're about, and it won't work. When my lawyer gets a hold of you, you won't have a cent to your name."

His body jerked as another door slammed, leaving him in silence. Nadir sank back. His stomach churned as he retreated from the bars. There was nothing left out there for him to pursue. No one would care. Drawing in a steadying breath, he turned to take in his prison cell.

It was worse than anything he had written. Rat droppings dotted the floor while the walls and corners were draped with spider webs. What little light came in through the filmed, barred panes above his head cast the room in a dingy haze. He ran his hands over his arms as a damp chill soaked through his shirt sleeves. They had stripped him of his jacket, his money, and his watch before dumping him into the cell. He had nothing left of his own. His heart thundered in his throat as he ran his eyes over the rickety metal cot with its disgusting, stained mattress. Drawing closer, he dared to hazard a sniff but drew back, immediately regretting it when he couldn't get the smell of thirty years of piss, sweat, and God knows what from his nostrils.

The impenetrable stone walls rose around him, snuffing out any delusions of returning to his old life. He glanced around for a place to sit but found nothing. Settling on the very edge of the filthy mattress, Nadir held his head in his hands and stared at the floor. This was real. He was trapped. Only a day before he had been strolling beside the earl and countess with a swing in his step, thinking of what he would do when he returned to London. He had even gotten a telegraph from his publisher saying that they loved his tenacious new heroine, that it was one of his best books to date. His hand curled into a fist. When word got to London that he was suspected of murdering a respected member of the gentry, how long would it take for them to terminate his contracts and throw his manuscript in the fire? Maybe someone would save it, add some salacious scenes to it, and publish it while he was in prison as some fictional addendum to his scandal.

He had been so careful. For half a decade, he had strategically chosen friends, seeking those who might take a shine to him and show him off to others. That's what they always did when they met Nadir Talbot. Their eyes would catch his motley outfits, studying the fine fabric and artful arrangement of line, before moving to his visage. He had been blessed with universally handsome features, straight white teeth and large eyes surrounded by long, dark lashes, made all the more appealing to his British friends by his noble nose and a wide mouth framed with full lips. Through the years, he had studied the exceptionals, the ones who pulled others along in their wake. By following their example, he cultivated his aloof charm and wit. Exclusive and haughty enough to fit in but just different enough to be a novelty that wouldn't be easily forgotten.

Nadir released a bitter laugh. What good had it done him? None of those men would flock to his side when he needed them. They were just like him: self-serving, driven, prideful. Having an acquaintance in jail wouldn't open any doors, and he would be swept under the rug as if he never existed. He was nothing more than an Egyptian trinket, like a mummy or bauble, and he had ignored and distanced himself from his family for what? For a few worthless acquaintances and a bit of notoriety. Nadir closed his eyes. Leona wasn't the only one who could have done better.

Chapter Twenty-Seven
The Earl & the Artificer

The morning sun trickled in through the gap in the heavy curtains, inching along the ancient planks before cutting across the bedspread. As his cheek grew hot, Eilian opened one eye and reached behind him with his prosthetic hand to grab his pocket watch. He brought it close, his eyes unfocused from sleep, but even as the numerals sharpened and fuzzed, he could make out that it was after ten. Dropping it back on the nightstand, he rolled over and buried his head into his pillow. At least Patrick had let them sleep. They had spent most of the night tearing apart the library searching for his great-grandfather's missing journal only to find that it wasn't there. By then, the clock was chiming four, and Patrick and the girls were already beginning to prep the fireplaces and their wardrobes for the day. The butler hadn't said a word when he saw them trudge out of the library empty-handed with only tired wrinkles around their eyes to show for their trouble. Eilian sighed, sinking deeper into the mattress's folds. The book had to be there somewhere. He would look later.

Keeping his eyes shut, Eilian inched his hand forward until his fingertips brushed against the warm, solid flesh of his wife's arm. He smiled. Hadley was still asleep. Careful not to disturb her, he slid closer until his prosthetic arm slipped under her side. He wrapped his other arm around her back and settled his head beside hers on the edge of the pillow, inhaling her familiar scent of cinnamon and cog-oil. Her breath came in gentle puffs only broken by the occasional deep sigh.

Leaning back a few inches, Eilian studied his wife. No matter how many times he awoke beside her, it still seemed odd to see her at rest. Her dark red hair clung to her cheeks as it had the previous night when she appeared in the study door, highlighting her strong jaw and soft cheeks. A dusting of freckles trailed across the bridge of her nose and reappeared on the caps of her shoulders and the swell of her breast where they became more diffuse until they were nearly invisible. Her lips, which were usually straight, had molded into a lax pout. If she hadn't been asleep, he would have lightly run his finger along them, tracing the soft curve of a cupid's bow.

A thought flashed through his mind. He swallowed hard and checked to make certain Hadley's breathing was coming in sleepy puffs. Through the coverlet, he could make out the planes and curves of her body. With a hesitant hand, he reached under the blanket and placed his palm on her side where it dipped in beneath her ribs. He waited, expecting her to stir, but she didn't move. Moving lower, he ran his hand along the firm, fleshy curve of her hip and thigh. It was warmer, softer than he had imagined. When she was awake, he had longed to become acquainted with her form as he would a statue, by touch and sight, but he had been too afraid to ask or act upon his whims. What if she wanted more when all he wanted was to observe? He had never touched or kissed anyone before Hadley, and it felt strange to want to do it and worse to say it aloud. Even thinking this way seemed foreign to him.

Pulling back again, he kept his eyes locked on her face and lightly rubbed the bare flesh of her upper arms. He skimmed his hand along her strong limbs, over the downy red hairs and slightly rough skin from years of working in her studio. With the edge of his hand, he followed the bend of her shoulders as they slid into her neck, feeling the flesh beneath his fingertips change inch by inch. It was times like this that he wished he had both arms. Then, he could close his eyes and burn the image of her form into his mind through touch, but now, he could only create half the picture. When he looked up from rubbing her neck, Hadley's light eyes were on his face and her mouth curled into a smile.

Eilian froze. He had expected her to get out of bed or give him a strange look for what he had done, but instead she held his hand in hers and pulled it close to her breast. Closing the gap between them, Hadley rested her forehead against his shoulder and shut her eyes. She intertwined her fingers with his and kept it close to her heart. He tensed at the warmth radiating from her body against his balled hand.

"Did I interrupt you?" she murmured drowsily.

He opened his mouth but the words dissolved on his lips as his cheeks burned. Clearing his throat, he whispered, "I'm sorry."

"For what?"

"For being presumptuous. I should have asked first."

Her grip on his hand tightened. "It's fine," she replied, her lips brushing against the rough stubble on his neck. "I told you I would be here if you ever wanted to try anything. I meant it."

Rising on her elbow, Hadley pressed her lips to his. His body arched, pressing against her stomach as his foot brushed against hers. Her hand ran through the wayward spikes of his hair while his clamped onto her back. When he began to tip back, she pushed against him, locking her arms around him. She landed on his chest as he rolled back with a smile. Lying on top of him, she kissed his forehead before planting a light kiss on each eyelid. Eilian closed his eyes and held her close. As she moved down his face, he caught her lips, drawing her in with a breath. His hands worked in slow circles over the gauzy fabric of her nightgown, never leaving her back. Swathes of gooseflesh rose over her arms and chest as his lips grazed hers and a soft slip of air blew against her cheek.

Hadley pulled back, licking her lips and inhaling the sandalwood of his skin. Pushing him too far would only make him retreat, but as she released her hold and sank against his chest once more, his arms cinched around her. He shifted beneath her until finally he let out a contented sigh. She smiled to herself. It hadn't been much, but in his vulnerable, sleep-addled state, Eilian had let his guard down enough to act on his curiosity. A faint pang of pride bloomed in her chest. At least he was making progress or trying to.

Resting her head over his heart, she said softly, "I want you to be comfortable with me, Eilian. I know it will take time."

"And I'm sorry about that. You probably never thought it would be this way."

"No, but I know you won't make me wait forever. I want you to know that I *want* you to come to me when curiosity strikes. Somehow, I doubt I will ever say no to you." She looked up in time to watch his eyes grow wide before turning thoughtful. "Do you understand what I'm saying, Eilian?"

"I do. It's just difficult though... to talk about it. I feel as if I shouldn't."

He swallowed hard. Speaking about it wasn't too difficult, but it left him with the fear of hurting her. Not saying how he felt meant eliminating that possibility. It felt impossible to talk of it though, especially when he lacked the words for how he felt. What *did* he feel? How could the absence of something be described when he had never felt the alternative?

His face reddened. "No one seems to speak frankly about these things. It feels odd to finally start."

"Yes, but I have seen the problems not speaking can cause. I don't want that to happen to us."

"What do you mean?"

"You know Adam and I weren't always on the best of terms. Recently, we have tried to talk more, and it works. We don't fight nearly as much."

"Really? What did you two—?"

245

Before he could finish, a knock came at the bedroom door.

"Your ladyship," Patrick called, "I hate to disturb you and his Lordship, but Mrs. Rhodes is here to speak to you."

She rolled off Eilian's chest and dramatically fell back on the mattress. "Can you ask her to come back later?"

"She seems quite distraught, madam. She says she will only speak to you."

Twisting her lips, Hadley lay with her arms crossed and stared at the gathered swags hanging above their heads. What did that woman want now? Eilian's hand wrapped around hers and gently squeezed until finally she released a tense breath.

"We had to get up some time," he whispered with a lopsided smile.

"Yes, but I had hoped it would be for a late breakfast."

"Your ladyship, what should I tell her?"

Hadley sat up and ran her fingers through her tangled hair. "Tell her I will be down shortly. Make an excuse for me, Patrick."

"Should I send up Charlotte to help you dress?"

"No, I will take care of it myself." As much as she liked her, the girl was too cautious when handling her gowns and hair and it took her twice as long to get dressed when she was around. "Eilian, can you help me?"

"Assemble my arm, and I will."

Sitting up, she picked the springs and leather pieces off the nightstand as her husband slid a clean cotton stocking up his arm. Without hesitation, she slipped on the couter and fed the spring muscles through the metal rings attached to it.

"What do you think Mrs. Rhodes is here for?"

She opened her mouth but then remembered he still didn't know who stole the Silphium. "I don't know, but it's probably nothing. I don't know what she could be upset about. Why?"

"I thought maybe you would want help."

"You don't have to stay while I deal with her. I will be fine."

He nodded as she affixed the final set of metal coils behind his elbow. "I was thinking of walking up to the dower house to see if

Laurence's journal ended up there. I imagine Nash walked off with them, along with a bottle of wine."

"I think I'm making out better then," Hadley replied with a smile as she hopped off the bed and dug through her dresser for clean drawers. "Dealing with Mrs. Nash is the last thing I would want to do."

"That makes two of us."

Eilian averted his gaze from his wife's form as she stepped out of her nightgown. A soft laugh escaped her lips, but he kept his eyes locked on the intricate weave of the Turkish rug.

"What's so funny?" he asked softly.

"That you still look away. I don't know whether to be insulted or flattered."

Eilian's cheeks burned. "It's rude to stare. Would you rather have me gawk at you?"

A wry smile crossed her lips as she lingered between shifts. "Sometimes."

Chapter Twenty-Eight
Obligations

Eilian poked his head out the backdoor of the servants' quarters. The rainstorm had ended in the early morning, leaving a film of hip-high fog and coating the countryside in a layer of varnish. The earl eyed his bicycle at the bottom of the steps. If he had been going anywhere else, he would have ridden his velocipede there without a care for how his trousers would look when he reached his destination, but he couldn't do that. Not today. Mrs. Nash would surely notice if the hems of his trousers were splattered with mud and flecked with bits of gravel. His grey eyes ran between the thick forest of yews and oaks surrounding the path and the bicycle. With a defeated sigh, he tucked it back into the house and shut the door behind him.

As he cut across the lawn to reach the dirt and stone path, he remembered that the steamer was parked in the old stables. He exhaled, watching his breath condense into a wil-o'-wisp. He could have taken it, but what if Hadley needed it or Patrick while he was gone? No, the steamer was better served at home. If he came rumbling up the drive, Mrs. Nash would see him coming and turn him away without even hearing what he had come for.

Gravel crunched beneath Eilian's boots as he followed the trail through his property. A small smile crossed his lips as he drew in a breath and tasted the scent of damp earth and wild flowers. Standing at the edge of the road, he looked back at the house. In the haze, he could make out Brasshurst's hulking form, complete with spires and bulbous glass protrusions. It still hadn't sunk in yet that the house and land was his. At any moment, it felt as if his father would appear to take control and send him back to Greenwich. Eilian's mind faltered before falling silent. That would never happen again.

Shaking off the thought, he continued on. As he rounded the corner of the copse that hid the family crypt, a familiar noise came from down the path. A steamer hurtled down the road, kicking up a hailstorm of gravel as it barreled toward him. Eilian staggered, his back colliding with the marble of the mausoleum. His hand slid against the slick, algal surface as he struggled to stay on his feet. He cried out as he fell to his knees, sinking into the top soil. Mud sprayed against his legs and hands as the cold air whooshed across his cheeks. Without looking back, the driver disappeared around the bend, fading away until all that was left was the faint chug of the engine and the stillness of its absence. Eilian's chest tightened as he stood on shaking legs. He clutched his remaining hand to his chest and counted his fingers to make sure they were all intact. The cab's wheels had been inches away from chopping off what digits he had left.

As he sunk onto the stone bench, his eyes trailed to the scholars and saints surrounding the mausoleum's portal, their all-seeing eyes nearly gone after centuries of rain and sea salt. Touching his signet ring, he let his head fall against the wall. Maybe someone was watching out for him after all. Listening for anymore rogue cabs, Eilian continued down the path toward the dower house. The moment the Georgian manor appeared through the trees, he knew something was amiss.

Where there had once been a walled flower bed stocked with wild flowers and lilies, there now was a smoking pit. Eilian looked for anyone who might stop him before hesitantly stepping closer and peeking inside. Amongst the wood and papers, piles of wool and charred linen appeared through the haze. Grabbing a branch from the garden, he prodded the smoldering pile and pulled out a man's shirt. The fabric had been all but eaten by the flames, but the sleeve was intact along with a few ribbons of the body. He dropped the shirt and poked around the ash. Spines of books and chunks of leather albums disintegrated at his touch. One lay intact against the edge of the stones. It was charred, but he recognized the book from when he intruded upon Nash in the back parlor. He hoped his great-grandfather's journal hadn't made it to the bonfire.

Eilian turned at the squeal of the front door opening behind him. He had expected to find Mrs. Nash glaring at him from the threshold, but instead, her slight lady's maid stood watching him with wide, grey eyes. Her face had paled even more than the last time he had seen her, and her face was drawn with fatigue. For the life of him, he couldn't remember her name.

"Is Mrs. Nash at home?"

"You just missed her, sir." The maid stared at her feet, her mouth tugged into a bitter line. "She's left for Poole."

"Do you know when she will return?"

"I don't know if she intends to return, sir. She left no word."

Disappointment settled over his shoulders, sinking him further into the mud as he stared up at the house's ivy-clad face. With an inward sigh, he turned, calling over his shoulder, "Thank you for your help, miss."

"Wait! Is there anything I can do for you? What did you need from the lady of the house?"

The maid had left the protection of the doorway and stood watching him, studying his open features as he faced her. He was nearly a foot taller than her, which wasn't unusual considering her short stature, but the urge to cower wasn't there as it was with most men and women. Her quick eyes flicked to the thick signet ring on his finger.

He was the kind lady's husband.

"You're the earl, aren't you? You're my master's cousin?"

He nodded. "Perhaps you can help me. If you don't think your mistress would mind."

"Even if she did, it's not as if she would know."

A smile crossed his lips as the maid wrung her hands and scowled. "I was hoping you could help me find something. It's a book."

"That may take a while."

•ઓ૭ ૭ઠ•

"It's right this way," the maid called over her shoulder.

She had led him deep into the house, far from the rooms he had seen during his first visit. The house didn't seem so large from the outside, but in the winding halls, it was easy to lose his bearings. Drawing an iron key from her apron, Pilcrow unlocked the door. It creaked open, washing the mahogany-paneled hall in sunlight. Eilian stood rooted in the door, his eyes wide as they ran over the endless piles of books and paper that littered Nash's private study. He had seen a glimpse of the mess when he snuck in to ask him about the silphium plant, but he had never thought it could be worse.

The room was stacked from table to ceiling with books. Some were placed neatly in the shelves as they should, but over the years a new row had sprouted in front and then on top of them. If there was space, a book had been crammed into it. In spare crevices too narrow for a book, papers jutted, yellowed and cracked from the sun. Sitting on every spare surface were notebooks filled with newspaper clippings and scraps of paper. Much like Laurence's journals, they were labeled by year and series number but appeared to be laid in no particular order. Eilian's chest tightened as he stepped into the rows of tables and shelves, the piles looming over him, threatening to fall in.

"Are you certain it's in here? I don't know how we could even begin to find it."

"Yes, sir. If it's something of his grandfather's you're looking for,

251

he wouldn't have kept it where others could find it."

Eilian cocked a brown brow.

"My master was a very private person."

Pilcrow watched from the door as the earl carefully walked between the narrow alleys to the desk and pulled out the drawers. With light fingers, he lifted the piles of paper, never looking at their contents. After making quick work of the desk, he moved to the nearest bookshelf, scanning the titles for what he was looking for. She wanted to help him, it seemed like the right thing to do, but she couldn't imagine laying a hand on her master's books and papers. A slap of pain rang through the top of her hand as she watched a stick come down over her knuckles. She massaged the sore bones. It had been years since it happened, yet she had never forgotten. *Don't you* ever *go through my things. Know your place, child.* She thought for sure he was going to fire her there and then, but he didn't. He scolded her, he hit her, then his eyes softened, and he went on like nothing was amiss.

She could never explain the Nashes behavior. His wife hated her most out of all yet kept her closest. He barely paid her any mind, but sometimes he would show her bits of his history in his grandfather's papers or some piece of embroidery his grandmother created. Each time it was done with a proud grin, as if he were passing something important onto her. Of course these history lessons were always done out of sight when, he knew his wife and the other servants were unlikely to walk in.

Her eyes landed on an oil painting of the manor's greenhouse hanging on the far wall. She was going to let the earl try to find it, but maybe she should just tell him where her master had hidden his special papers.

"I know I already asked, but will your mistress be cross with you for letting me in?"

"I suppose she might." The words hung on her lips. They still hadn't sunken in yet. "That is, if she were coming back."

The earl stopped pulling books from the shelves and turned to watch the little maid's thin lips nearly disappear into her face.

"Mrs. Nash won't be returning from Poole?" He shook his head. "She couldn't possibly have abandoned this place. She barely packed up. What did she take? Only her clothing?"

Pilcrow shifted uncomfortably. "Would you like any tea or refreshments while you look, your lordship?"

"No, thank you, but I would like it if you would tell me more about Mrs. Nash."

"I don't know what to tell you, sir. She's gone to Poole, and I don't know when she will be back."

"I understand that much," he replied as he set the books aside and drew closer, perching on the edge of a table. "She didn't tell you how long she thought she would be gone?"

She shook her head, her hands trembling as she stuffed them into her apron pockets. "No, sir."

"So you're out of a job now?"

"I don't know, sir. I'm the only one left."

"What happened to the others? Did she take them with her?"

With his lax posture and open features, she could nearly forget his station; he spoke to her like the butcher boy did. She made to speak but thought better of it. "I shouldn't bother you with my problems, sir."

"Don't worry about that; I asked you. Anyway, I like a bit of chatter while I look."

"Very well. If you insist, sir. They left not long after the funeral when she—," Pilcrow drew in a long breath, "when she said she would no longer need us. Well, most of us. She took the butler, I think."

"Why didn't you leave?"

"My mistress hadn't left yet. She fought with Mr. Nash all the time, always threatening to leave, but she never did. I thought she would back out this time, too. I didn't think she would leave me behind. I thought she needed me."

She stared out the tall window at the view of the forest filled with crooked trees. Pilcrow bit her lip and took a step toward the lamp where books sat stacked at its feet. Grabbing a handful, she shuffled the papers into a straight pile and carefully arranged the books by size. Slow boot-treads crossed the boards and lingered only an arm's length away. Whether it was an arm's length or a mile, it didn't matter. The gulf between them would never shorten.

"I hope you don't mind me prying, but what are you going to do now?"

Pilcrow kept her eyes and head down as she pulled a cloth from her apron and mopped the dusty tabletop.

"Did she give you a reference for when you look for employment? Did she at least tell you where she would be staying?"

She shook her head.

His voice sharpened with a tinge of anger meant for another. "Then how are you to get another job?"

"I wouldn't know, sir. I've never had to get one. I've worked here my whole life. I don't know how to go about it."

Her thin chest tightened as she raised her hand to her lips. She had said too much. Quickly apologizing, she excused herself and darted down the hall. Rounding the corner, she sunk into a niche that had once contained a vase she broke as an adolescent. After twenty years, it had never been replaced by another but served as the perfect hiding place for a maid who needed a moment of additional invisibility. Closing her eyes, she rested her head against the cool, damp plaster. What was she going to do? Now that she had said it aloud, it all seemed so hopeless. No one in town would take her in after she acted as Nash's messenger. At first, she had been curious about what her master had written, but upon seeing the volatile reactions of those she delivered them to and the weight of the coins and bills that came in reply, she made up her mind to never read them. She didn't think she could stomach knowing so many things people longed to keep hidden.

But why hadn't her mistress taken her with? Her throat tightened as her face and neck grew hot. How could she abandon her to fend for herself after a life spent only in the dower house and its grounds? Over twenty years should have been enough to prove her loyalty, to prove her skill. Maybe she really wasn't the model maid she took herself to be. Maybe she had only been kept on because her mother used to work for Nash's grandfather at Brasshurst. When push came to shove, familial loyalty would only carry her so far. Setting Mrs. Nash's hair, mending her dresses, writing her letters, succumbing to her abuse and rages, it all amounted to nothing in the end. With her master gone, there was nothing left for her.

"Excuse me," the earl's soft voice called beside her.

Pilcrow jumped, her back ramming into the wall as her eyes flew open to find the nobleman watching her. He quietly stepped out of the way to let her slip from the niche.

"I would like to propose a solution to your problem. You are under no obligation to accept, but my family deserted you and I want to make it right."

Her eyes searched his face. "Yes, sir?"

"My wife and I have only been married a few weeks, and she doesn't have any staff to speak of. She has been putting it off for a while, but she needs a lady's maid. Would you like to join us?"

She drew in a tight breath, trying to ignore her pulse thundering in her temple. "Thank you, your lordship, that's very kind of you, but I can find work on my own. You needn't feel obligated to help me."

Eilian frowned as the maid shifted her face into a tight grin and moved as if to walk away. "It isn't merely a sense of family obligation," he added, hoping she would turn. "We are in desperate need of a lady's maid. One of our chambermaid's has been trying to help out when she can, but her skills are limited. Lady Dorset has been mending her own gowns and setting her hair. With the lifestyle she will now be living in London, I don't quite know how we will manage without a proper lady's maid. That was your position, wasn't it?"

"Yes, sir."

"I thought we might have to go through an agency, but you never know who will turn up at your doorstep when you do that. It would be so much better to find someone who we know did a good job and who was only let go due to unforeseen circumstances. If Mrs. Nash returns, we will happily let you go back, but it would be a job for at least for now."

The words churned through her mind. Mrs. Nash had never been fond of her, but Lady Dorset had treated her like a person. That hadn't happened often. "Would I be coming with you when you return to London?"

"Of course."

Her light eyes brightened at the prospect of a fresh start. London was miles away. Anyone she ever brought a letter to would be nowhere in sight. She could finally go out when she had free time and not feel the cold stares of those who hated her for the task Nash made her perform. But doubt crept into the back of her mind. She had never been so far from Dorset before. Her whole life had been spent in Folkesbury, and London seemed so massive, so grand compared to what she was accustomed to. What if the other staff were better than her or more posh? It didn't matter. It would still be a fresh start.

"If you think it's best, your lordship, then I would be honored to serve her ladyship."

A wide smile spread across his cheeks. "It's settled then. Now, there's one condition to your employment."

"Sir?"

"You must help me find that journal."

Chapter Twenty-Nine
The Fall

In the alcove at the bottom of the steps, Hadley Sorrell collected herself. Drawing in a deep breath, she exhaled her frustration. She couldn't let Mrs. Rhodes see the petty anger in her eyes. How was she to know that her call was interrupting a lovely morning? Hadley smoothed a hair behind her ear and straightened her jacket before stepping into the great hall with a measured smile. Her guest stood with her back to her, her hand resting on the lion jutting from the hearth.

"Mrs. Rhodes, to what do I—"

The voice died in her throat as Leona turned. Her eyes were puffy and rimmed in red. Upon seeing the noblewoman enter, she sucked in a breath and bit back her tears. Hadley paused at the sight. Nadir Talbot's cousin, for all of her cultivated airs in public, had seemed so strong and put together that for a moment she wondered if Patrick had been mistaken about who was there. She had heard what had happened at Nash's funeral service, but she hadn't been able to reconcile the two women she knew. A few strands of black hair had come loose from her bun and hung across her full cheeks. With emotion brimming behind her eyes and her blue taffeta dress, she could have been a Renaissance Madonna.

"What's going on? What happened?" Hadley asked, crossing the room.

Leona Rhodes cleared her throat and straightened her spine as she met Lady Dorset's concerned gaze. Her voice came pinched and low when she said, "It's Nadir. He's been arrested."

"For what?"

"What do you think? For Murder."

"Murder? But how? That doesn't make any sense," Hadley sputtered, her mind reeling.

Leona left her place at the hearth and stared the countess down with tears in her eyes. "It doesn't have to make sense. Purcell came and arrested him all the same."

"But someone shot him! Is the man insane or does this town hire imbeciles?"

"Purcell doesn't care who really did it. He has Nadir, and that's all that matters."

Shaking her head, Hadley looked over her shoulder to confirm her coat was hanging near the door. "We need to do something. Have you spoken to the police? Do you know when the magistrate will be here?"

"Purcell said the trial would begin in a few days, but when I tried to speak to them again, they shut me out. They won't let me speak to Purcell or even see Nadir. I sent telegraphs to a few names I found in his datebook, but no one has sent a reply. I don't know what else to do." Her lips blanched as she bit them and closed her eyes. "I don't have enough money to afford a lawyer for him, and without speaking to him, I don't know who else to contact."

"You think *I* do?"

"Lady Dorset, you and your husband are the only ones in town who know for certain my cousin is innocent. Isn't there someone in London you could telegraph? Someone you could contact who would be willing to help him?"

She met Leona's eyes, red and sore with desperation. If it had been her brother sitting in jail, she would have done the same, but she knew no one of value. "I will see what I can do. My cousin and her husband move in circles with law enforcement. They might know someone. I will telegraph them, but right now, we need to go to that jail. Grab your coat, Mrs. Rhodes."

Dabbing her eyes with her handkerchief, Leona shook her head. "I don't think I can do it again. I keep picturing Nadir in there and—"

Leona faltered, her face clenching against the emotion welling threatening to spew out. Releasing a frustrated sigh, Hadley wrapped her arm around the woman's shoulders and steered her toward the door.

"Now is not the time to fall to pieces, Mrs. Rhodes," Hadley said as she pulled the bell for Patrick and handed the other woman her coat.

Mrs. Rhodes drew in a ragged breath but resolutely pressed her lips together.

"Your cousin needs you. Have a cry later once this is all sorted, but for now, we must fight."

⁘⁘⁘

Leaving Mrs. Rhodes safely deposited on her own sofa with a fire in the grate, Hadley sat in the idling steamer. Parked in front of the tea house, she inhaled the sweet, warm aroma of scones and tarts as Patrick looked down the road at her destination before turning back to his employer with a weary frown.

"Are you sure you don't want me to accompany you, your ladyship?"

"No, Pat. The less people involved the better." The image of Eilian's butler handcuffed and thrown into a cell flashed before her eyes. She couldn't let that happen. Dipping her hand into her clutch, she withdrew her derringer. "Hold this while I'm gone. If I don't come back in half an hour, go to Poole and get the authorities."

Patrick's eyes widened as she dropped it into his palm. He stared at it, holding it at arm's length before placing it gingerly on the seat beside him. Before he could ask her why he would need to fetch the authorities, she was out the door and walking toward the police station. She held her head high, fighting the stiffness in her neck and back that might alert the men inside to her true motive. At the haberdashery windows, she stopped, using the reflection to watch the two constables across the street through the windows of the old Georgian building. Purcell was nowhere in sight. Narrowly avoiding an ambling steamer cart, she crossed the road and slipped inside.

"Lovely weather, isn't it?" she said as the two constables' eyes locked onto her.

Constable Lyall flashed a smile and gave her a shallow bow from his table.

"May we help you, your ladyship?" Constable Osgood asked flatly from the front desk, his brows furrowed.

"I hope so." Removing her gloves and leaning against the tall desk, she sighed. "Is Sergeant Purcell in?"

"No, he's in Poole."

She smiled inwardly at her luck. "Oh, what a pity. I wanted to ask him if he had any news about Mr. Nash's murder. Lord Dorset and I will be leaving town in a few days, and we were so hoping to have it all sorted before we left."

"We arrested the murderer this morning, ma'am," Lyall piped up from the back corner. "The magistrate will take care of him by the end of next week. What a coincidence that you stopped by today."

"Yes, that is quite a coincidence," the other constable murmured.

"Really? Who is it? I hope it wasn't anyone from around here. That would mean the murderer was probably at my party."

"You're right, ma'am, he was at the party. It's Mr. Talbot."

"Mr. Talbot? But how? There has to be a misunderstanding. Mr. Talbot seemed so nice."

"You never know with some people. I saw them fighting not long before, too."

"Would it be possible to speak with him? I should really like—"

"Nice try, Lady Dorset. I know you and Talbot are friends," Osgood said, straightening behind the desk as he glared at her.

"I can't speak with him for just a moment?"

"No. Lyall, show her ladyship out."

Dropping the act, Hadley waited for the lanky young man to unwrap his legs from the stool and bound over to her. Fighting back would only get her a cell beside Nadir. The constable slipped his arm into hers and gently led her out the door.

"I'm sorry, ma'am, but the Sergeant said not to let anyone speak to Mr. Talbot."

"But why?" she asked as Lyall's head swiveled up and down the street, stopping when he noticed her steamer.

He shrugged. "I'm just following orders. Oh, my wife wanted me to tell you how much she enjoyed your party."

Hadley stopped so quickly Lyall nearly ran into her. "But that doesn't make sense."

"I know Mrs. Rhodes fainted and all, but—"

"No, not that. I mean, arresting Nadir Talbot."

"How do you figure, ma'am? He was the last one to see Mr. Nash, and you found him near the body."

"Yes, but he had been shot in the head. Someone tried to kill him, too."

"The sergeant thinks that was self-inflicted. Mr. Talbot's a clever one. He probably did it to throw us off."

"But where did he get the gun and where did it go? You didn't find one on him or in the orangery, did you? How could he have shot himself without a gun? You should ask your sergeant about that before you toy with a man's life." As the constable puzzled over the gun problem, Hadley patted his arm and extricated herself from his loose grasp. "If you will excuse me, constable, I need to send a telegraph. Let the sergeant know that I will be finding a suitable lawyer for Nadir Talbot and contacting Scotland Yard."

ഛ

Hadley drew in a deep breath. If she was to deal with Leona Rhodes again, she would need all of the composure she could muster. When she stepped through the careworn curtain, the woman's dark eyes locked onto her, pleading for an answer. Shaking her head, Hadley settled into the seat opposite Mrs. Rhodes. Her lip quivered, but she quickly bit down on it and turned back to her needlepoint before the tears could work free.

"I contacted my cousin in London. She or her husband should know someone. They should send a reply by tomorrow. I'm sorry I couldn't do more for Nadir, Mrs. Rhodes, but they turned me out as well."

"Thank you for at least trying, Lady Dorset. I don't know how we can repay you."

Hadley paused, the words hanging on her lips, unable to be ignored. "I would like you to tell me the whole story. Then, we will be even."

Leona froze, her heart thundering in her ears. Catching herself, she shook her head and replied, "What do you mean? I told you about the silphium."

"I think there's more to it. Nadir told me that the reason he was in the orangery the night of the murder was because he received a letter from Mr. Nash. I think the letter was meant for you, not him. I think Nadir suspected something as well and tried to protect you. If I am to help him, I want to know from what."

"What if I don't tell you?"

"Then, I will go to the police and tell them you know more than you're letting on. If Purcell won't listen, I will speak to the police in Poole."

"But I didn't kill Randall! What happened didn't cause that."

"How do I know that your cousin isn't sacrificing himself for you? How do I know you weren't there, hiding in the orangery waiting for him? What I do know is that Nadir Talbot didn't murder Mr. Nash while *you* have been behaving strangely. It has to be something grave if you aren't willing to divulge it to save your cousin."

"Even if I did, it wouldn't matter," she cried. "Purcell's mind is made up."

Leona looked up from her lap to see the countess staring at her, waiting. The only one who knew was dead. There had been so many times she felt the words on her lips, but at the thought of Nadir abandoning her for good, she stayed silent. Every choice had been hers to make. Any shame she felt came from another's cold glare or reprobation. Soon, Lady Dorset would pack up and leave for London, and any additional scorn she felt would leave with her.

"If I tell you, you have to promise not to tell anyone else. No one else needs to know. In the end, it won't help Nadir either."

"We don't know that."

"I do," she snapped. "Do you *promise* to keep this between us?"

"I promise."

"Come, we will discuss it in the study."

Mrs. Rhodes led her into the next room without ever looking back at the younger woman trailing behind. Motioning for Hadley to sit at Argus's desk, Leona shut the door and leaned against it as if she feared it would be thrown open at any moment.

"What I'm about to say can't leave this room. My husband can never know." Drawing in a deep breath, Leona steeled herself against what she was about to say. It had gone on for years, but to say it, was to acknowledge all of her wrongs. "Randall— Randall Nash and I were involved."

Hadley cringed. "You were having an affair?"

"Yes," she replied, gauging the redhead's reaction, "but you didn't know him like I did. He didn't treat me like he did the others."

"It's not just that. The age difference alone—"

"I know. He was *much* older, especially when we met, and married, but he never loved his wife. He had been pressured into marrying her. You wouldn't understand. It's never happened to you."

"But you would know? Surely you and Argus…?"

Leona shook her head, a few loose black curls breaking from her coiffure. "You must understand, Lady Dorset, Argus is a sweet, kind man, but we have nothing in common. He has no ambition or drive. Randall wasn't like that. He returned to Folkesbury when I was barely seventeen. I went to him because I heard he had gone to Cambridge and I wanted to learn Latin and Greek, so I could read the classics like Nadir. My parents wouldn't pay for a tutor to teach me. When I asked him, he tossed me out, yelling that he wasn't the schoolmaster, but I kept coming back, poorly reciting the phrases I had taught myself, and he relented.

"At first, he really did teach me Latin and Greek, but things progressed until it was beyond our control. I knew they wouldn't approve of him teaching me, so I would tell my parents I was visiting my friend for tea. We met at the dower house when his wife was at her meeting, but as we became closer, he started bringing me to Brasshurst Hall. The house had been boarded up since his grandfather's death, so we would go through the old aqueducts as not to draw attention. He loved that house. We spent many a happy day there." She let out a dry chuckle. "It must sound foolish to you, a young woman ruining herself with a married man twice her age."

Keeping her voice level despite the knot growing in her chest, Hadley said softly, "He seduced you. He should have known better."

"There was no seduction. His wife was a shrew, and my parents' control and heritage ensured that I had no suitors. I was never so foolish as to expect him to leave his wife or that we would ever be anything more than lovers, but he made me feel pretty and smart, which was all I ever wanted." She smiled. "He made me feel like I was worth something."

Leona's eyes softened as she pictured Nash's face fifteen years younger when they would lay across the orangery's mosaic floor among the cut-glass crustaceans and cephalopods. The cool damp of the tiles soaked into her bare back as she gazed up at the leafy palms soaring high above them, the sun's rays warm across her cheeks and arms. Without looking, she knew Randall would be no more than an arm's length away watching her. Those sharp, grey eyes drank her in, and she willingly gave herself over to them.

"And Nadir didn't know?"

She shook her head, pacing back to the door to listen for any signs of her husband on the other side. "He was long gone by then at boarding school. When he did return, I made sure to cover my tracks better. We went on like that for years. Every few days I would visit 'my friend.' Then, my parents found out. I don't know how they knew, but I think Rubella finally had enough and decided to get her husband back once and for all. Later, I found out I wasn't the first of his trysts, but I was the last."

"What happened?"

"My parents reacted as you would expect. I was practically banished from society. They hated me. They hated Nash. Even if they never caught us in the act, I was soiled. If he had been some young cad, they would have simply forced him to marry me, but they couldn't. Instead, they found the next best thing: a young naive man with an inheritance who would never notice that his bride was soiled." Leona bit her lip and sucked in a sharp breath. "When Argus arrived in town, they found their solution. He knew nothing of my history or of Nash's. By then, rumors had begun to circulate. My father spoke to Argus, and suddenly, we were courting and engaged. Please make no mistake, Lady Dorset, Argus is the best person I could have married under the circumstances and he is a good man, but it's not what I wanted."

Hadley sat rooted at Argus's desk. Her heart echoed through her chest, and when she went to speak, she found the moisture had evaporated from her mouth. "What did Nash do?"

"After we were discovered, he left to escape the scandal and lived in France with his wife. I didn't see him for nearly five years. I thought I would never see him again, but then, last year he turned up out of the blue."

She had rounded the corner with a basket of groceries hanging on her arm when she looked up and saw him standing in front of the post office. He was older, the lines of his face deeper and the color had finally leeched from his hair, but his eyes were the same. They pinned her where she stood. For a long moment, they simply stared until inch by inch the crowd carried them closer and the questions and lost history poured out. In an instant, it was as if no time had passed.

"I didn't intend for it to happen again. I hadn't realized how much I missed him, how alone I really was, and apparently his feelings never changed. My parents had left for Alexandria, though they stopped speaking to me long before that, and Nadir was in London. I had my chance, and I took it." A faint smile crossed her lips as she stared into the empty hearth. When she turned back to the countess, her eyes burned with waiting tears. "Now, he's gone."

"The child was his, wasn't it? That's why you needed the silphium."

Leona nodded.

"But if you loved him, why did you get rid of it?"

"I panicked. We had gotten away with it for so many years only to have that happen." For a second, she locked eyes with her reflection in the mirror above the fireplace, barely recognizing the woman before her. Refocusing, she looked past herself to Lady Dorset. "When I realized what had happened, I went to him. I knew it could only be his and that he still wouldn't leave Rubella. He said he wouldn't do it, that it would create a scandal. I didn't expect him to, but I wanted for him to either help me leave Argus or take care of his child. Despite all of the money he extorted from others, he wouldn't help me. He wouldn't even give me the silphium, so I stopped seeing him.

"You were right though, I loved him, but he forced my hand. For all these years, he had used me. Why else would he refuse to help me and his child? When I ignored him, he started sending notes with his maid begging me to meet him. He even tried to blackmail me. What could he have taken? I mean, just look at this place," she said gesturing toward the cracks in the ceiling and the faded wallpaper. "We already had to sell the steamer and fire the cook and maids. If he exposed me, he exposed himself, and he had much more to lose than I did. I told him so, but he wouldn't relent. All I had left to use was his precious silphium. He had to have known what it did, and he still wouldn't give it to me."

"He wanted you to have his child," Hadley replied, the words rushing out the moment they formed in her mind.

"I realized that after a while, but don't you see? I couldn't do that and still live here. I would have loved our child, but I couldn't let Argus go on thinking it was his. That's why I wanted Randall's help. He could have put me up in a little house or apartment somewhere that I could be anonymous. I could raise the baby, and he could come visit once in a while. As long as I had his support, I could have done it." She closed her eyes, banishing the thought with a scoff. "Foolish fantasies. In the end, I knew I wouldn't be able to live with myself if I had to pretend Argus was the father, that we were a happy family."

"Would he have known the difference?"

"No, but I would. I would be constantly reminded of my missteps. What if the child had his eyes? Everyone would know. There was no other way for me to have some semblance of a normal life except to rid myself of all traces of Randall once and for all. That's how it was with him. All or nothing."

"Did you tell him what you were planning to do?"

She shook her head. "Not about the silphium. He knew I wanted it and still did nothing. After what he did to me, he didn't deserve to have it."

"I saw the look on his face when you collapsed at the party. He knew what you had done."

"Good, I wanted him to. I wanted him to feel the sting of loss, to have him understand that his actions had consequences and that for once he shouldn't have only thought of his own well-being. Unfortunately, Nadir saw him, too. I still don't think he's put it all together, but he realized Randall and I were involved somehow. While I was recovering, Randall came to visit me and Nadir scared him off. I never got to speak to him again."

Hadley's eyes brightened with clarity. "Nadir said he snuck into the orangery because he received a letter from Nash. It *was* yours."

"Yes, but I don't know how he got it. When Dr. Sturgis brought him back to us bandaged and drugged with morphine, I knew what Nadir had done. The letter was right on his desk." She drew in a wet breath and squeezed her eyes and lips shut. "I burned it. I was so afraid he had killed him. I still don't know how he knew where to go; Randall never said. If it hadn't been for the wound, I would have thought my own cousin guilty. Who else would want to kill him?"

Hadley could think of a few and the countless others who had been victims of his extortion. There had been times when she was tempted to draw her gun.

Pushing away from the desk, Hadley stood at Leona's side as she covered her face. Hadley gently patted the dark-haired woman's shoulder. Everything was so much clearer. Nash's pallor when she hemorrhaged at the party, Nadir sneaking into the orangery, her strange behavior at the funeral. No one else had been so overcome with emotion, not even Mrs. Nash.

"First, I lost Randall. Now, I'm going to lose Nadir, too."

"No, you won't. Not if I have any say in the matter. As soon as I hear from my cousin, I will go back to the police."

"I'm surprised to hear you say that. After hearing my sordid story, I'm amazed you even want to associate with me. Anyone else would think me a whore or worse. What *do* you think of me?"

What did she think? What if she had met Eilian after he had become engaged or married to a woman of his parents' choosing? She would have liked to imagine that she would have been virtuous, that she would have ignored any feelings she had for him and gone back to her lonely life. When she first realized Eilian had feelings for her, she had braced herself for the possibility that he might not want to marry her, but under different circumstances, could she have been his mistress? Knowing him and what being a mistress entailed, she couldn't imagine it, but if he had been a different man with different needs, would she have allowed herself to be drawn into that role?

"I can't say. I have never been in your situation, Mrs. Rhodes. If I loved someone very much and they happened to be married, I don't know what I would have done. It's possible that I would have done the same, especially if they were in a loveless marriage. It isn't right, but it happens. Men do it all the time with little guilt." Hadley watched Leona dab at her eyes and steady her breathing. When she seemed to finally compose herself, she asked, "Do you regret what you did?"

"Which part?"

"Any of it."

"No," she replied, keeping her face lax despite the well of pain rising behind her eyes, "I loved Randall. I will never get that back, and I doubt I will ever love another the way I loved him. Without experiencing that, I don't know where I would be now or who I would be." Leona looked up to see the countess watching her with a puzzled look. "You must think it strange to hear me say that after all you have heard. You must understand that Randall and I had a long history together. The tumult of two months can't erase the decades of my life I love the most. My time spent with Randall Nash was some of the best, no matter how brief or covert. I like to think that if circumstances had been different, we could have had a good life together."

The two women stood in silence. Hadley didn't want to leave and have Mrs. Rhodes believe she was fleeing her sins. Even if she wanted to, the shock and guilt from forcing her to reveal what she had done weighed heavily on Hadley's conscience. It was not her secret to know. She knew how easy it could be to fall into the trap of mistresshood. If Leona hadn't been married to Argus, she could have had more freedom than most married or widowed women. She could have worked, had a lover, and possibly even a marriage, if she chose. It was what men had done for centuries with little retribution.

"I'm very sorry this had to happen to you and to Mr. Nash. I didn't know him the way you did, but he seemed to have cared a great deal for you. You must have other things to attend to, Mrs. Rhodes, so I will be on my way. I'm sorry if I caused you any pain; that wasn't my intention."

"I know," Leona replied softly as she reached for the door.

The door swung back to reveal Argus's broad face. He stared at the women within with pleading eyes, his head shaking in time with his mutely working mouth.

"Is it true?" he finally wheezed.

The air squeezed from Hadley's lungs as Leona held his gaze, unable to speak but free of pain or remorse. With a final nod of her head, he slowly turned and retreated down the hall. Hadley took a step forward, but Leona's hand locked around her arm.

"Let him go. It's what I deserve."

Chapter Thirty
His Eyes

It was dark by the time Hadley arrived back at Brasshurst. The warm spring rain lapped against the panes of the great hall, casting the room in curious shadows and creating a steady din within the ancient walls. Water dripped from her hair and ran down her neck where it was wicked up by her sodden dress. She had lingered on the beach too long. Sitting against the rocks, she had stared out at the boats tossed by the angry waves rolling in with the storm. They clawed at the sand, tearing shells and bits of sea glass from the shore. Wind whipped her hat until she pulled it off and let the sea spray tear the pins from her hair.

For hours, she turned Leona Rhodes's story over in her mind. She and Nash had been lovers. Part of her was appalled that she had betrayed the docile man she married on so many fronts. Maybe if Argus had been cruel and Nash had been a handsome young suitor, things would have ended differently. The other part of her understood that it was impossible to control attraction. Leona didn't have to act on her

271

feelings, but she did. Knowing that what happened with Nash hadn't been a transient infatuation somehow made it easier to stomach yet harder to imagine. Now, the man Mrs. Rhodes loved was dead along with what could have been their child, and her husband had left when he learned the truth. That had been Hadley's fault. What would Leona do now, especially if Nadir was convicted?

By the time she had given up on sorting through her thoughts, the air had grown heavy with rain and her teeth were coated in salt. Walking through the cobbled streets that soon dissolved into white gravel, Hadley wondered if she had made the right decision in pressing Mrs. Rhodes to tell her more. The woman had been right when she said it wouldn't help Nadir. Hadley's curiosity had ruined a marriage and left her with only the hollowness of shame.

"You're home!" Eilian called behind her as she pushed open the door.

When she turned to see Eilian approaching with his arms wide, her eyes lit up despite herself. Her husband's arms closed around her, pulling her to his chest. He planted a kiss on her forehead as his arms cinched around her. Hadley shut her eyes, burying her face deep into the folds of his shirt and jacket. The warmth of his body against hers and the pressure of his arms against her back were what she needed most.

"Had, you're soaked to the bone," he said, pulling back and gently wiping her cheeks with his sleeve. "What happened? I thought you took the steamer, but then, I came home to find Pat setting up for dinner without you."

"I did, but I stayed too long at the beach. I needed a bit of time to myself, so I sent Patrick home. You understand."

As Eilian stepped back, still holding her by the arms, he finally saw her face. In his excitement, he hadn't noticed the tired sag of her eyes or the heaviness in her countenance. "What happened?"

I botched it.

Hadley smoothed her hair and dress as she bit her lip. Before she could continue, Eilian wrapped his arm around her shoulders and steered her toward the great hall's stairs. Passing Pilcrow where she leaned into the shadows between the tapestries and woodwork, he motioned for her to follow them. She silently padded ten feet behind them, the countess none the wiser of her husband's new hire. At the bedroom door, the wisp of a maid slipped into the dressing room out of sight.

"Here, let me help you, Had."

It took little coaxing to get her into the cushioned chair in front of the vanity. Her eyes darted from her reflection when it fell across the dark circles rimming her eyes and her bedraggled hair, which hung in limp, soggy locks. She couldn't bear to look at herself. When she finally raised her eyes, she caught her husband smiling behind her as he carefully pulled out the pins that had once held her hat. Putting them aside, he removed her hair pins, dropping them in her palm beside the others.

"So how was your day?" she replied when he began unhooking the buttons running the length of her neck. Closing her eyes, she savored the sensation of his fingertips skimming her neck and the hitch of her breath when the cold pearls brushed her skin. "I hope it was better than mine."

"I went to the dower house. I was able to find the journals that were—"

A soft knock sounded on the other side of the bedroom door. Thinking it was Patrick, Hadley called for the visitor to come in. Upon noticing the countess at the vanity, the maid's colorless face brightened with a wide grin.

"I'll have your dress ready in a few minutes, m'lady. I just wanted to see if you needed anything."

Hadley's eyes flicked between her husband and Pilcrow. "No, thank you."

When the door clicked shut behind her, Hadley turned to Eilian with a questioning look.

He shifted uncomfortably, resting his hands on her shoulders. "I was about to get to that. I found the journals... and Pilcrow at the dower house."

"Why is she tending to my clothes? I thought she worked for Mrs. Nash."

"Mrs. Nash has packed her things and gone to Poole without her servants."

"Are you joking?"

"No, all of the other servants left." He dropped his voice. "It didn't seem right to leave her behind. Poor thing didn't know what to do with herself. She's never worked anywhere else, and I thought you might need someone to help you get dressed and mend your clothing. I know you aren't thrilled with Charlotte."

She released a snort as she slipped from his loose grip and began tugging the dress from her shoulders. "I can dress myself. I have been doing it my entire life."

"I know, but having her tend to your clothes and hair when you go out is one less thing for you to worry about, which would mean more time to work on your projects. You would also free-up Charlotte and let her resume her usual duties."

Stepping out of her wet dress, Hadley rubbed her arms and slipped on her robe. She stood at the hearth, watching her husband regard her with a lopsided frown. Having a lady's maid to do her hair or pick her clothing meant something. It was another long step from her old life where she relied on no one but herself. In marrying Eilian, she had gained the freedom that comes with being a married woman of class and standing, but she had lost her anonymity and the ability to say she did it all on her own. No longer was she merely a craftswoman. Her products no longer spoke for her. Instead, her person came with a name, a vision of what the Countess of Dorset ought to be, and a congregation of helpers. Since her mother died nearly a decade ago, she had prided herself in being the one to get it all done with as little help from others as possible.

As if reading her mind, Eilian said, "I have Patrick to help me with my things. I didn't mean to spring it on you. I thought she would be a help. We could always have this be on a trial basis. If it doesn't work out, she can join the other girls as chambermaids."

"That would be a demotion," Hadley replied, keeping her voice low so the maid couldn't hear her through the wall.

"It's better than no job and no references."

Hadley rubbed her temples. "I'm not going to turn her out if that's what you're worried about. I'm not as cruel as Mrs. Nash. I know what it's like to not know where your pay will come from." Drawing in a tight breath, she sat on the edge of the bed and listened to the rain patter against the mullioned panes. If she closed her eyes, she swore she could hear the waves lapping beneath the soft snapping of the fire in the grate. "Tell me more about your day. I want to forget mine."

The question hung on his lips, but from her dour expression and her peevish plucking of the quilt, it was obvious that she didn't want to talk about it. When she was ready, the story would pour out.

In the most cheerful voice he could muster, he began, "Well, I found the journals. Nash hid them in a nook in his study behind a painting of the orangery. It seemed funny at the time that he should put them there since he was always popping up in it until I remembered the murder. Anyway, there was also a jar of dried silphium seeds. I'm hoping I can plant them in Greenwich, and give some to a few botanists I know. Pilcrow was actually the one to find—"

He stopped, watching as Hadley bit her lip and stared at the bare planks of the floor. Her nails dug into her arm to staunch the tide of emotion collecting behind her lower lids. Eilian had only seen her cry twice before they came to Brasshurst, once in the desert and once when she called off their engagement, and after the latter happened, he could never erase the image from his mind. Seeing her so vulnerable still startled him. Dropping to his knees beside her, he held her hands in his and tried to catch her downcast gaze. She clamped her lips shut against the hiccupped sobs even as her body rocked in protest.

"Hadley, what is the matter? Please tell me. Was it something I did?"

She shook her head, her breathing coming in tight squeaks. Raising her eyes to meet his, she swallowed against the lump in her throat. His expression was soft with concern as he searched her face for some hint of what had occurred. Her eyes burned. She knew saying it would unleash every thought she had tried to suppress. All she could see was Mr. Rhodes with his eyes full of hurt, before he disappeared out the front door. The pain he must have felt.

"I botched it!"

The words fell heavy from her lips as the torrent of wet sobs escaped with them. Before she could clasp her hands over her face, Eilian wrapped his arms around her. His mechanical arm ran the length of her back as his other hand trailed into her hair to keep her close. Pressing her face into his collar, every frustration poured forth. She could never be a countess. She would never live up to his mother or the women hanging in the portrait gallery. All she could see was Randall Nash snapping at her in the orangery, the vein on his broad forehead pulsing; the void beside the pool where the silphium used to grow standing empty while Leona Rhodes lay bleeding; Nadir locked behind iron bars while Nash's killer ran free. She was supposed to fix things, that was the natural order, but she couldn't do anything anymore. How had it all gone so wrong?

Eilian held her close in hopes that it would quiet the cries wracking her body despite her best attempts to stifle them. Rubbing her back with his prosthetic hand, he whispered for her to take deep breaths. When she couldn't, he hugged her closer and kissed her temple.

"I'm sure you didn't botch whatever it is."

"No, I did. I ruined everything," she replied, her voice rough with tears.

The bedroom door creaked open, but when Eilian's grey eyes met Pilcrow's, she nodded and ducked out without a word. Turning back to his wife, he slipped from under her grasp and gently brushed the sweat-soaked hair from her cheeks.

"Don't say that. Tell me what happened."

"Nadir Talbot's in jail. Mr. and Mrs. Rhodes have split up, and that's all my fault."

"I'm sure it isn't—"

"Trust me, it is. She's the one who stole the silphium plant. She needed it— she needed it because she had an affair with Nash and was with child. Argus overheard us talking and stormed out."

"What? What are you talking about?"

Using the edge of the quilt, Hadley dabbed her eyes and sniffed as Eilian settled beside her. "I'm sorry I didn't tell you. You had so much on your mind at the time, and I wasn't sure about the silphium or Nash until she told me. I— I didn't mean to keep it from you. It just never came up. I didn't know the rest of it until now."

He kept his gaze soft, hoping he wouldn't add to her pain and guilt. "Tell me everything."

The whole tale poured out. She told him of how Leona used the aqueduct to break into the orangery in order to steal the plant and how she smashed the window to make it look like a burglary. All the pieces fell into place as she recounted how Leona's "stomach troubles" at the party had really been a miscarriage. She was about to tell of her affair with Nash when she paused. *Damn secrecy*, Hadley thought at her momentary hesitation of sharing the details with her husband. Secrets had never helped Nash or Leona, and they certainly hadn't helped Nadir Talbot.

When she had finished, she sat back on the bed with her knees pulled up to her chest and her robe draped over her legs. Her eyes burned as she watched Eilian shake his head and rub his jaw. He was confused, but at least he wasn't angry.

"Why didn't you tell me sooner?"

"I don't know. Stealing the silphium didn't really harm anyone, and by the time I put it together, it was too late to do anything about it. She had used up most of the plant when she miscarried. It wasn't like we could put it back." She swallowed hard. "She had a good reason for using it, and I didn't want her to get in trouble with the police, especially after she— she nearly bled out."

His eyes trailed down to his prosthetic hand before returning to her tearstained face, which had puffed and reddened. "But why didn't you tell *me*?"

She averted her gaze from his and rested her chin on her knees. "I didn't know if you would understand, and I didn't want you to say anything to Mr. Rhodes. Men don't deal with these things. You won't even touch me, so how was I to know how you would react to someone having an affair or choosing to end a pregnancy? I don't know if any man can understand it."

Eilian fell silent. How would he have reacted? He knew little of Mrs. Rhodes, and what he knew of Randall Nash made him wonder why anyone would seek to have a close friendship with the man, let alone an intimate relationship. Then there was Argus. Mr. Rhodes seemed to love his wife, but there was no way for Eilian to know what went on behind closed doors. Maybe Argus was negligent. Maybe he treated his wife with the same indifference he treated the news of the silphium, or maybe he was like Eilian and couldn't do what his wife asked.

"I would have tried to understand."

"I know, and I'm sorry."

"Is there anything else I don't know?"

Hadley shrugged and pawed at her eyes with the heel of her hand. "I don't think so. I sent a telegraph to Eliza and James. Hopefully they can find a decent lawyer for Nadir. The police wouldn't let me speak to him or Purcell. I don't know what else to do."

Eilian rubbed her shoulders and gave them a gentle squeeze. "You have done all you can. I'm sure Mr. Talbot will be all right. He didn't kill Nash; a judge will see that. When the magistrate gets here, I will see what I can do. Maybe throwing around the family name will do some good."

"Thanks."

As his wife drew in a tremulous breath and cleared her throat, Eilian withdrew a clean handkerchief from his drawer and carried over the wash basin. The water had gone cold, but he dunked the cloth in and wrung it out one-handed. He hated seeing Hadley fall apart. She was the strong one, and while he was never certain what to do, he knew this was something he had to make right for her. Cupping the side of her face with his prosthetic hand, Eilian gently wiped the moisture from her cheeks and eyelashes.

"I promise I will get Mr. Talbot out of trouble. If this lawyer doesn't come through, I will call in some favors." When her face brightened into a weak grin, he added, "I'm still shocked Mrs. Rhodes fell for someone as dreadful as Nash. I shouldn't be; he apparently had a way with women."

"Oh? What do you mean?"

"While you were out, I started reading great-grandfather's journals. An illicit affair is what caused the big rift between Nash and my father. Nash was engaged to Rubella when he was caught by my father with one of the maids. Apparently, she found out she was with child after she was sacked, but by then, conveniently, Nash was already married and out of the country. Great-grandfather made sure of that."

Hadley released a dry laugh. "And history repeats itself." Clearing her thickened throat, she called, "Pilcrow, you may come in now."

The moment the words were out, the dressing room door opened and the petite maid bustled in with a clean dress trailing behind her. She flashed the couple a smile before standing at the ready for Hadley to slip into the gown. The countess inwardly sighed but gave herself over to Pilcrow's careful attention. After buttoning the back with nimble fingers, the maid stood before her to adjust the collar and brush her skirt. As Hadley lowered her gaze to meet Pilcrow's, the breath caught in her throat.

What if the child had his eyes?

Chapter Thirty-One
Bullets in the Yews

"Get up."

Nadir jerked awake as the sergeant's boot collided with the frame of his cot. His head pounded at the sudden exertion and the dank cell tilted and whirled around him. When his vision finally settled, he locked eyes with Purcell, who stood in the doorway with his hands behind his back. A small smile crossed Nadir's lips as he smoothed his rumpled shirt and brushed the bits of dirt and dust from his trousers.

"So, you finally came to your senses, Sergeant? Better late than never."

"Lady Dorset hired you a lawyer. He sent a telegraph saying he will be here tomorrow afternoon."

He turned and raised his eyes to the glowing full-moon peeking through the bars. How long had he been asleep in that stinking rat hole? Pain lanced through his stitches where hair had matted across it during his rest. With his fingertip, he picked at the wound.

"That is very kind of her. I will have to thank her."

"Yes, it must be nice to have such a benevolent benefactress. Too bad his services won't be necessary."

As Nadir finally freed the last bit of hair from the minute knots, the noose slipped over his neck. His arm slammed into his neck as Purcell yanked him backwards, driving the rough knot into his spine. He grabbed the edge of the cot with his free hand, his fingers tearing through the threadbare fabric. Nadir fell back, staggering and falling onto his knees. All that stood between him and strangulation was his hand, which had been inadvertently trapped in the loop of the noose, but when Purcell pulled with all of his strength, his wrist pressed into his throat. Nadir gasped, groping for air. Spots fluttered in front of his eyes as he groped for anything he could use to get Purcell off. The darkness pressed in around him, his hand only meeting the filth-slicked stone. The cell wavered. He gulped down the tang of sweat and cloying cologne. The sergeant's sweaty hand brushed against his neck where it slipped from the knot. Every sense heightened and flickered as he released a rasped cry. It couldn't end like this.

Reaching back with his free hand, Nadir clawed at the officer's face. A holler rose behind him as his fingers dug into the man's eyes and tore at the soft flesh beneath his mustache. The moment Purcell whipped his head from beneath his grasp, allowing Nadir pushed up on his heels and threw him off balance. The sergeant's hands groped for the length of rope, but Nadir spun away, his head reeling as he fell into the cot. Tugging the heavy cord from his neck with trembling hands, he drew in a lungful of air.

For a moment, Nadir and Purcell stared at one another. Nadir sat sprawled on the torn mattress, his chest heaving and his throat aching, while Purcell stood between the cot and the iron door. Keeping his eyes locked on the officer, Nadir stood. Purcell's sharp gaze caught every minute flicker of movement that might betray his next move. He shifted, his hand slipping to the holster hanging at his hip, but before he could reach the leather pouch, the writer was on top of him. Slamming his shoulder into Purcell's chest, he threw him into the iron bars. The officer reached for his hip and twisted beneath him, but Nadir's fist plowed into his face before he could slip his hand around the gun. Three rapid blows were all it took. The sergeant's head bounced off the bars of the cell as Nadir let go and he slid to the floor. His eyelids drooped and blood trickled from his nose onto his well-groomed mustache. Nadir didn't have much time.

Nadir crept into the deserted front room and looked out the window. The streets were empty. The only noise he could make out was the steady tattoo of rain and the scuff of boots down the hall. Grabbing his confiscated walking stick from behind the desk, Nadir threw open the door and disappeared into the rainy night.

He ran heedlessly down the street, his expensive shoes slipping on the wet stones as he sprinted past shuttered storefronts and darkened homes. The last time he had gotten into a real brawl was during his brief time at Cambridge, but his hands never forgot the technique he had practiced for hours after being jumped one too many times at his first boarding school. His throat ached as he swallowed against the bruised knot where the noose had been. He had to hide. He had to get away from the footsteps pounding behind him.

Through the haze of heavy rain, he could make out where the road divided up ahead. He could follow the bend toward Leona's house, but there would be no escaping once he was inside and he couldn't risk Leona getting hurt. Past the house were the rickety path and the aqueduct leading to the dower house. If he could lose Purcell— No, the officer probably knew the tunnel better than he did, and he would be an easy target in the confined space.

Stopping to catch his breath, Nadir's eyes trailed to the moon glowing through the threatening clouds. His heart thundered in his ears. The other path was a direct route to Brasshurst Hall. Glancing over his shoulder, he could make out a shadow rushing toward him only a few hundred feet away. Nadir locked eyes with the blinking windows of the manor and dove into the brush.

The Earl and the Artificer

๑๑ ๑๑

Nadir's head pounded with each footfall, but he couldn't stop. Sliding down a steep embankment, he closed his eyes against the nausea as dendritic branches scratched his face and tugged at his hair. The leaves and trees behind him snapped under Purcell's approach as he barreled after him. Nadir had expected to lose him a third of the way to Brasshurst, but he was right on his heels. Swinging his walking stick like a machete, Nadir scrambled through a patch of briars, feeling the pull and snap of his shirt sleeves tearing. The house loomed in the distance, a bulbous beacon. What if Purcell caught up with him before he could get to Brasshurst? What if he did and the Sorrells refused to help? Nadir banished the thought as he vaulted over a fallen tree, his ankle throbbing as he landed hard on an unseen stone. He was nearly there. He could make out the slick edges of the Gothic facade and the camphor trees illuminated within the massive dome. As he tumbled out of the thicket and into the clearing that marked the edge of Brasshurst's ornamental gardens, the forest fell silent. Nadir turned, staring into the trees for any sign of Purcell. Had he given up?

A crack of light erupted from the top of the hill followed by a familiar retort. Nadir dove for the overgrown hedges, but a searing pain ripped through the flesh of his bicep followed by a hot sluice of blood before he could reach it.

"Shit!" he cried as he staggered, his body reeling against the pain. He clamped his hand over the wound and crawled behind the nearest yew. Shutting his eyes, Nadir gritted his teeth and held his breath as three more shots rang out. Bits of bark and leaves exploded out around him. So this was how it would end: curled up against a tree with his left arm blown open, waiting for his murderer to find him. The paralyzing pain refused to ebb, engulfing his arm in a vicious throb. With his knees, he pulled the scabbard from his cane-sword and listened. Rain pattered against his face, running down his cheeks and over his half-healed stitches in rivulets. For a long moment, he sat in the darkness; the only sound his labored breath and the rustle of leaves. Moonlight glinted along the length of his sword as the sergeant's footsteps slowly retreated into the brush.

Nadir rose to his feet, tucking his injured arm close as he looked around the gnarled trunk. In the absolute blackness enveloping the woods, it was impossible to tell if Purcell was gone. A shiver passed through him. It didn't matter; Nadir had to get to Brasshurst whether Purcell was there or not. Holding tight to his cane-sword, he inched his bloodied arm toward the pocket where his talisman had once been. He pulled his hand back, taking his breath away with a sharp pain. His luck had run out. Drawing in a deep breath, he sprinted toward the manor.

He hoped to God they were still awake. He could scarcely make out his hand in front of his face, but the light in the lower windows was clear. Skirting the edge of the orangery, Nadir stared at the thick, murky glass. There was no way he could break it with his injured arm. As he reached the house's stone facade, he smiled at his fortune. Sitting in his dressing gown only feet from the window was Lord Dorset.

✦✦✦

Eilian whipped around at the sound of frantic rapping at the drawing room window. Dropping his letter to David Hogarth, he locked eyes with the ashen face peering in through the glass. For a moment, he wondered if he had nodded off. Then, the sodden creature stepped closer, and he could make out Nadir Talbot's long hair and full lips. He leapt from the sofa and pulled open the mullioned window with a burst of wind that nearly swept his letter into the grate.

"Mr. Talbot, what the devil are you doing here?" Eilian asked, his eyes roaming from the writer's torn shirt to the twigs and sprigs of thorny leaves entangled in his hair. "What happened? I thought you were in—"

"I was. I will answer any questions, but please, let me in, Lord Dorset."

He opened his mouth to ask why he hadn't come to the front door, but upon seeing Nadir's pleading eyes, he pushed the ottoman in front of the window.

"I'm going to need a little help, I'm afraid."

Climbing onto the footstool, Eilian held out his hand. Tossing his sword in ahead of him, Nadir wrapped his arm around Lord Dorset's shoulders and allowed the nobleman to pull him over the high sill. Nadir groaned through clenched teeth as he straightened and stepped into the warm room. Even with his hand clamped over the wound, blood ran down his arm, puddling at the edge of the carpet.

The nobleman's eyes trailed to the deep tear in Nadir's sleeve, careful not to look too closely. "Are you all right?"

"I've had another run-in with a bullet."

"I can send Patrick to fetch the doctor."

"Don't!" When the earl eyed him suspiciously, he added, "He can't know I'm here. I just need a place to hide for a little while. I didn't know where else to go."

"Mr. Talbot, what is going on?"

Nadir reached for the scrapes across his neck. Standing in front of the fire, his body jerked against the cold where it lingered in his hair and down his back, trapped between layers of fabric. How must he look to the earl? Covered in dirt, bloodied, and wielding a cane-sword like some noble-savage. Why should anyone believe him?

"Sergeant Purcell is trying to kill me."

"What? Why would he do that?"

"Because he killed Randall Nash and he knows Lady Dorset isn't going to let this go. Someone told him she was getting a lawyer for me—which I still need to thank her for—and he probably realized the best way to have the case swept under the rug would be to have the only suspect die. I couldn't have written it better."

Nadir let out a bitter laugh. It was all so absurd. No wonder the earl was shaking his head. "I know you don't believe me, but look," he added as he pulled down his soggy collar to reveal raw rope burns and the beginnings of bruises. "Purcell did that. Tried to string me up right in the cell, so I ran. What else could I do? Then, he shot at me. It nearly hit home, too. Luckily, I turned in time."

"Good Lord," the earl whispered, drawing back.

"I know you have no desire to harbor a fugitive, Lord Dorset, but I need a place to stay until I can get out of the country in the morning. After that, I will never darken your door again."

Eilian nodded and motioned for Nadir to follow him down the hall. "Hadley won't be pleased to hear that. There is no way she would let you flee the country without clearing your name."

"What?"

Watching Nadir stop mid-step, a weary smile crossed Eilian's features. "Mr. Talbot, you must know you have my wife's unwavering support. There is no way she would let Sergeant Purcell get away with dragging you back to jail or tarnishing your reputation further. When she finds out he did that to you," he continued, pointing to the hidden wound, "I don't know if I will be able to keep her from going to the constabulary in Poole until morning. Either way, you have our protection."

A knot in Nadir's chest, half from pain and the rest from overwhelming fear, loosened. His own cousin hadn't fully believed him, but Lady Dorset did. "I don't know what to say."

"You can thank her when you see her. I'm sure Hadley will let you stay in one of the guest rooms. In the meantime, you should at least have someone dress your wound. Are you certain you don't want us to get the doctor?"

"Yes, your lordship. I'm afraid Purcell will find out and—"

Nadir froze at the shrill peel of the doorbell.

Chapter Thirty-Two
Blotting a Stain

The color drained from Nadir Talbot's face. Swallowing hard, he tightened his grip on the ivory handle of his blade. He licked his dry lips and rasped, "He's here."

Eilian's eyes flicked between the front door and the bloodied man standing behind him, his left arm hanging useless at his side. "Maybe not."

"Who else could it be? I can't imagine you have late-night visitors often."

"Right. Just stay right here while I find Hadley. She doesn't like surprises."

Crossing the hall, Eilian spotted his wife racing down the steps to answer the door. The bell rang again, followed by the heavy thunk of a fist.

"For God's sake."

"Had! Had, wait!" he cried in a harsh whisper.

Hadley stopped mid-step, raising her henna brows at Eilian's pallor. "What's wrong?"

"It's Purcell. He's here looking for Nadir."

"But he's in jail. That man is a bigger fool than I thought. I will set him straight."

Catching her wrist, Eilian pulled her close and whispered, "Nadir's in the hallway."

She opened her mouth to reprimand him for joking, but her husband's grave face stayed her tongue. When she looked down the hall, a familiar form solidified in the shadows. Nadir Talbot smiled and gave her a stiff bow.

"How did he get in here?"

"I will tell you later, but we can't let Purcell find him. He killed Nash and wants to do the same to Nadir. Do you have your derringer?"

"Of course not." The pounding on the door grew louder as Patrick emerged from the hidden panel and made for the door. "Patrick, wait. Eilian, hide him in the servants' walk."

Hadley studied Nadir's careworn face as he emerged from the hall. His once lustrous hair now hung in snarls, and his Byzantine eyes were ringed with deep creases. He looked more tired than she had ever seen him. What was the scandal doing to him? Then, she noticed that his left hand wasn't gloved as she first thought; it was coated in dribbles of dried blood. Before she could find the source, Nadir ducked into the panel and pulled it shut behind him.

Sitting with her back to Nadir, Hadley pulled her dressing gown close and plucked a book from Eilian's research off the end table.

"Eilian, sit down. Act like nothing's wrong."

"I don't know if that's possible," he replied as he took up position behind her, blocking the camouflaged panel with his body. "Let him in, Pat."

Eilian held his breath as the clack of the sergeant's heels echoed through the great hall. Purcell appeared in the doorway sharp despite his rain-soaked hair and mustache. His light eyes flickered over the shadows just beyond the doorways and down the halls before coming to rest on the lord and lady on the sofa. Stopping before them, he gave a curt bow.

"To what do we owe the honor, sergeant? It seems rather late to be paying social calls," Hadley said.

"Lady Dorset, I'm here because Nadir Talbot has escaped. I have reason to believe he is headed this way."

"Really? But I thought you had him under lock and key. No one was even allowed to see him this afternoon, so how did he get out?"

"He overpowered me, your ladyship, when I went to tell him of your kind offer to pay for his representation."

Eilian swallowed hard. Keeping his eyes on the policeman, he shuffled across the back of the chair to where pale pink splotches of blood had formed on the edge of the rug. A few smaller drips trailed from the carpet to the paneling. With his slippered foot, he blotted the first stain.

"I would like to search the premises."

"Why? We haven't seen him."

Purcell's lip curled into a sardonic grin. "It isn't that I don't believe you, your ladyship, but I think Talbot may be hiding somewhere on the grounds. There are plenty of places to hide in and around a house this large. I promise I will not take too much of your time."

"That won't be necessary, Sergeant Purcell. I give you my word as a lady that Mr. Talbot hasn't been here. Now, please leave. I would like to turn in for the night."

Inching closer, Eilian put his foot over the second puddle.

"What have we here?"

Eilian's heart pounded in his ears as the policeman's gaze swept from the edge of his slipper to the trail of bloody water leading behind the woodwork. At Eilian's wide eyes, he tutted and shook his head.

"Harboring a fugitive is a serious offense, Lord Dorset."

Reaching into the holster at his side, Purcell withdrew his revolver and aimed it at the paneling.

"No!" Hadley cried, lunging from the sofa.

Eilian caught her arm and pulled her back as the sergeant turned the gun on her. She stared down the barrel, her chest heaving, her hand still reaching to stop him.

"Sit *down*, Lady Dorset. This doesn't concern you."

"Don't shoot him," she said, her voice a ragged whisper. Holding her breath as Purcell reached for the edge of the panel, she felt Eilian's arm tighten around her.

"Please, just let him go. I'm sure we can all forget this ever happened."

Ignoring the earl, the sergeant banged on the panel with the butt of his gun. "Talbot, come out!"

As Nadir shifted and scratched behind the wall, a pale face appeared in the shadows of the upper arcade between the vases and statues. The hidden hinge whined, and Nadir stepped out. Dust had settled into the folds of his dark hair and cheeks, making him appear spectral—old even. Nadir clenched his eyes shut as he tugged his injured arm through the narrow gap. Purcell kept his gun pointed at Nadir's heart as he stepped in front of the massive mantle still clutching his cane-sword. Locking eyes with the sergeant, Nadir threw the blade to the ground with a clatter.

"Sergeant, you know he's innocent. We all do," Eilian began, feeling Hadley silently plead for him to do *something*. "If you let him go now, this can all end peacefully. Isn't one death enough?"

"Let's go, Mr. Talbot."

Nadir met Hadley's red-rimmed gaze. There was nothing any of them could do. He shook his head, keeping it down so the others couldn't see his fear, and followed the officer. Hadley's body tensed beneath Eilian's hand, resisting the urge to charge after them. Her derringer was upstairs in her dresser drawer. Why had she not kept it on her? But would it have made a difference? Purcell had more experience, more strength. He held all the cards. Hadley shook her head. She couldn't let him take Nadir. Her eyes traveled to the sword-cane laying just out of reach.

Purcell walked backwards, his eyes sweeping over the nobles, his captive, and the butler, who stood frozen against the grand staircase.

When he neared the foyer threshold, a faint chink echoed through the great hall as one of the heavy porcelain vases lifted from its niche. Pilcrow's grey gaze met Eilian's, holding it for a long moment before a shadow passed across her features and she released the vase.

With a crash, it collided with the back of the sergeant's skull and shattered across the wooden floor. Purcell stumbled, grabbing the back of his neck, but before he could catch his balance, Nadir slammed into him. Hadley broke from Eilian's grasp, snatching the sword, and rushing toward the men as they fell against the wall in a pile of drenched silk and wool. Following close behind, Eilian took up the heavy fireplace poker.

Nadir fought the pain in his injured shoulder as he pressed his forearm into Purcell's neck. With his free hand, he held the sergeant's wrist, keeping his gun as far from his face as he could. Leaning against him with all of his weight, Nadir breathed in the tang of Purcell's sweat and the cheap whiskey on his breath. Nadir stared into the sergeant's stony eyes. His arms shook from the pain arcing through his shoulder and the strain of hanging onto his waning strength. Purcell grunted, kneeing Nadir in the gut. The moment Nadir recoiled, the sergeant ripped his arm away. As he pulled the trigger, the iron poker collided with his arm. Hadley screamed and ducked at the boom of the gun and the shattering glass of the skylight. When Eilian drew the poker back again, Nadir landed a blow squarely in Purcell's jaw. The gun dropped from his hand, skittering across the rug. Before the sergeant could recover, Hadley dove for the gun. The metal burned and the barrel smoked as she pointed it at the officer. Purcell glared at her and Eilian, who stood poised to strike if he dared to move.

"Nadir, are you all right?" Hadley asked, never taking her eyes off Purcell.

"Yes, but I should like my cane back."

Crossing the room on wavering legs, he shook out his hand and inspected the purpled bruises already forming across his knuckles. The sword-cane felt heavy as he took it from Hadley's outstretched hand and held the blade to the man's neck. For the first time in days, he could breathe again.

"Pat," Eilian called. The butler, who hadn't moved since the fight began, peeled away from the foyer wall. "Go into Poole and fetch the police."

Purcell sneered at Nadir. "You think they will believe you?"

"I know they will."

Chapter Thirty-Three
Uncertain Futures

Eilian and Hadley glanced up from the iron tea table at the sound of gravel shifting on the drive. The steamer chugged, letting out a belch of smoke as it stopped before them. Trunks and baskets littered the back bench and the roof where several more had been tied on. Hadley smiled to herself as Leona Rhodes and Nadir Talbot crossed the lawn. In his royal purple suit and gold ascot, he nearly looked like he did the night of the party. The practiced smoldering gaze complete with smudged charcoal around his olive eyes was still there, but in those eyes, he had lost a hint of his devil-may-care attitude. It was the same weary wariness he had when he spoke of the time before success bought him respect. She hoped that, with time, the gleam would return.

"Well, we're off to London!" Nadir called as he and Leona reached their table.

"So everything's settled now?" Hadley asked.

"Yes, thanks to both of you. The authorities in Poole have cleared me of any wrongdoing, but I will be back to testify at Sergeant Purcell's trial in a few months. I rather hope Mrs. Nash is never caught, so at least my life won't be interrupted again. Have you seen *The Times?*" When the Sorrells shook their heads, he continued, his left hand sweeping in wide gestures while his right remained stiffly at his side. "'Novelist Trapped in Web of Murder.' A ridiculous headline but fairly accurate. My publisher sent it to me demanding to know if it was true and if the whole mess was settled. Luckily, whoever wrote it did so *after* I was cleared. I still have a publisher, so no harm done." He lips curled into a rakish grin. "It also mentioned the heroic actions of the Earl and Countess of Dorset. Don't worry, it was very complimentary."

Eilian's cheeks burned. "That would explain the letter from my mother. I wondered how she knew. I was beginning to think she paid Patrick to spy on me."

"You're going to London too, Mrs. Rhodes?" Hadley asked, her eyes trailing to the woman beside him. Standing next to her motley cousin, she was nearly invisible in her dove-grey gown.

"Yes, I need some time away from Folkesbury to figure things out."

Nadir clasped his arm around his cousin's shoulders. "A little smog and lively company will do wonders. She will be staying with me in Bloomsbury, of course. When are you heading back? You *are* going back, aren't you?"

"Oh yes. With our families being there and my business, we can't stay away too long. We're still packing and figuring out what to take back with us, but we will be leaving some time tomorrow."

"I, also, plan on returning in late August to do some digging around the property," Eilian added as he offered Leona his seat, which she refused with a wave of her hand.

"Really?"

"I have been sending out inquiries to archaeologists who know more about Rome than I do, and a few seem quite interested in Brasshurst."

Leona opened her mouth to speak, but before she could get the words out, her face darkened and she fell silent.

Spotting the sudden heaviness of her features, Hadley said, "Will you be going to any parties, Mrs. Rhodes? There's at least another month left of the season. Hopefully, we will bump into one another."

"I don't know if I will feel up to it."

"Of course she will. That reminds me, I plan on throwing a soiree fairly soon to celebrate the completion of *The Harem Girl*, and you will certainly be receiving an invitation. I know that after reading that ridiculous article, my friends will be lining up for an introduction to the Earl and Countess of Dorset. You would probably like my set; they're a lively bunch. Writers, poets, adventurers, artists, anarchists, suffragists."

"I look forward to it. If you ever find yourself in Greenwich, be sure to stop by. Mrs. Rhodes, when you get settled in London, you should send a letter to Mr. James Elwood in Poole. When we inquired about Mr. Nash's will, your name came up. Apparently, he left you something after all."

Leona blanched but nodded. "Thank you, Lady Dorset. I will."

"Oh, before we leave, I must give something to your maid. I wanted to thank her. If it wasn't for her, I might not be here."

"That's very generous of you, Nadir. Patrick," Hadley called to the waiting butler, "please bring Pilcrow out."

Walking back to the steamer, Nadir returned with a paper-wrapped package. Pilcrow's umbral form inched out the door and along the Gothic facade toward the waiting crowd. Her light eyes flickered over their faces, lingering on Mrs. Rhodes and Mr. Talbot for any sign of disgust or anger. Mrs. Rhodes met Pilcrow's gaze but quickly averted it to her feet.

"You need me, your ladyship?"

"Mr. Talbot has something for you."

Her eyes widened as he held out the bundle. Keeping her head down, she tore the paper away and shook out the long, wool coat within. She ran her fingers over the soft fabric and shiny black buttons before giving the shoulder seam a tug. It was finer than anything she owned but not so fine as to draw attention. Pilcrow looked up to find the handsome Mr. Talbot regarding her with an apologetic smile.

"After what happened, I couldn't leave without making good on my promise. I wish you all the best here, Pilcrow. You deserve a chance at a better future."

Pilcrow lingered on Mrs. Rhodes' solemn features. "We all do."

⋖⋗

Hadley shut the door as the steamer disappeared around the bend and into the trees. Sighing, she gave him a half-hearted smile. "They're gone now."

"I'm sure we will see them again," Eilian replied, squeezing her hand.

"I know. I just enjoyed having a friend who isn't related to me. Besides you, I haven't had one in quite some time."

"Stay in touch with him. It's easy enough to find his address."

"I'm sure he has his own friends back in London. Well, I'm going to finish packing. Are you coming?"

"I will be up in a few moments. There's one thing I still need to do."

Leaving Hadley at the stairs, Eilian followed the familiar path to the library. He was going to miss Brasshurst. In the month he had been there, he had grown accustomed to the house's peculiarities, its groans and pulse, its crawling ivies and sculptural yews. Now he saw it as a not another *thing* to be dealt with but a giant slumbering within its garden. It was that vitality he would miss when he returned to Greenwich.

Passing rooms of white-draped furniture, he entered the library. Eilian slipped through the sliding doors and inhaled the familiar scent of polish and parchment. On the desk sat a stack of books he wanted to incorporate into his own library. Most were by ancient scholars and engineers, but next to them lay the massive family Bible. Carefully lifting the gilt cover, he drew a pen from the desk, traced the curling branches to his father's name, and drew a forked line. On one side he

296

inscribed, *Eilian Sorrell. Born 1864.*, and on the other, *Dylan Sorrell. Born 1866.* From them, he added Hadley and Constance along with the years of their births. Eilian stared at the sea of names and hoped he would never have to add the second half to the entries he wrote. Closing the cover, he piled the rest of his books on top of it and lugged them up to the bedroom.

At the end of the portrait hall, he nodded to Laurence. When he returned for the beginnings of the excavation, he would bring a portrait of his father to hang beside his great-grandfather. Maybe one day, when they were ready, he and Hadley would guard the entrance to the library.

Also by the Author

The Ingenious Mechanical Devices

The Earl of Brass (IMD#1)

The Gentleman Devil (IMD#2)

"An Oxford Holiday: An Ingenious Mechanical Devices Companion Short Story"

The Earl and the Artificer (IMD#3)

"The Errant Earl: An Ingenious Mechanical Devices Companion Short Story"

Dead Magic (IMD#4)

About the Author

Kara Jorgensen is an author and professional student from New Jersey who will probably die slumped over a Victorian novel. An anachronistic oddball from birth, she has always had an obsession with the Victorian era, especially the 1890s. Midway through a dissection in a college anatomy class, Kara realized her true passion was writing and decided to marry her love of literature and science through science fiction or, more specifically, steampunk. When she is not writing, she is watching period dramas, going to museums, or babying her beloved dogs.

Want a **free short story** along with lots of sneak peeks and behind the scenes goodies? Join my newsletter Her Ladyship's Missive at KaraJorgensen.com.

www.ingramcontent.com/pod-product-compliance
Lightning Source LLC
Chambersburg PA
CBHW020238180626
46810CB00006B/2254